High Praise for Fiona Buckley's Ursula Blanchard Mysteries

QUEEN OF AMBITION

"Ursula Blanchard, lady-in-waiting and espionage agent to Queen Elizabeth I, shows her usual flare in dealing with murder and intrigue in Buckley's fifth engrossing Elizabethan mystery. A student death, complicated ciphers and a runaway wife make for a suspenseful story. As in previous novels in the series, the author blends historical fact and fiction. . . . The challenging plot and winning heroine will satisfy existing historical fans and should attract new ones."

—*Publishers Weekly*

"As a spy and a 'pokenose' in the court of Elizabeth I, Ursula Blanchard has the ideal job for a woman of her intelligence and cunning. In her fifth outing in a richly researched historical series by Fiona Buckley, Ursula uses her subtle skills to investigate a potential plot against the queen as she prepares to take her 1564 Summer Progress to Cambridge."

—*The New York Times Book Review*

TO RUIN A QUEEN

"An absorbing page-turner."

—*Booklist*

QUEEN'S RANSOM

"Buckley's amusingly modern characters mesh successfully with the well-researched plot, and readers will be wrapped up in the sixteenth-century thrill of pitfalls lurking around every corner."

—*Publishers Weekly*

"Now is a nice time for Tudor fans to light a flambeau, reach for some sweetmeats, and curl up with *Queen's Ransom.*"

—*USA Today*

"Quick pacing, a sympathetic and modern heroine, and political intrigue make this sixteenth-century mystery series as complicated and charming as an Elizabethan knot garden."

—*The Tampa Tribune*

"*Queen's Ransom* is a fantastic historical fiction novel filled with royal intrigue. Renowned for her characterizations, Fiona Buckley is a creative storyteller who makes the Elizabethan era fun to read about."

—*Midwest Book Review*

"Buckley draws both Ursula and the secondary characters in three dimensions. *Queen's Ransom* is satisfying and thought-provoking. Buckley well demonstrates the political and emotional tension between Protestant England and the Catholic states in the early sixteenth century. I am definitely looking forward to the next volume in the series."

—*Over My Dead Body! The Mystery Magazine Online*

THE DOUBLET AFFAIR

"An intricate tale rich in period detail and vivid characters. Among writers of historical mysteries, Buckley stands out for the attention and skill she brings not only to suspenseful plotting but to the setting that supports it."

—*Publishers Weekly*

"Buckley's grasp of period detail and politics, coupled with Ursula's wit and intelligence, make the story doubly satisfying."

—*The Orlando Sentinal* (FL)

"A delectable novel that is must reading."

—*Midwest Book Review*

TO SHIELD THE QUEEN

"The debut of Ursula Blanchard, young, widowed lady of the Presence Chamber at Elizabeth I's court, combines assured storytelling and historical detail. A terrific tale most accessibly told."

—*The Poisoned Pen*

"A lively debut that's filled with vivid characters, religious conflict, subplots and power plays. Ursula is the essence of iron cloaked in velvet—a heroine to reckon with."

—*Kirkus Reviews*

"Buckley's tantalizing re-creation of Elizabethan life and manners is told with intelligence and gentle wit. A noteworthy debut."

—*Library Journal*

ALSO BY FIONA BUCKLEY

To Shield the Queen
The Doublet Affair
Queen's Ransom
To Ruin a Queen

Queen of Ambition

AN URSULA BLANCHARD MYSTERY AT
QUEEN ELIZABETH I'S COURT

FIONA BUCKLEY

POCKET STAR BOOKS
New York   London   Toronto   Sydney   Singapore

This book is a work of fiction. Names, characters, places, and incidents are products of the author's imagination or are used fictitiously.
Any resemblance to actual events or locales or persons, living or
dead, is entirely coincidental.

 A Pocket Star Book published by
POCKET BOOKS, a division of Simon & Schuster, Inc.
1230 Avenue of the Americas, New York, NY 10020

Originally published in 2002 by Scribner

ISBN: 0-7434-1030-0

First Pocket Books printing December 2002

10 9 8 7 6 5 4 3 2 1

POCKET STAR BOOKS and colophon are registered
trademarks of Simon & Schuster, Inc.

For information regarding special discounts for bulk purchases,
please contact Simon & Schuster Special Sales at 1-800-456-6798
or business@simonandschuster.com

Front cover illustration by Harry Bliss

Printed in the U.S.A.

This book is for my good friend Jean Wandlass
With thanks for her kind hospitality and her patient company
during that rain-swept visit to Cambridge

Queen of Ambition

1

Untimely Accident

He looked so young.

He was nineteen, so Edward Hawford, vice chancellor of Cambridge, had said, in hushed tones as he led the way to where Thomas Shawe, student at King's College in Cambridge, had been laid, on a trestle table in one of the side chapels of the lofty College Chapel.

Death had smoothed out the marks of growing maturity, and as I stood gazing down on his face, I thought that he looked no more than fifteen. But nineteen was young enough, too young. His whole life had been before him and it had been cut off because a horse had shied or stumbled and thrown him headfirst into a tree. There were bits of tree bark still in the bloodied dent between his right temple and the crown of his head, mixed with the splinters of bone where his skull had cracked as an egg cracks when struck with the back of a spoon. Around the injury, his hair, which was a striking shade of reddish blond, almost metallic in color, like brass, was matted with dry blood.

My eyes stung and I brushed a hand across them, and beside me, Rob Henderson, my good friend and the queen's good servant, in whose company I had traveled to Cambridge, noticed. "I know," he said quietly. "This is a terrible thing."

When the news of Thomas's accident reached me, I had sought Rob out as soon as I could. He was not at the lodging but my maid, Fran Dale, and my manservant, Roger Brockley, were there and were able to tell me that Rob was at Christ's College, conferring with Hawford, who was master of Christ's, as well as being vice chancellor of the university. Dale was much occupied with some stitchery and she was no brisk walker anyway, but I took Brockley with me, so that I would appear properly escorted, and set out, hotfoot, for Christ's. On arrival, I insisted, somewhat arbitrarily, on speaking to Rob at once. When, after some argument, I was taken to him, I found that Hawford already knew of the death and that they were actually discussing it. When he understood who I was, Hawford had personally brought us to see the body.

"I understand," Hawford said, "that his horse came back to its stable without a rider and the groom went out to look for him. He was found lying dead among the trees in King's Grove. He must have been killed instantly. It's very sad, very sad. He's an only son, you know. As it happens, the family live only ten miles away. His tutor went at once, in person, and has returned to say that the poor young man's father will be here tomorrow, bringing a cart. Someone will keep vigil with him overnight and the inquest will take place tomorrow morning. It will only be a formality. It's quite clear what happened. He had permission to exercise his horse on college land and he was riding through King's Grove on the other side of the river, when something upset the animal and this is the result."

He paused and then added: "And very disconcerting it is, under present circumstances. I want to show respect for the family's sake—in fact, his father is a connection of mine, albeit a distant one—and I don't want to sound heartless, but, well . . ."

I could see his point. In normal circumstances, King's College Chapel would have been a place of calm repose, where Thomas could have lain discreetly and his fellow students could have come quietly to say farewell to him. The vice chancellor of the university would not have been much involved, except to pay brief respects of his own, if he so wished, to a promising young life and perhaps an academic career, thus cut short.

Circumstances, however, were not normal. A royal visit was imminent, elevating what would otherwise have been a private tragedy into a public awkwardness worthy of Hawford's anxious and personal attention and destroying the serenity to which the dead are entitled.

In a week's time, Her Gracious Majesty Queen Elizabeth, reaching the main objective of her Summer Progress 1564, would arrive in Cambridge and for five successive evenings she would be entertained by dramas enacted here in King's Chapel. Workmen were building a dais for her to sit upon, a stage, and a retiring room.

The chapel just now was full of workmen and racket and a sense of urgency, the sound of hammering echoing from the fan-vaulted roof and the richly carved rood screen. According to the vice chancellor, King Henry VI, who had founded King's, had wanted an austere design, but he died long before the work was finished and subsequent rulers had had other ideas. The whole place, stonework and woodwork alike, was glorious with Tudor roses, portcullises, heraldic hinds and griffins and ornate crowns, all dappled with the rainbow tints of sunlight through the stained-glass windows—and all, just now, slightly dimmed by a layer of wood dust, which had also attached itself to our clothes, and drifted, on hidden air currents, even into the seclusion of the side chapels.

The one where Thomas lay was a step down from the main chapel's floor, and the trestle had been carefully placed away from the door, out of sight of the workmen. But although it was only a few minutes since the chaplain who was watching over Thomas had drawn back the sheet to reveal his face and the upper part of his body, dust was already settling on the boy's pale features and on the brown velvet doublet in which he had ridden out that morning. It was a heavy doublet for July, but he had gone out early, when the air was still cool.

"We thought of putting him on his bed in his lodging," said the vice chancellor unhappily, "but he shares the room with two others and where are they to go? Everywhere is full up now that people have started arriving from court ahead of the queen, and bringing their valets and maids and what have you. There are three manservants sleeping on the floor in the kitchen of my own lodgings! The university is having to accommodate ladies and their tiring maids. We are not accustomed to seeing women in the colleges."

Brockley, who was standing quietly back in a corner of the little chapel, beside the chaplain, caught my eye and, despite the solemn circumstances, permitted himself a flicker of amusement. Hawford gazed at me in a pained fashion, as though my female sex had somehow polluted his university. By the sound of his voice, he considered himself hard done by.

"It is a great honor for King's to entertain the queen," said Rob rebukingly. Hawford gave an exasperated sigh.

"I *know,* I was not referring to Her Majesty; of course not. But so many other women . . . and now *this*!" He turned to me. "Master Henderson asked me to bring you here, Mistress Blanchard, but may I know what the connection is between you and this young man? I understand that you are a lady of the queen's court, although I must say I can't recall having seen you hitherto and . . ."

He did not actually say *and despite your manservant, you don't look much like a court lady either* but that disparaging glance of his said clearly enough that he saw before him a young woman in a dull brown gown with no farthingale, a plain linen cap, and a plain linen collar instead of a ruff, whereas Master Henderson was the epitome of elegance in russet satin slashed with yellow, his ruff trimly pleated, and his neatly barbered fair hair adorned by a russet velvet cap complete with a sparkling jeweled brooch.

"My tasks for the queen have taken me outside the college," I said. "I have been concerned, for one thing, with this little playlet which is being arranged to amuse the queen when first she rides into Cambridge. We all wish to make sure that it is performed perfectly and doesn't take up too much time. Her Majesty may be tired from the journey. As for Thomas Shawe—I have met him in the course of my duties. He was involved in the playlet. It seemed only right to—pay my respects."

"And if an unexpected death occurs in a place which Her Majesty is soon to visit, her servants have a duty to inquire into it," added Master Henderson smoothly.

"But what is there to inquire into?" said the vice chancellor, still sounding querulous. "This was just an unfortunate accident. The inquest will declare as much and that will be that."

"Of course," Rob said. "Please give our condolences to Master Shawe's family. If you are ready, Ursula . . ."

"Yes." I was so very, very sorry for Thomas and his family, and also for the girl who had been in love with him. Leaning down, I kissed Thomas's brow on Ambrosia's behalf, as I had promised I would. It was as cool and hard as marble. Brockley came forward too, to look at Thomas for a moment. Then we turned away and together we all went out, leaving the chaplain to draw the sheet up once more over the still face, and resume his vigil. Returning to the main chapel, we paced through it to the south door.

Out in the courtyard, we paused. "Our discussion was concluded, I think," Hawford said to Rob. "There is no need for you to come back to Christ's with me. I have many things to attend to. I must be sure that the inquest is properly set up and that the boy's family will be accommodated as is fitting. This is so distressing."

"Come, come." Rob Henderson was bracing. "Accidents do sometimes befall lively young men on lively horses."

"I suppose so," said the vice chancellor gloomily.

He took himself off, walking briskly and brushing the dust off his gown as he went. Rob and I looked at each other. "Thomas's mare," I said, "is a placid, elderly nag, not lively at all. Thomas told me so himself."

"Horses can stumble," Rob said mildly.

I shook my head. "You and I haven't spoken together for some time, Rob. There is something you don't know. I was going to meet Thomas at three o'clock this afternoon; about now, in fact. He couldn't get away from his tutor and I couldn't get away from the pie shop any sooner. Thomas was worried and he wanted to talk to me about it. And now he never will."

My voice was grim. From the beginning, Sir William Cecil, the Secretary of State, had sensed that there was something amiss in Cambridge. He had known it in the marrow of his bones and now I knew that he was right.

"For someone," I said, "though I'm not sure who—I think this was a long way from being an untimely accident. For someone, it may have been very timely indeed."

2

Untimely Summons

Thomas Shawe rode out to his death through a pearly daybreak in July 1564. Only a month before, in early June, I was living quietly at Withysham manor house in Sussex and I had never heard of Master Shawe. For a young woman of thirty I had had an unconventional, not to say eventful, life but if anyone had told me then that within four weeks I would be dressed like a servant and working in a pie shop, rolling pastry, waiting on undergraduates, and putting up with it when the proprietor shouted at me or even clouted me around the head, I would have been skeptical to say the least.

I was expecting to be called away from home, yes, but to court, not to a pie shop, and indeed, a summons to court was what the royal courier brought to me on that beautiful June morning. Which was, ironically, the first morning at Withysham on which I had said to myself: *Yes, I do miss Matthew, but all the same, I'm happy here.*

Withysham, which was a former nuns' abbey converted to a manor house, with a home farm, a village, and a couple of smallholdings attached, had been given to me only a couple of months before by Queen Elizabeth in return for a service I had rendered to her. When I went there, with my eight-year-old daughter Meg, I found it sadly neglected. It had been in the hands of an aging caretaker steward for over three years, with depressing results. The hall roof leaked, there was an old wasps' nest in a corner of a disused bedchamber, and there were tapestries so moth-eaten that they were fit only for a rubbish heap. The floors looked as if they hadn't been swept for a century, and two of the home farm cows were so old that they could hardly stand up, let alone produce calves or milk.

Fortunately, I had some money and there were rents due that provided more. I set to work forthwith, pensioning the old steward off, promoting my excellent manservant, Roger Brockley, to take his place, and seizing the chance to instruct Meg in housewifery. I had never before been in charge of her education. She was the child of my first husband, Gerald Blanchard, and for many years, force of circumstances had compelled me to leave her with foster parents while I earned us a living. Now that we were reunited, there was much that I wanted to teach her.

Yet Withysham was not truly my home. Home was the French château of Blanchepierre in the Loire Valley, where my second husband, Matthew de la Roche, was living. During a visit I had made to England earlier in the year, plague had broken out at Blanchepierre and Matthew had written bidding me stay where I was until the summer ended. The plague always subsided when the weather cooled. Making the best of it, I decided to pass the time putting my new property at Withysham to rights, before joining the court and accompanying the queen on her Summer Progress. I had once been a Lady of Queen Elizabeth's Presence Chamber and during my stay in England I had found that in her eyes, I still was.

On that June morning, I had begun as usual by taking Meg with me to the kitchen to listen while I gave the orders for the day's meals. While we were there, our spit boy, who was sharpening knives, cut himself and Meg helped me to dress the wound, using an ointment prepared from herbs by Gladys Morgan, an aged woman from South Wales. Gladys had attached herself to me in a way that was often an embarrassment, for she was, to be candid, a dreadful old woman. I could insist that she washed and wore respectable clothes, but her few remaining teeth still resembled fangs and her laughter was a demonic cackle.

Roger Brockley, who had a kindness for the aged, had once rescued her from a charge of witchcraft and now I lived in dread that one day someone would bring the charge again. True, the Withysham people didn't dislike her as her former village had done. She had a gift for brewing medicines and ointments and had helped quite a few of them with her lotions for rheumatism and her potions for fevers. The old steward suffered from breathlessness and palpitations, and for him she had made a concoction of foxglove that had relieved him a good deal. I had cause to be grateful to her myself, for she had once saved the life of my woman, Fran Dale, and she had lately invented a brew that eased my occasional attacks of sick headaches better than the chamomile infusion I had used before.

She had, however, irritated the local physician quite a lot by her ministrations and I had had to be firm with both of them, telling Gladys to be more discreet and recommending the physician to mind his own business, attend the patients who called him in, and leave the rest alone (I felt no compunction about this; I was fairly sure that he killed as many as he cured and Gladys was better than he was about warning people of the difference between a healing dose and an overdose).

Gladys, in fact, was useful, but she was also a responsibility. After attending to the spit boy, I seized the chance of explaining all this to Meg, for I hoped that one day my daughter would marry well and have her own home and then she too would have to keep the peace among her servants.

Having finished with the kitchen, I had time for more intellectual pursuits. Meg and I were reading books of history and travel together, and I had bought a Latin grammar so that we could work on Latin, in which she already had a grounding.

It was an excellent mental exercise for me, too. I had lately become aware of how miserable women could be when their beauty began to fade, unless they had other interests. I had also discovered that such studies could be a defense against the languorous persuasions of summer weather, the scent of roses, the sound of grasshoppers, the voices of dove and cuckoo, and the eventide song of the blackbird. When I was concentrating on a Latin translation, I did not daydream about Matthew.

At court, I had often been impressed by Queen Elizabeth's own interest in learning and her gift for languages. Sometimes I wondered whether Elizabeth, determinedly unmarried and still only thirty, also found her intellectual pursuits a refuge from importunate desires.

I did not intend to give up my own studies once we were settled back in France, however. On the contrary, I hoped to find a tutor who could instruct both Meg and myself not only in advanced Latin but also in Greek. My education had been a matter of sharing my cousins' tutor, and although we had gone a fair way with Latin, my cousins had pleaded to give up Greek almost as soon as they began it, on the grounds that it was too difficult. We had learned the alphabet and not much else.

For the moment, though, Meg was only at the stage of basic Latin and that was occupation enough for us. I settled down with her in the small room that I had chosen as a study, which looked out toward Withysham's neatly thatched gatehouse, and to the home farm fields on the hillside beyond our encircling wall.

As she often did, my woman, Fran Dale—I still called her Dale although she was actually Mistress Brockley—joined us, to sit by the windows with some mending. Because the day was warm, two of the casements were open, letting in the sound of skylarks and the smell of new-mown hay from the fields. Meg sat with her head bent earnestly over an exercise concerned with the fourth declension, while I tried to puzzle out a grammatical point that had always confused me, involving the construction of the gerund. Though I remember, on that morning, I wasn't concentrating as earnestly as Meg. There were occasions when intellectual tasks didn't quite succeed in blocking out emotional ones. I kept on raising my head to look with affection at my daughter, who was becoming so very pretty.

She took after her father, Gerald, who had been a handsome man. Her glossy hair was dark just as his had been, and she had his brown eyes. I had dark hair too, but not quite of the same shade, and my eyes were hazel. I had dressed her in a lightweight crimson brocade, which suited her to perfection, and her little white linen cap was clean on that morning. Sitting there so studiously, she was such an enchanting picture that she distracted me from my books and from the sights and sounds of the outside world alike. I did not want to stop looking at her.

And I was realizing that despite the empty place beside me, which must always be there until I was reunited with my present husband, Matthew, here at Withysham in the company of my daughter, living this quiet life of domestic duties and peaceful study, I was surprisingly content.

It was Fran Dale who heard the distant clatter of hooves on the gatehouse cobbles, looked out of the window, and exclaimed: "Mistress Blanchard, ma'am, there's a royal messenger just ridden in, or my name isn't Dale."

"Well, it isn't, is it? It's Brockley!" said Meg with a giggle.

"Meg, don't be pert," I said absently. "Dale is sometimes known as Dale and sometimes as Mistress Brockley. In France, when we go there, I shall be Madame de la Roche, but in England I prefer still to be Mistress Blanchard. People aren't always called by the same name all the time." I rose and went to the window. The horseman was walking his mount toward the stableyard and he was near enough for me to see from his livery that Fran was right.

Well, I was expecting him. This was my summons to join the queen and prepare for the Progress to Cambridge. But it had come well before I looked for it, and I not only wished it hadn't, because it felt like an intrusion, I also wondered *why* it had come so soon.

It was my first intimation that something out of the ordinary was afoot.

When the time came for me to go to France, I intended to leave Brockley and Dale to run Withysham for me. I would have plenty of servants at Blanchepierre. But in England, I only had Brockley and Dale as personal attendants, so they would have to come to Cambridge with me. Therefore, I recalled the old steward, Malton, from his retirement cottage and put him back in charge with a lengthy list of instructions, which included taking the utmost care of Gladys. "I won't be here and Brockley won't be here, but if anyone harms Gladys while we're gone, you'll answer for it. I'll slash your pension."

"I'll do my best, Mistress Blanchard," said Malton bleakly. He had never known what to make of me but he was more than a little afraid of me, which just now was all to the good.

"You'll do more than your best," I said. "Call on the vicar for help if necessary." The vicar's living was in the gift of Withysham and he was afraid of me, too. I was young to be a husbandless lady of the manor and sometimes I had to put on fierce airs in order to get my authority respected. I sometimes feared that I was turning into a fair facsimile of a battle-ax.

Meg, along with her nurse, Bridget, would have to return to her foster mother, Mattie Henderson. Rob and Mattie were the owners of a big house near Hampton and Rob was a courtier, and a friend of Sir William Cecil, the Secretary of State. Rob was to join the Progress and Mattie had written to me that he was already at court. Mattie herself, however, was expecting a child and was to stay behind at their home, Thamesbank. Meg was well used to both Mattie and Thamesbank and would be contented enough there until I came back.

"Though I don't envy Mistress Henderson, having to stay at home while her husband goes off gallivanting among all the court ladies," Fran Dale said in sour tones. "And her nearly forty, at that. If I was her, I couldn't abide to see Roger going off like that and leaving me behind."

"No one's asking you to," I pointed out, somewhat brusquely, since I was extremely busy just then with the choice of gowns to pack and a further list of last-minute instructions for the harassed Master Malton.

The day before I set out, I had an unexpected visitor. Five miles from Withysham was Faldene, the house where I had been brought up, mainly by my uncle Herbert and my aunt Tabitha. My mother had been a court lady who was sent home in disgrace, with child by a man she would not name. I had been that child. Her parents and later on her brother Herbert and sister-in-law Tabitha had sheltered us, had clothed and fed us, and had even educated me, but they had not been kind. We had disgraced them, and they let us know it.

Later on, when my mother was dead and I was a young woman confronted with a life as Aunt Tabitha's unpaid maidservant and Uncle Herbert's unpaid clerk, I succeeded in stealing the affections of their daughter Mary's betrothed. I ran off with Gerald and married him. Finally, when Uncle Herbert became involved in treason, I was the one who got him sent to the Tower. He had been released long since, as an act of mercy, because he was a heavily built man who suffered from shortness of breath and attacks of gout, but understandably, he didn't feel inclined to forgive me.

In fact, for excellent reasons, I didn't like my uncle and aunt and they didn't like me and although I lived so near them, we had not seen each other during my sojourn at Withysham. I was very surprised when Brockley came to my chamber, where Dale and I were folding clothes into hampers, and announced that Mistress Tabitha Faldene was below, and wished to speak to me.

"Aunt Tabitha? Here?"

"Yes, madam." Brockley knew the situation and his

calm high forehead with its dusting of pale gold freckles was faintly wrinkled with surprise. "I have asked her to wait in the main hall."

I went downstairs and there, indeed, she was, thin, vinegary Aunt Tabitha, neat and prim in a stiff, narrow ruff, her housewifely dress of dark blue tidily draped over a modest farthingale. Aunt Tabitha did not care for showy garments.

"So there you are, Ursula. I won't ask you why you haven't called on us. Tact, no doubt, and in fact, you were right. Your uncle does not wish to see you and of course I respect his views. All the same, families should maintain the proprieties. I hear you are bound for the court again and I felt it was only proper that I should speak with you before you left. If you wish to visit your mother's grave in Faldene churchyard, you may do so."

"Thank you, Aunt Tabitha," I said in astonishment. Tabitha was a stickler for the proprieties she had mentioned, but I hadn't expected her to maintain them after what I had done to Uncle Herbert. I did indeed want to visit my mother's grave, and had been planning to go there very early one morning and do so before people were about. I didn't bother to ask how my aunt knew I was going to Richmond. Half the Withysham villagers at least had relatives in the village at Faldene.

I called for refreshments and asked after my uncle and cousins. My uncle's gout had been better of late; my cousins, all now married, were apparently thriving. My cousin Edward was actually married to a distant relative of Gerald's and now had a baby daughter.

"We were pleased," Aunt Tabitha said, "when we

heard that you had settled in France with Matthew de la Roche. We hoped you had seen sense at last and perhaps your husband would save your soul for you. We were also pleased, though surprised, to hear that Withysham had been restored to the two of you. But are you going back to France?"

"Yes, in the autumn. I shall take Meg with me."

"And in between, you are returning to court and the service of that red-haired heretic of a queen. It seems that you can hardly keep away from her." Aunt Tabitha and Uncle Herbert adhered to the old religion, which was how they had got entangled in treason.

I looked at her coldly. There had been an occasion, long ago now, in the days of the passionately Catholic Queen Mary, when she and Uncle Herbert had returned from witnessing a burning, and by way of warning me against heresy, had forced me to listen while they described it. I still had occasional nightmares about that. I would never either forget it or forgive it. "The days of the heresy hunts are over," I told her. "And people are grateful to Elizabeth for it."

"They may think differently when they reach the hereafter."

"I was sorry for Uncle Herbert, believe it or not," I said. "And I do have a sense of family loyalty. But—I have other loyalties, too."

"That is obvious," said Aunt Tabitha, and unexpectedly sighed. "Ah, well, I suppose we must be glad that at least you mean to return to your husband. Your first loyalty should be with him, after all."

We exchanged a few more desultory words and then she took her leave, repeating that I was welcome to visit my mother's grave though I should not come to the house. The whole visit had a very odd atmosphere. My aunt's attitude had been—well, not quite conciliatory but close to it—and she had been strangely lukewarm about the news that I was going back to France in the autumn. It was almost as though she didn't want me to go. I felt as if she had come for some purpose that she had not declared.

But I had no chance to pursue the matter. I did visit my mother's grave, very quietly, early the next day. And then it was time to load the pack ponies, mount our horses, and go. The court was beckoning.

And it really was beckoning. It was always the way. Once I had done with saying good-bye to Withysham and dried my tears on parting from Meg, my resentment and surprise at this early summons faded away. The prospect of the court, the exhilaration of it, the cut and thrust and double-talk of political maneuvers, and above all, the personality of Queen Elizabeth, glittering, dangerous, vulnerable, frightening, and lovable, began to seduce me. Elizabeth and her court were like a heady wine, and I was an addict who longed with all her heart to drink of it once more.

3

Nondescript and Importunate

I liked Richmond. With its ornamental turrets and sparkling fountains, and its well-lit, airy rooms, it was to my mind the prettiest of all Elizabeth's residences and for me it had good associations. After Gerald's death, when I was an impecunious young widow who was lucky to have friends who had found her a post at court, it was to Richmond that I had come, to enter a new life and it was there that my grief had begun, slowly, to heal.

It was there, in the summer, when the gardens were in bloom, that Matthew and I had first met.

This too was summer and as Dale and I, accompanied by a page and two men to carry our hampers, made our way toward the palace building, the sanded path led past flower beds ablaze with color. The air was full of the hum of bees and the beguiling perfume of lavender and roses.

A few gardeners were busy with weeding, and

courtiers, men and women, their costly doublets and embroidered skirts as vivid as the flowers, were strolling along the paths. One or two of them recognized me and called greetings. I returned the greetings but did not stop. The June day, so beautiful when one was sauntering through a garden, had also meant a hot and dusty ride from Thamesbank, where I had left Meg in the morning. Even the horses had been weary at the end of it. Brockley had taken them off to the stable, murmuring soothingly to them about buckets of water and fresh hay. Being used to riding, I was not unduly tired but I did feel the heat and Dale was drooping badly. She was in her late forties and she had never liked horseback travel. She had already said that she hoped the Progress to Cambridge would be the last long ride she ever undertook in her life. The sooner we were in a shady room, washing our faces in cool water, the better.

Once indoors, the page led us along a wide, flat-ceilinged corridor that turned a corner into an unfamiliar wing. Through the windows on one side, I saw sunlight flashing on the Thames, but I could not work out quite where I was. "I've never been lodged on this side of the palace before," I said to the page.

He glanced at me, sidelong. He was about sixteen, exquisite in white and silver brocade, and with a nascent beard around his lips. Pages, in my experience, fell into four broad categories: the cheeky, the timid, the circumspect, and the knowing. This one was on the cusp between circumspect and knowing. "There are a number of guests at court, Mistress Blanchard, and Lady Margaret Lennox is among them. As is her custom, she has brought a large retinue and they need a great deal of accommodation. I have myself had to move into different quarters."

I quelled a smile. His voice was almost completely bland, but there was the very tiniest trace of resentment in *had to move*. His new quarters were probably squashed and he would of course know all the court gossip about Lady Lennox. She was a cousin of the queen, since both of them were descended from Henry VII, and family propriety (Aunt Tabitha would have understood) required her to be treated with dignity. Elizabeth, though, had good reason to detest her, and did. Good courtiers followed Elizabeth's lead and detested her too, and young pages, when they mentioned Margaret Lennox, could afford to let their voices be tinged, *just*, with dislike.

Though wise court ladies did not encourage this. I didn't answer and was glad of that when, half a second later, a door on our left was flung open and through it strode Lady Lennox herself, no less, tall and commanding, her farthingale almost filling the doorway, her cream satin skirts adorned with enough embroidered flowers and sewn-on pearls to rival anything in Elizabeth's own wardrobe, and one beringed hand angrily straightening a pearl-edged headdress, which seemed to be on the verge of toppling sideways off her waves of crimped brown hair.

We stepped aside to let her pass, but ignoring us, she stopped short and swung around to face a nondescript little man in the dark gown of a scholar or cleric, who had followed her out of what I now saw was an anteroom, presumably to her private apartment.

"I have told you before! I will not have you imporr-rrtuning me in this fashion!" I knew that Lady Lennox had been reared in England, but her father had been a Scot and her Tudor mother had lived in Scotland long enough to pick up the accent. As a result, Lady Lennox had it too and the rolling northern *R*'s magnified the natural harshness of her voice. "Must I put arrmed guards on my door in the queen my cousin's verra palace, in order to have some prrrivacy?"

"But, my lady, if only you would listen!" The little man held up imploring hands, palms pressed together as if in prayer. "I came today to tell you that I paid heed to what you said when last we met! If only you would take me back, I would prove my worth to you! You wouldn't regret it! I would do wonders for you! I would do anything for you. I have no desire to displease you, only to return to your favor . . ."

"You would be grrreatly in my favor, Master Woodforde," said Lady Lennox furiously, jamming her headdress back into position, "if you were lying in your coffin with your hands folded on your heart and a carpenter at hand rrready to nail down the lid! Now get out of my sight and stay out. *Madge! Bess! Ladies!* Where the devil are you all . . . !"

In a flurry of skirts and feminine exclamations, Margaret Lennox's ladies came rushing through the anteroom to their lady's side.

"My lady, we are so sorry . . . !"

"Oh, what a disgrace! Is he here again? Be off with you, you pestilential creature!"

"Madam, do forgive us . . . !"

"Where *were* you?" demanded Lady Lennox. "I did

nothing but leave my rooms for a moment to speak with a friend, and the moment I returned, I found this . . . this nuisance waiting in ambush—here, within my own anterrroom!—and no sign of any of you! You are the senior lady, Madge; you should know better!" The noble Margaret made a gesture with her right hand that would have been a blow, had Madge not stepped back just in time.

"Madam, we were in the inner chamber, arranging your spinet music as you wished and . . ."

"I didn't wish you to neglect your duty at the same time and let this . . . *pairrson* in!" She glared at the non-descript man, who was standing quite still, his gaze fixed on her as though he did not know how to with-draw it. "*Will* you go away?"

The little man seemed to come to himself. He turned away but not, I saw, in any very chastened fash-ion. As he brushed past us, his gaze swept impersonally over us, as though we were inanimate objects rather than people. Then he glanced back over his shoulder and called to Lady Lennox: "But I meant it! One day I will earn your gratitude and your love, I promise!"

"*Love!*" gasped Madge. "Of all the impertinence!"

"Back inside!" ordered Lady Lennox. "Forget him!"

She swept them all away through the door to the anteroom. The door was shut. We were left feeling as though we had been invisible, ghosts observing the antics of people who did not know we were there. We looked at one another. The men with the hampers were rolling their eyes and pursing their lips in silent whistles.

"A remarkable woman," said our satin-clad page. "She attracts hangers-on, of course. Many ladies admire her greatly. Do you know she has not a single gray hair on her head?"

I did know. I had also heard that Lady Lennox's beautifully waved brown hair was a wig but I wasn't going to discuss such things with a page. It might not be true, anyway. Although she was in her forties, she was still very handsome of face and perhaps her hair had survived the onslaughts of time as successfully as her well-kept complexion.

"Never mind Lady Lennox," I said sharply. "I want to wash and change and would like to reach my room soon. Today, for instance!"

I had expected to find myself sharing a room with one or two other ladies but to my surprise I found I had a small room to myself. In the past, when at court, I had sometimes had a private room, but only for a special reason, which I hadn't thought would apply this time. I raised my eyebrows, and remembered once more that my summons from Withysham had come strangely early. Well, I would no doubt be told all I should know before too long. The page, indeed, had a message, to the effect that at five of the clock, I would be fetched to attend on the queen.

The room had been well prepared, with jugs of washing water and a set of towels in readiness. By the time the page came back for me, I was washed and rested, wearing a fresh gown and with my hair tidy. I followed my young guide through the passages until we reached familiar territory, and I saw before me the double doors to the queen's own rooms.

Guards moved aside to allow me past and the page, opening the doors, announced me. I entered. Queen Elizabeth was there, seated regally in an ornate chair, behind which stood her favorite lady, Katherine Knollys (a nearer cousin to the queen than Lady Lennox and much more beloved). Standing before the queen were Sir Robert Dudley, Master of the Queen's Horse and Elizabeth's favorite (though not her lover, whatever the gossips might say), and Sir William Cecil, the Secretary of State.

The atmosphere was tense. In fact, it could have been sliced up with a knife and served as well-matured cheese. As well as stepping into the royal presence, I had also walked into the midst of a quarrel.

4

A Ridiculous Entertainment

Elizabeth acknowledged my arrival and my curtsy with a single brief glance, but her attention was on Cecil. Her tawny eyes were bright with indignation. "We can see no harm in this notion, Master Secretary, no harm at all. Why should there not be a little lightheartedness on these occasions? It will take only a few minutes and satisfy the undergraduates' very proper and very loyal desire to play a part in our reception. They are surely hardworking youths. Let them have their reward. When this lady, whoever she is, is whisked out of our sight, let all be brought to a halt with a blast on a trumpet and let there be a distribution of largesse to the onlookers. Of silver coins—shillings and half crowns," added Elizabeth thriftily.

"Ma'am!" Cecil spoke protestingly. "It is my duty as your Secretary of State and also as the chancellor of Cambridge, to ensure that your royal visit there is conducted with the dignity due to your position and my reputation. Every man of note in the entire university will be assembled to greet you—at Queens' College and King's College Chapel and . . ."

"And my position and your reputation will be shipwrecked by a harmless jape which will allow us all a little laughter?"

"No, ma'am. But I am concerned for your safety as well as your dignity. A pack of shouting, overexcited young men, and swordplay—even with blunted blades—within a few feet of your person! What can you be thinking of?"

"Stuff and nonsense! Who will want to harm me in Cambridge? If in the whole realm there is a stronghold of support for me, it's in Cambridge. It was the seedbed of the English Protestants. These young men are my subjects as much as any of their elders. They are being kept away from the plays and dissertations, but if they wish to participate in my welcome for just a few merry, lively minutes, why not let them? Robin here is not indifferent to our safety, or our dignity and position—or his own, either—and yet he agrees with me. Do you not, my sweet Robin?"

The queen's sweet Robin, very splendid in the gold-slashed crimson that was his favorite color scheme, bowed to her and to Cecil. "I trust none of them will be threatened, whether deliberately or by accident. If Your Majesty wishes me to take part in a playful sword fight—elegantly planned and carefully rehearsed, of course, and at a safe distance from your person—I am at your disposal."

I eyed Dudley doubtfully. I had on occasion had reason to be grateful to him, but I did not like or trust him and Elizabeth's evident preference for him had often worried me—though, unlike Cecil, I suspected that she did not trust him either. Entranced by him she might be, but Elizabeth was one of the few people I have ever encountered who could look at a member of the opposite sex and distinguish between attraction and reliability. She knew a dangerous man when she saw one. Which did not stop her from now and then making alliance with him against the gravity of Cecil.

Like Elizabeth, Dudley now glanced in my direction. "Good morning, Mistress Blanchard."

I responded with another polite curtsy and Elizabeth, with a flick of her long, jeweled fingers, signaled to me to take up a position behind her chair, beside Kate Knollys. Obeying, I found myself looking straight into the faces of Cecil and Dudley. I observed at once that Dudley's swarthy face was grave, but that his dark eyes were agleam with malicious humor, while Cecil, despite the controlled tone of his voice, was pale with rage, the permanent worry line between his blue eyes deeper even than usual. As for Elizabeth, I had sensed her mood at once.

Elizabeth's moods were so marked that sometimes they amounted to different personalities. She could be a queen with all the splendor of sovereignty about her—and then change in a moment to a vulnerable young woman whose elaborate gowns seemed too heavy for her. She could be a railing fishwife, an ethereal moon goddess, or a pouncing, bright-eyed cat, ready on the instant to play or to claw. The latter Elizabeth was the version that most exhausted and exasperated the dignified Cecil, and this morning, most decidedly, he was trying to cope with a mischievous feline.

Even as I took my place, however, Elizabeth's mood altered. The cat slid out of sight and the queen edged into the ornate chair in its stead. Suddenly, the royal plural was not a matter of form, but was being wielded like a weapon. "Master Secretary, you are not to think that we do not appreciate your care for us. But in this matter, you are overruled. This began, if we understand aright, as a students' jest, and what Master Woodforde and his brother wish to do, is take the jest over, give it official blessing, and thus control it. If we forbid it, these hotheaded young men may think of some other jest, and perhaps then get themselves into trouble. No, let them play their little comedy, under official aegis. And now, gentlemen, we wish to be private with our ladies. I have not addressed a single word of greeting to Mistress Blanchard. Come round before me, Ursula. How well you look. The air of Sussex must suit you."

"Ma'am," I said, curtsying again as I came around to the front of her chair. Then I inquired: "Did I hear the name of Woodforde mentioned?"

"You did. What of it?"

"Is he a smallish man, not very striking, who looks like some kind of clerk or scholar?"

"We have not personally seen him," said Elizabeth. "But he is a scholar, yes. He is employed as a tutor at Cambridge. Cecil?"

"It sounds like the same man. I take it you have come across him? That is quite possible; he is at court just now," said Cecil, and then, changing the subject in a smooth fashion which I recognized as a warning not to pursue the matter of Master Woodforde, he added: "My wife, Lady Mildred, has a message for you—a somewhat lengthy one, concerning Meg. When your hours of duty are past, you will find me in my study. I have my usual Richmond quarters. Please attend on me and we can discuss what she has in mind. It may take some time."

"But I shan't release you until your duty is over," Elizabeth said, smiling. "I have not seen you for far too long and in a day or two you will be setting off for Cambridge. You are to be sent there with an advance party of official harbingers, led by Master Henderson, to see that all is in order for my visit."

"That is why I was recalled from home so soon?" I asked.

"It is, indeed. Master Cecil suggested that you should be included among the harbingers. You have always understood my requirements very well and your advice will be of value. Good day, Sir William," added Elizabeth, coolly dismissing them. "Good day, Robin."

I had no opportunity to see Cecil that day, for the rest of it was spent with the queen. With her other ladies, I attended on Elizabeth while she held an audience for the Spanish ambassador, walked in the garden, and watched a game of tennis. Later, we sat talking and sewing together, but within call, while she spent an hour, as she often liked to do, studying books from her considerable library of works on history and politics.

Then came supper, cards, and music, until at last, she withdrew with her ladies of the bedchamber and I could go to bed.

But in the morning, Elizabeth had a conference with her Treasurer and I was free at last to seek Cecil out in his study. It was a pleasant room overlooking the Thames. Reflections from the river rippled across the paneling and the flat ceiling with its crisscross of narrow beams and its exquisitely carved and painted Tudor roses of red and white. The leaded window was open and from outside came the gentle tinkle of the musical weather vanes which were one of Richmond's most charming features.

Cecil rose courteously to greet me and came around the desk, limping. "Is it your gout?" I asked him with concern.

"It is. No one seems able to recommend a cure. I try this diet and that, but my old nurse's medicines seem to work best, though heaven knows what she puts in them. Since I'm the chancellor of Cambridge, I shall have to accompany the queen—indeed, I intend to get there ahead of her to make sure all is as it should be. Dear old Nanny has agreed to come too, and bandage my gouty foot for me. To her, I think I'm still the little boy she used to scold for getting his feet wet."

I urged him to sit down again and he did so but not behind his desk. Instead, he moved to a settle just under the window and sank onto it, hitching the hem of his formal dark gown up so that it would not touch his swollen foot, which was bandaged and encased in a soft slipper. He beckoned to me and I took the other end of the settle. Studying his face, I saw again how marked was that line between his eyes, and noticed that his fair beard was fading from flaxen to gray. He looked tired.

"The queen," he said abruptly, "has a brilliant mind. Her grasp of political theory, of the motives of rulers and the art of diplomacy, never fails to astonish me. My wife is an intellectual woman but Elizabeth surpasses her by far. Most of the time, that is. At other times," said Cecil with feeling, "although she is now thirty years of age, a few months older than you, Ursula, she behaves as though she were playing games—*chess* games—with people as her pawns. She is doing it now and I am at my wit's end to know how to manage."

"What is she like in the council chamber?" I asked curiously.

"In council? She has a mind like a rapier. She makes her points like a swordsman thrusting. But the tone in which she makes them varies with her mood. And even in council," said Cecil gloomily, "there are times when I think she is playing with us. You have been away from the court for some time. Did you know that she has revived that business of offering Robin Dudley's hand in marriage to Mary Stuart of Scotland?"

"Yes." I nodded. The previous evening, while Elizabeth was reading, I had sat at the opposite side of the room with the other ladies, and in low voices, they had regaled me with the latest gossip. "But surely," I said, "she doesn't mean it."

"God knows what she means! I don't think she knows herself. I can see the point of offering Mary a husband of Elizabeth's own choice, yes. It would put a stop to the ambitions of Lady Lennox. She hasn't recently mentioned aloud that she has a good-looking son who would be interested in uniting two descendants of Henry VII by marrying Mary himself, but I doubt if she has forgotten it. An uneasy prospect. What if they had a healthy son!"

I nodded. "England would have a Catholic dynasty-in-waiting and the risk of a party gathering round it."

"Precisely, especially if Elizabeth goes on refusing to marry and produce an heir of her own." Cecil turned away from me for a moment to stare through the window. He had given his devotion to Elizabeth and to the Protestant movement in a public way from which there was no retreat. The day a Catholic ruler ascended the throne of England, Cecil would have to flee or risk death.

"Though even young Darnley might be better than a Spanish marriage," Cecil said as he turned back to me. "At least we have his mother here in England as surety! But what we need most of all is an heir of the queen's body. Again and again, the council has *pleaded* with Elizabeth to take a husband. She fobs us off by promising to marry when it should be convenient. As far as I can see, it will be convenient the day after the Last Trump, and meanwhile, Mary of Scotland is her likeliest heir. Getting Mary married off to a Protestant with no royal blood would be an excellent idea. She's welcome to Dudley! Except for the small difficulty that she has made it clear that she isn't in the least interested in him—the queen's horsemaster, she calls him—and Dudley has made it equally clear that he isn't interested in her, and as for Elizabeth, well, if he did suddenly pack his saddle-bags and announce that he was off to Scotland to seek his fortune, I think she would have him carried off to the Tower between two huge Yeomen of the Guard with his feet six inches off the ground. She'd never let him go! I don't know what she's about. Whatever game she's playing, I don't understand the rules. And now, my dear Ursula, we have this royal Progress to Cambridge University."

"I gathered yesterday that there was a . . . a difficulty."

"Difficulty!" It came out as an explosion. "I should think there is! This visit, Ursula, is a significant occasion. As you no doubt heard the queen remark, Cambridge was where the English Protestant movement began, the place where Martin Luther's ideas first took hold. A visit by Queen Elizabeth means something—it signals very clearly that she and her council have chosen to be on the Protestant side of the religious divide. It has to be a success—*has* to be. And in the middle of all the preparations . . . !"

He broke off, as if lost for words. I said quietly: "Who is Master Woodforde?"

Cecil studied me thoughtfully. "You apparently managed to come across him before you'd been at court for five minutes. You have the oddest knack in these things. How did it come about?"

"It was pure chance. I was passing the door to Lady Lennox's chambers when she burst out of it, in the middle of an argument with a small man in a black gown. She addressed him as Master Woodforde. He was saying that he would do anything to get back into her favor and she was saying that she would favor him most if he were in his coffin. I think he'd got into her rooms uninvited and been lying in wait to plead with her."

"Yes. That is the man. His name," said Cecil, "is Giles Woodforde—Dr. Giles Woodforde, strictly speaking, although he never seems to use the title. He likes to say that he's an unassuming man. He was once in Lady Lennox's service, as a tutor, originally to her son Henry Darnley, and after Darnley outgrew him, he stayed on to instruct other young people in her household. Then he was dismissed for some reason—I don't know exactly what except that he managed to displease Lady Lennox in some way. Maybe religion had something to do with it. She's a Catholic sympathizer and he's from a good, solid Protestant family. He was born in Cambridge and studied at the university. After he left Lady Lennox's service, he went back there and became a tutor in Latin and Greek at King's College. He's here now in the company of some other university representatives who have come to discuss details of the queen's visit with me. Which brings me to the matter we were discussing when you joined us yesterday."

"It sounded more like an argument than a discussion," I said.

"It was! This is the situation. The queen is to arrive in Cambridge on the fifth of August. Now, these days, some of the students go home in the late summer, ostensibly to help their fathers get the harvest in, but some have slack modern attitudes and use that as an excuse to slip away early."

Contemplating slack modern attitudes, the hard-working Cecil sniffed disdainfully. "And just for once," he said, "I wish more of these youths were modern idlers! I also wish that they were controlled as they were in the last century when they weren't allowed into the town at all unless a senior university member accompanied them. Now they have more freedom—and I am sorry to say that few of them are leaving the university early this year. The prospect of seeing the Queen is too exciting. Most will still be there on August fifth, ready to make pests of themselves if given the ghost of a chance. So, from the start, I have made it clear that the students are *not* to create a nuisance during the queen's visit. They may be allowed to cheer respectfully from a distance as she rides in but no more.

"At least," said Cecil with irritation, "that is how I planned it. But now . . . it seems that Woodforde has a half brother. Same mother, different fathers, which accounts for their different stations in life. While Giles Woodforde is a scholar, his older half brother, Roland Jester, runs a pie shop in what is called Jackman's Lane in Cambridge, and it is a place where undergraduates are permitted to go. They are still not allowed to frequent taverns and aren't encouraged to mix with the townsfolk, but nowadays they have to have *some* places in which to congregate and Jester's Pie Shop is one of them. It serves meat pies and cheese and small ale which can be consumed on the premises. By agreement with the university authorities, it closes in the afternoon so as not to encourage students to linger over midday gatherings. But gather there they certainly do, and it appears that Jester overheard them planning a rag."

"To do with the queen?"

"Yes. As she comes into Cambridge, she will pass through Jackman's Lane and there she is to pause briefly, dismount, and take a seat on a small dais with a canopy, and a lady chosen to represent the women of the town will present her with a nosegay. Then she will mount her horse again and ride on into Queens' College to receive a more official address. The students, apparently, conceived the wild notion of kidnapping the lady who is to present the flowers! Jester overheard them arguing over whether to do it after the presentation or before!"

"But . . ."

"But why didn't he just report them to the authorities and put a stop to the whole thing? He did in a way; at least, he reported it to his half brother, Woodforde. But Woodforde apparently has sympathy with young people and instead of crushing this nonsense instantly," said Cecil in tones of fury, "he promptly invented a mad scheme under which the rag would become part of the official welcome. The lady—a Mistress Smithson—that's all I know about her—would present her flowers and then some students would rush up and a couple of them would have a brief mock fight with the queen's guards while the others would whisk the lady out of sight into the pie shop. It would be a playlet, more or less. It would start with one of the students bowing before the queen and begging to be allowed to take Mistress Smithson away as a keepsake, or something equally absurd. And somehow or other," said Cecil, "Wood-forde persuaded Jester to agree and then actually con-vinced the fellows of the university that this scheme should be presented to me!"

"And you don't like it?"

"*Like* it? Violence—even mock violence—right beside the royal dais? People waving swords about? But all the queen says is: oh, let the young men take part in the welcome and have their innocent fun! And now, as an afterthought, Woodforde has asked Dudley to be the queen's champion and take part in the fight and that . . . that madman Dudley has volunteered to fight a mock duel with one of the students! Bah!" snorted Cecil.

"Dudley sees no harm in it either?"

"Dudley is taking the queen's part, partly to annoy me because provoking me always amuses him but also because he wants to please her. He's afraid of being sent to Scotland against his will. I am perfectly sure that he's in no danger of any such thing but oddly enough, Dudley is less certain."

I said: "And is all this something to do with the rea-son why I have been called from Withysham so much sooner than I expected? I have been told that I am to go to Cambridge almost at once, to make advance preparations for the queen's visit. But have I other work as well? Are you afraid that there may be some-thing behind this?"

Cecil sighed again, moving his bandaged foot uneasily. "Yes, I am, though I can't imagine what it can be. Cambridge is as much a Protestant stronghold as ever it was; that's true enough. During Queen Mary's heresy hunts, there were a lot of very frightened people there; in fact, I gather from Woodforde that one of his relatives spent most of the previous reign in a state of terror and not without reason. His home was searched for heretical literature once, though nothing was found. Nowadays, the undergraduates nearly all come from families who are staunch supporters both of Elizabeth and the Protestant faith. But there is that link with Lady Lennox."

"I doubt if it's much of a link," I said. "She obviously couldn't bear the sight of Woodforde and wanted him out of her way. Is anything known against either Woodforde or this brother of his—Jester?"

"No, nothing, and don't imagine I haven't looked for something. Let me tell you about them. They're both middle-aged. Woodforde is said to be forty-one and Jester is four or five years older and the only flaws in their otherwise virtuous pasts are that Woodforde once worked for Lady Lennox and was dismissed—and neither of those is actually a crime—and that Roland Jester's wife left him.

"And I can understand that all too well," Cecil said, with a glint of amusement. "Because the chief drawback to those two brothers as far as I can discover, is that they are inconceivably boring! It's my belief that Mistress Jester ran away to avoid dying of ennui. I've been reading their correspondence—they write to each other whenever they're apart—and more tedious letters you couldn't imagine."

"Really?" I frowned. I had, after all, seen Woodforde, hands pressed together as if in prayer, pleading with Lady Lennox for her favor, and I had seen the dignified and wealthy Lady Lennox, after an encounter with him, looking as harassed as though a pack of hounds were snapping at her heels. I hadn't seen Jester, but there was surely more to Master Woodforde than a tedious mentality.

I said as much. Cecil shrugged. "Maybe. But if you saw those letters, you'd think otherwise. While Woodforde has been here, his brother has written twice, paying out for a courier, and Woodforde has written back both times. Because of my suspicions, I had the letters intercepted—both ways—and I also had Woodforde's quarters at court searched. Some old letters were found that Jester wrote to him while he was with the Lennoxes. The way they were written made me more suspicious than ever at first. They were rambling and disjointed, and sometimes awkwardly phrased, and at once, I thought: a cipher! So I had them tested, but . . ."

"Without success?" I prompted, since Cecil had stopped in midsentence.

"Completely without success," said Cecil. "There wasn't a trace. They obviously weren't the kind of cipher that replaces letters by strange symbols or by other letters; but there are other ways of writing secret messages. I have heard of codes in which one takes every third—or fourth or fifth or sixth or whatever— letter or word to extract the message. It takes skill to write a letter that conceals a message in that form and still reads in an ordinary, sensible fashion, but it can be done. Sometimes there's a pattern of intervals; you have to take the second, fourth, sixth, eighth letter or word, and then start the sequence again. That sort of code can be difficult to break but I have clerks who can do it, all the same. They applied their best efforts to the correspondence between Woodforde and Jester and found nothing but gibberish."

He sighed again, irritably. "We even tested for a double cipher—I mean applying letter-substitution ciphers to the gibberish. There was still nothing. No sign of a code. The brothers aren't exchanging secret correspondence on treasonous plots. The letters are just what they seem—dull, trivial outpourings from dull, trivial minds."

"What sort of things do they say?" I asked curiously.

"Well, Woodforde's first letter back to Jester starts off quite reasonably with his impressions of the court and the meetings he's attended but then he drifts off into a stream of haphazard banalities. He doesn't like jesters—except for his brother and his niece!—there's a creeper rattling near his window at night, he can hear sheep in the distance, he's bought a new blue doublet . . . all his letters meander on in the same way. Roland Jester isn't much better. They go in for occasional poetic flights—Woodforde's, mostly. Jester's the duller of the two. *He* bothered to hire a courier in order to complain that the girls who work in his shop giggle too much and that his furniture is getting old!" I had rarely heard Cecil sound so acid.

"But you're still suspicious?" I said.

"Yes. I'd be glad to be proved wrong—but yes."

I thought hard. "Judging by the exchange I witnessed between Woodforde and Lady Lennox," I said, "the link between them doesn't look significant. All the same . . . how much would Lady Lennox grieve, I

wonder, if anything were to happen to Elizabeth? I
fancy she'd attend the funeral in a heavy black veil to
hide her laughter."

"Really, Ursula!" Poor Cecil looked quite shocked.
"You have the most salty way of putting things sometimes."

I smiled. My husband Matthew's pet name for me
was Saltspoon. "But even if harm is planned against
the queen," I said, "she will be a public figure in Cambridge! If anyone is lying in wait with a firearm or a
crossbow, they will have many chances to shoot without having to create one in this elaborate way."

"She won't be a target on that dais in Jackman's
Lane if I have anything to do with it," said Cecil. "It
will have a canopy and sides and no vantage point from
the front that an assassin could use. But I'm not happy,
Ursula, no. I feared that the queen would be obstinate,
but I did convince her that you should go to Cambridge early as one of her harbingers. I remarked on
the importance of this visit and said that you would be
an ideal choice: you would cast a feminine eye over the
arrangements, and you are highly observant. From my
point of view, you are also discreet. I believe in discretion. Plots against the queen are not a subject for gossip in my opinion. I prefer the very idea to be unmentionable and, therefore, unthinkable. You, I know, will
not gossip."

"Thank you," I said.

"The queen raised no objection. These arrangements are my responsibility anyway," said Cecil. "But
your real purpose will be to discover, if you can,
what is going on, and if this silly playlet, this ridicu-

lous entertainment, is what it seems, or not. How you are to do it, I don't know, but you are good at finding ways, in my experience. Investigate that pie shop, find out all you can about the half brothers and their associates, and the students, too. Look out for coincidences. In my view," said Cecil, with another glint of amusement, "if there were an eleventh commandment, it would be Never Trust Coincidences. You will not be alone in your task. I have also discussed it with Rob Henderson. You know that he is to lead your party of harbingers, of course. That is at his own request. He will be conducting the same inquiries as yourself. Sometimes two heads are better than one. Rob is the official leader but I wish you to cooperate as partners in the inquiry. Both of you will be paid for your services as harbingers *and* as inquiry agents."

Putting Withysham to rights was eating money. I thought about the extra income and inclined my head. "I will do my best," I said.

I might be, strictly speaking, Madame de la Roche, wife of Matthew de la Roche of Blanchepierre in the Loire Valley. But when I was in England, I was Ursula Blanchard, Lady of the Queen's Presence Chamber and widow of Gerald Blanchard, a man who had once carried out secret tasks for one of Elizabeth's great men and who had inadvertently taught his wife a good deal about such things.

I always wore an underkirtle and a divided overskirt and inside the overskirt I stitched hidden pouches where I could carry, among other things, a small dagger in a little sheath and a set of lockpicks.

I had never used the dagger, although I had been responsible for sending men—and one woman—to their death by other means. I had used the lockpicks quite often.

When I was in England, I was a secret agent, on behalf of Elizabeth, in the direct employ of Sir William Cecil.

5

Respectable Employment

The Hendersons had been friends of Sir William
Cecil's for many years. I first came to know them
when he arranged for them to foster Meg for me at a
time when I could not care for her myself. Rob Henderson was one of the few people who knew of my
secret work, and at Cecil's request, he had often helped
me with escorts, armed assistance, and the like, backed
up by a mandate from Cecil to carry out arrests if
required.

He had done that for me during the task I had
recently carried out on the Welsh border. Nevertheless,
things had changed during the two years before that,
when I had been away in France. I had gathered by
now that Rob Henderson had in the interim become a
full-fledged agent. His good-looking, candid face, with
its fashionably trimmed beard, and the dashing clothes
he liked to wear, were an advantage because they
amounted to a disguise.

"You don't look like an agent," I said as we made our plans for the journey. "Any more than I do."

"You," said Rob frankly and not for the first time, "are a young woman and in my opinion you shouldn't *be* an agent. I know you're good at it, but all the same, I wish you could have stayed at Thamesbank and kept Mattie company for a while. I'm worried about this new baby. We didn't expect another so late in life. Oh well. We must put Elizabeth's interests first and both do our best, I suppose."

The other members of our party included three court officials: a Yeoman Purveyor, whose special task was to make sure that when the queen and her enormous entourage took the road, they would always be properly fed; a junior Gentleman Usher, who was to make certain that everyone would be accommodated in suitably furnished rooms; and a conscientious junior Officer of the Wardrobe, who had to ensure among other things that there was space for everyone's clothing, and robing rooms for Her Majesty wherever she was likely to need them. He was the one who later on caused a stir in King's College by insisting that a retiring room be built in its chapel.

We would be followed, a week or so before the arrival of the queen, by a party of senior Gentlemen Ushers, who would make sure that everything we had arranged was as it should be, and they would in turn be followed by Sir Robert Dudley and Sir William Cecil in person, to make sure that the Gentlemen Ushers hadn't made any mistakes either. Our party was the first and the humblest and also the one with the most work to do.

We had our own assistants, of course. Along with us rode a gaggle of valets and clerks, the latter with slates and abacuses sticking out of their saddlebags, and of course we had our entourage of personal servants, which in my case meant Dale and Brockley, and in Rob's case meant three of his menservants, all former soldiers and all equipped with swords as well as fashionable cloaks and dashing hats.

Giles Woodforde and the university dignitaries were due to return to Cambridge but they did not ride in our company. I had begun to have a shadowy idea about a way of pursuing my investigation and I didn't want Woodforde to know who I was. I didn't think he had noticed me during that encounter in the corridor; he had been too taken up with Lady Lennox. "As far as he's concerned, I ought to stay unnoticed. I think I should keep out of his sight," I told Cecil.

Cecil obligingly made sure that the university men went off separately, ahead of us. Since Cecil was the Secretary of State and the chancellor of Cambridge as well, no one argued.

The other harbingers had also to examine the arrangements at the houses where the queen would stay on her way to Cambridge, but Rob and I had no time to lose. The queen was due in Cambridge in less than three weeks. If there was anything to discover, we must find it before she got there. Again, Cecil had smoothed our way by giving straightforward orders. The rest of the harbingers were to deal with the intervening houses as they went along; Rob and I were to go straight on to Cambridge, the royal destination, and begin work there.

Even at that, we took four days to reach it, because we had packhorses and they slow one down. I was annoyed but Dale was thankful, for she always found riding a trial. The journey was interesting, though. I had not seen East Anglia before. Gradually, the land grew flatter and marshier and more seamed with waterways, and the sky above seemed to grow wider every day, stretching from horizon to horizon. We had one wet day and we could see the cloud coming from the west long before it reached us, a heavy blackness with the rain sweeping below it in pale, hazy curtains.

The local people, whenever we had occasion to speak with them, had broad, slow accents, often hard to follow, and some curious skills. We were startled one misty morning to see two towering figures, at least ten feet high, thin and spindly, moving about on the boggy ground to the right of our track—until we realized that they were men on stilts, wading through the mud.

In the evening and the early morning, wild geese often flew overhead in a formation like a V, honking in wild voices. On the third morning, I was riding beside Rob Henderson, talking to him about my plans for when I reached Cambridge, when a flight of geese swept by above us, and looking up at them, I said: "Their calls always seem to be full of salt winds and vast empty spaces."

"You like them, don't you?" Rob said, and withdrawing my gaze from the sky, I found him regarding me quizzically.

"Well—yes, I do," I told him.

"That says something about your nature," he said.

"Will you ever settle for domestic peace? I wonder. Or will the wild geese call to you for the rest of your life?"

I was startled. Rob and I were friends, although we were not and never had been anything more. I would have said, though, that we knew each other well. But never before had handsome, stylish Rob Henderson, who adored his bubbly wife, Mattie, and his growing family, looked at me so searchingly or assessed my nature so shrewdly.

He was right, too. No matter how much I missed my husband, no matter how much I enjoyed peaceful days as a chatelaine of a manor, no matter how many tears I might shed on parting from my daughter, once I was abroad in the world on the queen's business, seeking out miscreants, another part of my nature took over. There was another Ursula in me, a huntress who needed to chase a quarry now and then in order to be really happy; who could not resist the call of adventure. Who responded and perhaps always would respond to the cry of the wild geese.

Rob's remark made me uncomfortable. Detaching myself from him, I rode forward to catch up with Brockley, who was just ahead. I wanted to talk to him, too, concerning my Cambridge plans.

"In my opinion," he said to me presently, "this whole venture is a wild-goose chase," and then he looked surprised, because I burst out laughing.

Brockley often sighed over the peculiarities of my character, and as for poor Dale, though she was deeply attached to me, she found me a most exhausting employer. We reached Cambridge just after noon on the final day of the journey, but only because on the previous day, I had grown irritated by our slow progress and begun urging us to hurry. Dale, roused early before she had anything like recovered from the long ride of the day before, bundled onto Brockley's pillion after hardly any breakfast, and then forced to endure more miles on horseback, was even more worn-out by the time we reached the city than she had been when we arrived at Richmond.

Coming into Cambridge, we saw, to either side of us, tangles of narrow lanes crowded with traffic, horse and foot, and heavily shadowed by overhanging upper stories. Every now and then we glimpsed the roofs and spires of colleges and churches, and sometimes, to our left, the glitter of the sunlight on the River Cam. I tried to fix an idea of the city layout in my mind but Dale's obvious weariness distracted me. The university dignitaries who had returned ahead of us had arranged lodgings for us all and it was well we found them without difficulty because my poor tirewoman really seemed about to topple out of her saddle altogether.

In her youth, Fran Dale had had smallpox and it had left her slightly pockmarked. The marks were not very obvious; most of the time, one noticed her well-shaped face and large blue eyes rather than the pocks. They showed up, though, when she became upset or overtired. When she started unpacking in our chamber, I saw how noticeable they were and told her to leave the hampers.

"Just help me into a clean gown," I said. "Brockley

will be here as soon as he and Henderson's men have settled the horses—the stables our landlord suggested are quite close, it seems. Then we'll have a meal and you can sleep." If she became much more exhausted, I knew she might fall ill. On the way, Henderson had mentioned that because of the marshlands, there were fevers peculiar to East Anglia, which could strike at any season. "You can finish the unpacking this evening. We shall have to go out tomorrow morning, though not very far," I told Dale.

"Where will we be going, ma'am?"

"Well . . ." I began doubtfully, and then turned at the sound of Brockley's familiar tap on the door. I called to him to come in and the moment he did so, I said: "What is it?" Brockley did not have an expressive face but I knew him well enough to recognize the signs of exasperation.

"We were recommended to leave the horses at Radley's Stables, madam, and I'm sorry to say that there was nowhere else to leave them but I only hope they'll be all right. We've had to waste a lot of time over it."

"What's wrong with Radley's?" I asked him.

"Wrong with it!" Brockley snorted. "When we got there, the owner was clouting a weedy under-groom all round the yard, shouting at him to do this and finish that and bellowing that they were all behind because the fellow had come in late in the morning *again*. The noise was upsetting the horses. I could hear them stamping and whinnying in their stable. We stopped at the gate and I left one of Henderson's men to hold my Speckle, and slipped into the stable for a look round. Our respected Mr. Radley was too busy knocking the daylights out of the groom even to notice he'd got custom!

"I found a young student in there, patting a nice-looking mare. *He* told me he'd come to explain that he couldn't take her out for his usual early morning ride tomorrow, and wanted someone to exercise her, but he couldn't get a hearing either and he wouldn't recommend anyone to stable a horse there; he wouldn't do it himself only the place is cheap and it was the only way he could afford to keep his horse in Cambridge at all. He said the hay was usually dusty and I had a look, and it was. He suggested the Eagle Inn in a place called Benet Street and told me where to find it. So I went back to the others and to the Eagle we went and the stabling there is all it should be, as a lot of people obviously know because it was full. So in the end we had to go back to Radley's and this time we got some attention from the ostler. But I've taken it upon myself to pay him extra to buy good-quality hay. I hope I did right, madam, but your little mare is choosy about her food and won't eat up unless it's to her liking. I don't want her losing condition."

"Nor do I. Yes, of course you did right."

"I also told Radley that if all our horses weren't well cared for, I'd warm his lugs and his back for him, personally, and Master Henderson's men all said they'd lend a hand. We've put the fear of God into him, I trust. But it's not the kind of stable I'd choose if I could help it."

"I'm sure you did your best, Brockley, and with you to keep an eye on the horses, I'm also sure they'll be all right," I said briskly. "Now, I want a word with you. About tomorrow . . ."

"We are to visit the pie shop?"

"Yes."

"You are serious about this, madam?"

"Brockley, you know I'm always serious about my schemes." I turned to Dale, who was looking at us in a puzzled way. "Brockley and I had a discussion about this during the journey," I said. "I daresay you noticed us talking together."

"Yes, ma'am," Dale agreed.

"I also talked to Master Henderson. It was about these plans that Brockley has just mentioned. The journey has taken longer than I wanted. The queen will be here now in a fortnight. I must find a way to get near the heart of the arrangements for this confounded playlet. I've told you that it involves a pie shop in a place called Jackman's Lane. Tomorrow, we are all three going to visit it. And after that . . ."

Our lodgings were in a timbered four-story house only a few minutes' walk from either Queens' or King's Colleges. Rob and I had asked to be in the same lodgings but we were decently separated, with my rooms at the top of the first flight of stairs, and Rob on the topmost floor, right under the roof. The arrangements could hardly have been otherwise, though, for we had as landlady a middle-aged widow, whose sparkling white ruff, apron, and cap, and cowed maidservants, were proof of her sublime respectability. After changing my clothes and taking some food, I climbed two flights of stairs in search of Master Henderson.

We had left the other harbingers behind on the road but when they arrived, they would want to know about the advance work we were supposed to be doing. I didn't want word getting back to the court that I wasn't attending to my duties, because as far as Elizabeth was concerned, a harbinger was all I was, here to cast a female eye over the arrangements in general, especially the Provost's Lodge where she was to sleep, and the rooms her ladies would use.

"I want to be seen to be doing something," I said to Rob when I had found him. "I may be otherwise engaged very soon."

"Let's go over to King's College and see what we can inspect straightaway," Rob suggested, and then added: "We can talk at the same time."

We found that the rooms in the Provost's Lodge were being swept and sweetened and were not yet ready for our inspection. The rooms that had been set aside as audience and council chambers could be seen, however. "Very well," said Rob. "We'll look at those."

Court business had to go on wherever Elizabeth was, even if ambassadors wishing to present their credentials had to chase her around the country. Therefore, she had to have audience and council chambers always available. Both needed space and dignity and a dais for the queen; the council chamber must also have good light, tables, seats, and writing materials, and her servants must be able to fetch refreshments without delay if required. There must be an ample supply of candles, which must not be scented. Messengers must be constantly available and have somewhere to wait. And so on and so on. The list of requirements, which we had in writing, was formidable.

Rob produced the list and we set off, guided by a minor university official, who was fortunately overawed by the importance of the arrangements and by us, and who was easily dismissed when we told him to leave us by ourselves to inspect the rooms, at leisure. We walked around them, noting shortcomings—there were several—but meanwhile, in quiet voices, we discussed other things.

"I intend to interview all the students who are to take part in the playlet," Rob said. "I will speak to them officially, one by one. Look, Ursula, there's really no need for you to go through with this pretense you have in mind, but if you insist . . ."

"I do."

"Very well. If necessary, I'll see that your disappearance is explained. I can say I sent you back to one of the houses where the queen will stop on the way here, because during our journey, I noticed one or two things I wasn't happy about."

I nodded. "Yes. That will do, I think. Now, as well as talking to the students, what about talking to Woodforde? Cecil says he has looked into Woodforde's character already, but nevertheless . . ."

"I know." Rob frowned. "Woodforde seized on the idea of this playlet, didn't he? Well, he's back in Cambridge now. As a woman, you can't haunt the university but I can. I'll see what more I can find out about him." He considered me gravely. "What does Brockley think about your wild scheme?"

"He's shaking his head over it."

"He always shakes his head over your schemes," said Rob. "This time I feel he's right to be uneasy. I don't like it, Ursula. It isn't fitting."

"What has that to do with it? There's no time to waste. I must find out what, if anything, is going on in that pie shop. Should we not arrange for supplies of paper for note-taking during council meetings? And inkstands at each place round the council table?"

Rob groaned, but said no more.

Next morning, having borrowed one of Dale's drab working gowns (although it still had an open overskirt, into which I had quickly stitched one of my secret pouches), I set out for Jackman's Lane and Master Roland Jester's pie shop. Dale and Brockley were with me but not in the characters of maid and manservant. For the moment, the three of us were trying to look like equals—in fact, relatives.

I had sent Brockley out in advance to find out just where the place was and he led us straight there. Jackman's Lane was a short street that turned off from Trumpington Street, the main road in from the south. Jackman's ran, slanting, in the general direction of the river but came out in Silver Street, close to Queens' College.

Elizabeth would pass through Jackman's on her way to hear an address of welcome at Queens', and there in the lane, she would pause, to receive her gift of flowers from a woman of Cambridge. The dais where she would be briefly enthroned for this purpose hadn't yet been put in place although its position had been roped off and was already causing a fair amount of nuisance to the ordinary traffic of the lane. It had been placed toward the Silver Street end, which was a little wider than the rest, and Jester's shop was very close to it.

On the side of the lane opposite the pie shop, the buildings were just cottages, small and solid and each in its own little garden, and not all the same size. The pie shop side, however, was quite different, consisting of a row of shops and houses, all adjoining and obviously all built at the same time. They were handsome affairs, with redbrick ground floors, overhanging timber and plaster stories above, and attics with dormer windows peeping out of the thatched roofs. Their architect had had a sense of style, for he had given them chimneys with decorative brickwork, and finished the line of buildings off at each end with four slender, faceted buttress towers, one at each corner. These were of redbrick as well, patterned to match the chimneys, with gray stone to pick out the facet edges, and ornamental crenellations on top.

The shops sold a variety of wares, and all of them had substantial living quarters above, with private side entrances beside the shopfronts. The pie shop itself was at the end of the lane, the last one before Silver Street, and had a walled garden that ran around it from front to back. Facing on to the lane was an open shopfront with a counter where passersby could purchase hot pies to take away. This was manned by a pink-faced lout with a bull's voice, which he used for bellowing requests for fresh supplies back to the kitchen inside. Those who wished to sit down and eat indoors, though, could go around the end of the counter, give orders from their tables, and be waited on.

We studied the place and then Brockley looked at me inquiringly. "We go in," I said.

It was dark inside, but clean enough, with fresh sawdust on the stone-flagged floor, and a partly open door at the rear, showing a glimpse of the kitchen beyond. Intriguingly, it also allowed us to hear that in the kitchen, a man was shouting and a girl was tearfully protesting, and as we seated ourselves at a rough table, some of the words clarified.

". . . and I'm a-tellin' you, Ambrosia, I've other plans for you and Thomas ain't one of them." The man's East Anglian voice was aggrieved, almost shrill. "He's not our sort and his family'll say that, same as I do. They're gentry even if they ain't of the richest. We're trade and the two don't mix. If only your mother was here . . ."

"I wish she *was* here! She'd understand!" This was accompanied by a loud clatter as though the girl were rattling pots and spoons together in a fury.

"Aye, maybe she would at that! Come to think on it, your mother never did have the sense she was born with or know her own good luck when she had it. Maybe she *would* lead you on to make a fool of yourself! Well, I won't! You'll not leave this place without I say you can, and someone'll allus go with you, till this here nonsense stops."

"That's not fair! That's not right!" *Clatter! Crash!*

"You'll thank me one day, my girl! Once this business of the queen's visit is over and done with, I'll see Thomas never sets foot in here again. Now get out there and serve; I've heard someone come in or my name ain't Roland Jester!"

"Mercy!" Dale whispered. "What a merry household."

"It happens," I told her. "You should have heard Uncle Herbert and Aunt Tabitha when they found out that there was something going on between me and young Master Gerald Blanchard, who was supposed to be marrying my cousin Mary. Roland Jester in there's a dear little baa-lamb by comparison."

"The girl is coming out," muttered Brockley. "Quick, madam, talk of something else."

"I wonder who did the carving on this settle," I said clearly. I was facing Dale and Brockley across the table and although they were seated on a bench as rude as the table, I was on a settle with wooden arms that ended in heavy, carved lions' heads. I fingered the mane of the lion immediately beside me and then withdrew my finger with a startled "Ouch!" and used my teeth to remove a splinter.

"They were all right when they were new but all our seats and tables are old now," the girl said in a dull voice as she came up to us. "With the queen coming to visit Cambridge and all, we're having new seats and tables made. Father thinks maybe courtiers might come in." She didn't sound as though she shared her father's optimism. Even in the poor light, I could see that her hands were callused and chapped with work, and that her eyes were reddened; she walked as though bowed with depression. She had a dark stuff gown on with a stained white apron over it. "What'll you eat and drink?"

I opened my mouth to ask what was on offer and then remembered that I was not here as Ursula Blanchard, court lady, but as Ursula Faldene, cousin to Roger Brockley. I had decided to use my maiden name, in case Jester should happen to mention me to his half brother, and in case Giles Woodforde had heard my name at Richmond. I subsided and looked at Brockley, silently asking him to do the talking instead.

Brockley, therefore, inquired what was to be had. "We've got chicken and onion pasties," said Ambrosia. "Or chicken pies without onion. The chicken was fresh-killed today. We don't hang poultry in summer. We've got some of the mutton pie from yesterday left as well, and that's all right, too. Or there's bread and cheese, and radishes. With small ale or milk to drink."

She rattled it all off efficiently, in an accent a little more educated than the man's, but she sounded as though she had said it at least a hundred times that day and would probably be reciting it that night in her sleep. We settled for chicken pies, Brockley and Dale with onion and myself without, and small ale to go with it. Brockley gave her his best and pleasantest smile, and as though we had heard nothing of the quarrel, asked if she had worked there long.

"All my life. I'm Master Jester's daughter," she said, and whisked away.

"What an odd-looking girl," whispered Dale.

"Yes, very unusual," I agreed. She had been facing the light from the open front of the shop and I had seen her features as well as her hands and eyes. Ambrosia Jester had the kind of face that is ugly or attractive according to your personal taste. It was slightly squashed from brow to chin, as though someone had put her chin on a tabletop and then placed a heavy weight on top of her head. Her lips were a fraction too thick, her nostrils a fraction too splayed, and her dark eyes were deep-set under brows that swept dramatically upward at the outer corners.

Yet it was a face with character and even passion, and judging from her father's strictures, she had found a focus for that passion. She was no clod—and her indignant parent, whatever Cecil might say about his style as a correspondent, hadn't sounded like a bore. That word didn't fit Master Jester, any more than it fitted Giles Woodforde, whose impassioned outburst I had witnessed in the corridor at Richmond.

"This family," I remarked, "begins to look interesting."

"You mean to go through with this?" Brockley asked me.

"I think I must. We're not going to find out very much just by sitting here and eating their pies. I've got to get right inside the place."

"Are you sure, madam? After all, I understand the scheme was started by the students and has been taken up by this man Giles Woodforde, who is inside the university."

"But it will involve this shop," I said. "I'm leaving Woodforde and the students to Henderson, because he can roam round the university more easily than I can. But the shop must be investigated, too. I'm going to try."

Our food and drink arrived, brought this time by a different girl, a skinny young one with timid blue eyes and pale hair trailing like wisps of straw from under her cap, and we stopped talking until she had gone.

Then I said: "I can't think of any other way of finding out anything at all! I know you won't be far away."

"I certainly will not!" said Brockley. "I wish, madam, that you wouldn't rush into these things so eagerly. You always say that you will be all right, that you won't court danger, but . . ."

"I know, Brockley. I'm sorry."

I smiled at him, my dear, reliable Brockley, with his gold-freckled skin and his level gray-blue eyes. Like his wife, Fran, he was in his late forties, and his wiry brown hair was now receding fast and streaked with gray. But he was, as ever, reassuringly solid in build and his calm voice with its trace of country accent never changed. The hands that were now breaking up his pie were the strong, steady hands of a horseman. Before entering my employment, he had been a groom and in the past, for a time, he had been a soldier. He smiled back at me and I saw Dale glance quickly from him to me and then look down at her food, and secretly, I sighed.

Brockley and I were not just employer and servant; we were also friends and colleagues. Once, during a terrifying night we had spent shut in the same dungeon, we had come perilously close to becoming lovers. We had not yielded, but nevertheless, somehow or other, Dale was aware of the attraction between us. Just as Mattie Henderson was aware that for all his charm and good looks, I had no desire for Rob Henderson, nor he for me.

That awareness was why I had made such a point of explaining to Fran that when Brockley and I talked so earnestly as we rode toward Cambridge, we had only been discussing plans about the pie shop, and it was also the reason why she had been so sour about Rob Henderson going off to Cambridge and leaving his wife behind. She had been saying to me, in cipher as it were: *I feel that there is something between you and Roger that leaves me out in the cold.*

I said: "It's a great relief to me that you will both be at hand. That is, assuming that we manage to arrange what we've come to arrange. Brockley . . . ?"

Brockley rose and went to the kitchen door. He called, and the girl Ambrosia appeared again, this time with a floury rolling pin in her hand. Brockley spoke to her quietly. She glanced quickly past him to look at me, and then disappeared into the back regions. Brockley returned to our table and a few moments later, a man came out into the shop. I saw at once that he could very well be related to Giles Woodforde. He was bigger, but he had the same oddly nondescript air about him. Five minutes after parting from him, you would be hard put to it to remember the color of his eyes or the shape of his face.

"This is the owner of the shop," Brockley said to me, not quite in his usual respectful tones. "His name is Master Jester. Master Jester, this is my cousin, Mistress Ursula Faldene. She is in need of respectable employment . . ."

6

The Pie Shop in Jackman's Lane

Life in Jester's Pie Shop was hell.

It was nearly as bad, I thought bitterly, as I crawled out of bed at half past four after my third night there, as life at Faldene House had been, when I lived there on sufferance with Uncle Herbert and Aunt Tabitha, never knowing from one moment to the next when my aunt or uncle would decide I had said something impertinent or failed to perform a task quickly or adequately enough, with painful results. Looking back, I wonder now if I encouraged, not to say seduced, Gerald Blanchard, my cousin Mary's betrothed, because he was a way of escape.

On the face of it, of course, I could have walked out of the pie shop at will, since I was there under false pretenses. Brockley had told Jester that he and his wife, Fran, were taking service in Cambridge, but that he wished to look after his widowed cousin Ursula and had, therefore, brought her to Cambridge as well and was seeking a good live-in post for her. It had occurred to him, said Brockley, exuding flattery, that Cambridge was about to become very busy and perhaps such a flourishing business as the pie shop might want an extra hand. Oh yes, his cousin Ursula could cook!

Fortunately, this was true though I had come to it comparatively late. I didn't learn much about cooking at Faldene, because while my mother still lived she had resolutely defended me from my aunt's attempts to turn me into a kitchen maid, and made sure I was educated. Later, Uncle Herbert found my education useful, since he could make me into an unpaid clerk, to keep his accounts. But I had picked up a good deal of culinary lore once I was married to Gerald and again when I became mistress of Blanchepierre. I could act the part required.

And act it I must. The freedom to walk out was a privilege I could not use. I was here for a purpose and to achieve it, I had to put up with whatever the pie shop demanded of me and whatever Master Jester chose to throw at me: accusations of impertinence, wooden platters, or blows. In referring to him as a baa-lamb in comparison to my uncle, I had been horribly wrong. Jester and Uncle Herbert were kindred spirits.

Above the pie shop, I shared not only a room but also a bed with Ambrosia and the thin maidservant Phoebe. We rose at half past four, washed faces and hands in cold water, scrambled into our clothes (mine were all commandeered from Dale), and sped down to the kitchen to break our fast with whatever rolls were left over from the day before, smeared with dripping and washed down with small ale, swallowing it all as best we could while simultaneously starting the bread oven, rousing up the fire, and putting the giant stockpot on to heat.

Then Phoebe would uncover the basins of dough that had been made the night before for today's bread and pastry, and start shaping and rolling. I, however, had been given a different job. Jester, who to be fair to him was always down before time, and Wat, the pink-faced lout who manned the street counter, and slept beside the fuel store on the ground floor, would soon be busy killing the day's supply of poultry. Master Jester, it appeared, set great store by the excellence of his ingredients. He had many regular customers, including some who did not come to the shop but had pies delivered to them, and he intended, he said, to keep their goodwill. He bought only a limited amount of meat from butchers, especially during the summer months. There was a fenced run in the back garden where he kept a dozen ducks and hens for eggs, along with the birds that were regularly bought live on market days and slaughtered as required. As Ambrosia had told us, during the summer he did not even let the birds hang.

Jester bought what he could get—capons, ducks, geese, or wildfowl brought in by fowlers from the fens—and mixed the meats if need be. I had to help Wat pluck and draw the birds and cut them up for the pot. "He never gets 'em done quick enough. Needs another pair of hands," Jester had told me. "I was thinkin' to get someone else, with the extra custom there'll be while the queen's in the city. Ambrosia's got the fowls to feed and the eggs to collect and the saw-dust to spread and I've got the marketing to do. You've come as a bit of luck."

When Wat and I had finished, the pieces went into a cauldron with some ladlefuls of stock, to be stewed slowly till they were tender. Then the meat could be stripped from the bone, cut small, and mixed with mushrooms, oatmeal, onions, and spices to make pie fillings. When Jester did buy from butchers, he usually purchased sheep or pig carcasses, and these were simi-larly prepared. He never bought beef. It was twice the price of mutton and, therefore, too expensive.

We had to toil hard but it could have been com-panionable if we could have worked together in a friendly fashion. Alas, instead of amiable cooperation, we had Roland Jester continually finding fault in the shrill, aggrieved voice that went so ill with his big physique.

"Phoebe, what're you doin' with that dough? Get the loaves into the oven for the love of God; we'll have the customers poundin' at the shutters afore long. Hurry *up*, girl, or I'll be after you with a stick, I will. Ambrosia, take that basket of eggs to the pantry afore someone knocks 'em clean off the shelf! Ain't them fowl drawn yet? What are they—freaks? They got twice as much inside 'em as ordinary fowl? You've not got time to stand still and eat, Wat. Leave off guzzlin' that roll and get busy with the cleaver . . . and don't answer me back, you great loon; I'll give you *I'm working as fast as I can, Master Jester!*" And with that, Roland Jester's cal-lused palm would crack against the back of Wat's head.

The most frequent victim was Wat, because he was

the only one who deliberately answered back. Wat himself paid these onslaughts little heed, because he was so hefty that he merely shook his head when Jester's palm landed, as though to discourage a blue-bottle.

For all his loutish appearance, though, Wat had a chivalrous streak. Once or twice, Jester had hit him for stepping in the way with a disapproving, broad Norfolk: "Aisy naow, aisy!" when the real target was Phoebe. Phoebe, who could be no more than fourteen, was too timid to do any answering back, but she was sometimes awkward and often drew Jester's ire by dropping things or clattering them.

Wat seemed shy of me and so far I hadn't had any-thing like a conversation with him; indeed, because his accent was so broad, I found it hard to understand him. All the same, he had twice come wordlessly to help me haul the insides out of a difficult bird.

However, he wasn't always there to interfere on Phoebe's behalf and as yet hadn't actually tried to defend me from Jester, though I would have been grateful if he had. I was deft enough and I tried to be respectful, but I seemed to have a positive knack of inadvertently saying things that Jester considered impertinent. Phoebe and I were both liable at times to find ourselves ducking a hurled platter or seeing stars as Jester's powerful palm sent one or the other of us reeling across the kitchen.

He didn't, I noticed, hit Ambrosia or throw things at her. When one morning her father actually knocked me flat on the kitchen floor, Ambrosia picked me up and since Jester had by then marched out of the room, she explained, in apologetic tones, why she was exempt.

"I have to give orders when he's not here and he thinks I'll be respected more if the rest of you don't see him knocking me about, so most of the time he doesn't—though it happens now and again. He used to treat my mother very badly, though. I hope you're not much hurt. Sit here for a moment."

She helped me to a stool. A wave of her heavy dark brown hair slid free of her headdress as she did so. Ambrosia had beautiful hair, although no one ever saw much of it because her father made her wear very concealing caps. I opened my mouth to ask her how long it was since her mother left, but my throbbing head managed, just in time, to remind me that I wasn't supposed to know anything about the household. Instead, I said: "Is your mother dead? How old were you when you lost her?"

"She isn't dead," said Ambrosia. "She ran away five years ago. I miss her but I don't blame her for going. My father cried after she went—sat and sobbed, if you can believe it—but he'd made her life a misery and that's a fact."

Roland Jester certainly made his servants' lives a misery. It was no better once we started serving customers. We were hurried and harried every moment, constantly urged to produce pies more quickly, although it was a mystery to me how we were supposed to make the oven bake pastry faster. The time that Jester knocked me down, it was for saying so. I was too used to speaking my mind, I suppose, and couldn't get out of the habit.

Time and again—because the simple fact that I was

not really Master Jester's helpless employee meant that
his blows made me more furious than frightened—I
yearned to storm out of that hateful shop and send
Roger Brockley or Rob Henderson (or better still, both
of them together) around to have a few words with its
proprietor. I had fantasies of the two of them putting
him in bed for a week. Meanwhile, I strove to suppress
my fury and endure. The days were passing and what,
so far, had I found out? I had tried my best and until
now I had achieved next to nothing.

My efforts in the last three days had included trying
to eavesdrop when Master Jester talked to anyone—his
daughter, his customers, or his neighbors. We had no
neighbor on the Silver Street side of the pie shop, of
course, but the adjoining house on the other side was
occupied by a Master Brady, a bronzesmith who had
separate business premises elsewhere, and his wife and
family. So far, this had revealed such breathless secrets
as the fact that the weather was very warm, that the
prospects for the wheat harvest were good, and that
students were an unruly breed.

I had also tried to pump Master Jester by asking art-
less questions. When he bothered to answer me, which
wasn't always, his replies were just as unhelpful. Yes, of
course, he was looking forward to the royal visit. He
was a loyal subject of the queen and hoped that her
presence in Cambridge would bring in business. It was
an honor for the shop to be involved in this playlet that
the students and his half brother had concocted. A
blank sheet of paper would have told me more.

Rob Henderson had furnished me with the names
of the students involved in the playlet. So far, they had

come to the pie shop only once. This was a lively occasion because they broke off in the middle of their meal to rehearse the sword fight for the playlet, with one of them pretending to be Dudley. They did it in slow, stylized fashion, but I had with some amusement watched Master Jester snatching tankards off tables, out of the way of the sticks they were using instead of actual swords, and listened while a young man called Thomas Shawe, who had an engaging grin and an extraordinary head of hair, which was neither fair nor red but was the color of slightly dulled brass, kept insisting that the boy who was taking Dudley's part must turn *this* way, not that, "or the public won't see properly and Master Woodforde says we've to give a proper show."

I understood that Dudley had been told of the moves and would have studied them in advance and that when he reached Cambridge, there would be a further rehearsal with him but probably only one, for lack of time. I wondered if the Master of the Queen's Horse realized how very amateurish the whole affair was going to be.

I had also gathered from Ambrosia that Shawe was the Thomas she was in love with, and that he was the one who had actually thought of the original rag. She told me about him by way of explaining why her father wouldn't let her serve at the tables when he was in the shop.

"We want to marry but Father was so angry when he found out. He won't hear of it. Maybe you overheard him shouting at me about it the time you first came into the shop."

"I did hear something, yes," I admitted.

"And it's not just that I'm trade and Thomas isn't," she said resentfully. "Father just doesn't want to lose me. I work hard and he doesn't have to pay me. He'll stop me marrying at all if he can."

"Oh, my dear!" I said, suddenly very sorry for her indeed, and conscious that I was at least ten years older than she was and had had two husbands. I felt I ought to be able to advise her, but couldn't think how.

Unexpectedly, however, she said: "I understand him, in a way. We're not hard up—far from it—but he was poor as a boy and he'll be tight with money all his life. And he's not good at . . . at"—she frowned, as though she had never sought words for this before and was finding it difficult—"at impressing people, making them do what he wants, so he shouts and hits out. I sometimes feel I ought to stay with him to look after him. He's my father, after all." She saw the sympathy in my face and added: "When I was younger, Uncle Giles—he's my father's half brother; he teaches at the university nowadays—urged Father to get a tutor for me so that I could be educated, and Father agreed, though I think my uncle helped with the fees. I had a good tutor, too. Dr. Barley, his name was. He taught me Latin, though with Greek I never got much further than the alphabet . . ."

Just like me, I thought, but remembered in time not to say so. Such accomplishments would seem very odd in a hired cookmaid.

"Dr. Barley is old and retired," Ambrosia said, with affection in her voice, "but before he left he told me to keep up the Latin he taught me, and Father lets me read a little most afternoons when we all have some time off. That's because the university insists on the shop being closed, if the students are to come here. Did you know that was the reason?"

"Yes. Master Jester explained that. I can understand your liking for books," I said, thinking with sudden wistfulness of Withysham, and those peaceful hours of reading with Meg.

"My father wants me to be happy, really," Ambrosia said earnestly. "But he wants the business to prosper, too, and to feel safe from poverty."

It wasn't my business. The Jesters weren't my family. I said no more.

On the day when the students came in, Phoebe and I were told to serve them and I tried to seize the chance to talk to them, but Jester caught me wasting time, as he put it, and promised me a drastic beating with a wooden ladle if I did it again. When I told him that my cousin Roger would half kill him if he did, he laughed.

"Masters have rights over servants. Your cousin's a servant hisself and he knows," he told me.

One day, I said grimly to myself as I went down the steep wooden stairs on that third morning, one day, please God, may I see Master Jester weeping at my feet and begging my pardon.

As I reached the bottom of the stairs, unexpected noises of thumps and bumps and male expletives reached my ears. I started interestedly toward them, rounded an awkward corner where the passageway bent and narrowed, and almost collided with Phoebe as she emerged from the storeroom with a pile of aprons. The living quarters of the pie shop were neatly enough arranged above stairs, where the bedchambers and parlor were, but on the ground floor, the store-room, which housed the linen and some odd pieces of furniture—Jester put extra tables in the shop at busy seasons—had apparently been pushed in as an after-thought between pantry and stairs. It stuck out into the passage and people were forever bumping into each other at that corner. Whoever had designed the build-ing had been less than perfect at his job.

This time, having edged around Phoebe, I discov-ered Wat and Jester crossing the passage between the shop and the kitchen and carrying one of the benches from the shop between them. They disappeared through the kitchen, Wat walking backward and being exhorted not to knock into things, and I heard the door to the backyard being kicked open.

Investigating further, I found that early though it was, a cartload of new tables and settles, elaborately carved with leaves and fruit, was being brought in, while the old furniture was being carried out, and that a carpenter was also busy putting up a screen to shield customers in the shop from a view of the kitchen.

"If great folk from the court come in," said Wat, reappearing in the shop, "we 'on't want 'em able to look across the passage right to where the cookin' goes on. They'll want to eat their pies, Maister says, not watch the maids rollin' pastry and stirrin' the cauldrons."

"No more they will," snapped Jester, stumping back into the shop. "And they'll want decent benches to sit on, not ones that put splinters in their fingers. I'll chop the old stuff up for firewood this very day; useful, that'll be. What you gawpin' at, Mistress Ursula? Sometimes you act as if you thought you were a fine lady instead of a cookmaid. Get back inside and start seein' to they fowl. We got three customers want pies delivered in time for dinner, an' when I promise to send things round in time, I mean in time!" He sounded thoroughly irritable. I went to work in a hurry.

Sometime later, when I had my hand inside a chicken, trying to get a grip on what seemed to be extraordinarily well-anchored innards, Jester came into the kitchen and said shortly: "You and Phoebe'll do all the servin' again this mornin'. One o' they students just came by and they'd all be in again afore noon today an' I 'on't have Ambrosia out there when that fellow Shawe's there. You hear that, Ambrosia? You'll stop in the kitchen."

Ambrosia, who was by the fire, stirring a pan of stock with a long-handled spoon, nodded without speaking.

I did not speak either, but I was thinking quickly. Today I would have another chance to talk to the students. Somehow or other, whatever Jester did to me, I *must* make use of it.

Time was pressing. The queen would be here in little more than a week. I knew now that Jester wouldn't tolerate gossip, so there was no question of casually talking to the students, winning their confidence, and dropping a few well-chosen questions in. This was not a prey that could be stalked with too much caution. This time, the huntress must show herself and hope to start the quarry out of covert.

7

Assignation

" . . . and if you muddle your lines again, young Morland," the metallic-haired Thomas Shawe said, swallowing a mouthful of chicken pie and banging ominously on the top of one of the brandnew tables with the hilt of his meat knife, "one of us will do it instead. The name of the lady who is presenting the flowers is Mistress Smithson—*Smithson*, not Smitherson—and your first words are *Your most gracious majesty*, not *Your m . . . m . . . most glori-gracious majesty.* You look right for the part but what use is that if you stammer? *Why* do you stammer? *I* don't stammer!" He certainly didn't. Thomas's voice was as resonant and unhesitating as though he had spent his life as a strolling player. He waved impatiently toward me as I was handing a supply of pies to Wat at the street counter. "More bread, my wench! Francis Morland's got to feed his brain!"

"And his tongue!" said one of the others.

I fetched the bread very quickly, only too glad of

another legitimate chance to get near to my quarry. As I put it on the table, the youthful Morland was going once more through his speech for the playlet. He hadn't all that much to say, as the play was mainly action. Apparently, the gang of students—there were five of them—were to be dressed as wild rustics, in green and brown breeches and jerkins, with leaves in their hair and earth smeared on their faces. As soon as Mistress Smithson of Cambridge had presented her flowers to the queen, they would rush up to the dais, pushing aside a few other people, students and towns-folk, who were to be placed there for the purpose of being pushed, and then they would halt, and bow most humbly and Master Morland, who was tall and comely and would indeed look impressive as a leader of wild men or outlaws, would declare that they were dazzled by Elizabeth's splendor and would never never offer any offense to her person, but, oh, would she heed their pleas and let them take Her Majesty's hand-maiden Mistress Smithson away with them as a keep-sake.

It was in my opinion a very silly speech and a reason in its own right for jettisoning the entire performance. Once it was over, Dudley, who would be at Elizabeth's side, would spring gallantly to the defense of the hand-maiden and Thomas would engage him in their brief pretend duel, and while they were thus occupied, the other students, winking and nudging to draw the attention of the crowd to their cleverness, would whisk the lady away into the pie shop where refreshments would await her, and musicians would play to her to soothe her alarm.

No one had suggested that she should take part in the rehearsals. She would be warned—probably on the day itself—of what was to happen and had only to accept events in good part. Even the students, I gathered, had never seen her.

"Your most gracious majesty," Morland was reciting nervously. "Light of our firmament and guiding star that shines through the leaves of the forest to lead forlorn souls such as we back through the night to our bleak campfires, behold the humblest of your servants, wild men who for their many sins must dwell in the greenwood far from all the comforts of . . . of . . ."

"Hearth and home," said Thomas Shawe irritably.

". . . heart and home . . ."

"Angels have mercy on us all. *Hearth* and home!"

". . . hearth and home and the bright eyes of fair ladies . . ."

I was here beside their table. Roland Jester was busy somewhere else and couldn't see me. If this wasn't an opportunity, nothing was.

"I'm not surprised Master Morland is nervous," I said brightly, acting the chatty maidservant. "What an honor, to perform before the queen's own self! Aren't you nervous, too, Master Shawe? Suppose something goes wrong! Suppose the swordfight goes amiss and a blade gets too near the queen? Ooh!" I made big eyes at Thomas. "You could end up charged with treason!"

So much of my work, so often, meant listening to conversations that told me nothing, reading letters of no importance, asking questions that failed to get interesting answers, angling for confidences that no one wanted to make. But now and then—just occasionally—the sweet goddess of luck would smile, and the quarry would not only break from the covert but jump straight into my arms.

I saw Thomas Shawe's face change. Unexpectedly, the self-confident young cockerel who didn't stammer and couldn't understand why anyone else did, faded out. In its place was a youth whose bold talk was for his peers; who used it to hide his secret shyness and doubts of himself. I was suddenly very aware, as I had been with Ambrosia, that I was at least ten years his senior.

"There are times," he blurted, "when I wish I'd never started this business."

Carefully, I said: "My cousin Master Brockley, who brought me to Cambridge, has taken service with a courtier—a Master Henderson, who is one of those overseeing preparations for the queen. If you're worried about anything, my cousin would advise you and help you to speak with Master Henderson if you wanted to."

Thomas seemed to shrink into himself. "I've seen Master Henderson. He's talked to us all. If I had anything to tell him, I'd have done it then. I haven't. I'm not worried about anything. At least, not anything serious." But his eyes were saying otherwise. I kept my own gaze on his face. He stood up abruptly. "We'd better practice the sword fight before we're too full of food to move. I've got permission to use the roped-off space outside, in front of where the platform is going to be, so we can do it properly. We'll come back to finish eating, but I'll settle up now. This is on me, lads. What do we owe?"

I told him and he paid. I looked at him again and felt that he was trying to give me an unspoken message but I didn't know what it was. I wanted to say something to encourage him but he moved off to the door with the others and I could not pursue him without being obvious. Disappointed, I turned to go back to the kitchen. I had heard Roland Jester's voice in there and knew I must not linger. But as I made to go around the end of the newly erected screen, I heard footsteps behind me and turned around again to find Thomas on my heels, holding out a coin.

"I forgot your gratuity. Here." Then, with his other hand, he caught my wrist and with a quick glance toward the kitchen, drew me into the shelter of the screen.

"I don't want to talk to Master Henderson. He's a courtier." He looked at me shyly, all his boldness gone. "My family's got land, enough to let out a couple of farms, but we're only small gentry—Father calls himself a yeoman farmer. Anyhow, we're not court folk and I don't feel easy with them. Master Henderson said we had a responsibility for the queen's safety and to tell him if anything's on our minds but I'd be afraid to go to him. I might be all wrong. I want to talk to someone but I might get into trouble for saying things . . . and I might upset Ambrosia . . . she and I, we're . . ."

With a finger on my lips I signaled that he should keep his voice down. "My cousin is very discreet," I whispered, "and he knows Master Henderson well, truly. Tell me what the matter is and I'll pass it on. I'll say I just heard it from a student. I won't mention your name. No one would blame you for wanting to be careful, when the queen herself is involved."

"I suppose that's so." Thomas's expression was wistful. "I'd like to talk to you," he whispered back. "You're a woman and it doesn't seem so official . . . and I'd like to talk to *someone*. Only I need time to explain—it's complicated. Could you get away very early tomorrow morning? Say, at five?"

"Not in the morning," I whispered. "What about the afternoon?" A din broke out in the street, of clashing staves accompanied by shouts and laughter. The rehearsal had begun. A clerkly man in the usual dark gown, who was sitting by himself at a nearby table and trying to read a book while eating his pie, jumped and tutted, but Thomas flashed a smile at him and reluctantly, he smiled back.

"Pity," Thomas said to me. "I keep a horse in Cambridge and I exercise it early. My mare's a placid old nag but she needs her daily trot and canter. But the afternoon might do—say about three of the clock? Tomorrow—not today." Boylike, he forgot once more to keep his voice down and again I put my finger to my lips. "I'm seeing my tutor in the afternoon today," he explained in a whisper.

"Three o'clock tomorrow afternoon?" I was careful to keep my voice low. "Yes. I think so."

"By the river? People are always strolling there. We could meet by chance, as it were. Just for a few minutes. You'll really come?"

I nodded.

"God bless you," he said. The racket outside crescendoed again and the clerk once more looked annoyed. "I'm sorry about all that noise," Thomas said to him, letting his voice reach its normal pitch. "We're a spirited lot, we students."

The clerkly individual snorted but once more, reluctantly, let himself smile. "I was the same once," he remarked. "One grows out of it."

Thomas laughed. Then, with a last nod to me, he hurried out of the shop. No one else needed serving; indeed, there were only three people left altogether, the clerk and a couple of very young students sitting in a corner. Customers tended to take themselves off when Thomas Shawe and his noisy band of friends were there. I picked up some used wooden platters and empty tankards from nearby tables, carried them into the kitchen, and set about washing them. Jester was taking a batch of pies out of the oven. "Anyone out in the shop that wants anything?"

"Not just now," I said. "Though the students will be back in a little while."

"They're more trouble than they're worth, sometimes," Jester grumbled. He scowled at the pies, which were slightly overdone, and when Phoebe accidentally clattered her pans, turned on her with a petulant recommendation to be more careful or he'd clip her ear for her. I attended to my washing up, trying not to draw attention to myself.

The rest of the day dragged but at least, at last, I was on the track of information. Next morning, I was up at four and was in the kitchen preparing the stockpot and the bread oven well ahead of Ambrosia, and even of Master Jester, who came downstairs as usual just before five to find half the early-morning tasks already done. He actually raised an approving eyebrow. "You're up betimes. That's good. You can take your breakfast sitting down while I get on with killing the capons and that goose that's just about ready for eating. Here's Ambrosia. Want your breakfast, girl?"

We broke our fast in comfort for once, joined after a while by Phoebe and Wat, and set about our morning's chores with all the better will for it. I was tending the stewpot and Ambrosia was out in the shop, sweeping the floor and humming as she worked, when someone pounded on the shutters that closed off the front of the shop from the street.

"Lord save us, who's that bangin' on the shutter at this hour?" Jester, who was making out a market list on a slate, looked up in surprise. "Ambrosia!" he shouted. "Go and open up and see who that is!"

We heard Ambrosia pull back the bolts of the shutters and speak to someone. Then we heard her cry out.

Jester dropped his slate, I dropped my spoon, and together we tore into the shop, Phoebe and Wat crowding after us. Ambrosia was standing there, tears pouring down her half-ugly, half-attractive face, and wailing that something couldn't be so, couldn't have happened, please, please tell her that it wasn't true! Beside her, awkwardly patting her shoulder with one hand and clutching his hat in the other, was Francis Morland. "I'm afraid it *is* true. I knew . . ." He glanced at Jester and started stammering again. "I . . . kn . . . knew he'd w . . . want someone to tell you. So I came. I'm so . . . so sorry. Something must have frightened his horse, it seems. He . . . he can't have known much about it. He was thrown headfirst into a tree. He m . . . must have been killed at once."

"Who?" I asked. I didn't stop to wonder if it was my place to ask questions, but this time no one was worrying about such niceties.

"Thomas Shawe," said Morland miserably. "Thomas Shawe is dead."

According to Francis Morland, Thomas had gone out as he usually did, early in the morning, to exercise his mare. "The groom at Radley's says he always collects her at five, and that this time was the same as always."

Before half past five, it seemed, she had come back without him, and since his route was known, the groom had gone to search for him. In King's Grove, a patch of woodland on the far side of the river, he had found Thomas lying at the foot of a tree. The poor boy had now been carried to King's Chapel, Morland said, and his parents were being sent for.

Ambrosia begged to be allowed to see him but her father would have none of it. "I'm sorry you're upset, girl. Anyone'ud be upset, hearin' of a young fellow dead like that. But for all your girlish dreams, he's naught to you and . . ."

"That's not true! He was everything to me." Ambrosia faced him, clenching her fists. "You would never listen," she said fiercely. "But we loved each other and we would have married."

"That's nonsense and you know it," said Jester roughly. "All apart from he's farming gentry and you're trade, he had his studies to do and two years teaching at his college and he wouldn't be let to wed till he'd finished. I've told you and told you."

"He wasn't going to finish his studies," said Ambrosia tearfully. "He was going to go home and help his father run their farms. They've got three. His father might have let us have one for ourselves. Thomas was going to go home and take a bride with him. Me! We'd settled it. We . . ."

"You settled nothing!" Jester went crimson in the face. "He wasn't for you, or you for him!" He noticed the rest of us and made a furious gesture that sent Phoebe and Wat hurrying out of sight. Morland, however, continued to stand about looking like the leftovers on a plate and I moved behind Jester, so that I was out of his sight. His attention, anyhow, was now fixed on his recalcitrant daughter. "Oh, if only your mother were here!"

"She'd have helped me! I told you before! She . . ."

"She was fool enough, I grant you, but I wouldn't have let her! I'd have made her talk sense to you! Oh, God, I need her here! Runnin' off an' leavin' me to manage on my own, the silly bitch. If I could get her back," said Master Jester, with horrific savagery and a complete lack of logic, "I'd cut her heart out for what she've done to me an' you!"

"You can't say that! Not about my mother!"

"Why not? Left you to shift for yourself as well, didn't she? Well, now, you're all I've got! I got to look after you. I won't let you go and marry a randy scholar that can't even keep hisself to hisself long enough to get his degree and do his teaching! You just go and wash your face and stop this nonsense. You're not goin' moonin' round his body, pushin' yourself forward and makin' a show of yourself, and that's the end of it."

"I *am* going!" Ambrosia was pale and shaking with the effort of defiance. "I *am* going! I . . ."

Jester's palm shot out and cracked against the side of her face. She crashed sideways, collided with a table, and fell, sobbing, onto the floor. Morland, coming to life, helped her up and sat her on one of the new settles, where she huddled in misery. "You may be her father, sir, but you should not have done that."

"Aye, I am her father and I know my own business best, and hers," Jester snapped. "You've brought the news, which you had no call to do, though I daresay you thought you were doin' right. Well, now you see what's come of it. Time you were off."

He advanced on Francis Morland, who retreated in alarm, and fairly shooed him out of the shop. He then came back to glare at his daughter and also at me. "You still here, flappin' your ears, Mistress Faldene? As for you, Ambrosia, just pull yourself together and . . ."

"I'm going to faint," announced Ambrosia in a blurred voice, and slumping forward, she slid off the settle. I caught her just before she struck the floor, and lowered her. I looked up at Jester. "Please fetch some water. She really has fainted."

"Tchah!" said Jester. *"Phoebe!"*

"And a basin!" I added hurriedly. Ambrosia was stirring and I knew what was likely to happen next.

Phoebe brought the water and the basin just in time. Jester, making a disgusted face, withdrew from the spectacle of me holding Ambrosia's head while she threw up her breakfast. "When she's reasonable again, tell her she needn't work today. Tell her to go and sit in her room and read. She likes doin' that an' it cost enough havin' her educated, God knows." He then vanished into the back regions and I seized my chance.

"I'll go to see Thomas for you," I whispered into her ear. "I'll kiss him good-bye for you and tell you how he looked. This afternoon. Will that do?"

Feebly, Ambrosia nodded. Phoebe knelt down beside us. The water was cold and she had thought of adding a cloth. Gently, she soaked the cloth and held it to the crimson bruise on Ambrosia's face. "I was a-peepin' out of the kitchen and I seed him do that. You'll have such a mark, Mistress Ambrosia. But the cold water'll help."

Phoebe was a timid thing but she had a good heart. "I heard you say you'd go to see Master Shawe," she whispered to me. "I won't tell anyone. Promise."

I gave her a smile. "I never thought you would," I told her.

8

The Quiet Grove

In the company of Edward Hawford, vice chancellor of Cambridge, Rob Henderson, and Brockley, I viewed Thomas's body and for Ambrosia's sake, I kissed him farewell, wondering all the time if he had died because of the assignation he had made with me. I knew, as we left the chapel, that his young face, already stamped with the terrifying calm of death, would haunt my dreams for a long time.

In the courtyard outside the chapel, when Hawford had gone, Rob listened thoughtfully as I said that I didn't think this was just an untimely accident.

"It looks like an accident to me," he said.

I shook my head. "It was far too pat," I said.

"So that was Thomas Shawe. Poor lad," Brockley said sympathetically. "I've seen him before, you know, madam. If you remember, when we first came to Cambridge and I went with the other men to stable our horses, I told you that I met a young man in

Radley's stable, and that he warned me against the place?"

"Yes. Was that Thomas?"

"For certain it was, madam. There's no mistaking that hair."

"No, indeed." I turned to Rob. "I want to see the place where it happened. I have time."

"I should hope so! The pie shop doesn't own you, I suppose," said Rob.

Brockley said uneasily: "Madam, if you believe that Master Shawe was killed, who do you think did it? Do you suspect Master Jester?"

"No. It can't have been him." I said it reluctantly. I would very much have liked to put the blame on the odious Master Jester but it wasn't possible. "Francis Morland brought us the news and he told us that according to the groom at Radley's, Thomas went out at five in the morning as usual, and the horse came back within half an hour. So Thomas must have been killed between five and about twenty minutes past. I was up and about before half past four, and Master Jester came downstairs not long after me. All he was killing during that half hour was poultry. I don't think he could have overheard me making an appointment to meet Thomas, anyway. He was in the kitchen and we were out of his sight and keeping our voices down. But it looks as if someone knew."

I frowned, trying to think. "Whatever was worrying him, Thomas didn't want to talk about it officially. He didn't want Jester to hear and I don't think he'd have said anything to Woodforde. But he could have mentioned it to another student, who went and repeated it to someone—Woodforde, for instance. Rob, can you . . . ?"

"Talk to the students again? Yes, I suppose I should do that."

He didn't sound overenthusiastic. I looked at him in surprise and some distress. "Rob, I really do believe that Thomas was killed, and it's horrible. But there is this—it does at least mean that we're not chasing shadows. There's something to be found."

"You may be right. Well, if there is, I've no doubt that you'll find it," said Rob. And then surprised me by adding quite sourly: "Even if I don't."

The curious momentary sourness vanished, however, as I repeated that we ought to see the place where Thomas had died. "Yes, indeed we should," Rob agreed. "The groom at Radley's will know where it happened." We set off there at once and found Master Radley, stocky, weather-beaten, and surly, standing in the yard, holding a piece of paper and muttering, while the harried under-groom scuttled about with bales of straw. "Bill for corn," Radley said when he saw us. "Bloody ould disgrace, it is, what corn costs in the summer, afore harvesttime. Times I see a bill like this, I wish my ould dad hadn't had me taught to read."

"The corn would still cost the same, whether you could read the bill or not," said Rob. "We want to talk to your groom—the one who found Master Shawe."

Radley obviously didn't want us to waste his groom's time, but equally obviously was impressed by Rob's fashionable garments and commanding mien.

He shouted for the groom, whose name appeared to be Jem, to come over and Rob did the questioning.

"We have just been paying our respects to the poor young man who was killed this morning. I understand it was you that went out to find him when his mare came home with an empty saddle?"

"Aye. Thass right." Brockley had said the groom was weedy and he was right. Jem was undersized and thin, with brown teeth, a nose that had at some time been broken, and stooped shoulders, possibly because he spent so much of his time bent nearly double under bales of hay and straw, and also, as like as not, because he had been hit so often that cowering had become habitual. "I get here of a mornin' afore five. Master Radley sometimes don't come into the yard till later, but I start the day's work, like, and saddle up Master Shawe's mare for him, most days, too. Thass how it was this mornin'."

"What time did Master Shawe go out today?" Rob inquired.

"Everyone keep on axin' that. Five or thereabout. Same as usual," said Jem shortly.

"We'd like to see the exact place," Rob told him. "Will you take us there?"

Master Radley cleared a disapproving throat. Rob fished a gold sovereign out of his belt purse, took Radley's right hand, pressed the coin into the palm, and closed the ostler's callused fingers over it. Radley murmured: "Well, thanks, sir. That's real gentlemanly," and thereafter, kept quiet.

"Take you all, sir?" Jem asked. "The lady, too?"

"I am here on someone's behalf," I said. "Someone

who can't come herself. She and Thomas were secretly betrothed."

The groom grinned lasciviously, met my cold eye, and became serious. "I can show you the place all right. Now?"

"Now," Rob confirmed.

King's Grove, the scene of Thomas's death, proved to be a fair walk away. We had to cross the river on the bridge from Silver Street and then make our way along the farther bank, with the river on our right and the city beyond it, and on our left, a wide flat expanse of fields where corn was ripening and cattle grazed. When we reached the grove, we found that, being private, it was fenced around. Jem, however, led us to a gate, which turned out to be unlocked. The King's College authorities evidently expected people to respect their boundaries without the aid of padlocks.

Beyond the gate was a narrow track that wound among the trees and joined a broader track, coming from a different direction. Jem took us along this for a few yards and then stopped. "Here, it were. Under that there tree."

The tree was an oak. There was little now to see; even the flattened grass where Thomas had lain had almost sprung up again. Only by looking closely could I see the few bent and flattened grass stems that remained. Jem, without speaking, and with an anxious glance at me, pointed to a small brownish smear on the bole of the oak, perhaps four feet from the ground. "Thass where the poor young gentleman went headlong into the tree, seemin'ly."

We looked at it carefully and then, of one mind

without needing to discuss it, we moved about, examining the ground. Apart from the little patches of green grass that flourished here and there, and the odd spindly bush or sapling, there was hardly any undergrowth, nothing but decaying leaves. There were hoofmarks in them and footmarks, too, where people had come to carry Thomas's body away. If there had been any other and more informative footmarks there, they had been trampled to destruction. Nothing was lying about which could have been used as a weapon.

There was nothing to be learned here. It did indeed look as though what had killed Thomas was the collision with the tree. We came back to it and stood there for a few moments in silence.

I was trying to take the surroundings in so that I could tell Ambrosia about them. The grove was cool and quiet, except for a little birdsong. The leaves filtered the July sunshine into golden dapples. It was no place to die. Though there were worse ones. If whatever Thomas knew had really led him to his death, then someone somewhere was playing a dangerous game. Perhaps a game that could lead to a dungeon and a gallows.

Once away from his bullying employer, Jem seemed sensible enough. After showing us the mark on the tree, he had moved tactfully away and now we could speak to one another in privacy.

"There's no evidence here," I said. "But I stand by my belief. I don't think this was an accident. Jester didn't do it, but what about Woodforde? You've been investigating him—have you found out anything useful?"

"I wish I had, but no," Rob said. "I searched his rooms here, just as I did at Richmond . . ."

"It was you who did it at Richmond, then?" I was intrigued.

"Yes. I now understand why searching people's correspondence is a job you hate," said Rob wryly. "At the time, I knew Woodforde was closeted with Cecil and his manservant was out on an errand. Cecil promised me he would make sure of it and he did. But every moment I was in Woodforde's chamber, I was straining my ears for footsteps and expecting him to come through the door or step out from behind the bed curtains and ask me what I was doing there. But to get back to the point: I found nothing amiss at Richmond and nothing amiss here in Cambridge either. There were some dull and interminable letters from Roland—Cecil has told you of those, I believe—and there were bills from tailors and bootmakers and a livery stable—not Radley's—and lecture notes and some students' exercises with rude remarks in Latin, scribbled in the margins in Woodforde's writing. As a tutor, he goes in for sarcasm. *But . . .*"

He gave Brockley a conspiratorial glance. I looked at their two faces with interest. "You two have been hatching a scheme of your own?" I asked.

Somewhere in the distance, carried on the soft July wind, a clock struck the half hour. "It's half past three," I said. "I need to get back. Can we talk as we go?"

Rob signaled to Jem that we had finished and we started back, parting company with the groom outside King's Grove because he said that Master Radley wouldn't like it if he took too long, sovereign or no sovereign. "Here," said Rob, groping in his purse once more. "Have one of your very own."

"My thanks, sir. Thass real generous, that is!" Jem pulled his forelock, favored us with a wide, discolored grin, and then added: "But 'scuse me all the same. Master Radley's not a patient man, no he ain't," and sped off ahead of us to resume his purgatorial existence at the stable.

We followed more slowly, once more taking the track along the riverbank toward the bridge into Silver Street. It was very warm. Sweat prickled under my arms and Brockley, also feeling the heat, took off his fustian doublet and strolled along in his linen shirtsleeves. Rob, always attentive to his appearance, remained encased in linen ruff and peacock-hued doublet but his face was crimson, with perspiration trickling down his temples.

I was anxious to know what new plans my companions had made but Rob murmured warningly that we should not talk until we were sure that no one could possibly overhear us. There were only a few other people about in that heat, but there were still some: a couple of workmen, in calf-length breeches and no shirts at all, coming from the fields with mattocks over their sunburnt shoulders, and behind them, a man in a long black gown, with gray hair trailing from under his dark cap, wandering along with his hands linked behind him and a preoccupied frown on his ascetic face.

Our view ahead was blocked until they had all passed us and then we saw that just ahead was an artist, busily sketching at an easel, his back partly turned toward us. At the sight of him, Rob slowed down and

Brockley said softly: "Careful, Master Henderson, sir . . ."

Rob stopped short. "I'll contemplate the ducks on the river," he said in a low voice. "Wait for me on the bridge. What are you gaping at me for, Ursula? Don't you see who it is? Brockley pointed him out to me when we saw him here the other day. Best if he doesn't see Mistress Faldene, pie shop cookmaid, chatting like an old friend to Master Henderson, gentleman employed by the Secretary of State. You're strolling with your cousin Roger, Ursula. I'm nothing to do with you."

Still bewildered, although I supposed that they probably knew what they were about, I walked silently on with Brockley. And then, at last, I realized that the back view of the artist was familiar. Though its owner was about the last person I would have expected to find in that capacity. That morning I had seen him wringing chickens' necks, making out a marketing list, and quarreling violently with his daughter. The spectacle of Roland Jester inscribing lines on paper with delicacy and precision was odd to the point of being weird.

"Do we stop?" Brockley whispered in my ear.

"Better. It would look more natural," I whispered back.

I could see now that Jester was working with charcoal, and that the sketch he was making, of the skyline of Cambridge, was quite remarkably competent. "Master Jester!" I said, halting beside the easel. He glanced up at me.

"Mistress Faldene. Takin' the air with your cousin, I

see. Mind you get back into the shop in half an hour. Good day to you, Master Brockley."

"You draw so well," I said, in admiring tones. "Why, sir, you could earn your bread at it!"

"I'd not enjoy it then," Jester said, sketching in the roofs and tower of a distant building, which, now that I knew Cambridge a little, I recognized as Peterhouse College. "A man has to have his relaxations. You oughter be grateful. I'm not let to keep the shop open all afternoon so I use my free time for amusement, and I'm such a generous and good-hearted man that I grant the same to the rest of you. Unless there's work still to do, that is, or you've put my back up—and we make up for it on Sundays, you'll find," he added ominously. "And now away with you. I don't like bein' watched when I'm drawin'."

We hurriedly murmured farewells and walked on. Once out of earshot, I said: "Well! I never would have thought it. That drawing was good! Whoever would have guessed that Jester was a secret artist? Now, Brockley, there's no one near us just now, so what is this scheme that you and Rob are laying?"

"It depends on your consent, madam. Master Henderson has arranged a chance for me to become Master Woodforde's manservant. We are pretending that I was formerly in Master Henderson's employ. I meant to come and speak to you this evening. It's settled, except, of course, that if you don't agree, I can back out. If I do join Woodforde, Master Henderson's men will keep an eye on the horses at Radley's. I made a point of that."

"How in the world did Rob . . . ?" I was astonished but also impressed. "It's an excellent idea, if it's possible. Would you have to live with Woodforde? I hope Fran won't mind."

"It would hardly be for long, madam, and Fran is much occupied."

"What precisely is she doing?" I asked.

"Embroidering cushions for the Provost's Lodge where the queen will stay. That Officer of the Wardrobe that we rode some of the way to Cambridge with; he's got here now and he's decided that some of the cushions and so forth in the Provost's Lodge need repair. He's hired seamstresses but since Fran is there and you're not using her, he's ordered her to help. He isn't paying her, either," said Brockley crossly. "He says there's no need since she has wages from you!"

"Well, I can hardly object, since I don't need her just now. But look, getting back to your plans, what about Woodforde's present manservant? I know he's got one."

"Had one, madam. The man wishes to leave."

"How very convenient!"

"I think, madam," said Brockley, "that Master Henderson—er . . ."

"Delved into his purse and brought out some sovereigns. All the same, if it was a good post . . ."

"According to Master Henderson," said Brockley, with a blank face but a gleam of laughter in his eyes, "the fellow was quite glad of a chance to leave. Master Woodforde isn't the easiest of men to work for. He's rough with his servants."

"Indeed? Brockley, the idea of you entering his service is a most promising scheme and of course I consent. But I hope it won't be too unpleasant."

"It can hardly be more unpleasant than the life you're leading at Jester's," Brockley said. "I'm concerned for you, madam. It sounds to me as if Woodforde and Jester are two of a kind."

We halted, halfway across the bridge. With one mind, we moved to lean on the parapet and look down at the flowing water of the Cam. "How do you know about that?" I asked.

"I've managed to talk to some of the students, in casual fashion, madam, and Master Henderson, of course, has talked to them officially. We learned nothing useful, but we did hear a few remarks about Jester and the way he treats the folk who work for him. I can only hope, madam, that Jester has offered you no offense."

"I've had a bad moment or two but if the worst came to the worst, I could walk out. Except that I don't like walking out with a task unfinished."

"No more do I," Brockley said. "But if when it's all over, Jester's not been found guilty of anything worse, if he's raised his hand to you, he'll have a bill to pay and I'll present it, never fear."

I turned my head to look at him. "You're a good friend, Brockley."

"I would hope so, madam. You need friends. I know you'll think this is just singing an old song that you've heard too often, but I wish you weren't doing this. You should be at home with your daughter in Withysham, or else both of you should be back in France with the Seigneur de la Roche."

"I wish I were, Brockley. With all my heart, I wish I were, but . . . if . . . if anything happened to Matthew, I would need a home in England and so I need Withy-sham. The queen gave it to me for services rendered, but although she didn't put it that way, I think that while I remain in England, she still expects services. They are part of the payment."

"I think you would still choose to serve her whenever possible, madam."

"You may be right." Suddenly I pounded a fist on the parapet. "Why must there always be plots and . . . and people who want to harm her? Above all, why here? This is Cambridge. Elizabeth has put an end to heretic-hunting; she has made England Protestant and in England, Cambridge is where the movement began. Here, of all the places in the entire realm, she should be valued; she should be safe! All along, I've hoped that this business of the playlet is just a mare's nest. But now that Thomas Shawe is dead—oh, dear God, he was so *young* . . ."

I hadn't expected to burst into tears. They overtook me without warning and although I tried to stop them, they began to fall on the parapet and on my hands as they rested there.

"Thomas Shawe ought *not* to be dead!" I said furiously. "He should have had years before him, and a chance to marry Ambrosia, too—they were in love, Brockley. Ambrosia's heartbroken now . . . !" Brockley put a tentative hand on my shoulder. It was warm and kind and at once aroused a new longing, to be back again in Matthew's embrace. But Matthew was far away, embattled in Blanchepierre in the midst of a plague epidemic, and I could not go to him. There was no comfort for me anywhere, except in the person of the friend at my side. I turned to Brockley and for one moment stepped into his arms and pressed my face into his shoulder, wetting his shirt with my tears.

He patted my back, as though I were a baby, but then put me gently away from him. "We mustn't give way, either of us," he said, and I knew that there was a double meaning in the words. I mustn't give way to grief over Thomas Shawe, and neither of us must yield to the secret thing that ran between us.

Least of all just now, for as I stepped back, dashing the tears out of my eyes and attempting to smile, I realized that a familiar figure was coming toward us over the bridge. We at once went to meet her, hoping that she hadn't seen.

"Roger! Ma'am! I've finished my stitching for today and I thought I'd take the air again awhile. I didn't expect to meet you here."

She curtsied to me, and smiled at Roger, a wife greeting her husband and a tirewoman encountering her mistress. "We are waiting here for Master Henderson to catch up," I explained, and began to tell her of Thomas Shawe and our visit to King's Grove and our encounter with Roland Jester and his easel.

Fran listened respectfully and made the right exclamations in all the right places, but I observed, with a heavy heart, that her eyes were full of pain.

Yes. She had seen.

9

Waiting My Chance

There was nothing to be done. Any attempt to explain why I was embracing Brockley could be interpreted as trying to explain it away, instead. It was for Brockley to deal with it later, in private with Dale. As we stood on the bridge, I stared down unhappily into the sun-dappled river. The water was not sparkling quite as it had been. The ripples were oily now and the sun-flecks duller. The air was growing humid and the sky was dimming. From the corner of my eye, I caught a glimpse of peacock-color and turning, I saw Rob approaching. "Here comes Master Henderson," I said brightly.

I knew that I should be on my way to the pie shop but I still had things to discuss with Rob. When he came up to us, I said briefly: "Let's lean on the parapet while we talk. I'm short of time so let's get to the point quickly. I repeat what I've said before. Thomas Shawe's so-called accident is proof, to my mind, that something is wrong about that playlet. Can we bring the coincidence—I mean Thomas's plan to meet me in secret, and his sudden death—as evidence at the inquest? In fact, can we cast enough doubt on the innocence of the playlet to justify canceling it on our own responsibility?"

"I wouldn't gamble on it," said Rob. "This looked so very much like sheer mischance. I'm still not sure that it wasn't, frankly, Ursula. Thomas's worries could have been about nothing worse than fear of pinking Dudley by mistake or thinking that some of the students are plotting a secret extra rag of their own."

"I don't think so," I said.

"Well, you always have your own strong views, I know," Rob said. "You *may* be right." Again, I was startled by a sourness in his voice, and he made a movement that was remarkably like an irritable shrug, but his voice was pleasant enough as he added: "Has Brockley told you yet about our scheme to get him into Woodforde's service?"

"Yes, and I've agreed."

"Good." Rob mopped his brow. "How close this weather is. We shall have thunder soon, for sure. Now, listen. Let us assume that you're right, Ursula. We could try to start a murder scandal at the inquest but we might not succeed. It's thin, to my mind. We could also go ahead and cancel the playlet, and brave the annoyance of the queen. I doubt if she would actually clap us into the Tower for it. But if we do simply quell the whole thing, and after all there *is* a plot of some kind . . ."

"And the inquest jury brings in a verdict of accident," I finished for him, "then we have muffled an attempt against Her Majesty but we are no nearer learning just what kind of attempt it is, and who the plotters are."

"The wolves," put in Brockley in his level voice, "would still be at large."

"Yes," I said slowly. "Yes. I do see."

"All of which," Rob said, "is an argument for letting the inquest go and continuing to investigate. What kind of man *is* Jester? Is he likely to have political interests? Or Catholic ones? You must know him quite well by now."

I thought that over. "No," I said at length. "I don't know him well. Cecil said he was a dull man—he writes dull letters, apparently—but I haven't found him tedious, not at all! He keeps on startling me. Oh, not about religion. I've never heard him mention it, but according to Cecil, he and his brother are both Protestant and that's probably true. I've been told that everyone from the pie shop worships at St. Benet's in Cambridge on Sunday.

"*But*—he has a violent temper and his wife ran away from him. And I've heard him speak of her in a way that wasn't just violent—it was . . . it was *vicious*. As though he'd never heard of the laws of God or decency. And then I come across him sitting at that easel, making a charcoal drawing that wouldn't shame Hans Holbein. I don't know what to make of him at all. I feel I haven't the slightest idea what he's really like. He could be anything, under the surface. And so could his daughter."

Hesitantly, I found myself putting into words

something that I had felt for some time. "Ambrosia's got a strong face; I think she's got strong feelings. And yet—I don't know what she's really like, either. She was in love with Thomas but I can't guess what she would say, or think, if anyone told her that Thomas was involved in something . . . treasonable or dangerous. Would it make her draw away from him or defend him? I can't tell." Out of the corner of my eye, I noticed another familiar figure approaching the bridge. "I think," I said warningly, "that Jester is on his way home. We should move on before he gets close to us."

We did so. Dale walked at Brockley's side, silent as she had been throughout the discussion, but somehow making it plain by the very way she moved that she was at this moment far more Mistress Brockley than tirewoman Fran Dale. I smiled at her once but her response was faint.

Striding at my side, still mopping his brow now and then, Rob said: "So we leave the inquest alone and go on as we were? Is that agreed?" His tone was irritable and looking at his flushed face, I wondered if this was merely due to the heat or if he was unwell.

"On reflection, yes, I think it best," I said mildly.

"I agree. And you are happy for Brockley to enter Woodforde's service?"

"Yes, if he's willing. Brockley?"

"I'm willing," Brockley said. "It will be tomorrow. As yet, I don't know when I'll get a chance to get away and report on anything I find but I'll manage."

"If you find out anything useful," Rob said, "try to tell both of us. I can't pass news on to Mistress Blanchard because I can't call on her. Courtiers and cook-maids don't mix. But I'm about in the university a good deal; you should have chances to speak to me, and I suppose you can visit the pie shop or meet her outside. You're supposed to be her cousin, after all."

"I'll do my best, sir."

"And, Dale, try to come with him," I said quickly. "I shall be glad to see you both. Meanwhile, I think I must poke my nose a little more earnestly into the Jesters' affairs. I've gone about for days with my ears and eyes open and I've learned next to nothing. Talking to the students was different—that would have worked, if only Thomas hadn't been . . ."

Remembering that still young face with the flecks of dust from the carpentry work in the chapel, and the hard cold brow that I had kissed, I was nearly over-come all over again. I had seen death before, many times, and I had thought I was hardened, perhaps more hardened than a young woman has any business to be, but Thomas Shawe had moved me deeply. I blinked the tears away. "I *hate* prying into other people's personal documents; you're right there, Rob—but I think I must try it. I will see if there is anything, any-where, in writing that will help."

I reached the pie shop rather late, though well ahead of Master Jester, but I found that Phoebe, Ambrosia, and Wat were back already and full of lamentation because Wat had just dropped a trayload of pies on the floor, and a pile of chopped chicken that had been in the pantry meat safe, awaiting its turn in the stockpot, had gone off in the sultry heat. Ambrosia, already upset enough over Thomas's death and her quarrel with her father, was in tears.

I was also upset about Thomas, very tired, and far too hot. I would have sold my soul to retreat to my bed, strip off my dress, and fall asleep. Pie shop servants, however, can't indulge themselves like that. I had to buckle down to work. When Jester arrived and heard Ambrosia's account of the various disasters, he cursed us all roundly and raised his fist to Wat, who dodged behind one of the nice new tables and by way of excuse shouted he was that sorry, but he was tryin' to get the pies set out on the street counter all in a hurry and on his own and he'd only got one pair of hands!

Whereupon, Jester rounded on me, demanded to know why I hadn't been back in time to help and for the second time during my short employment at the pie shop, I found myself sprawling on the floor with my head ringing like a gong.

He did himself no service. As he stormed off toward the fowl run to execute a couple of mallard he had bought that morning at the market and brought back in coops on a handcart, I picked myself up, brushed sawdust off my clothes, thanked Wat coldly for his kind and helpful remarks, and then while poor Wat, who was really a most amiable soul, stumbled an apology, I came to a grim conclusion.

Almost every task I had undertaken as an agent had eventually led me to poking my nose into other people's private letters and although one of the reasons why I detested this was my dread of being caught, it wasn't the only one. I also hated it because it made me feel like an intruder.

But not this time. This time, I would still be afraid of being caught by Jester but I wasn't going to worry about intruding. I would positively enjoy invading my unpleasant employer's privacy, and I hoped I would find any number of embarrassing and undignified secrets.

I worked hard all the rest of the day, while my head throbbed where Jester had struck me, and I poured with sweat under my servant's dress. I told myself that I was lucky in a way, for I had an open linen collar instead of a ruff and at least did not have starched linen pleats irritating my neck as the fine ladies did. The fine ladies, however, didn't have to stand in a sweltering back room and yank the guts out of mallard ducks, or stir bubbling stewpots next to the fire in a kitchen as hot as Hades, or serve pies and small ale at a run. I managed a few private words with Ambrosia and told her that I had seen Thomas.

"He looked very serene. I'm sure he never knew what had happened to him," I said, trying to comfort her as best I could. "I gave him your kiss. His family are taking him away tomorrow."

"And I can't go to his burial," Ambrosia said bitterly. But she thanked me, nevertheless, and gave me a wan smile. It struck me that when her mother ran off, Ambrosia had probably been younger than I was when my mother died. I had missed mine badly enough; Ambrosia might well have missed hers even more.

She had a forlorn look, as though she had lacked mothering.

Rob's promised storm arrived that night, with a majestic display of lightning and a roar of thunder that had Phoebe squeaking with fright. It brought relief from the heat, which for me had made sharing a bed with two other people nearly intolerable. The only person I would have welcomed in the same bed as myself was Matthew. That would be different, I thought longingly. The heat of a sultry night and the glow of Matthew's skin would melt and blend together into the heat of love, and after love came sleep, no matter how stifling the weather. But Matthew was far away. I must endure as best I could.

The storm and Phoebe's pathetic fear of the sizzling lightning and the prowling thunder took my mind off both my discomfort and my yearning. Because of the heat, we had left the window open and when the rain began, it blew through the window and spattered our faces. Ambrosia got up to shut it, remarking that we were lucky that her father had had the thatch repaired in the spring. "It was leaking then and we were all glad we weren't sleeping on the attic floor."

"What's on the attic floor?" I asked casually. "If no one sleeps up there, what's it used for?"

"Father has a study there," Ambrosia said. "He does his accounts there. And I'm allowed to keep some books there and sometimes I go up there to write to my old tutor. There's a lumber room too, with all sorts of odds and ends in it, leftovers from my grandfather's day. He had this whole row of houses built, did you know?"

"Did he?" I was surprised. "Was your grandfather wealthy, then?"

"Yes, quite. He was my maternal grandfather—my mother's father. There's money in the family. She had very little with her when she fled, though," Ambrosia said bleakly. "It's a hard world for women."

That must mean, I thought, that the money was now in the hands of Roland Jester, which surely cut out one motive for getting involved in a conspiracy. He wouldn't be doing it because he was desperate for money. He might still be greedy for it, of course, but it was less likely as a motive. So why should he be plotting harm to Elizabeth? It was a puzzle.

The thunder crashed again and Phoebe whimpered and started to pray to God and the angels to protect her. I patted her shoulder consolingly and because her petition had brought religion into my mind, I remarked that I wondered what it was like in Cambridge during Queen Mary's reign. "I've heard it was a hotbed of what she'd have called heresy."

"There was something called a visitation when I was eleven or so," Ambrosia said as she got back into bed. "I didn't understand it very well then. But officials from the university and from court came and searched every stationer's shop and a lot of private dwellings for what they called heretical books, and two heretics who were already dead and buried were dug up and their coffins were burned. I saw that. My grandfather was still alive then and he was frightened, I know. He had some heretical books but he hid them. This place was searched but they weren't found. We're all Protestants here. Most people in Cambridge are the same, though everyone did a bit of pretending in Queen Mary's day."

Lightning flashed again and thunder crashed as if making a species of cosmic comment. But there was no reason why Ambrosia should lie to me, I thought. If Jester was involved in anything he shouldn't be, then an impassioned desire to restore Catholicism by getting rid of Elizabeth and replacing her with Mary Stuart of Scotland was an even less likely reason than money.

But if neither of those, then what? Perhaps he had nothing to do with any plots at all. If there was a plot, it might have its roots elsewhere. Perhaps the pie shop and the students were being used by someone quite different and Jester was unaware of it. Perhaps Woodforde was fooling his brother. Perhaps . . .

I was so very tired and my head was still throbbing. Both Ambrosia and I now had spectacularly bruised faces. The storm was moving away.

I slept.

I now knew exactly where to direct my search, which was useful. Obviously, the attic floor. But on the next day, which was a Saturday, I had no opportunity. I had to work in the shop all morning and as it rained all day from dawn to nightfall, no one went out in the afternoon. On the contrary, Jester spent the afternoon up in his attic study, presumably with his account books, and Ambrosia went up there as well, to read, she said.

She was an odd sort of girl to find in a pie shop, I thought. Most girls in her position could hardly write their names and were as likely to spend an afternoon over a book as they were to spend it slaying a dragon or studying astronomy. It was Uncle Giles who had made the difference, of course, by persuading her father to employ a tutor for her. Although I had seen nothing of Giles Woodforde since I came to the shop he was evidently an influence here.

It was an exhausting afternoon. Before going upstairs, Jester, still annoyed with me for being late the day before, gave me a stream of jobs to do in the kitchen and warned me that even if it hadn't been raining, he wouldn't have let me out of the place this time, just to teach me a lesson. "I told you, good-natured, that's what I am, letting you all go out of an afternoon. But don't ever rely on it!"

I spent the afternoon peeling onions, making pastry dough, scrubbing greasy shelves, and wondering from time to time whether Rob had yet had a chance to interview the students again. Then customers began to reappear and I was working, cooking, serving, and clearing up, until late into the evening.

The next day was Sunday, the thirtieth of July, and although the shop didn't open, no one who lived there was free of surveillance for a single moment. Master Jester was most certainly of the Protestant persuasion. He took his household in its entirety to early service at St. Benet's, and then again in the afternoon, and in between, we were required to gather in the first-floor parlor while he conducted a private service of his own for us, with prayers and texts. The prayers, I noticed, included a plea that the Almighty would even now soften the hard and recalcitrant heart of his vanished wife, Sybil, and cause her to repent and return to the home she had so wickedly abandoned, and to the hus-

band who loved her, and to her duties as spouse and
mother and helpmeet, and to submit humbly to the
natural penances that must befall unnatural women
such as herself.

Many householders hold private prayers in a similar
way. Some are reverent and touching. Master Jester's
efforts were not. My bruised face ached and so, I daresay, did Ambrosia's. I hoped that wherever Sybil Jester
was now, she was being kindly treated.

That day, I learned why Jester had said that his gen-
erosity over our free afternoons would be made up for
on Sundays. In the intervals of the religious exercises,
Phoebe, Wat, and I were set to cleaning the living
quarters completely while Ambrosia and her father
cleaned the pantry and the shop. The Sabbath was
assuredly not a day of rest in Jester's Pie Shop.

But on the next day, Monday, the thirty-first of July,
everything changed.

10

Greek Letters

On Monday, opportunity could hardly have smiled
more enticingly. The sun shone. In the afternoon,
Master Jester marched out carrying what I now realized was a box of sketching materials and a folded
easel. I had seen him with them before without understanding what they were. Phoebe went out to spend
some of her meager pay on a new ribbon for her
churchgoing cap; Wat trudged off to heaven knew
where although probably not to his home. (According
to Phoebe, his father was a wildfowler out on the
marshes, which local folk called the fens, but Wat
wasn't following the family trade because he was so
big and heavy that when he went plodding through
the marshes on stilts, to retrieve trapped birds from
nets, the stilts sank too far into the mud and were
liable to crack.)

Ambrosia said she was going to St. Benet's. "We're
not supposed to pray for the dead but would God

really mind, do you think, Ursula, if I just knelt and asked him to look after Thomas? I needn't pray aloud. No one would know, even if they were at my side."

"I'm sure God would understand," I said. "I've prayed for the dead myself, secretly, in the same way."

"What will you do this afternoon?" Ambrosia asked.

"I'm tired," I said. "I'm going to lie down on the bed and sleep."

I duly went upstairs and took my shoes off, ready to arrange myself on the bed at short notice if Ambrosia or Phoebe should come in. But I kept stealthy watch from the window and one after another, I saw all of them leave the premises. Pushing my feet back into my shoes, I made haste to the topmost floor.

The staircase up from the middle floor was a narrow spiral that emerged in a corner of the attic at the Silver Street end of the house. Sunlight streamed in through the dormer window and the thatch was immediately overhead. The place had the warm and dusty smell that is characteristic of attics in summer. A quick survey revealed that there were three rooms up there, leading out of each other across the width of the house. Jester seemed to be using one as an office and Ambrosia's books were in another, while the third, as she had said, was full of disused furniture and other bits and pieces.

Jester's room was the one into which the staircase led. It was the biggest and the best lit, because as well as the dormer window, there was a flat glass skylight let into the thatch on the other side. It had a small hearth, unused in summer. A few books and some piles of correspondence were arranged on shelves fixed to the wall at one end. The furnishings were a walnut desk with a silver writing set, a stool to match the desk, and an oak settle under the dormer. I set to work to examine whatever I could find.

It wasn't a difficult task. In fact, it was the easiest search I had ever undertaken. I knew the house was empty, which gave me confidence, and by pushing one of the dormer windows slightly open, I could be sure of hearing if anyone came home. Down below, the shutter that closed the shop was bolted from within, and anyone returning would come in at the private door alongside. This led into a small lobby with inner doors to the shop and the other ground-floor rooms. It wasn't locked during the day but its hinges squeaked. I wasn't likely to be taken by surprise.

There were some account books on the shelves, and I quickly discovered that Roland Jester had a firm grasp of the principles of double-entry bookkeeping, that his arithmetic was accurate, and his shop highly profitable. I learned nothing further. I then turned to the correspondence and found the two letters which Woodforde had sent to his brother from Richmond, and which Cecil had had intercepted and described to me so scathingly as dull, trivial outpourings from dull, trivial minds.

I found the letters not so much dull as peculiar. As Cecil had said, the first began in quite reasonable fashion with an account of Woodforde's journey to court and the people he had met and talked to on arrival, including Cecil and Dudley. He added sadly that he had seen Lady Lennox but that she continued cold to him. Remembering the remarks I had heard her make to him, I felt that this was putting it mildly.

After that, however, the letter, which was lengthy, became oddly muddled, drifting from one topic to another and back again in haphazard fashion. He commented on the queen's appearance, noting her liking for gowns in white and cream and silver, and said that he had seen her with ornaments of white jade in her hair. This was true, but it was observant of him to have noticed it and why, I wondered, should he mention the white jade but not the pearls, which she wore far more ostentatiously and often?

There were several references to food, including the surprising statement that pease pottage appeared quite often at the noon meal. This was *not* true. I couldn't remember ever seeing pease pottage at court. It is a peasants' dish. He complained primly of the frivolity at the court and he undoubtedly loathed jesters—*although I make an exception for you and for my dear niece, your daughter. Sometimes, I think the humor of the professional ones is too unkind and full of pepper.*

Touchingly tenderhearted, I thought, and an interesting remark from a man whose personal servant said he was badly treated.

I read on. There was a romantic description of what he called a faery dawn at Richmond, pearly with dew and with just a trace of silvery fog drifting over the Thames. In the next paragraph he said he had bought a new hat and his companions had admired it, and a few lines later he was grumbling again about the prevalence of jesters, one of whom had irritated him so much during a mealtime that Woodforde had longed to throw something at him. For some reason, he specified that the something he wished to throw was the vinegar. Why the vinegar in particular? I wondered.

Then came another of the comments that Cecil had mentioned, about the rattling creeper that had kept Woodforde awake. He had nailed it to another creeper stem to keep it still. Why, he asked rhetorically, should one have to spend so much energy and zeal on such matters?

The second letter was in much the same style. I could see why Cecil had suspected a cipher. The rambling, the disjointedness, the awkwardness, was in places very marked; small incidents like the rattling creeper taking up too many words; flights of fancy about faery dawns and pearly dew mingling with repetitious references to jesters, clothes, and food. But Cecil and his code breakers knew their work. If they hadn't found a cipher, then there wasn't one.

I gave up on the letters and went through to Ambrosia's room, which was beyond the lumber room, as though she wanted to keep a distance between herself and her father. In contrast to Jester's sanctum, this was poorly furnished with a rickety table and stool, and just one wall shelf, though here too there was a little hearth for warmth in winter. The shelf held a couple of histories, a book of poems, a Greek primer, and *Caesar's Gallic Wars* in Latin. On the table was a battered wooden box and beside it, the one good item, a writing set of brass and polished wood.

The box contained letters and to my surprise, when I picked them up, I found that although Ambrosia had told me that she hadn't got very far with Greek, they were in the Greek alphabet and presumably in that language. Perhaps, I thought, she was not of a boastful temperament and hadn't wanted to flaunt her education in front of someone she thought to be humble. Or perhaps her tutor—what had she said his name was? Dr. Barley, that was it—was continuing her instruction by letter. I looked at the letters with interest, wishing that my own Greek had gone further than the alphabet and a very small vocabulary. I could still remember most of the alphabet. Picking a few words at random, I murmured the sounds of the letters under my breath.

And realized, with a jolt under my breastbone, that the sounds I had just made, if run together, did not come out as Greek at all. They came out, more or less, as *aking ioints* and *Iama sikoldman.*

Aching joints? I am a sick old man? I whispered on, stumbling a little where my memory proved rusty. *I seem to acquire a new ailment every season. My digestion will no longer let me eat some of my favorite foods, and I grow breathless when I walk far. My physician makes me take an infusion of foxglove for it, which helps a good deal . . .*

In passing, I thought that her correspondent's physician and ancient Gladys Morgan back at Withysham clearly belonged to the same school of medicine. The signature, when I had deciphered that as well, was *Edward Barley.* Ambrosia and her tutor were corresponding in English, using the Greek alphabet.

There were awkwardnesses here and there where the Greek letter didn't quite match the English sound. An initial "J" or "Y" was always an "I," for instance. But on the whole, to anyone who knew the Greek alphabet reasonably well, the letters were perfectly clear. Barley's handwriting was a little shaky, the hand of an elderly man, but it was legible enough. I thought he was a kindly soul. Every letter began by thanking Ambrosia for writing, and the whole tone was one of affection.

There were about a dozen letters altogether, though, and my halting recollection of the Greek alphabet made me slow. I could not read everything. I flicked through the sheets, pausing here and there at random, in case anything interesting should emerge but not expecting that it would. Even if there were plots afoot in this shop, and Ambrosia were privy to them, she surely wouldn't chat about them to her tutor. Then, in the middle of the third letter I picked up, two words caught my eye. *Iour mother . . .*

Iour . . . that would be *your*. Your mother. Ambrosia's mother? The one who had run away from Roland Jester? Frowning, I tackled the surrounding text.

Your mother sends you her love, but still forbids me to tell you where she is living. She thinks it best that you do not know. She bids me say again that she would not have left you, only she feared for her life. She hopes and prays that your father will continue to treat you well as he always did in the past. She longs to see you and hopes some day soon that she will see you, though you, perhaps, will not see her . . .

Mysterious! Searching further, I found other references to Ambrosia's mother.

Your mother is well. She misses you but rest assured that she is safe and well provided for . . . Your mother does not forget that your birthday is this month of May . . . Your mother asks if you still use the writing set she gave you just before she went away . . .

So, through her tutor, Ambrosia was in touch with her mother, and because all the correspondence was in the Greek alphabet, there was little chance of Jester finding out, even if he went through her letters. Jester, presumably, did not know any Greek.

But none of this was any help to me. I put everything back where I had found it and went back to Jester's study, where I suddenly realized that there was one thing I hadn't inspected. I went to the oak settle and found that, yes, it had a lift-up seat and a storage box beneath. Here, it seemed, Jester kept his artistic efforts. There were two sets of charcoal sketches inside, one with the sheets punched at the corners and fastened together with a thong, the other just a pile of loose sheets. I took both sets out for a closer look.

There was no doubt that as an artist, Jester was amazingly talented. The loose sketches were mainly buildings, landscapes, and skylines like the one I had seen him drawing by the river. They were excellent, with carefully done fine detail.

The set of drawings that were fastened together were different. They were small sheets, only about nine inches by six, and leafing through them, I found that they were a wild medley of subjects—rather like his letters!—well executed on a small scale. The top one, for instance, showed a boy or a young man—he was rather casually sketched—giving a tidbit to a horse. In the background was a field and a little church. The artist had given reverent attention to the church, which was drawn in detail, and had also lavished great care on the dappled coat of the horse and the apple which the boy (or man) was offering.

The same mixture of casual and careful delineation appeared in quite a number of the drawings, as though some, though not all, of the pictures had been abandoned when not quite complete. Some of the sheets had more than one sketch on them, too. The top half of one such page showed people dining, one helping himself to salt from a saltcellar that was much more elaborately and beautifully depicted than he was, and beneath this was a picture of a woman apparently buying cloth, holding a length of it in one hand while giving money across a counter to the man who was selling it. The woman was a mere outline but the cloth was meticulously drawn—with highlights, showing that it was a gleaming material such as silk or satin.

Another sheet with two pictures on it showed a girl who looked vaguely like Phoebe, working in a kitchen, and below that, a girl who looked a little like Ambrosia, walking in a formal garden. Here again, the background was more carefully shown than the figures of the girls. I shook my head, puzzled, and put the sketches carefully back in the settle. Disconcertingly, something had stirred in the depths of my mind but was refusing to surface. I had had this experience before. I had noticed something but did not myself know what it was. It would come to me, or so I hoped.

I was looking around, to see if I had missed anything, when I heard the squeak of door hinges from below, and then the sound of voices.

I glanced swiftly about to make sure that I had left everything as I had found it and then, as quietly as possible, I sped down the spiral stairs. I blessed the peculiar architecture of the house now because the door of the bedchamber was not visible from the lower flight of stairs, the one leading down to ground level. I was able to dart into the bedroom unseen. Then I heard someone coming up the stairs, and Ambrosia's voice called my name. "Ursula! Are you there? Your cousin wants to see you!"

A picture of innocence, I emerged from the bedchamber with my shoes in my hand, just as Ambrosia arrived at the door. "Did I wake you? I'm so sorry. But your cousin Roger . . ."

"Is he here? I'll come down at once. Thank you, Ambrosia."

"I've pulled the shutters down a little," Ambrosia said. "You'll be able to see each other's faces."

The pie shop wasn't due to open for another half an hour. Brockley was waiting for me, therefore, at a table in an otherwise empty shop, cool and dim although Ambrosia's thoughtful arrangement with the shutters did let in a little light. Seating myself opposite him, I could just about make out his face. "What news?" I asked.

"I got away from Woodforde for a while. He's not a man I'd work for from choice. He threw a pair of boots at me this morning, out of sheer bad temper, and his aim is good," said Brockley. "I understand that he did some training with arms when he was with the Lennoxes, and that he goes to the college butts every Saturday and practices with the crossbow. I daresay it keeps his eye in." He peered across the table at me. "I can't see you too clearly but is that a bruise on your face?"

"I'm afraid so."

"Roland Jester?"

"Yes."

"If at the end of all this, he isn't gallows meat," said my manservant coolly, "I promise you, madam, I'll kill him myself."

"Please don't. I don't want you to become gallows meat too! What brings you here, Brockley?"

"I've some pieces of news, madam. Whether they're important or not, I don't know, but I wanted to tell you about them. One's a pretty little bit of gossip I got from the man I replaced in Woodforde's service. He stayed on for half a day to show me what to do. He didn't like Master Woodforde and he talked out of malice but it was interesting malice. I now know why Woodforde was thrown out of Lady Lennox's service."

"Oh?"

Brockley let out his rare chuckle. "He fell in love with her and kept on writing her love letters and leaving them on her pillow, accompanied by roses, and finally, her servants found him one evening hiding under her bed."

"He fell in love with Lady *Lennox*? The man must be out of his mind. One might as well fall in love with . . . a stone monument!"

"Ladies sometimes don't quite understand how men see other ladies. Lady Lennox is a handsome woman still, madam, and there is something about her—an air of banked fires, if you understand."

"I understand very well," I said, "but—banked fires in Lady Lennox!"

"Yes," said Brockley calmly. "I've seen her at court, of course. I wouldn't call her a stone monument. A she-dragon, perhaps. And dragons breathe fire."

"I suppose you know what you're talking about. No wonder she threw him out! Good God! Did her husband know?"

"Oh yes, and laughed himself silly, according to the fellow I was replacing," said Brockley. "I tell you, that man hates Woodforde. He'd been beaten with a riding whip and had everything you can think of thrown at his head—not just boots but pewter tankards, glassware, even a knife on one occasion though that time Woodforde did have the decency—or the caution—to miss."

"Brockley, if he tries to whip you, or throws anything dangerous at you, you may leave his employment at once and knock him down on the way out."

"Thank you, madam."

"Is there anything else? You said you had pieces of news, plural."

Brockley nodded. "There is something else and this may be important though I can't quite see why. It's just a feeling. You'll know, perhaps, that the lucky lady who is going to be kidnapped by the students and brought into the pie shop is a Mistress Smithson?"

"Yes."

"I am wondering, madam, if that's her real name."

"Really? What is her real name, then?"

"This morning, Woodforde sent me on an errand," Brockley said. "I had to ride out to a place called Brent

Hay Manor just outside the city and deliver a letter to this Mistress Smithson. She may have been Cambridge born but it seems she doesn't live in the town itself. She's a companion to a Mistress Grantley, who is a widow and the owner of the manor. From something Master Woodforde casually said, I think the letter was to do with what kind of dress Mistress Smithson should wear for meeting the queen. I was allowed to see her privately, in a little parlor, and give her the letter. She read it in my presence."

"And?" I asked.

"She's not young," said Brockley, thoughtfully. "About Fran's age, perhaps, and she has a . . . a tired look about her. She said I was to tell Master Woodforde that she understood and would follow his instructions. She also said—to me, this wasn't part of the message—that she couldn't refuse this honor, that Mistress Grantley had put her forward for it and wouldn't permit her to say no. Then she gave such a heavy sigh, madam, and looked at the letter again and, as though she were talking to herself, she said: "'Jackman's Lane. Well, well. Still, surely nothing can go wrong in the presence of the queen.'"

"You mean she seemed afraid that something *would* go wrong?"

"Yes, it sounded like that. And then the next thing she said was: 'I suppose it will only take a few minutes. I'll give the queen my flowers and then slip away into the crowd.' She obviously hasn't been told yet about the playlet and the kidnap, so she doesn't know she's to be brought into the pie shop. I would have told her that myself, madam, except that I didn't start to wonder until I was already halfway back to Cambridge. I'm not always such a quick thinker, I'm sorry to say. But once I'd started wondering—well—Master Jester's wife ran away from him, didn't she? She would certainly be frightened of having to come back to Jackman's Lane. Could this Mistress Smithson be her? Living under another name?"

I gazed at him in astonishment. "I suppose it's possible. But . . ." A thought occurred to me. "I'm living here as Mistress Faldene, but I'm still using my own Christian name of Ursula, because I'm used to it. If this is Mistress Jester pretending to be someone else, she might be doing the same. Do you know what Mistress Smithson's first name is?"

"Yes, madam. The letter I carried today was addressed to Mistress Sybil Smithson."

"Oh, my God," I said, remembering Master Jester's household prayers on Sunday and the way he had importuned the Almighty for his wife's return. "Yes. You're quite right. *Sybil!*"

11

The Eleventh Commandment

"It *could* be," said Brockley cautiously. "Though Sybil's a common enough name."

"I know. But if this particular Sybil is afraid of coming to Jackman's Lane—then we have a coincidence." I could hear Cecil's voice in my mind. *If there were an eleventh commandment, it would be Never Trust Coincidences.* He was right, too. I knew that from experience. Coincidences do exist but when they occur in suspect situations, one should look at them twice, or three times, or even four, before believing that they are what they seem.

"If Mistress Smithson is really Mistress Jester, then she is Woodforde's sister-in-law," I said. "Does he know, I wonder?"

Brockley frowned. "Master Woodforde—well, in the university people call him Dr. Woodforde—didn't say anything about being related to her or even knowing her. He just gave me a letter to be delivered to Mistress Sybil Smithson at a manor known as Brent Hay, out on the road to the north of Cambridge. 'On the right, half a mile past some cottages and a smelly place where someone's rearing pigs,' he told me. I found it quite easily. When I got back, he simply asked if I had delivered the letter safely and when I said yes, he nodded. That's all."

"It doesn't make sense." I was trying to puzzle it out and feeling more lost every moment. "If Woodforde does know who she is, then he also knows *where* she is, so why hasn't he told his brother? He surely knows that Roland wants her back. The two brothers are close, they must be. They write interminable letters to each other whenever Woodforde is away from Cambridge."

"Perhaps he's on Mistress Jester's side," Brockley suggested. "Why did she run away, after all? Did Jester hit her, as he seemingly hits his servants?"

"I think so," I said. "Ambrosia told me that he treated her very badly and the way I've heard him talk about her—yes, indeed, I think so."

"Maybe Woodforde's in sympathy with her," Brockley said, "and doesn't want to tell his brother where to find her. Only in that case . . ."

"He doesn't sound the sort of man who would be in sympathy with her and in any case, if by any unlikely chance he *is,* why on earth is he arranging for her to be kidnapped right outside the pie shop and then brought into it?"

"So he probably *doesn't* realize who she is. Someone from the university must have seen her and talked to her before settling the arrangement, but maybe it wasn't Woodforde."

"Which brings us back to a coincidence," I said restively. *"And I don't like coincidences!* I don't like the feel of this at all, Brockley, but I can't make sense of it." I put my head in my hands and gripped my temples. "I can't make sense of any of these *people!*" I groaned. "I've never met anyone quite like them in my life. I've met oddities, but these . . . !"

I had undoubtedly met oddities. I had once met a man who tried to build a flying machine. I had encountered a merchant adventurer whose delight in the adventuring part of his calling verged on the suicidal, and a woman in her sixth decade who fell in love with a boy of twenty. I had even—though I didn't want to believe it—once encountered a ghost.

And, to my sorrow, I had met the love of my life and found that he was a sworn enemy to my queen.

But mostly, those people had been odd in ways that sprang from their own natures. It was possible to understand them. For instance, Matthew's innocent belief in Mary Stuart's claim to Elizabeth's crown sprang naturally from his Gallic upbringing. Never before had I come across people like the Jesters, whose characters seemed to be made up of hopelessly incompatible facets.

"Look at them!" I said to Brockley. "A pie shop owner who has the temper of a devil and sketches like an angel. A pie shop owner's daughter who writes to her former tutor in English, but in the Greek alphabet. That's Ambrosia—I've just found out about that.

"And now there's a runaway wife who quite by chance, it seems, is going to be brought within her husband's reach, through the agency of a brother-in-law who doesn't realize who she is . . . and by a strange coincidence, this is to happen as part of a peculiar scheme to turn a students' rag into an entertainment for the queen, which has Cecil gnawing his beard with worry—and I think he's right. Thomas Shawe thought something was amiss and where is Thomas Shawe now? By the way, did you find out where Woodforde was when Thomas was killed?"

"Yes. I asked the fellow I replaced," said Brockley. "I was pretending to be asking questions about his routine. The answer was: in bed with a touch of the marsh fever and being waited on hand and foot. He certainly wasn't out in King's Grove murdering Thomas."

"But what happened to Thomas *can't* have been an accident," I said mulishly. "That would be just another impossible coincidence." I sat up, pushing my cap back from my forehead. "Look, Brockley. One thing is certain. If Mistress Jester and Mistress Smithson really are the same person, I want to warn her. Because from what I've seen and heard here, I don't want to see her thrown back into Roland Jester's power—not against her will, anyway. You'll have to take that ride again and tell her about the playlet and the kidnap and that she's going to be brought right into this very shop! Then she can decide what to do, for herself."

Brockley scratched his head. "Madam, I can't. I have another hour or so and then I must be back at my duties. If I fail, I could be thrown out and then I'll have lost my chance to study Woodforde, or keep watch on him."

"Then tell Master Henderson and let him arrange a messenger . . . now what is it?"

"I have several pieces of news," said Brockley gloomily. "That's another one. Woodforde isn't the only one who's had the marsh fever. Master Henderson can't leave his bed. I called at his lodgings before I came here—to report all this to him—and he could hardly raise his head from his pillow and obviously didn't want to talk. He woke up yesterday morning with a high fever on him."

"*What?*"

"Don't be too alarmed, madam. The physician was there—Henderson's man had called him. He said that Master Henderson would probably recover quite soon—that he was strong and that this type of fever rarely lasted long. But . . ."

"He didn't look well when we saw him on Friday," I said. "So you had no chance to ask if he'd yet talked to those students, to see if Thomas Shawe confided in any of them?" He shook his head. Another thought occurred to me. "Is there an outbreak of fever in Cambridge? If there is, the queen's whole visit could be canceled." I would be heartily relieved if it was.

But once more, Brockley shook his head. "There are always a few cases. Woodforde is prone to these attacks, apparently, and I understand that Master Henderson had been out to the fens on some errand or other to do with arranging fuel supplies. They use peat a lot in this district. The fever breeds in the fens. Her Majesty won't be going anywhere near them. But I don't think Master Henderson will be much help to us for a day or two and I haven't got the right to give orders to his men.

"In any case," added Brockley in his expressionless

way, "there's a big fuss going on for other reasons. All the harbingers have reached Cambridge now and they and their servants and Master Henderson's men are running here, there, and everywhere. It seems—I got this from Master Henderson's valet—that there's been a muddle over the list of household servants who are to accompany Her Majesty. No lodgings have been arranged for the sewing maids and laundresses and the vice chancellor has only just found out that the queen is bringing her own dining plate. He's upset as apparently King's has some fine silver plate which he wanted to show off and he wants to arrange to use it for at least one dinner and he's actually arguing about it and making a to-do . . ."

"Oh, for pity's sake!" I said.

"And there's another to-do involving Master Woodforde," Brockley said. "He's quite a connoisseur of wine, it appears, or thinks he is. It seems he took it upon himself to advise the vice chancellor on which vintages should be served to the queen. But the vice chancellor consults his butler on these matters and when the butler heard that Woodforde was interfering, he actually came round to Woodforde's rooms to tell him to keep his nose out of other folks' business. I was there when the butler arrived and there was a fine old shouting match. And on top of all that, the Gentlemen Ushers are expected tomorrow, to inspect all the arrangements . . ."

I peered suspiciously across the table at Brockley. His voice and face might be expressionless but I knew him well enough to detect the glimmer of amusement in his eyes. Like most people, he quite enjoyed a panic as long as he was allowed to watch it and not join in. But if he didn't feel directly involved in this particular panic, I did. If Brockley couldn't go to Brent Hay, and Rob and his men couldn't take a message for me, either, someone else must do it instead. I took a deep breath and raised my voice. *"Ambrosia!"*

She had been upstairs, but the urgency in my voice brought her to us at a run. "What is it? Ursula?"

"Sit down," I said. "Here at the table with us. Roger, tell Ambrosia what you have just told me, about your errand to Mistress Smithson, and what she said to you."

Ambrosia sat, linking her hands together on top of the table. Brockley embarked on his account. When he had done, I said: "Ambrosia, I don't want to pry. But is it possible that this Mistress Smithson of Brent Hay could be your mother?"

I looked down at her laced fingers. They were trembling.

"Yes. It might be so. It might be," she said unsteadily.

"I take it," Brockley said, in his slow, calm voice, the voice which was so good at soothing the fears of nervous horses, "that Mistress Jester, your lady mother, had her own good reasons for leaving home. I've seen the world, mistress. I know what life can be like for a woman when she is not kindly treated."

"My mother," said Ambrosia, "used to be scared that one day, my father might actually kill her. I used to try to stop him when he was beating her, but he'd always just get hold of me and run me into another room and lock the door. The day she ran away from here, she had a black eye and so many welts and bruises . . . she showed me before she went. She went in the morning when Father had gone to the market but she warned me first. She said I was old enough to understand why she was leaving me. She said I could come with her, if I wanted, only it would be harder for two of us than for one and my father didn't hate me as he hated her. . . ."

"He really does hate her, then?" I hardly knew why I asked, since Jester's treatment of his wife was so detestable that the reason behind it was scarcely relevant. I think I was just curious about the extraordinary Jester family. "I've heard him say terrible things about her," I said, "but at prayers on Sunday he did say he loved her and you said he cried when she left him."

"Oh, don't you understand?" said Ambrosia impatiently. "He says he loves her—yes, he did weep when he found she'd run away—but he used to treat her as though he hated her and besides, she's his, she belongs to him, he thinks she had no right to desert him. I know more about it now than I did then. Listen . . ."

She plunged into a description of her family history. Roland Jester's father had apparently been a Cambridge tavernkeeper. "He didn't own the place, just rented it," Ambrosia said. "Though it was doing quite well, I believe." He had died when Roland was little more than a baby and his brother and sister-in-law, who until then had been keeping another inn, very small and far from prosperous, in Yarmouth, had seized their chance and moved in to "help" the poor widow, left with a tavern and a small child on her hands.

Mistress Jester, however, had meanwhile caught the eye of a good matrimonial prospect, an educated man called Geoffrey Woodforde, who was employed as secretary to a Cambridge merchant. She had handed the lease thankfully over to her husband's relatives ("They paid her something, I think," Ambrosia said. "Not much but I suppose it was a dowry of sorts") and married Woodforde. While she was about it, she handed little Roland over to her husband's brother and his wife, as well. They had no children of their own and Geoffrey Woodforde, apparently, was not enthusiastic about being a stepfather.

"I think he wouldn't have married her, if he'd had to take the child on as well," Ambrosia said. "All the same, he was fair. He got my father educated. Uncle Giles was born a year after the marriage and when he was old enough to have a tutor, Master Woodforde arranged for Father to come and share the lessons. Father can read Latin!"

"And Greek?" I asked innocently, and Ambrosia shook her head, and even showed some amusement.

"No. He didn't get far with that, any more than I did. He said the funny alphabet was too much for him. But Latin, yes; he learned that and he's kept it up. He reads Latin poetry sometimes. So his mother and stepfather didn't ignore him even if he didn't live with them. When he married, Master Woodforde took a rented cottage near his employer, and that's where Father went for his lessons, so his mother—my grandmother—saw him quite often. He told me once that when she realized he was clever at drawing, she encouraged him. He wanted to be an artist. But his uncle said that no one could earn a living as an artist and wouldn't have it. His mother took his part but neither his stepfather nor his uncle agreed with her. I didn't know them; they died before I was born, but I remember my grandmother—she didn't die till I was ten. She used to scare me rather. She always seemed angry, somehow. She had a very strong, fierce way with her."

She sounded just like Lady Lennox. Possibly, to Giles Woodforde, Margaret Lennox really did represent his ideal of womanhood. Giles Woodforde was beginning after all to make sense.

"Anyway," Ambrosia told us, "his uncle died when Father was about twenty, and the landlord thought him too young to take over the lease. His stepfather helped to set him up as manager of a pie shop so that he would have a business of his own. It wasn't this shop; Jackman's Lane was built only nine years ago. That was when my maternal grandfather bought the land on this side of the lane and designed the buildings and had them put up. He was an architect by trade."

I nodded, remembering what she had told me previously. Ambrosia reverted to her original narrative. "I believe that my father's stepfather was really quite kind when Father said he wanted to be an artist, but he wasn't prepared to support him. He said my father had got to earn his living. He could draw for amusement, but that was all. Father himself told me once that he was upset at the time but that now he thinks Geoffrey Woodforde was right. He likes money. I don't mean that he's tightfisted," Ambrosia added hastily. "But he's, well, provident."

I was listening intently, finding that Roland Jester too was beginning to make sense. From childhood, he had been torn between the tavern in which he was born, and the quite different world of his educated stepfather, and on top of that, he had had this improbable talent for draftsmanship, which had been crushed by his uncle and by the need to earn his bread and by his own fear of insolvency. Yes, it matched the man I knew.

"Then," Ambrosia said, "Father met my mother."

It had been a remarkable romance, for Roland Jester, pie shop manager and at that time anything but well-off, was hardly an ideal match for Mistress Sybil Jackman, daughter of John Jackman, architect, who had full coffers and fur-trimmed gowns.

"My father's sketching had something to do with it," Ambrosia said. "The story goes that my mother was out walking one day, with her maid, and saw my father sitting by the river with his easel. She was amazed by the work he was doing, and stopped to talk, and then came back next day and did the same thing and in the end they fell in love and she insisted on marrying him. Her father gave her a good dowry but he never liked the match. Later on, when he did the building here in Jackman's Lane, he put almost all his money into it and when the work was finished, he sold all the other houses, except for this one. He gave this to my parents on condition that he should live here with them and have their company now that he was getting older. He'd got his money back, selling the others, but he did something with it so that when he died, my father wouldn't have it. It's with bankers in London, until I have children and then it will go to them. If I don't have children, it goes to a distant cousin and his descendants."

"Indeed!" I said. Jester wasn't as well off as I thought. His business was solvent enough but, I thought to myself, he does like money.

"We didn't find out till Grandfather died—I'd just turned fourteen then. It was a bitterly cold January and he caught a chill that went to his chest. After he was gone, the will was examined and oh, my father was so angry!" Ambrosia said. "That was when he turned against poor Mother. She tried to hold out, but it was too much in the end. She ran away in the June. And now you tell me that she may be brought in here—right into my father's hands! I've got to let her know! I've got to warn her!"

"Quite," I said. "That's why I called you down here. Could you find Brent Hay Manor, do you think? Neither Brockley nor I are free to go ourselves and besides, you are her daughter, anyway."

"Find Brent Hay—oh, there's no need." Ambrosia brightened, as I had hoped she would. "I can't go either," she said. "Father wouldn't let me go off like that and if I went without asking, there would be the devil to pay when I got home. It would be where have you been and who have you been with . . . he doesn't usually hit me but he would for that. But . . . a year or so ago, my mother got in touch with me, through someone else. She said I was old enough now to keep a secret and that she trusted me not to let Father know we were exchanging messages. I don't want to say any more but yes, I could get word to her. At least, if this

Mistress Smithson *is* she. She wouldn't tell me where she was or whether she was calling herself by another name. But the . . . the person who is passing messages between us will know."

"I won't ask you to tell me any more," I said. "But do it, Ambrosia. Warn her."

"Mistress Brady, the bronzesmith's wife next door," she said, "doesn't mind sending her serving boy on errands for me, if I pay her something and give him a coin or two as well. I have a small allowance. Thank you for telling me about this, Ursula, Master Brockley. Thank you."

She sprang up and raced out of the room. I heard her feet going up the stairs, one flight and then two. She had gone to her attic. Brockley and I sat on, talking about Woodforde. Brockley had learned a good deal about his habits and interests. Archery with either the longbow or the crossbow was long outdated as an art of war, but it was still a favorite sport, and as many men did, he practiced it after church on Sundays; there were butts attached to King's College and Giles Woodforde had won several crossbow contests. I pricked up my ears at that, but Brockley shook his head. "It's a commonplace, madam. It doesn't turn him into a villain."

"All the same . . ."

"You've seen the arrangements for the queen when she comes to Jackman's Lane." The dais had been built by now and the supports for the canopy were in place. "Her Majesty will be shielded by the canopy from all directions except in front and the open front faces straight along the lane into Silver Street. There are no dangerous vantage points, not even up on a roof."

Cecil had said the same. "But I still don't like it. I wish to God," I said, "that Cambridge could have a really fierce outbreak of marsh fever! Then the Progress would be canceled and we could all go home. I'm missing Meg so much, and my husband even more . . ."

Memories suddenly flooded back and I checked myself. "I'm sorry. I wouldn't really wish the marsh fever on anyone. People can die of it, can't they? One might as well wish for an outbreak of plague or small-pox! I'm afraid all the time that Matthew will fall vic-tim to the plague. I've had no news from Blanche-pierre lately. And . . . I remember how my first husband, Gerald, just caught the smallpox and was gone in days . . ."

I was near to tears again, just as I was on the bridge, which had led to Dale finding me in Brockley's arms. This time, however, they were stopped by the return of Roland Jester. The private door creaked open and then Jester, carrying his sketching gear, strode through to the shop, impatience billowing before him like smoke. He dumped his easel on the nearest table, unbolted the shutters, wrenched them open to let in light and air, and burst into speech the moment he realized that the shop wasn't empty.

"I'm late . . . we're due to open again . . . good God, girl, what you doin', sittin' there a-gossipin'? Come to see your cousin, Master Brockley? Well, fair enough but now she's back on duty and if you want to buy a pie and some ale you can stop, but if not, don't clutter up the premises. And why ain't you swept the sawdust up and put down fresh, Ursula? Get to it or else! An' get some pies out here on the counter. I met Wat, comin' back, and sent him round by the charcoal merchant so he won't be here yet; you'll have to take over. Where's Phoebe got to?"

Phoebe appeared at that moment, breathless. Jester shooed her into the kitchen, exclaiming that Wat's counter needed stocking and he had deliveries to make to two customers who had ordered pies for their supper. Ambrosia came down the stairs, looking quite normal, glanced into the shop, gave me a nod, and then called quite openly to her father that she just wanted to send off a letter to her old tutor. "All about the queen's visit. It's so exciting! To think she'll be just outside this very shop!"

"She writes to her tutor but she doesn't hide it from her father, it seems," Brockley whispered, as Ambrosia went out to the street.

"Why should she? I told you—she writes in the Greek alphabet and Jester can't read it," I whispered back. "Just before you came, I was upstairs looking at her letters."

"Risky, if you ask me," Brockley said. He stood up to take his leave. "He might look over her shoulder one day, point to a sentence, and say *what does that mean?*"

"She's sharp enough to invent something convincing," I said. The threatened tears having receded, I managed a chuckle. "I find it rather delightful. Roland Jester strikes me as one of those people who are put on earth for other people to sharpen their minds on—thinking of ways to deceive him."

"I'd best go, madam," Brockley said. "But I'll be by the river tomorrow afternoon, if I can."

"I hope to see you there," I said.

He went out of the shop. Presently, Ambrosia came back, smiled at me, and then went calmly to the kitchen. I wondered how soon the letter would leave the bronzesmith's house and begin its journey to Mistress Sybil Smithson. It would be a relief, I thought, when we knew for sure that the message had reached her. I would also be glad to know whether or not she really was Sybil Jester.

The following afternoon, I met Brockley by the river as arranged. I was rather disappointed to find that Dale was not with him. I had hoped she would be, because I was sorry for her and did not want her to think that my meetings with Brockley were anything other than business.

Brockley, however, said he had tried to fetch her from his lodging but found her frantically stitching at a huge embroidered curtain that was to be used in one or the other of the queen's apartments in Cambridge. "She couldn't come," he said. "She hopes you'll come back soon so that she can simply work for you and not be made use of by all and sundry! Madam, Sir William Cecil is due here on Thursday, the day after tomorrow and Sir Robert Dudley too. I thought you'd like to know."

"Yes, indeed. I must report everything that I've learned, such as it is," I said. "Including the death of Thomas Shawe. Very likely, Cecil will think that the playlet should be canceled and take the matter out of our hands."

We strolled for a few moments more in silence, among the other townsfolk who had come out to walk by the river in the sunlight. The weather was fresher since the storm. As we turned to retrace our steps, we saw a woman in the black gown and veil of deep mourning, hesitating by the bank of the river. Brockley caught his breath and we both quickened our pace, thinking for a dreadful instant that the woman intended to jump into the water. As we started toward her, however, she stepped back and walked away, and we halted. Beneath the thin material of the veil we had glimpsed the generous ruff—the only bit of white in her costume—of a lady of means, who would probably not want to be accosted by a serving man and cookmaid. She was alone, with neither groom nor maid of her own, which probably meant that she had left them behind deliberately, out of a wish for solitude. She had a lidded basket on her arm and as we watched, she turned toward the bridge back to Silver Street and the town.

But her walk still spelled dejection. "Poor soul," Brockley said. "Lost her husband, I daresay. Madam . . ."

"Yes, Brockley, I know."

"Madam, you should be with him. Forgive me. I mean no disrespect. But you *should* be with your husband. It isn't right for you to live alone and—well, life is never certain. You lost your first husband. You and Master de la Roche need to be together while you can."

"I'm only waiting for him to call me back to France, when the plague is over. I'll go to him immediately then."

"I hope he calls for you soon. This present state of things—isn't good for you."

Or for us. The words were not said; we never, never referred in words to that night in Wales when we had nearly, oh, so nearly, abandoned the roles of employer and servant, and forgotten the boundaries of his marriage and mine. But sometimes reminders came without words.

"It's time I went back to the shop," I said abruptly.

I returned in good time. The moment I had stepped through the lobby into the passage to the kitchen, however, I heard the sound of sobbing, somewhere upstairs. I found Ambrosia in our room, lying on the bed, weeping bitterly.

"Ambrosia?" I said, putting my hand on her shoulder.

She raised her face, blotched with crying, and without speaking, pulled a letter from under her tumbled skirts and handed it to me.

It bore the name of Dr. Edward Barley, and it was sealed. I looked at her questioningly. "I don't understand."

"Dr. Barley was my tutor. I used to write to my mother through him," Ambrosia said dully. "When she ran away, she took shelter with him first, though I didn't know it, of course, until she began sending messages to me through him. When I wrote yesterday, I sent the letter to him as usual. I don't *know* that this Mistress Smithson at Brent Hay is my mother, you see, so I couldn't write direct to her."

I nodded gravely. "Go on."

"I gave the letter to Mistress Brady next door," said Ambrosia miserably, "and she said her serving lad would take it today. He's just got back and he brought the letter back with him." The tears began to flow again. "My poor tutor. He was so very old and he's been ill for a long time—his housekeeper was there, the boy says, crying her eyes out. He had some sort of attack on Friday, just after eating his supper, and died the next day, on Saturday. The funeral is today—it couldn't be delayed longer because of the heat. The letter hasn't reached my mother—and I'm sure at heart that you're right and she *is* my mother—and poor Dr. Barley is dead, like Thomas, and I couldn't go to say good-bye to either of them!"

12

Winged Mercury

My first thought was: *another* coincidence. Though how it fitted, I couldn't see. Dr. Edward Barley hadn't been making assignations with me to discuss suspicions of the students' playlet. I stood there, patting Ambrosia's shoulder, trying to think it out. "You say he had been ailing?" I inquired carefully.

"He had breathless attacks and pains in his chest sometimes," Ambrosia said, still sobbing. "He told me in his letters."

And so indeed he had, and there was nothing strange about it. Such things were common enough in old people; my own grandfather had died after similar symptoms. One must not see plots and murder everywhere. Old, ailing men do die, sometimes suddenly, and there *are* such things as genuine coincidences. This was surely misfortune, pure and simple. Mistress Jester's misfortune, very likely, if we didn't act swiftly.

"Ambrosia," I said, "get up off that bed, go straight upstairs, write a new letter of warning to your mother. You can address her as Mistress Smithson, but make sure you tell her that when she comes to Jackman's Lane, she'll be brought into Jester's Pie Shop; that will be warning enough. Then get next door's boy to take it straight to Brent Hay. *Quickly.* Your father will be back any moment and he mustn't have a chance to see who you're writing to and question it."

"Oh, do you really think I'm so stupid?" Ambrosia snapped. "I've done that! Or tried to!" She sat up, dashing the tears from her eyes, and from under the pile of pillows at the head of the bed (one advantage of plucking all those fowl was that we did have soft pillows), she pulled out a second sealed missive. "I worded it the way you've just said, too, but I signed it *Ambrosia Jester.* If Mistress Smithson is my mother, she'll realize at once that I know where she is and what the warning is all about. But next door's boy can't go this time! They're expecting guests—a married son and his family. The boy and the maidservant in there are far too busy to run errands for me today or probably all week, either. Sometimes it's like that. It's never mattered before."

I gnawed at my lip, thinking fast. I would of course be free to go out the next afternoon and although I wouldn't be able to get as far as Brent Hay, I could hand the letter to Fran or one of Rob's men then. But I hoped to meet Brockley then and hear anything further that he had to report, and besides, a day would have been lost and the more warning that Mistress Smithson-cum-Jester had, the better. Also, I couldn't quite trust to being free tomorrow afternoon. I had only to irritate Master Jester—which was never difficult—and he'd make me stay at the shop and peel onions. I wanted to get this letter safely on its way *now,* before anything happened to prevent it.

"Are there any customers needing pies to be delivered?" I asked her.

"Only one," Ambrosia said. "The Hardinge family—the people in that cheap jewelry place three doors along."

"Yes, I know where you mean. I need an errand to take me out of the shop," I said. "I could deliver that order, take it along early. When your father comes back, say you sent me . . . no, wait, just taking pies up the lane won't give me anything like enough time—is there anything else I could get while I'm out? Can I make a dash for the market and bring back some . . . some . . ." Ambrosia tended a herb patch in the back garden so we never bought herbs from the market, but there were other things. " . . . some mushrooms or peppers? We use a lot of them."

"Yes, we do. Get both," Ambrosia said. "I'll say I told you to. What are you going to do?"

"Find a messenger," I said. "Give me that letter. And wash your face, for the love of heaven! Your father mustn't see you like that."

I was afraid of meeting Jester on my way out, but there was a quarter of an hour still in hand and he was no doubt still sketching somewhere. Armed with a basket of pies, I sped to the jewelers and delivered them, murmuring something about them being freshly baked and they'd heat up nicely or would be just as tasty cold. Then, carrying my basket with Ambrosia's letter in the bottom of it, I sped on, making for the heart of Cambridge, where the produce stalls were, and the lodgings where I had originally meant to stay.

From the start, I had insisted that a small room be hired there for Brockley so that he and Dale could sometimes be together. Married though they were, my unfortunate servants often had to sleep apart because ladies' maids were supposed to share rooms with their mistresses. I used to send Dale to her husband at regular intervals, though, and when I first moved to the pie shop, I thought it would be a good chance for them to have a few connubial nights. Now, of course, Brockley had moved into Giles Woodforde's rooms. But I hoped to find Dale in our lodgings.

I arrived breathless and very hot, my face shiny and dust on my plain brown skirts along with traces of the flour I had used that morning making pastry. The ultra-respectable landlady opened the door to me, looked me up and down, and raised inquiring eyebrows.

"Is Frances Brockley here?" I inquired.

"And who might you be?"

I blinked and then realized that she hadn't recognized me in my servant's garments.

"I am Mistress Ursula Blanchard," I said with dignity. "I have lodgings here although I am not at the moment using them. I am also the employer of Frances Brockley. Is she here?"

"You're Mistress Blanchard? You don't look much like her, I must say. She's a court lady."

"*I'm* a court lady," I said sharply. "I'm dressed like this because I am making a private inquiry on behalf of the queen and need to look like a plain working-woman. Now, is Frances Brockley within?"

"I don't know what game you're playing, my good woman, but I do know this—court ladies don't go round dressed as cookmaids with flour on their skirts and no one sends a woman to make private inquiries as you put it, for Her Majesty or anyone else. Private inquiries for the queen, indeed! Be off with you!"

I was aware of time sliding past, being wasted, while Master Jester was by now, no doubt, back in the shop and wanting to know why there was quite such an urgent need for mushrooms and peppers. Ambrosia and I had laid our plans in haste and I had an uneasy feeling that there was a basket of each on the pantry shelves.

"Fran will know me," I said through my teeth. "Please call her."

"Mistress Brockley's working for the queen, right enough, and proper woman's work, at that. She's sewing and she's got a lot to do and I'm not disturbing her for the likes of you."

"Oh, for the love of heaven! *Fran!*" I bawled. "*Fran! FRAN!*"

"Stop that! Shouting like a fishwife on my very doorstep! I never heard the like. And me with a sick man upstairs who isn't to be disturbed! What are you? Some kind of gypsy woman with no manners? *Oh!* Now see what you've done! There are my neighbors looking out of their windows to see what all the uproar is about. You're making a spectacle of my premises. Go

away at once—at once, do you hear, or I'll send my girl
for the constable!" She made a violent shooing gesture
with one hand and started to close the door with the
other. I rammed my foot into it.

"Stop being ridiculous! I *am* Mistress Blanchard
and . . ."

"How *dare* you? Joan! *Joan!*"

"*Fran! FRAN!*" It was turning into an absurd
shouting contest. People really were putting their
heads out of upstairs windows to see what it was all
about.

Mercifully, the racket had roused people inside the
house as well as outside. One of the landlady's cowed
maidservants, presumably Joan, now came running up
from the basement, just as Fran herself, holding a
threaded needle, and Rob Henderson, wrapped in a
bed gown and looking wan, came down from their
rooms above stairs.

"Ma'am!"

"Mistress Blanchard!"

"What is it, madam? Is it one o' they nasty vaga-
bonds?"

"*Is* this Mistress Blanchard?" inquired the landlady,
addressing Fran and Rob together, and folding her
arms in an outraged fashion.

"Yes," said Henderson. "It is. Come in, Ursula."

"Very well, Joan. Back to your work. I never heard
the like. No one's more loyal to Her Majesty than I
am, but I must say her coming to Cambridge is doing
Cambridge no good. Why, they said a Cambridge
woman was to give her flowers and they picked someone who doesn't even live in the town anymore, as if

them that do aren't good enough, and I have to say that I don't care for her taste in her court ladies!"

"Mind your tongue, woman!" said Rob, managing to summon up a commanding tone from somewhere. "Better come up, Ursula."

The three of us went into the Brockleys' room, where the settle was heaped with a mass of green and silver silk, on which Dale had presumably been working. "It's curtaining," she said as she pushed it aside so that I could sit down. "Oh, ma'am, there's so *much* of it; I'm right tired of it. I can't abide being told to embroider fast. It spoils the work."

She herself took a stool and Rob sank down onto the window seat. Eyeing him with anxiety, I asked him how he was. "Brockley told me you had the marsh fever."

"I have but I'm better," Rob said. "The fever died out by sunset yesterday. I'll be about again by tomorrow. The physician said I should rest today. Never mind about that. What's brought you here, pounding on the door and in such a hurry that—well, I heard our landlady say you had flour on your skirt and so you have. Didn't you even stop to brush it off?"

"No," I said brusquely. "I haven't had time. I have a letter to be taken to a place called Brent Hay Manor, just to the north of Cambridge. It's urgent. I would send Brockley but he isn't free. I thought Fran might go . . . unless your manservant could?" I looked at Rob hopefully.

"I'd send him or any of my other men gladly but I've lent them all to the Gentlemen Ushers for the day. There's so much going on and I've been too sick to work—I thought at least I should provide what help I could," Rob said dispiritedly. "And Fran here is stitching away, as you see. She's been seconded to the Wardrobe, as it were. She's not free either."

"Oh yes, she is. Dale is my tirewoman and I never gave permission for her to be seconded to anyone." I was too hot and exasperated to waste time being tactful. "Dale, I would go on this errand myself if I could, but I can't, not if I'm to keep my place at Jester's. I'm in the same position as Brockley. You must go instead. Be my Mercury, my winged messenger! Here's the letter." I opened my basket and took it out. "It is to go to Mistress Sybil Smithson at Brent Hay Manor, on the north road out of Cambridge. I believe it's quite easy to find and if it's a manor house I expect it's fairly big. You can ask the way. Take my mare, Bay Star, from Radley's. I'll give you a note for Radley so that he'll know that it's all right to let you have her. He can read. The letter is very urgent indeed. The embroidery will have to wait."

"Mistress Smithson? Isn't that the woman who is to present the flowers?" Rob asked. "What on earth can you have to say to her, Ursula?"

"Her name isn't really Smithson," I said. "It's almost certainly Sybil Jester and she's the wife who ran away from Roland Jester and it seems that this playlet is going to bring her straight back into his pie shop and she doesn't realize it. She thinks she is only coming to Jackman's Lane. She's worried enough about that! Her daughter is horrified and so am I. I've had some experience now of Master Jester. The daughter and I are trying to warn her!"

I looked around and cursed because the need for a note for the stable had only just occurred to me and I hadn't brought one with me. "There's nothing here to write Radley's note on. Just a minute while I go to my chamber and see to it."

"What a fuss you're in!" said Rob. Illness seemed to make him querulous. Ignoring this, I raced to my own chamber, found everything undisturbed and my writing set on the table, scribbled the note, raced back again, and thrust it into Dale's hands. "Go on, now, Dale. Don't delay. I have to get back to that pie shop. Don't just stand there. Hurry!"

Sometimes, getting people to cooperate was amazingly difficult. It could be like trying to move a boulder or shift a balky mule. Dale never did like being harried and it took several maddening minutes to get her shoes changed and her hat on and to make sure she had some money with her in case she had to ask directions from the kind of person who needs tipping. I got her on her way at last and then I made further kindly, if brief, inquiries after Rob's health, took my leave without seeing the offended landlady again, hurried off in search of mushrooms and peppers and remembered, too late, that in all my anxiety to communicate with Mistress Jester, I had forgotten to ask Rob if he had talked to Shawe's fellow students yet. Well, it was too late now.

It was the wrong end of the day for buying produce. I found some peppers but there were no mushrooms to be had. When I brought my inadequate booty back to the shop and took it through to the pantry, Jester was there, poking about on the back of a shelf. He spun around at my entrance and I saw that he was in a thoroughly bad temper.

"And just where d'you think you've been? Mushrooms and peppers indeed! We're not short!" Reaching back, he snatched a couple of baskets off the shelf and brandished them at me. "What're these then? Just because they've somehow got pushed to the back, Ambrosia can't see them! She ought to use her eyes and so ought you. Wasting good money like this! Now get to your work before I lose patience with you altogether!"

I obeyed him, joining Ambrosia in the kitchen. She looked pallid, as well she might. But no, she said, he hadn't struck her. "I pushed the peppers and mushrooms behind a crock of lard," she said, "and pretended I thought we'd run out. I think he believed me."

"Your letter is on its way," I said.

"Thank God," said Ambrosia. Then, miserably, she said: "Sometimes, I'd give anything to have my mother back again but I wouldn't want her to come back to be used as she was, and Barley told me that she couldn't have me with her wherever it is she's living now—this place Brent Hay, I suppose. I don't know why. I know I've got to do without her. She's not dead," said Ambrosia, with sudden and startling bitterness, "but sometimes I think that she might as well be, as far as I'm concerned."

I had a troubled night, thinking things out, trying to make sense of them. The next day was Wednesday. On the day after that, Cecil and Dudley would arrive. I would lay whatever I knew before them and then the responsibility would be theirs and not mine.

I only wished I could tell them more. What, after all, did my discoveries amount to so far? There had been two unlikely coincidences. Thomas Shawe, who had suspected that something was amiss with the playlet, had been thrown from his horse and cracked his skull, and through the playlet, a runaway wife was to be brought within reach of her husband, apparently by chance.

In addition, a sick, elderly retired tutor had suddenly died, an event that could have stopped Ambrosia from warning her mother of her peril.

Assuming, of course, that Mistress Smithson really was Sybil Jester, and that someone had reason to think that Ambrosia knew it, and was also in touch with her mother. It didn't add up to very much. If the someone was Woodforde, why on earth hadn't he just *told* Roland Jester where his errant wife was? Neither Woodforde nor Jester could have killed Thomas, either.

As it happened, I managed not to irritate Master Jester that morning, and in the afternoon I was able to go out as usual. I went first of all to the river where Brockley had said he would meet me if he could. His duties had evidently kept him, however, for he was not there, though the woman in the mourning garments was, alone as before. This time she was not lingering by the riverbank but merely strolling, and as before, she turned away into the town. Newly bereaved, I supposed, pitying her, for I feared for

Matthew and still at times remembered Gerald, and I knew what the loss of a husband was like. In time, one hoped, she would heal, as I had done. I could not tell her age but I didn't think she was very young. If she had some wealth, a new marriage might present itself in due course but in the early days of bereavement, one didn't believe that.

I didn't wait long, for I also wanted to see Dale. Presently, I set off into the town to visit our lodgings. The landlady let me in without protest this time though she still bristled with disapproval. I found Dale sewing again, sitting where the sunlight could fall on her work. I startled her by coming in unexpectedly and she exclaimed and sucked her finger where she had pricked it. "Ma'am! I didn't expect you today."

"Don't be silly, Dale! Naturally I want to know how your errand to Brent Hay prospered. Did you get the letter there?"

"Yes, ma'am. Yes, I did. Oh, there now, I've dropped blood on this work . . ." Dale found a handkerchief and furiously scrubbed at a minute fleck of red that no one would ever be able to see when the curtain was hung unless they went right up to it and peered at the material with a magnifying lens.

"Just put your work down for a moment. I want to make sure of this. You found your way to Brent Hay and delivered the letter personally. I take it you found someone to tell you the way. I hope it wasn't too long a ride. What sort of a place is it?"

"I didn't take it in much, ma'am. There now, I've made a knot in this thread, and it's real silver thread, silver leaf wrapped round silk. I was told to be so careful with it . . ."

"Dale, will you please put that needle down and attend to me?"

Dale stabbed her needle into the curtain fabric, and laid it all down on a table beside her. "It wasn't so very far, I suppose, only it seemed as if it was. I can't abide riding alone like that . . ."

"I know, Dale, I know. There are all sorts of things you can't abide." That phrase was all too familiar. "But you got there?"

"Yes, ma'am. It was a big house, like you said. I found someone along the road who directed me. A woman like a housekeeper said she would give the letter to Mistress Smithson. I couldn't press to see her in person. I didn't like to, in a big place like that, and besides, I was needed back here. There's this silver embroidery to finish repairing and then a cushion cover that has to have white flowers embroidered on it . . ."

Dale sounded thoroughly fussed. Her eyes looked tired and I noticed with disquiet that there was a big box of candles on the window seat. "Dale, have you been stitching at night and spoiling your eyesight? What are all those candles for?"

"Oh no, madam, I haven't been doing that, at least not much. But I get nervous, sleeping in this room all alone. I know there's others in the house, but still, I never could abide being alone at night. So I have a lot of candles. But I put them out before I go to sleep; I'm careful."

"All right, Dale, all right. But why don't you ask our

delightful landlady if one of the maids can share the room with you till Brockley comes back?"

"I thought of it, ma'am, but I'd feel foolish. She'd make me feel foolish."

"I daresay!" I could believe that. "Well, Brockley will be back with you in a few days. All our pretenses will end when the queen arrives. But you are not to sew by candlelight. You don't have to worry about neglecting that stitchery. I'm your employer, not the harbingers. Have you seen Brockley since yesterday? I hoped to meet him by the river before I came here, but he wasn't there."

"I haven't seen him either, ma'am," Dale said in a miserable tone of voice. I looked at her anxiously, realizing that she was probably lonely, probably missing her husband badly, and certainly being bullied by the harbingers.

"You had better finish the silver stitching," I said, "but after that, you are not to work for anyone else but me. Leave the cushion cover and its wretched white flowers. They'll have to be done by someone else who will at least be paid for it. I'll have a word with Master Henderson . . . oh, Rob, there you are."

I had left the door open behind me and Rob had come quietly in. He was dressed, and looked decidedly better.

"I heard," he said. "I'll see to it. I agree with you. I think Dale has been put-upon. Never mind, Dale. The queen's visit begins on Saturday. The inquiry must end then, for good or ill, so whatever happens, you will be reunited with Roger by the end of the week. I am glad to see you, Ursula. My fever has completely gone. I feel a trifle weak but nothing worse and I feel the need of the open air. I intend to walk over to King's College Chapel to look at the retiring room before the Gentlemen Ushers get to it. They are going to inspect it later on today. I daresay you'd like to come?"

13

Leaden Feet

We left Dale stitching again, still with a despondent air even though she admitted that she had only an hour or so of work to finish and was glad to be told that she need not do the cushion covers.

We were going out on the queen's business, and although I hadn't much spare time, I thought it worthwhile to exchange my dull gown and un-bleached kirtle for something more dignified. Dale interrupted her task long enough to help me into a decent tawny overgown and cream kirtle, and fasten a neatly pleated ruff into place. The overgown, of course, had my usual hidden pouch and I transferred my lockpicks and dagger from my cookmaid's dress. I wasn't likely to need them in the chapel, but I was rarely without them.

I made her hurry. "The minutes slide away when one is rushing here and there round Cambridge," I said to Rob. "But I'd like to see the retiring room. I would rather have been a real harbinger, you know, than an imitation one, using it as a cover for these inquiries that lead nowhere."

It took longer than I liked to reach King's College because Rob was still shaky from his illness and did not walk fast. However, when we did get there, we were pleased with what we found. The chapel was much quieter and cleaner than when we viewed Thomas Shawe's body there. The workmen had gone, taking their saws and hammers with them. The dust had been swept away, the dark, richly carved timber of the rood screen glowed with polish, and on top of it, the retiring room in the rood loft was complete. The air now smelled of beeswax rather than wood shavings. Two men on ladders were still busy cleaning some of the intricate carving over the west door but otherwise the work was finished.

"That's better," said Rob thankfully. "I have been going nearly mad, lying on my bed and wondering if the chapel would ever be ready on time. At one point, when the fever was very high, I had a terrible dream about Her Majesty arriving and being all mixed up with workmen. I'm not really here as a harbinger, any more than you are, but all the same, in spite of all the Yeomen of this and that and the Gentlemen Ushers, I still feel responsible."

"Here *are* some Gentlemen Ushers, I think," I said, as the south door opened, letting in a stream of sunlight and a group of dark-gowned personages. "I know what you mean. I feel exactly the same. Rob, when exactly is Cecil due to arrive tomorrow?"

"He and Dudley should both be here by midday.

They're expected to dine with Hawford, the vice chancellor."

"I must see Cecil as soon as I can. He'll be expecting a report and if there isn't much that adds up there are certainly some interesting factors . . ."

"Dear Ursula, you sound like a mathematician!"

"I'm serious, Rob! The last time we were here, we were looking at a young man's body and . . ."

"What's the matter?" Rob demanded as I dropped my voice to a mutter and moved hastily around to the other side of him.

"Woodforde's with those ushers," I hissed. "He's in his university gown but that's Woodforde all right. He mustn't see me. He might come to the pie shop at any time and he mustn't realize that there's a court lady there in disguise."

Peering around Rob, I saw that the new arrivals had turned to look up at the carvings that the workmen were cleaning. For the moment, they had their backs to us. We were close to the rood screen. Stealthily, we retreated into the shadow of the deep arched door through the center. "We can go through and into one of the side chapels off the choir," I whispered. "If we kneel down and hide our faces in prayer . . ."

"Stop!" said Rob, peering warily out of the arch toward the choir. I peered too and saw that the choir wasn't empty. A stage had been set up there and a dais built, with a thronelike seat on it for Elizabeth to occupy during the disputations and the Latin plays, and three men were examining it. I recognized them and they would recognize me. They were the Yeoman Purveyor, the junior Gentleman Usher, and the junior

Officer of the Wardrobe with whom we had traveled part of the way to Cambridge.

"What are *they* doing here?" I muttered.

"Everyone's been panicking. People are doing jobs that aren't really theirs, just to get things done at all," Rob whispered. "Like Dale."

"What are we to do?" I glanced back and saw that Woodforde and the ushers were now moving toward the rood screen. We were trapped in the archway.

"Up here!" said Rob. "Into the retiring room. Quick!"

I saw now that there was a door in the side of the arch. Softly, Rob opened it, revealing a stair. We slipped through, closing the door after us, and climbed quickly up. "I just hope," I said as we emerged at the top, "that we haven't made a horrible mistake. If they come up here as well . . ."

I found that I was frightened, which in itself was interesting. It told me just how sure I was, in the depths of my mind, that Thomas Shawe had not died by accident. It also told me that although neither Jester nor Woodforde could possibly have killed him, I nevertheless believed that they had arranged it.

If they thought I was a menace to whatever schemes they were laying, well, accidents could happen to cookmaids, too, especially in kitchens. In kitchens there were fires and meat cleavers and . . .

We looked around us. On one side of the room there were glassed windows overlooking the choir. From these, we at once moved cautiously back. The room held a press for fresh clothes, a settle-cum-chest, upholstered in blue and silver brocade, a small curtained bed where the queen could rest, a toilet stand with a modern glass mirror, and a padded stool in front of it. There was some more curtaining at the far end, but when I looked behind this, it revealed only a privy.

From where we were, we could hear the approaching footsteps of Woodforde and the ushers. They reached the rood screen and then, to our horror, we heard Woodforde's voice, which I recognized by its high-pitched tone, suggesting that they should inspect the retiring room. "They *are* coming up!" Rob said. "Well, officially we're harbingers. We'll have to brazen it out and hope no one connects you with that pie shop."

I had no desire to do any such thing. The bed curtains were drawn back, but the bed itself was gracefully draped with a shimmering blue cloth of silver coverlet on which red and white Tudor roses had been embroidered. The edges of the coverlet swept the floor. "Just pray they don't look under the bed in case someone's hiding there as Woodforde hid under Lady Lennox's," I said, and dived into concealment.

"Did he?" asked Rob in a bemused voice, stooping and lifting the hem of the coverlet to talk to me.

"Yes, he did, and Rob, try to get into conversation with Woodforde and see if you can find out whether or not he knows who Mistress Smithson really is. Probably is, I mean."

"You give orders like Her Majesty in person!"

"Rob! It isn't funny. *Please!*"

There was no more time. The Gentlemen Ushers and Woodforde were climbing the stairs. Rob let go of the coverlet and straightened up. A moment later I heard him say: "Good day, gentlemen! Master Robert Henderson at your service! I haven't had the pleasure of meeting you before as I have had to keep my bed for a few days, but I am one of Her Majesty's harbingers. As you see, I am about my duties again. I have just been making sure that all is clean and orderly."

"Quite, quite. Just as you should." That fussy voice belonged to an usher I knew slightly, having met him at court. He had a most unsuitable surname, for Sir Walter Large was no more than five feet four inches tall. He was also a great one for asking questions about fine detail. "This all seems quite satisfactory. The room is smaller than I expected but there is no time to alter that now. What's through there?"

I heard the rings of the privy curtain rattle and then a grunt as Sir Walter observed the arrangements it concealed. The curtain rings rattled back again. Rob was inquiring the names of those he had the honor of addressing, and I heard Woodforde explaining who he was and that he had been given the task of showing the ushers around the chapel, and introducing his companions by name. "Sir Walter Large . . . Lord Dunwood . . . Sir William Mallow . . . Roger Brockley you know, of course. He formerly served you, I believe."

No wonder Brockley hadn't met me by the river. He was giving Woodforde status by attending him. The ushers themselves, more sure of their dignity, had left their servants behind.

I lay still, breathing slowly and softly, relieved that there really had been some thorough sweeping under the bed. There was no dust to cause coughs or sneezes.

I heard the door of the press being opened and shut and the lid of the settle being lifted.

Then I heard Rob remark: "Master Woodforde, I wonder if you could spare me a moment. There is something I particularly wish to ask you, about this lady who is to present the flowers to the queen when first she arrives. I had heard that she is to represent the women of Cambridge but I now understand that she actually comes from outside Cambridge. Now how does this come about? Indeed, just who is she? Between one thing and another and my illness, I haven't been able to pursue this matter."

Clever Rob. As smooth and easy an entrance into our inquiry as anyone could have devised. He ought to be a success as an agent.

"Ah. Now this is a point I too wish to raise." That was Large. "The vice chancellor assures us that she is a suitable person but it is our duty to examine everything and everyone concerned in Her Majesty's visit."

"Oh, Mistress Smithson is ideal, I promise you," said Woodforde. "She is Cambridge-born although she is at present in the household of Mistress Catherine Grantley of Brent Hay, just outside the city. When the idea was first mooted of having a Cambridge lady to present the flowers, a proclamation was issued asking for nominations, and Mistress Grantley put forward the name of her companion. Mistress Grantley is a woman of some wealth and she has been most generous in making gifts to the university. I think the authorities felt that to accept her choice would be a graceful return compliment."

It was nerve-racking, under that bed. At any

moment, someone might take it into his head to lift up the coverlet and peer in. Even so, despite my thudding heart, I grinned. Cambridge, supposedly a seat of learning, of intellectual growth and avant-garde ideas, was as venal a place as any. Money talked in Cambridge just as it did everywhere else.

"But," Large was saying protestingly, "surely someone went to see the lady? Have you met her yourself?"

"The vice chancellor has visited her," Woodforde was saying. "I can assure you that she wasn't accepted without being interviewed. No one unsuitable would ever be permitted to perform such a task, sir. No doubt the vice chancellor can tell you more, if you apply to him."

The subject of Mistress Smithson seemed to die out with my question unanswered. One of the ushers remarked in authoritative tones that they would now inspect the stage, and that he was wondering whether voices would carry clearly from it to the queen's chair. "I would like to try it out. The chair can be moved forward if necessary, I fancy."

"I was thinking the same thing, my lord." That wasn't Large's voice. It was presumably Mallow's, since he used the words *my lord* and so must be replying to Lord Dunwood.

"Perhaps you would attend us, Master Henderson," said Dunwood. "Your opinion would be of value, I feel sure."

"After you, sirs," said Woodforde.

Rob had no alternative but to go as bidden, leaving me where I was. Feet moved toward the door and started down the stairs. I could still hear someone in

the room, though, and peering from under the coverlet, I saw a pair of feet in buckled shoes and another
pair in boots, following the others toward the door.
They halted, however, just as Brockley's voice, pitched
for harmlessness and ingenuousness, a fraction slower
and an iota more countrified than usual, remarked: "If
I may make so bold, sir, I've heard tell that this lady,
Mistress Smithson, is some relation to you. Would that
be right?"

My splendid Brockley had grasped Rob's intentions
and picked them up where Rob left off. In view of
Woodforde's habit of assaulting his servants, I felt that
Brockley was showing not only initiative but a good
deal of courage. To my surprise, however, Woodforde
answered him quite calmly. "So you've heard that, have
you? Well, well. How gossip gets about. A man's business, and his family, ought to be his own. I learned
only today that there's been talk among the students
that I've some secret scheme in hand, and I'm using
their playlet to further it! Had you heard that too?"

Under the bed, I stiffened. Brockley, his voice still
even and harmless, said: "Really, sir? No, I hadn't
heard anything like that."

"Well, I'll tell you something, fellow. Not that I
want you talking about my private business to anyone
and certainly not to Master Henderson . . ."

"Like I said to you, sir, I was glad to leave his
employment. He's the last one I'd go chattering to,"
said Brockley. I had never heard him sound so surly. I
had once told Roger Brockley that he would have
made a good strolling player and he greeted the idea
with horror, but it was perfectly true.

"Just as I thought. But you may say, if you hear such talk from other quarters, that you know for a fact that there's no harm intended to any through the playlet. As it happens, I do have a secret scheme, but it's as innocent and happy as a child's lullaby, you can be sure of that."

"Indeed, sir?" said Brockley, on a questioning note.

"It's perfectly simple," said Woodforde, somewhat irritably. "Maybe if there is talk going about, I had better tell you. Then you'll know what's going on and you'll know better how to answer—provided you don't let out to anyone what the plan really is. It's true enough that the lady's a connection of mine though I didn't know that until after she'd been chosen to present the flowers to the queen. She's my sister-in-law. Her real name is Jester, but she is calling herself Mistress Smithson just now. Due to a sad family misunderstanding, she is estranged from her husband although I must hasten to say that the matter is not one of scandal. She's been living decently enough in good service, with Mistress Grantley. It was quite by chance that I learned who she is. I was calling on an old acquaintance of mine, a retired tutor called Dr. Edward Barley, who is one of Mistress Grantley's tenants. That reminds me, when we leave here, we must go to my brother's shop and break the news that Dr. Barley is dead. I have just heard. My niece was fond of him—he used to be her tutor. In fact, I recommended him. Well, to continue, as I approached his house on the day of my visit, I was most surprised to see my sister-in-law coming out of his gate. She didn't see me and I didn't call to her. I didn't like to, in view of the estrangement.

"She turned up the road toward Brent Hay and I went on to pay my call. I wondered where she was living, though, and in casual fashion, I asked Dr. Barley who was the lady I had seen. He said she was Mistress Smithson, who had come with a message from Brent Hay.

"And I confess," said Woodforde confidingly, "that when all this business of the students and their mad scheme to kidnap the lady sprang up, it occurred to me that I might now engineer a means of bringing my brother and his estranged wife together. It could be a most happy outcome of the royal visit, and I admit that I like the notion of doing it through a little playlet—it will add a touch of drama, a pretty conceit."

"I see," said Brockley, sounding blank. "Or rather, I don't see. I mean, sir, how exactly . . . ?"

"The playlet will proceed, the lady will be whisked away into her husband's very shop where he will be waiting for her—and what happens when they meet will be for them to decide. I wish for your discretion now, because it is possible that if the court harbingers knew of the plan, they might dislike it and spoil it, though I am sure that if, later on, the queen were to hear that she had been part of a joyful scheme to reunite two loving people, parted by a foolish muddle, she would be delighted. What do you think, Brockley?"

"I'm sure you're right, sir."

"I am looking forward very much to seeing the queen here in Cambridge," said Woodforde. "I much admire such great ladies. I was once in the employ of Lady Lennox, you know."

"Were you, sir? I have heard of the lady, of course, though I have never seen her."

"She treated me ill, I'm sorry to say," said Woodforde with a sigh. "Yet still," he added, "I have the greatest regard for her. She . . ."

"Where have you got to, Woodforde?" Rob had come back into the retiring room. "Your ushers are waiting for you. I would like to sit down here and make notes at that toilet table—I have seen one or two minor things that need attention, which have escaped even the ushers. Did I hear you talking about Lady Lennox as I came up the stairs?"

"You did. A great lady, and an excellent wife and mother; an example to all women. She lives for her sons."

"And for the furthering of their ambitions, I believe," Rob agreed.

"Is that not a sign of a devoted mother?"

"When one of the sons aspires to the hand of the Scottish queen," Rob said, "it could also be the sign of an ambitious mother. I prefer Queen Elizabeth to Lady Lennox, any day."

"Oh, but I assure you!" Woodforde sounded flurried. "I meant no disrespect to Her Majesty . . ."

"Oh, go and catch your Gentlemen Ushers up. I must finish here."

Peering from under the bed, I saw Woodforde's buckled shoes and Brockley's boots go out the door. I lay still as they receded down the stairs. Then Rob said softly: "Ursula?" and I crept out from under the bed.

"We got away with that," he said with a sigh of relief.

"We did more," I told him. "He had a fascinating

conversation with Brockley after you'd gone. Brockley was superb. Listen . . ."

"Yes. I can imagine it," Rob said when I had done. "Some men are indiscreet with their servants. Woodforde is one of them, it seems. He wouldn't tell anyone in authority about his shoddy little scheme. He'd know they wouldn't take kindly to being used. But given half an excuse, he'll boast to his servant. I've met the type before. Well, so now we know."

"Know what?"

"What's behind all this playlet business, of course. The mystery's solved."

I stared at him. "Solved? What about Thomas Shawe? Who would murder him just to stop a reunion between Master and Mistress Jester? Anyway, if Woodforde really just wants to bring them together again, he only has to tell Jester where his wife is! Why play games over it?"

"The inquest on Thomas Shawe duly took place, you know," said Rob patiently. "And the verdict was death by misadventure. Accident, in other words."

"Well, we expected that. And I still don't believe it."

"Well, I do. Especially after what you told me just now. See here, Ursula, why don't you ask yourself, really ask yourself, how anyone but you and young Shawe could have known about your plan to meet? From what you've told me, both of you wanted to keep it a secret. You haven't inquired yet but as it happens, I did speak with some of the students before I fell ill . . ."

"I kept meaning to ask about that and then being distracted. What did they say?"

"Even you lose the thread sometimes, don't you, Ursula? Well, I'm glad to know you're human and even womanly on occasion. They said little to the point. As far as I can ascertain, young Shawe never said a word to any of them about any assignation on the afternoon of the day he died. He *did* mention to Francis Morland and some of the others that he had some unspecified worry or other about the playlet but he never told them what it was, or hinted that he meant to tell anyone else. I'm quite certain in my own mind, however, that we now know all about it, and for the love of heaven, how *could* Shawe's death be murder? His fellow students obviously didn't know he was meeting you and you said on Friday that Roland Jester isn't likely to have overheard the two of you arranging your assignation. So how could anyone have found out?"

"I don't *know*. But . . ."

"But what?" said Rob impatiently. "Are you suggesting that there are *two* schemes behind the playlet?"

"Yes . . . do you know, I think I am. Because it does make a sort of sense. You've just said that Thomas admitted to Morland that he was worried, and Woodforde himself said that today—just today—he learned that there were whispers among the students. I heard him say so. What if Woodforde took fright and decided to let something out to Brockley as soon as a chance arose, by way of laying a false scent? Yes, there is a hidden scheme, but it's only a matter of ending a family estrangement . . . when all the time, something else, much more serious, is being plotted."

"Oh really, Ursula! This is all so far-fetched."

I was still pursuing my own line of thought. "He talked about an estrangement due to a misunderstanding," I said angrily. "Bruises and a black eye, according to Ambrosia. Not too easy to misunderstand, in my opinion! And all because her father didn't leave his wealth to her and Roland but tied it up so that Roland couldn't get at it! But the point is, if anything else— untoward—happens during the playlet, Woodforde now has a witness who can assure people that he knew beforehand what Woodforde's plan really was and it had nothing to do with—whatever the untoward event may be. Woodforde will exclaim in horror that he has been made use of by some miscreant! That will be his story if he needs one. Clever!"

"I find this very difficult to swallow, Ursula," said Rob tiredly. "It seems to me that you are just tilting at shadows."

"I'm not. I'm sure I'm not." I hardly knew why I was so sure, but now I rummaged in my mind for the reason, and found one. "Brockley heard you tactfully questioning Woodforde and I think he was trying to follow your lead. When he began asking questions I was afraid that Woodforde would be angry, but he wasn't, not at all. He answered fully and he was very very pat. It *was* as if he'd been waiting for a natural-seeming chance to talk about it."

Rob sighed. "I don't agree with you but have it your own way. Let Cecil decide, when you speak to him tomorrow! I shall see him when he first arrives—he's going to lodge at St. John's College—and I'll ask him to be ready to receive you during the afternoon. I suppose you could leave the pie shop now, though."

"I'll stay until the moment comes to see Cecil. I'll give myself every chance to find out more. And now I'm going to be late back. I've got to go back to our lodgings first and change my clothes again! And I've got to get out of here unnoticed, somehow."

Luckily, a quick, cautious glance through the window to the choir showed us that Woodforde, the ushers, and the three other harbingers were now all busy with the dais and the stage. We slipped quickly down the stairs and with the rood screen to shield us, we hurried to the south door and escaped unseen. We hurried back to the lodgings as quickly as the convalescent Rob could manage, and I resumed my cookmaid's clothes before setting off alone for the pie shop.

I was half an hour late by now and I thought grimly that I could expect trouble from Jester when I got there. I was in no mood to tolerate it. That afternoon, I had once more become Mistress Ursula Blanchard, court lady, and now I was finding it difficult to turn back into Ursula Faldene, humble cookmaid. I had said I would stay until tomorrow, but if Jester as much as raised his hand, I decided, I would walk out after all.

Which would be a pity, because in the course of the afternoon, it had come into my mind that I would very much like another look at that odd set of drawings I had found in Jester's study, the ones that seemed in some cases to be not quite finished. For some reason, they were nagging at my mind. I hoped I wouldn't have to forgo the attempt in the interests of self-preservation.

In my experience, oddities in general follow the same rule as coincidences. If you find one in conjunction with any sort of mystery, there often turns out to be a link, however unlikely this may seem to begin with. I had once made a journey in company with a man who for no apparent reason pretended to be ill. There didn't seem to be any connection with the mission I was on . . . but it was there, all the same. Those drawings might, just possibly, reward further investigation.

I need not have worried. When I reached Jackman's Lane, I found the Jester shutters half closed, which meant they were set to let in light, but not to welcome business. Entering quietly through the private door, I heard voices in the shop and went in, catching my breath as I did so, for the first people I saw in the shadowy interior were Woodforde and Brockley. They paid me no attention and silently thanking heaven for the sanctuary of the queen's bed, so that Woodforde had not seen me less than an hour ago dressed as a court lady, I moved around them, to find Ambrosia sitting at a table and softly weeping while her father sat at her side, patting her arm but looking irritable. Wat and Phoebe were standing awkwardly by.

"Oh, Ursula!" Ambrosia caught sight of me, wiped her eyes hurriedly, and spoke to me with valiant aplomb. "My uncle Woodforde has brought such sad news! My old tutor Dr. Barley is dead!"

"Oh. I'm . . . I'm so sorry," I said.

Jester said: "Where in God's name you been, girl? What time d'you call this? I want to open up but what with all this and Ambrosia carryin' on as though I were dead instead of an old tutor she ain't seen in years . . ." He didn't, however, sound as though he

were really interested in my movements. Guessing
that they had all been in the shop for some time, I said
righteously: "I beg your pardon, sir. I heard you in
here when I came in and not wanting to intrude on
family matters, I went upstairs and have been sweeping." Ambrosia gave me a ghost of a conspiratorial
nod.

"Mistress Ambrosia's told me a little about her
tutor, sir," I said to Woodforde, addressing him, I
realized, for the first time in my life. The daylight
through the partly opened shutters gave me my first
really good look at him. I could see the petulant lines
around his downturned mouth and the cold gray
stare of his eyes. I didn't like him. "Was it a sudden
death?" I asked him civilly.

"Yes, but not exactly unexpected. I've known him
for many years. He's been ailing a long while. His
housekeeper sent me word and I was sorry to hear of it
but not surprised," Woodforde said. "I was too busy to
attend the burial but I sent my condolences and a con-
tribution to the funeral expenses." He paused, continuing to stare at me. His next words were alarming.

"Your name's Ursula? Doesn't sound familiar and I
haven't seen you here before that I know of, but I'm
sure I've seen you somewhere."

My insides did a somersault. "I haven't worked here
long, sir," I said mildly. "Perhaps we have passed in the
street. I go out on errands now and then."

"Perhaps." He went on staring for a couple seconds
more and then gave it up. "Dr. Barley seemed much as
usual when I saw him last, maybe a little short of
breath. But there—a man of his age—sooner or later

God is bound to call him. The message from his housekeeper said that he fell ill after supper on Friday evening, and then had a final seizure on Saturday and was gone."

Ambrosia's tears were flowing again. "Oh, go upstairs and wash your face, girl!" her father said to her. "Can't you control yourself? Ursula, take her up and get her calm so you can both get on with your work. The man was old and ill and God's called him, as my brother says. There's no need for all this. Wat, open the shutters. Go on, Ursula, see to Ambrosia."

Ambrosia rose to her feet. Going to her, I put my arm around her and guided her away. We went up to our chamber and I sat her on the bed. "That was a splendid performance," I said. "Anyone would think you really had just heard the news! The second message went off to your mother yesterday. It's all right. She's got it."

Ambrosia looked tearfully up at me. "But she hasn't."

"What?"

"That's why I'm in such a state. Uncle Giles came and I was called down, and I was trying not to cry— and then when he came out with the news about my poor old tutor, at least it gave me a chance to let go." Once again, she fished under her pillow and brought out a letter. "This came just after you went out. A gardener's boy from Brent Hay brought it. I was going out too and found him hanging about, waiting for me. He said he'd had orders to give it to me in person and not to let anyone else know, and that a lady at Brent Hay had paid him well to bring it."

She handed me the letter. It bore the date of Wednesday second of August. "Today!" I said. It was from Ambrosia's mother. It said that she had heard of the death of Dr. Barley, expressed grief for him and went on to say that since she could no longer write through him, she had decided to write direct to Ambrosia this once. She had news she longed to impart and a request that she must make. She had decided to reveal the name she was now using and where she was living, because it was likely enough that Ambrosia might learn this soon in any case and she could only hope that Master Jester didn't learn it, too!

She hoped to find a replacement for Dr. Barley soon so that she and Ambrosia could go on communicating through a third party, which would be safer, as then there was a chance that their correspondence might remain a secret from Ambrosia's father.

And now for my news. I am living as Mistress Smithson in the household of Mistress Grantley of Brent Hay. You must have heard, dearest girl, that when the queen comes to Cambridge, she is to pause in Jackman's Lane and that a lady called Mistress Smithson is to present flowers to her there. I am that lady. This very day I have also learned that there is to be some sort of little jest and I am to let some students kidnap me and snatch me away. Perhaps you have heard about this, too. It seems that I have quite an important part in the welcome for the queen!

I would have had to tell you in any case, dearest girl—for not to do so would be unbearable. My darling, I couldn't bear to be so close to you without you knowing. Perhaps, just for one moment our eyes will manage to meet. I shall be looking out for you. It has been so long, so very long, dearest daughter, since I last saw your face. I wonder if you have changed much in the five years since I fled? I hope you will know me when you see me; but will I also know you? I pray with all my heart that I shall do so.

But I am also telling you this news because I need your help. This task is a great honor which I could scarcely refuse when it was offered to me, but in spite of this and much as I yearn to be near you again, I am very much afraid of coming to Jackman's Lane. I want you to recognize me, but what if your father recognizes me, too? I shall be dressed very grandly in a gown that Mistress Grantley is lending me and, of course, the crowd will be kept at a distance, so perhaps he won't. If he does, well, I tell myself that in the queen's presence and with students all about me to protect me, he can surely do me no harm then and there. But the secret of my present name and whereabouts will be laid open to him and in that case, please, Ambrosia, warn me as quickly as you can, for I shall have to leave my present home and adopt yet another name.

Apart from this, it would be safer for you not to write to me here or try to see me.

I am sending this by one of Mistress Grantley's garden boys who often runs errands both for her and for me. I have told him that it concerns a very private family matter and that he must make sure that he gives this letter to you and to you only and that without anyone else nearby. I have told him that we resemble each other though I said that we are but cousins. If he can identify you, and I trust he can, then surely I will do the same myself, and next Saturday I will know you.

We had been right to think that Mistress Smithson was Mistress Jester, then. She had taken a serious risk in revealing her name and whereabouts to Ambrosia and writing to her in such candid terms without a third party in between but the desire to see her daughter again and to be recognized by her breathed out of the letter.

"She doesn't know," said Ambrosia desperately. "She *still* doesn't know! What went wrong?"

"I don't know," I said faintly, passing the letter back to her. "I can't think—I was sure . . ." I was thinking quickly. I hesitated and then plunged. "I'll try again to get word out to Brent Hay. And there's something else I might do—look, I . . . well, my cousin Roger works for a courtier and the courtier works for Sir William Cecil . . ."

"Who's he?"

"The queen's Secretary of State," I said shortly. "He will come to Cambridge tomorrow. I think I can speak to Roger's employer and tell him about this. You see, it sounds as though—well, your uncle Giles encouraged the students in their nonsense, didn't he? I'm wondering why, that's all. What if he knows that Mistress Smithson is your mother and has some scheme to throw her back into your father's power? Perhaps that's why he wanted to make the playlet official! But I don't think that the people of the court would like that. From things Roger has told me, I think that if they even suspect such a thing, they'd put a stop to it. They wouldn't like being used. If I'm right, then if I tell what I suspect, the playlet will be canceled. If you love your mother, just don't repeat what I've said to anyone but leave it to me to do my best and tell lies for me if I have to go out at difficult hours."

"Is it true?" Ambrosia asked wonderingly. "*Could*

you? Would you dare—go and talk to these great people?"

"Roger will help," I said.

I would see Cecil tomorrow. I would get the playlet canceled if I could and I would make sure, once and for all, that Mistress Jester knew what had been planned—and knew, too, what I had learned while hiding under the bed in the retiring room: the fact that her brother-in-law did indeed know who she was and where she was. She could decide for herself what to do, I thought, but in her place I would fall diplomatically ill, keep well away from Jackman's Lane, and set about finding a new name and hiding place forthwith!

And I would also, I thought grimly, make a point of seeing that leaden-footed Mercury of mine, that anything but winged messenger, Fran Dale.

14

A Time for Tears

I wanted to rush out of the shop and go to Dale then and there. But when Ambrosia and I went downstairs again, after Woodforde had gone, we found a surge of business. The queen's entourage was arriving in force by now, and some of the less exalted ones, the grooms and wagoners, the laundresses and scullions, were roaming around Cambridge in search of cheap suppers. The shop was full, and Jester in his most chivying mood.

Since I really did want another look at those drawings, I needed to keep my character as an employee and as such, I had no more chance of getting out of the shop that evening (or of getting up to the attic either) than of growing wings and flying to the moon. At the end of the day, when at last we all went wearily to bed, I found that Ambrosia was still worrying about her mother. "What if you can't get another message to her and can't get the playlet stopped either?"

"I *will* get word to her, whatever happens. There's still time. Leave it to me and don't worry."

But she did worry, to the point of lying sleepless. I knew this because I was seething with such impatience that I was sleepless too. I tried to calm myself, because a dull ache had started above my left eye and I was afraid of developing a sick headache. In the event, the ache eventually faded, but sleep I could not and as I lay there, I now and then turned my head and saw Ambrosia's open eyes gleaming in the dark. Once or twice I thought that she was crying.

Toward morning I dozed but was wakened early by Ambrosia, who was getting up. She was too restless to stay abed, she said when I heard a distant watchman proclaiming that it was four of the clock and all was well, and protested. In the dawn light, I saw that she looked exhausted and from her reddened eyelids, I knew that I was right; she had wept in the night. When we were alone for a moment because Phoebe, who had also woken up, had carried our chamber pots out, she said to me: "You promised."

"I know. I'll see to it. I'll go as soon as I can."

I felt dreadfully weary as I went downstairs with Phoebe, and at first, I could not think how to get away. I would have to ask Ambrosia to invent an errand for me, I thought, at some moment when her father wasn't within hearing. However, Ambrosia, who had gone down ahead of me, had eaten quickly and gone straight out to the yard to save Wat a task by helping her father kill fowl, so that I couldn't speak to her at once.

Instead, however, I ate my breakfast comfortably at

the table, along with Phoebe and Wat. Some rolls and drippings and a good drink of small ale, taken for once in peace and in company that didn't include Roland Jester, had the effect of clearing my mind as if by magic.

Suddenly I saw that I had been trying to do too many things at once and had failed to put them in order of importance. The vital things I had to do today were to dispatch a new message to Brent Hay and to see Cecil. I must see Dale too because I needed to know why the message I had entrusted to her had miscarried.

Snooping in the attic, however, was a lesser matter. I could try persuading Cecil to have the premises searched officially and the drawings confiscated. But if he would not and I returned from seeing Cecil and Dale to find that Jester no longer wished to employ me, then I must let the search of the attic go.

And I had better set out at once, while Jester was still engaged in slaughtering poultry. I gulped the last of my ale and stood up. "Phoebe, Wat, I'm going out. I'm going without permission but I have . . . I have a family matter to see to and I must call on my cousin. Will you tell Mistress Ambrosia? I'll be back later on today."

"But Master Jester will be so angry!" Phoebe's eyes were round.

"Tell Mistress Ambrosia," I said again. "She knows something of the matter already. Let her tell her father. And, Phoebe, try to work deftly this morning; don't give him any reason to take it out on you if he's annoyed with me. You can be deft if you try."

"I'll keep my eye on 'er," said chivalrous Wat. "And 'im!"

The morning was warm and I had with me everything I needed. When rising, I had put a purse of money into my pouch with my lockpicks and dagger. Now, equipped for the day, I simply walked out of the shop. The front of it was still shuttered, but I went out through the private door, cursing when it creaked, although it wasn't likely to be audible in the backyard where Jester was. Once outside, I set off rapidly to my first objective.

In the long dark hours, I had done some thinking. When I asked Dale to describe her visit to Brent Hay, I had noticed that her manner seemed odd, but I had thought she was merely feeling harassed. I could have been right. It was just possible that Dale had not been seriously at fault. She had given the letter to a housekeeper, she said. Perhaps the housekeeper had forgotten to give it to Mistress Smithson, or not done so until after Mistress Smithson had written and dispatched her letter to Ambrosia. I should be fair to Dale and make sure of my facts before pouncing on her with questions. Cecil would not be in Cambridge yet. I had a little spare time. I would begin, I thought, with Radley's stable.

Cambridge was busy. The queen's wagonloads of goods—the personal tapestries and bedding for her bedchamber and the chambers of her principal ladies and courtiers, the boxes of clothing and documents, and the plate that had so disappointed the university vice chancellor—had started rumbling into the town the day before and they were still coming. There must have been over two hundred wagons altogether. Most of them had six horses; the fields on the other side of the river were already filling up with grazing animals, and when I reached Radley's, I found that whatever its shortcomings, it didn't have a single stall to spare. Indeed, the hay bales had been shifted into a mountainous pile in one half of the hay barn so that makeshift partitions could be put up to make extra stalls in the other half.

I made a quick inspection of my own animals and found with relief that they had been groomed and that their standard of feed was adequate. Brockley and Rob Henderson's men had terrorized Radley to good effect, I thought. Going outside again, I found Radley arguing with a carter over the proper treatment of a draft horse that had gone lame. Ruthlessly interrupting them, I demanded to know whether, the day before yesterday, a Mistress Brockley or a Mistress Dale had brought a note from me, requiring her to take my mare Bay Star out on an errand and asking for the mare to be saddled up for her.

Radley recognized me, fortunately, but said that it was the groom, Jem, that I wanted. "It was him she dealt with—Mistress Brockley she were calling herself."

He bellowed Jem's name in a roar that must have been audible two streets away. The harried groom appeared at a run. "Where've you been hiding yourself?" Radley asked him. "Never in sight when you're wanted. Late again this morning," he added to me. "Too idle to get out of bed on time, even though he knows I'll be waiting for him with a strap. All right, Jem. You tell the lady about your errand the day afore yesterday, for Mistress Brockley."

"Errand?" I queried. "It was Mistress Brockley's

errand. I gave her a note so that Master Radley here would let her have my horse, Bay Star. I had to send an urgent message to a Mistress Smithson at a place called Brent Hay."

"Oh yes, ma'am." Jem gave me his brown-toothed smile. "Yes, Mistress Brockley, thass right. Only she was scared of riding alone, she said, and Master Radley here, he said I could take the mare and the letter. Get Mistress Brockley to tell you 'zactly where you're to go, he said to me, him being busy at the time, trying to fit up that there hay barn to take hosses instead of hay. So I did what he said."

"I see. And when did you take the message?" Dale had passed on the errand to someone else, and she would hear from me about that, but it was possible that if Jem hadn't taken it until yesterday, it had reached Mistress Smithson-cum-Jester safely enough after all, but not until after she had written and sent off her own letter to her daughter.

But no. "I took it right away," said Jem, slightly affronted.

"The day before yesterday, you mean? And you found Brent Hay and gave it to Mistress Smithson herself?"

"I think so. Leastways, I misremember exactly what the names were, but Mistress Brockley, she said the letter was for a Mistress Sybil someone or other at a place called something-hay and I got directions and there was a Mistress Sybil there all right. She opened the door to me."

"And just where was this place?" Radley joined in. "What did it look like?"

"It weren't as big as I thought it 'ud be, from what Mistress Brockley said," Jem said. "She said it 'ud be like a manor house, but it was just a sort of biggish cottage, along the road out northward, opposite that place where they breed pigs and there's allus such a stink that I wonder how folks can stand to—"

The clout that Radley now administered to the side of Jem's head sent the unfortunate groom staggering. He bumped into a horse trough and Radley, leaping after him, grabbed him by the neck and dunked his head into the water until Jem, struggling, started to bubble. "You damned stupid . . . I took good money for that there errand . . . and let you have your tip and . . . this is how you serve me . . . you oaf! . . . You lackwit! . . . You addlebrain!" Between each enraged exclamation, he shoved Jem's head back down into the trough again.

"Here!" I caught at Radley's arm. "I want to know just where he really took that letter and how can he tell me if you drown him?"

"He don't need to tell you!" Radley desisted, however, and Jem, soaked and purple in the face, sagged against the trough, coughing into it. "*I* can tell you where he took it!" Radley snarled. "I know that place! A biggish cottage, opposite the fellow that breeds pigs? Thass *Rose*hay, that is! Belongs to Brent Hay, but Brent Hay Manor house is another half mile on. What did the lady look like as took the letter, Jem? Come on, you tell Mistress Blanchard here. What did she look like?"

"Just a woman!" Jem spluttered. "An old sort of woman, skinnylike. No cap. Seemed all amazed when

I said I'd got an urgent letter for her. 'Who's writin' me letters?' she said to me."

"I'll wager she did!" said Radley with contempt. "Her name's Sybil, right enough. Sybil Lessways, that 'ud be. No wonder she said who was writin' letters to her. No one would as knew her. She can't read nor write."

"But she took the letter?" I said persistently.

"Well, I said as it were for her, so, yes, she took it," Jem said sullenly, wringing his hair into the trough.

"And I can tell what she did with it," said Radley helpfully. "Or more or less. Chucked it in her fire, or twisted it up for a spill to light candles with, come the dark."

"Thank you," I said. "I'm most grateful. Do drown him if you want to, Radley." I brought out my purse, found a gold coin, and pressed it into Radley's hand. "Here's something for your pains."

It was still too early for Cecil to have reached Cambridge. I made straight for Dale.

She was in the lodging, on the settle by the window, stitching a cushion cover against my orders and when I marched into the room, she dropped it and pushed it furtively aside, misinterpreting the anger in my face. I corrected her at once.

"I don't care a straw about the cushion cover. I want to know just why you lied to me when you told me you had delivered my letter to Mistress Smithson at Brent Hay. I told you to take it yourself. I now know you didn't. You passed the errand to a fool of a groom who took it to the wrong place! You said you were afraid of riding alone. You may not be the world's finest horsewoman but you're more than capable of riding my nice well-mannered Bay Star for a few miles on a warm summer day and you know it! And then to lie! I want an explanation!"

Dale stared at me, read just how intense and implacable my anger was, and burst into tears.

"Stop that! Stop it at once!" Crossing the room, I seized her shoulders and shook her. "Just *stop* it! Now tell me. Why wouldn't you go to Brent Hay for me? And why did you pretend you had?"

"I'm sorry. I'm sorry!"

Unlike Queen Elizabeth, who threw things at people and slapped her ladies whenever she felt like it, I had never gone in for striking the people who served me. After being brought up by Aunt Tabitha and Uncle Herbert, I knew all too well what it felt like and if time had blurred my memory in any way, Roland Jester had now refreshed it. But I was never nearer to striking Dale than I was at that moment. There was still ample time to warn Mistress Smithson, and with luck, Cecil would stop the entire playlet anyway, but it would have been all the same if there had been no time to spare and no Cecil to intervene. Above all, the lie stuck in my gullet.

"I don't care whether you're sorry or not!" I shouted at Dale. "I want to know *why*!"

"Oh, ma'am . . . !" Dale's tears, far from ceasing, intensified. Wailing with abandon, she threw herself at my feet. I hauled her up again and put her back on the settle.

"*Will* you stop it? Now—talk sensibly and explain!"

The explanation came, in a stream of words so incoherent that at first all I could make out was that Dale loved Roger Brockley desperately and he was all she had, which hardly seemed to be the point. Dale, however, was nearly hysterical and out of sheer pity for her, I damped my anger down. Bewilderment replaced it. I sat down beside her.

"I wish I knew what all this was about! Dale, do try to sound rational. What has Brockley to do with this? I know you love your husband, of course I do. But why did that stop you from going to Brent Hay and make you lie to me about it?"

"I didn't want you to know, ma'am."

"Know what?"

"What I feel like, ma'am. What I'm afraid of. You've been so good to me and Roger's so dear; I can't believe either of you 'ud do anything wrong but I've always known . . . I've always known . . ."

"Known what? Dale, please! There's something here that I don't understand, it seems, and I ought to understand. Just tell me."

Dale gulped and then looked me in the face. She straightened her back. I saw her pull dignity, a peculiarly feminine dignity, around herself as though it were a robe. "I have always known, ma'am, that you and Roger mean a lot to each other. You've got your private jokes, your special way of looking at each other, and . . . it's as though you're more than manservant and lady, and then, here in Cambridge, when I met you that afternoon on the bridge, I saw you in his arms."

"I know you did. But surely Brockley explained?" I

said. "He was only comforting me because I was missing my own husband! I gave way and he provided a shoulder for me to shed a few tears on."

"Yes, ma'am. So he said to me. But . . . I've sensed something . . . even in France I did, and it got stronger after we came back to England. I'm an ignorant woman in many ways, ma'am, not like you with your Latin studies and so forth, but there are things I'm not likely to be mistaken about, all the same."

"But what has this to do with Brent Hay?" I asked again.

"I haven't liked it," said Dale steadily, "that you and Roger have been meeting, and me not there."

"We have only met to discuss the inquiries we're making—Brockley must keep me informed of anything useful that he learns. He can't do it through Master Henderson. Even if Master Henderson hadn't been ill, he couldn't come visiting a cookmaid. It's not been easy, with me at the pie shop and Roger now with Master Woodforde. We've had to meet when we can."

"Yes, ma'am, so I understand. But after seeing you on the bridge that day . . ."

"Yes, well?"

"I've been keeping watch on Roger!" Dale burst out. "I've been following him. I watched you both meet by the river once, and another time I saw you there, waiting for him, though he didn't come. You came here after that—I only just got back ahead of you. That was when you sent me to Brent Hay, but I couldn't go, ma'am, I just couldn't go. I thought—I was afraid—I don't know what I thought! That perhaps you'd manage to meet him again and it would be here and you wanted me to be somewhere else and . . ."

"You were watching? We never saw you! Where were you?"

"You did see me, ma'am, and so did Roger but you didn't know me. I wore black and put a veil over my face."

"You were the woman in the mourning veil!"

"Yes, ma'am."

"But she had a big ruff on, not the sort of thing you ever wear . . . oh, I see! I *see*! You used one of *my* ruffs!"

"And that old mourning veil, ma'am, that's always with your things."

"I've had that since I was a child," I said distractedly. "I used it for my grandparents' funerals, and my mother's and Gerald's."

"Yes, ma'am," said Dale wearily. "I'm sorry, ma'am. I didn't harm your things. I washed the ruff and pleated it fresh and I folded the veil away, just as it was . . ." Her dignity fell from her again. She sagged back, turning her face away from me, waiting to hear her fate.

I said nothing for a moment, for I was badly shaken. I was also thanking heaven that although it was true that Brockley and I had once nearly forgotten our marriage vows, we had not actually done so.

I took her chin in my hand and turned her face toward me again. She met my eyes miserably, searching them for the answer to a question she dared not ask.

"Never mind about the ruff and veil," I said. "Now, listen. Be assured—and I will swear it on a Bible if you wish—that there has never been any impropriety between me and Brockley." I hoped she would believe me. Among the items of gossip I had gleaned during my visit to court had been the fact that while I was in France, Elizabeth had fallen sick of the smallpox and when she believed herself to be dying, had sworn that there had been no impropriety between her and Robert Dudley. I had reason to know that she spoke the truth but plenty of people didn't think so. Words are cheap, after all.

"Brockley and I are friends," I said. "We have shared peril together. But I promise you, his heart is yours. When we first went to France and you fell into danger, he was nearly out of his mind with fear for you. As for me, my heart belongs to Master de la Roche and the sooner I am home with him again, the better. You know very well that I intend to leave Brockley behind at Withysham as its steward, and you with him as its housekeeper."

I had decided on that because my husband, Matthew, had himself concluded that Brockley and I were rather more than just friends; but Dale mustn't know that. "You have nothing to fear from me," I said. "Nothing. You can go on any errand I choose for you in the perfect certainty that nothing amiss is happening behind your back and you need never lie to me."

"Is it possible," said Dale, "for a man and a woman to be friends and nothing more?"

"Many people think not," I said. "But the queen manages it."

"Dudley?" asked Dale, a little too acutely. She knew the court gossip just as well as I did.

"Yes, in a way," I said. "She and Dudley aren't lovers, though she loves him—and what she meant by offering him to Mary of Scotland as a husband, I can't imagine. You know about that?"

"The whole court and half the world knows it, ma'am." Dale was calm now, reassured because I was willing to gossip with her.

"The queen would never let Dudley go," I said. "Cecil said as much and I think he's right. But nevertheless, they are *not* lovers. We were speaking of friendship between men and women. The queen and Dudley are one kind of example. She and Cecil are another. They are genuine friends, and there are many others in her council whom she trusts and regards with friendship. It can be done, and one needn't be a queen, either."

We sat in silence for a few moments, letting the wound between us heal. Then I said: "I still need to get word to Mistress Smithson. I will write another letter. I now know for sure that she *is* Mistress Jester. While I am at it, I may as well ask her whether she knows of anything else that her husband and brother-in-law may be planning. I can put it to her that if she does, she should speak before they fall deeper in. What if her daughter were somehow to be dragged in as well? Bring me my writing things. Then, Dale, you must again set out for Brent Hay Manor house, and this time, for the love of God, *go*! Make sure that you actually see Mistress Smithson, who lives as a companion to a Mistress Catherine Grantley, and give her the letter in person. Once more, I can't go myself. I need to call on Cecil."

15

The Lonely Mouse

Rob Henderson was not in the lodging, but I hoped
that he had kept his word and asked Cecil to expect
me. I changed into a suitable gown and waited for a
while, since it was too early for Cecil to have arrived,
and I hoped Rob would come back. However, he did
not, and eventually I set out for St. John's College
alone, since I had dispatched Dale to Brent Hay.

When I reached it, people were coming and going,
carrying fuel and supplies through an imposing
entrance, and the work was being supervised by a
porter, an extremely dignified figure with a gold chain
of office. I inquired of him whether Master Robert
Henderson was there. He immediately called an
underling and I was led through the archway into a
wide, splendid quadrangle surrounded by buildings in
rosy brick, with graciously mullioned windows and
towers at the corners.

I was shown in at the door of a tall, slender tower,

its angles picked out in gray stone, and topped with crenellations. Although it was larger and less ornamented, it was in many ways so like the buttress towers that finished the terraced houses of Jackman's Lane that I thought Jester's father-in-law must have imitated them. I was taken up some stairs to a set of rooms where I discovered Rob busily harassing a number of clerks, who were checking baggage items against a list.

"Yes, he's arrived," Rob said to me. "But his gout is troubling him. He made the journey in his coach, for comfort, and he's sent instructions that the college dignitaries aren't to wait on him until he summons them. He's brought his old family nurse to attend to him, with her simples and her bandages. I haven't had a chance yet to ask if he'll see you. I didn't think you'd be free until this afternoon, anyway. Since you're here, I'll ask him now, but . . ."

Shaking a dubious head, he went out, leaving me to gaze irritably out of the window into the quadrangle, while behind me, the clerks went on checking baggage and giving me inquisitive looks. Rob was not long, however. "You can come through," he said, reappearing in the doorway, and I followed him into a paneled chamber where Cecil was resting on a settle with his bandaged foot up, while an elderly woman, with a soft, wrinkled face and a very neat cap and apron, crouched nearby on a low stool, stirring a pot in which she was brewing something sweet and aromatic over a small portable brazier.

Rob took himself back to the clerks and the baggage. Cecil's face was drawn with pain but he gave me a smile. "You find me at a disadvantage, Ursula. These attacks always come at the most inconvenient moment. Will you dine with me? I am about to have a very plain meal with no spices or pepper or white wine. My physician says it will help if I avoid such things. Nothing makes any difference that I can detect but I try to follow orders."

"If you followed my orders, my boy," said the elderly woman, "you'd have stayed at home and sent some trustworthy fellow or other to see to things in Cambridge. That 'ud be my advice but there, you always did go your own way."

"And you're proud of me for it, Nanny," said Cecil.

"Maybe. Maybe. Going your own way's got you into high places, I grant you. But there's a price for everything, that's what I always say."

"I know, Nanny. As I think I once told you," he added, addressing me, "to Nanny I am still the little boy whose grazed knees she had to bathe when I'd fallen down . . ."

"Fallen out of a tree, more like, after you'd been told a dozen times not to climb it!"

I laughed. The affection between them was heartwarming and obvious. I became sober again very quickly, however. I was there, after all, on serious business. Cecil read my face and said: "You have something to report?"

"Yes. And I want to ask you to do something for me."

I hesitated, since we were not alone, and Cecil, again, understood. "There is no need to worry about Nanny. She understands discretion. I've known more talkative tombs."

"Now, don't you go chattering about tombs; it's unlucky," Nanny said reprovingly. She wrapped her hands in her apron, lifted the pot off the brazier, and set it down on a couple of bricks that were ready at her side. "There, that can cool. A dose of that this evening and you'll sleep easy tonight, sir. Is the lady dining? If she is, I'll go to the kitchen and ask for extra."

"I'd like to dine. Thank you," I said. Nanny gave me a grin that was nothing short of mischievous, and said: "Well, now you can talk all the scandal you like and no one to hear," and departed in a cloud of conscious tact as palpable as the aromatic fumes from the brew.

"Ursula?" said Cecil.

"I haven't discovered any plots," I said. "But there's been a death . . ."

Cecil heard me out. As I talked to him, I felt more strongly than ever that my narrative lacked cohesion. A silly, unnecessary scheme to bring Mistress Jester back to her husband's home, when all Woodforde really needed to do was tell Roland Jester where she lived. A worried student, who wanted a secret meeting to discuss vague suspicions that had probably been aroused by nothing more sinister than the said ridiculous scheme. The death of the same student—but in what seemed to be a simple riding accident. Nothing more, except for a persistent sense of something wrong.

"And that's all," I said. "But I can tell you this: Roland Jester is an unpleasant man and if I had been his wife I think I would have run away too. I have sent Dale off to warn her against taking part in this playlet and warn her too that Woodforde knows where she is. You may call it interfering, but I am on her side."

"You can be quite militant at times," Cecil said. "Rob Henderson has been saying as much. You've been ordering him about, he says, as though he were your slave."

"Oh." I felt uncomfortable. "I'm sorry. But I'm worried and I needed his help to find things out."

"Yes, I know. He's told me some of it though he made it clear that he doesn't agree with your conclusions. I'm not sure if I do, either. No, it's all right." He raised a hand to stop me as I was about to speak. "With the queen, I will not take chances. Thomas Shawe's death is enough on its own to make my mind up for me. She will agree, I think, when she hears of it. The playlet will indeed be canceled, and I think we will have both Jester and Woodforde brought in for a little questioning. Even if it *is* just a matter of Woodforde using the playlet to set up this melodramatic reunion, he has no right to make use of the queen in such a fashion. He isn't showing proper respect. He seems sadly lacking in that particular virtue. I wonder if that was the reason why Lady Lennox dismissed him?"

"In a way," I told him. "I suppose one could call it lack of respect. He wrote love letters to her and one evening he was found hiding under her bed."

"He was *what*?" Cecil, caught between laughter and disbelief, moved jerkily, jarred his swollen foot, and subsided with a gasp. "A thousand curses on this malady. Who told you that?"

"Brockley," I said. "He had it from Woodforde's previous manservant."

My explanation had included Brockley's new position as our spy in the enemy camp and indeed his
impressive piece of information extraction in the
King's College retiring room. Despite his obvious
pain, Cecil smiled.

"So that was it. Hid under her bed, you say? Like
you in the retiring room—or rather, *not* like you. Lady
Lennox would have had a shock if her servants hadn't
found him before he jumped out on her. Well, well,
well!"

Cecil was a man of propriety. In my presence, I
never knew him to utter a single word that could not
have been said in the presence of archangels. In his
presence, I too was always a perfect lady. We were,
however, a man and a woman of the world. For a few
silent moments we each privately considered Giles
Woodforde's unlikely passion for Lady Margaret
Lennox and imagined it in consummation. At least, I
did, and I don't think I misinterpreted the sparkle in
Cecil's eyes.

Then he said: "To business," and shouted for Rob.
Within moments, he had dictated a note and Rob had
been dispatched with orders to Cecil's retainers to
bring Woodforde and Jester to us. "I'll question them
myself," Cecil said.

Rob returned presently to say that the men had set
off, and a few moments later, Nanny also reappeared,
followed by a string of servants with our dinner. While
the three of us and Nanny sat eating it, in informal
fashion, Cecil brought Rob up-to-date on all that I had
told him and I explained, when Rob asked, that I had
come unattended because I had had to send Fran to

Brent Hay, although I didn't say why her first attempt to take a letter to Mistress Smithson had miscarried, only that it had.

The meal was heavenly, I must say: a shoulder of veal with a sweetened mustard sauce that Cecil didn't take, capons in a bland sauce that he did, cabbage, peas, fresh manchet bread, a salad of radishes and cucumber, a fruit pie, some orange- and nutmeg-flavored custards (which Cecil also passed by with a regretful sigh), and red wine to wash it all down. In the pie shop, we snatched food at midday much as we did at breakfast—usually some of the stewed meat that went into the pies—and had our main meal together in the kitchen in the evening, after the shop was closed. It was more varied then and there was always enough, but it couldn't compare with this.

We had just finished when two of Cecil's officers arrived, looking worried and accompanied by Brockley. I knew both of the officers, having had them as part of my escort when first I went to France. Stocky, sandy-haired Dick Dodd was solidly reliable, and the brindle-bearded John Ryder had been a good friend to both Brockley and myself. Dodd had apparently taken a couple of men to the pie shop while Ryder, also with two men, had gone to collect Woodforde from his rooms. Both had returned without their quarry.

Ryder had found only Brockley alone in Woodforde's lodgings. "Master Woodforde went out two hours ago and he didn't say where he was going," Brockley said, repeating to us what he had already told Ryder. "Master Jester came to see him early in the morning and spoke to him in private. Then they went off out together. I tried to follow, but I couldn't risk getting too near them and I lost them in Cambridge. So I went back to the lodging to wait. They were going toward the pie shop, I think, but that's all I know. Only, there's something I want to tell Mistress Blanchard," he added, turning to me. "When I saw you the other day in the pie shop, madam, I was with Master Woodforde and I couldn't speak to you then."

"Would that be," inquired Cecil, "that you have found that Master Woodforde knows very well who Mistress Smithson really is?"

Brockley blinked. "How did you know, sir?"

Cecil explained for me, while all those present listened with burning interest and visible astonishment. At the end, however, he said: "But this is not the matter in hand just now. What we are interested in just now isn't the whereabouts of Mistress Jester; it's the whereabouts of Master Jester and his brother. You didn't find your man either, Dodd?"

"No, sir. Master Brockley is right to think that he and Woodforde were going to the pie shop but we found it closed, and inside it nothing but a young girl acting all distracted. She said her father went out this morning and came back with her uncle Woodforde right enough, but that the two of them went off again and she didn't know where they'd gone or why and she was scared. It seems the shop employed another girl to cook and wait at table, and a fellow to man the street counter . . ."

"Phoebe and Wat," I said.

"Those're their names? According to the girl, before Jester and Woodforde went off together, Jester paid them off and told them to take their things and go back to their homes. The wench—she was Jester's daughter—said her father wouldn't tell her anything but she knew something was amiss, and she was left there wringing her hands and crying, not knowing what's afoot or why. We asked her a lot of questions but she didn't seem to know any answers and we had no orders to bring her in, so we left her for the time being. We can go back for her if need be."

Cecil looked at me. "Have you any idea where Jester and Woodforde could have gone?"

I shook my head. "No, I haven't. But I think I should go back to the shop. Ambrosia's there alone. I may be able to help her—or if she *does* know anything helpful, I may find it out. Besides"—the memory of those curious sketches came back to me—"there's still something in that shop that I want to pry into, if truth be told."

"I've got a dog like you," Rob said to me unexpectedly, causing everyone to look at him in astonishment.

"A dog?" Cecil queried.

"Yes. Oh, a very lovable dog! But he's the most inquisitive animal God ever made. I call him Pokenose because that's what he does—pokes his nose into everything. Twice he's been caught with it stuck in a jug—a jug of milk once, and wine the second time. Once he got it stuck in one of my boots. I found him crashing round our bedchamber, trying to shake it off. You're just the same, Ursula. You're inquisitive—and you've been in danger before now because of it. I'm always afraid that one day you'll get into danger that you can't get out of."

"In the autumn," I said, "I'm going home to my

husband, in France. I shan't run into danger anymore then."

"Seriously," said Rob, "I'll be glad. You ought to be at home. You worry me—and if you and your husband hope for children, you shouldn't leave it much later."

"Are you very worried about Mattie?" I asked him suddenly, and he nodded.

"Yes, I am. Nearly forty is late for having a child even if it isn't her first child. You should be at home with your husband, Ursula, having your children *now*!"

"I hope I soon will be," I said, not letting him see that his remarks were making me uneasy. In France, I had had a stillborn son and nearly lost my life in the process. I was still afraid of trying again.

It occurred to me that perhaps I should also be afraid of returning to the pie shop. Yet, what use was I as either wife or agent, if I gave in to fears?

"For the moment," I said, "I feel that I have to go back to that pie shop anyway. I *can't* leave Ambrosia alone there."

Brockley at once said that he would come with me, but just as I was drawing breath to thank him gratefully, Cecil vetoed the idea. "Brockley still has his place as Woodforde's manservant and I would prefer it, Brockley, if you went back to his lodgings in case he returns. If he does, let us know. By *us*, I mean myself and Sir Robert Dudley, who arrived in Cambridge with me and is lodging in Trinity College. I will make sure that he is told of all this. I am sure you need not worry about Mistress Blanchard. She has an established place at the shop and I trust she can go back there without running into danger."

Cecil's wishes, like the queen's, had the force of orders, no matter how politely he expressed them.

So I went back to the pie shop alone, drawn thither by Ambrosia, and by a set of partly finished drawings, just as a mouse is drawn by cheese, straight into a trap.

16

Rambling, Disjointed, and Awkward

The afternoon was wearing away by the time I reached the pie shop, where I found closed shutters and a group of disconsolate students, waiting hopefully for signs of life. One of them was Francis Morland, who hailed me eagerly. "Have you come to open up? What's amiss?"

I said I wasn't sure but had heard that a family friend, Mistress Ambrosia's former tutor, had died. It was the first thing I could think of. "I don't know much about it—I'm not family—but the shop may not open today. I'm sorry."

They made polite noises of condolence and began to drift away. I tried the private door, found it open, and slipped inside.

The place was silent. I went quickly through the ground floor: shop, kitchen, pantry, fuel store, and windowless cupboard of a room next to it, where Wat slept. His bedding lay there, folded for the day. There was no sign of Ambrosia downstairs but when I went up to our bedchamber, I found her there. Once more, she was lying on the bed. She looked ill. "Ambrosia?" I said questioningly.

She sat up, staring at me. "You've come back? I wondered if you would. Where did you go?"

"To get on as quickly as possible with getting that playlet stopped," I said. "Which I have done. Another letter has gone to Brent Hay, too. You can stop worrying about your mother. I was scared to come back, I don't mind admitting, but after all, this is where I live just now and I need the work. Is your father very angry?"

Ambrosia gazed at me without speaking and I rushed on with remarks that I hoped were suitable to my character as Mistress Faldene, Brockley's widowed and hard-up cousin.

"I'll have to tell him some taradiddle or other, I suppose. I have a child, as it happens, being fostered. I can say that I had a message that she was ill, but that I found her recovering, so I came back at once. But, Ambrosia, why is the shop closed? Where's your father?"

"I don't know," said Ambrosia blankly. "He went this morning to see my uncle and then they both came back here, shut the shop, and sent Wat and Phoebe away. Then they went out again, together. I don't know what's happening or what's going on. There was a bit of a scene with Wat and Phoebe. Phoebe thought she'd done something wrong and she's afraid of her own father; she said if she lost her job and was sent home, he'd just kick her out again. She started crying and then Father was angry and shouted at her to stop and raised his hand, and Wat stepped in and told him to leave her alone and, yes, what *had* she done, or what had Wat himself done, come to that. . . ."

"And then . . . ?"

"Father calmed down and said that neither of them had done anything wrong but he just wanted to close the shop for a while, and he paid them off. He paid them a month's wages each!" said Ambrosia.

I shared her amazement. It sounded most unlike the provident Master Jester.

"And now . . . ?" I said, leaving the sentence unfinished.

"Now I don't know what to think or what to do!" Ambrosia put her face in her hands and once more began to cry, in a deep, unhappy way that worried me because it sounded as though it were coming from something more intense than a closed pie shop and a father who had gone out one morning in the company of his brother, and had as yet been away for no more than a few hours, all of them in broad daylight.

I considered her thoughtfully. "Have you had any dinner?" I asked.

"Yes. Some stewed lamb that should have gone into pies for this evening, and some bread."

"Good. Now," I said briskly and, I hoped, with an air of authority, "I think you should rest. Try to sleep. I'll go and tidy up so that all's in good order when your father comes back."

"All right," said Ambrosia with a sigh. She rolled over, drew up her knees, and closed her eyes, and I went out quietly, shutting the door after me. I went down the stairs and along the passage as far as the awkward corner by the jutting-out cupboard, letting my feet clatter a little, but then I stopped, took off my shoes, and holding them in my hand, I crept back again, stole up the stairs and past the bedchamber door, and went on up the spiral staircase to the attic floor.

Making straight for the settle in Jester's office, I lifted up the seat. The drawings were still there. I took out the set of small sheets that bore the curious array of semifinished sketches.

They had been nagging at my mind ever since I first saw them. Somehow, in some way, they had reminded me of something . . .

I stared again at the first one, in which a man or youth was giving an apple to a horse and once more noted that the apple, the dappled coat of the horse, and the church in the background were vastly more detailed than anything else in the drawing. I turned to the second, which was one of the sheets with more than one drawing on it. At the top was a sketch of a woman reading by a window. A humble bee was buzzing on the pane.

The woman was a mere outline but the book and the bee were painstakingly shown. One could even see the furriness of the bee's fat body. There was no such patchiness, however, in the picture beneath, which was a lively depiction of a battle, with visored knights and warhorses and foot soldiers, all flourishing weapons, and all very clearly drawn. I looked at that for some time, wondering.

The third sheet also had two pictures on it: a rather

good rendering of a stormy sea, and beneath that, a cat lapping from a saucer. Here, too, everything was properly drawn. But on the fourth page, which showed a room with a rising or setting sun visible through a window, the only really finished items were the sun, which had striking rays and was half visible above the horizon, and the door on the other side of the room.

I flipped on through the set, looking at sheet after sheet. Some had quite a number of little drawings on them. One was dotted all over with small sketches: a schoolmaster looking with pop-eyed disapproval at a pupil who had dropped blots all over his work; the sea with an island in the distance; a wall covered in creeper; people skating on a frozen river.

I noticed that Jester must have spent a very long time indeed over the triangular leaves of the ivy on the wall, on the wide, indignant eyes of the schoolmaster, and the gleam of the blots, but other details were scarcely roughed in. The picture of the island was properly finished, but the feet of the skaters and the furrows their skates left in the ice were much better drawn than the people themselves.

A couple of pages further on I came to the sheet that showed a girl in a carefully depicted kitchen, with, below her, a girl walking in a formal knot garden. The girls did look as though he had used Phoebe and Ambrosia as models, but all the same, he had lavished far more love and care on the kitchen hearth and the pots and pans, and the plants and flowers in the garden.

The following page showed two very elegant ladies, one of them playing a lute. Ladies and lute were all carefully drawn. On the next page, for some incomprehensible reason, was a picture of a woman milking a cow under a crescent moon. The moon was strongly outlined and so was the stream of milk as it plunged into the pail. The cow and the woman were merely silhouettes.

This one had a second picture below it: people dancing in a great hall, with a band of musicians in a minstrels' gallery above. The musicians and their instruments were very thoroughly delineated but though the dancers had clearly drawn smiling faces, their bodies were vague.

Further on came another page that I remembered: people dining, one helping himself to salt from an elaborately detailed saltcellar, and in a separate scene below, a woman buying cloth. The highlights on that cloth really were clever draftsmanship. I noticed that the coins the woman was handing to the vendor were disproportionately large.

I moved to and fro through the set. There was a royal hunting scene, although the huntsmen and the hounds were casually outlined. Clearly drawn, however, and right in the foreground, was a queen, possibly Elizabeth although the resemblance wasn't striking. She had a detailed crown on her head, however, and she carried a longbow and a quiver. The quiver, with its protruding arrows, had been shown in most loving detail, even to the flight feathers on the shafts.

I went back to the top page. Apple. Dapples. A small church or chapel. Apple. Dapple. Chapel. The nagging idea in the depths of my mind, which had brought me back to look once more at these pictures, began to take a definite shape. It seemed far-fetched and yet . . . I turned again to the second sheet. This emphasized a book and a bee and below that, a battle. The third, a sea and a cat. The fourth . . . that was the room with the door on one side and a rising or setting sun beyond a window. In my chest, my heart began to thump like a pounding fist. Rapidly, I counted the sheets.

There were twenty-six of them.

Twenty-six sheets. Twenty-six letters in the alphabet. Was this—could it *possibly* be?—an aide-mémoire to a cipher? A rather extraordinary cipher, in which the letters of the alphabet were represented by *words,* usually nouns, but not by the same one every time!

A is for *apple*—it had said that in the hornbook from which I took my first reading lessons. *Dapple* and *chapel* rhymed with *apple.* It would make them easier to remember, perhaps. *B* is for *book* . . . or if you say it aloud, what does it sound like? *Bee!* And the third sheet . . . *C* is for *cat.* Or, if you say it aloud, *sea.* In the fourth . . . a door and a sunrise . . . sunrise! . . . no, daybreak, dawn!

If these pictures were the key to a cipher, how would such a code work? It would mean . . . long, rambling, disjointed letters often awkwardly worded . . .

And what kinds of letters did Jester and Woodforde write to each other?

Long, rambling, disjointed missives, often awkwardly worded . . .

I needed time and secure privacy to study these. I folded the sheets double and thrust them quickly into my hidden pouch. I had better take something to work on, I thought, and went over to the shelves where I had found Woodforde's letters. Yes, here they were. . . .

I had them in my hand when I heard a sound behind me and swung around.

"And just what," said Ambrosia, staring at me, her dark, slanting brows drawn together and her eyes hard with suspicion, "do you think you're doing, poking about among my father's papers?"

17

Legacy from a Queen

"I was just . . . looking. I've never been up here before," I said untruthfully. "But I wondered if your father had left any . . . any note or sign of where he had gone. You were resting—you don't look well, not well at all—and I thought, if I could find something helpful . . ."

It wasn't good enough. Ambrosia strode up to me and snatched away the letters I was holding. She stared into my face. "You're not just a cookmaid, are you?" she said. "You don't even speak like one, or not all the time. You didn't just now. You sounded like a lady. . . ."

"I was educated above my station," I said. "My . . . my mother worked for a lady who let me share her daughters' lessons." It wasn't far off the truth. Aunt Tabitha had made my mother run errands just as, later on, she made me run them. I had shared my cousins' tutor very largely at my mother's insistence and my uncle and aunt considered me to be lower down the social scale than they were, even if I didn't agree with them.

"Then why pretend, and sometimes talk like a common person and at other times, when you forget, sound like a court lady?" I clearly had much to learn about working in disguise, I thought grimly. "You know people above your station as well as talking like them!" Ambrosia said. She stared at me more intently than ever. "You were so sure you could get that playlet stopped, so sure you could get word to important people and be listened to. And the queen will be here in a couple of days. You're a court spy, that's what you are!"

"A court spy? Spying on what? Spying in a *pie shop*?" I attempted a light laugh. "No, really, Ambrosia, I never heard such nonsense. . . ."

Ambrosia raised her voice. *"Father! Father!"*

It was no rhetorical appeal to an absent parent, but a shout to attract the attention of one very much within earshot. There was a scraping noise behind me and I spun around once more, just as a whole section of the wall where the shelving was swung inward, shelves, books, papers, and all. The shelving was attached to what was actually a hidden door and in the doorway, as hard-eyed as his daughter, stood Roland Jester, and behind him, looking over his shoulder, was his half brother, Giles Woodforde.

"She's a spy!" said Ambrosia hysterically. "I didn't know. I didn't realize. I'm sorry! She *knows* court people! I wouldn't be surprised if they sent her!"

I whirled again and would have fled, but Ambrosia barred my way, springing into my path again when I tried to dodge past her. I tried to thrust her aside but she withstood me and then Jester's hands closed on my upper arms and dragged me backward, through the secret door, with Ambrosia following. When we were all inside, the door was shut. On the inside, it was a perfectly ordinary door with a latch and a bolt.

"I told you this morning you were a fool of a girl," Jester said breathlessly to his daughter. "Now you've done another damn daft thing! Why did you call to me like that? Now she knows our hiding place!"

It was a very uncomfortable hiding place, just a cramped, stifling, boarded-off space at one end of the attic. The only light and air came from what seemed to be a long, narrow grating just under the eaves of the thatch at the rear of the house. From the outside, it would be overshadowed and nearly invisible. There was also a very small skylight that from its position looked as though it were one end of the bigger skylight in Jester's office.

In the resultant murk, I could just make out the faces of the others, and see the meager furnishings: a couple of stools, a very small square table, an iron-bound chest pushed up against the thatch, where it came down to meet the floor at the front of the house, and a lidded pail. Despite the lid, the pail smelled.

"I tell you, she's a *spy*!" said Ambrosia. "I had to stop her getting away! Lord knows what she's learned. I found her looking at your letters."

"I don't know what you're talking about! Have you all gone mad?" I took refuge in a panicky bluster, which wasn't difficult, for I felt very panicky indeed. "You were in a great fuss because you didn't know where your father was—you *said*"—I scowled at

Ambrosia. "So I thought I'd look in case he'd written a note you hadn't seen. And all the time he was in here and you knew it—and what *is* all this about spies? Why have I been dragged in here? What's going on?"

"I wanted that playlet stopped and she said she could do it! I told you!" Ambrosia threw the words not at me but at her father. She sounded completely frantic. "For my mother's sake! I told you that, too! I don't want her dragged back here to be hit!"

"Will somebody *explain*?" I shouted, partly in the hope that someone, somewhere would hear and come to my rescue, though it was hardly likely, since the building was empty except for us.

Ambrosia at last paid me some attention. "I know, I said to you: go and stop the playlet if you can. But as soon as Phoebe said to me that you'd gone, I started thinking. I got frightened. My father's still my father and Uncle Giles is my uncle. I . . . it isn't just that you've tried to use the queen's visit to fetch my mother back, is it, Uncle Giles? There's something else. You and my father . . . I've been worrying and wondering for a long time. You've been talking together in private so much and I know Father's been anxious over something and . . ."

"For the love of God, girl, will you hold your tongue!" shouted Woodforde.

"I told Father where you'd gone," Ambrosia said to me, ignoring her uncle. "I told him you'd gone to see your cousin because he worked for someone who was from court and you hoped to get the playlet canceled. I had to! I had to warn him!" I stared at her in amazement. She looked back at me defiantly. "When it's your own father and your own uncle; when it's *family* . . . and now I find you in my father's office, fiddling with his things . . ."

"If only you'd minded your own business in the first place. Would've thought you'd want your mother home yourself!" Jester snapped. "Suppose I should be grateful you at least took some thought for me and your uncle but I tell you, this could be the end of us all!"

"Mother's not to be fetched back to be knocked about by you!" Ambrosia almost screamed at him. "You shouldn't have treated her like that in the first place. And what do you mean, this could be the end of us all? What are you *talking* about? Oh, I knew it, I knew it! There *is* more, something important, isn't there?"

Woodforde stepped across and gripped my chin, turning my head this way and that. He wasn't in a scholar's gown this time, but in a dull brown doublet of some thin and, from the smell of it, none-too-clean material. "I knew I'd seen you somewhere before," he said as he released me. "I saw you at Richmond. Oh yes, I did! Dressed very fine, you were, coming along a passage with a maid at your heels and people carrying luggage for you. You're from the court all right! What are you doing here, pretending to be a cookmaid? How much do you really know? I wonder."

There was an awkward, almost comical, silence while we all peered at one another with intense suspicion, no one knowing quite what anyone else knew for certain. Except that it was now quite plain that there was far more to this than a needlessly complicated plot to drag Mistress Jester back to her husband. *This could be the end of us all,* Jester had said. Like Ambrosia, I was wondering just what that meant.

One thing it clearly meant, however, was that although whatever else was being planned remained a mystery to me, it had to be serious and dangerous. In some way, surely, it involved a threat to someone and in all probability, that someone was the queen.

The silence lasted for several moments. I would call it a frozen silence except that the heat in that confined space under the sun-warmed thatch was nearly unbearable. Then Woodforde drew a dagger.

Ambrosia gasped and said: "No, Uncle, please!" and Jester said protestingly: "No, Giles. You can't kill a young woman."

"I want to know what she knows," said Woodforde. "Just hold on to her, will you?" He took hold of my chin again and laid the blade against my throat. Jester let out a moan but kept his grip on me. Ambrosia stared with huge eyes, biting her lips. "Now," Woodforde said. "Just why did you want to look at Master Jester's papers? Just what did you expect to find?"

"A note to say where he'd gone! That's all! And I should tell you that Cecil knows I'm here! I saw him this morning. Yes, all right, I come from the court. Cecil sent me to Cambridge in the first place to find out if the playlet was all it seemed to be. Which," I added desperately, "it obviously isn't!"

"Hark at you," said Woodforde. "Cecil. Not *Sir William Cecil.* Not *Her Majesty's Secretary of State.* Just Cecil. You're on familiar terms with him, that's plain enough. Very well. Go on."

"That's all! *Sir William* was suspicious of the playlet," I said. "And no wonder. A snare to catch Mistress Jester—and something else as well, it seems! I have told *Sir William Cecil*"—I was sardonic on purpose, to hide my fear—"all about the snare, at least, and the whole business of the playlet will indeed be stopped."

"Why," lamented Jester, "did God have to saddle me not only with a faithless wife but also a wantwit of a daughter?"

"And Cecil knows where you are," Woodforde remarked to me. To my relief, he withdrew his dagger from my throat, but still kept it unsheathed. "But he can't know about this little hidey-hole and he'd better not find out."

A wish to ease the tension combined with genuine curiosity made me say: "What's this place for, anyway? How did it come to be made?"

"One could call it a legacy from Queen Mary," Jester informed me. "My father-in-law, Master Jackman, he was an ardent Protestant, and in Queen Mary's day he was scared all the time he'd be taken up for heresy. When folk started sayin' that heretics were goin' to be hunted out, he got nightmares. Sybil and me slept in the next room and he used to wake us up, screamin' out in his sleep. So he planned how he'd escape bein' caught. When he built the houses on this side of Jackman's Lane, he used builders—a father and two sons—who thought the same way as he did. They were the only ones that knew about this hidden room. Dead and gone they are now—with the lung-rot, last winter. The houses were built very quickly, in a matter of weeks." (That, I thought, explained the afterthought air of the linen cupboard and the resultant awkward corner in the passage. Haste never did equal efficiency.)

"This room," Jester was saying, "was made as a place to hide and there're ways out of the house as well, so that if hiding wasn't enough, if someone needed to get right away, out of Cambridge and away to the river and the sea, they could. My father-in-law always had arrangements in place, a boat ready on the river and contacts among ships' captains at Lynn."

I wondered where the ways out were. I couldn't see any sign of one in the attic, which seemed an unlikely starting point for such a thing in any case. Perhaps he just meant hidden ways of escape from other parts of the house.

Woodforde said impatiently: "Oh, stop wasting time. And keep your voices down. We've got to deal with this . . . this interloper."

"There's no need," said Jester. "The playlet's going to be canceled and that's the end of the matter, ain't it? I don't see why we have to hide here anyway. We've done nothin'. This mornin' Ambrosia tells me that her tutor, the one that's just died, that she used to write to all innocentlike, left a message to be sent to her, sayin' that this Mistress Smithson is her mother and that you were plannin' to get the students to hand her back to me." Ambrosia, by telling that lie, had evidently made some sort of attempt to protect me. "I come and tell you that the court folk are goin' to find out about it," said Jester in aggrieved tones, "and you get in a panic, but I don't see what about. That's all anyone knows, ain't it? We've done naught wrong yet!"

"I'm still not sure she doesn't know more than she's saying," said Woodforde, glaring at me.

Jester snorted. "It's not wrong for a man to want his wife back and I'm not afraid to say it to Cecil's face. Why shouldn't I? I got a right to my wife's company, ain't I? She swore to be bonny and buxom for me and always faithful, and then she ran off and I tell you and I'd tell Cecil, too, or the queen her own self, that I need her. I love her, for all her father cheated me. I can't do without her!" There was a startling note in his voice, like the whine of a hurt dog, or one deprived of the essentials of life, like food or water. "Why should the queen mind that? If we just leave it at that . . ."

"We're not going to leave it at that." Woodforde spoke with steely obstinacy. "Your wife has you under a spell and you can't do without her, you say. Well, there's things I can't do without, either. You want Sybil; I want . . . what I want. We can both have what we want but that means you keep to our bargain."

They were talking to each other as though they were alone together. More than that; as though each, inside his mind, was gazing upon some dazzling vision that blinded him to everything else: to me, to Ambrosia, even to the reality of a world that contained powerful people like Queen Elizabeth and Sir William Cecil, who did not like to be used and would not tolerate threats.

The two brothers resembled each other in the color of their hair and the nondescript design of their faces, but in other respects they weren't very alike. Woodforde was weedy, while Jester was by comparison almost burly, and their speech was different, Woodforde's being educated while Jester spoke roughly. Their minds, however, seemed cast in the same mold and I did not like what I sensed about that mold.

What were the visions that obsessed them? In Jester's case, it seemed to be his absent wife. But Woodforde's obsession was presumably Lady Lennox. I could not see how that fitted in. Whatever it was, though, I was sure now that it had driven Woodforde beyond reason and that he would kill for it.

"What I want to know," Jester was demanding angrily, "is how you think I can keep to the bargain if there's no playlet."

"There might be another chance," said Woodforde. "Even if the queen's party doesn't stop in Jackman's Lane, they may still ride through it."

"Oh, I wish I knew what you were both talking about!" wailed Ambrosia. "And what about Ursula!" She clenched her hands and shook them in the air. "Oh, dear God, I only wanted to protect my own family; I didn't want Ursula hurt, but she's here and you're talking in front of her and . . ."

"What about Ursula, you say? What about Sybil?" Jester hardly seemed to have heard. "What about my *Sybil*? I want her back, I tell you! I dream of her at night. I've dreamed of her just about every night since she ran off and left me. She belongs to me and sometimes I think if I got her back, I'd kill her and sometimes I think I'd throw myself at her feet—but dead or alive, I want her in my arms!" Although he was behind me, I sensed that he was glowering at his daughter. "You say you don't know where your mother's living; that Barley only told you she was Mistress Smithson but not where Mistress Smithson's to be found, and maybe that's true and maybe it ain't. Come to think of it, I reckon maybe it ain't and though I know my dear brother won't tell me, maybe I could beat it out of you if I tried . . ."

"You couldn't! *I don't know!*" Ambrosia said shrilly. *"And nor,"* she added for good measure, *"does Ursula!"*

For a fraction of a second, through the gloom, her eyes met mine with a look of appeal. *Don't tell them! Don't tell them!*

I felt as though the words *Brent Hay* must be written across my forehead in letters of fire. In a shaky voice—which was no pretense—I said: "I don't know where Mistress Smithson lives and you'd be wasting your time trying to make me tell you. I could have inquired but I didn't. I was doing Ambrosia a favor—and a pity you weren't more grateful, Ambrosia!—but I didn't want to get too deeply entangled in what isn't my business."

"You were minding your own business? A spy who minds her own business. That's a contradiction if ever I heard one," Woodforde observed.

"If I thought either of you girls did know . . ." Jester began ominously.

"The wenches can be easy. I won't let you beat them," said Woodforde cynically. "I don't want them telling you. They can rely on me."

Jester's grip on my arms hardened in fury, digging painfully in. "Damn your dark soul for all eternity, Giles. *I want my wife back,* and how can I have her if she's not brought into the shop, and you won't tell me where she lives!"

"You help me," said Woodforde, "and I'll tell you where to find her. You don't help me, and I won't. It's that simple."

"You'll get us both hanged!" Jester shouted. I thought he was the less obsessed of the two, but I doubted if that would help me much. Woodforde was too dominant. As for Ambrosia, she clearly didn't know very much more than I did, but despite the muddle she was obviously in, she was loyal to her family. However, she did now make a protest on my behalf, with another wail of "Yes, but what *about* Ursula?"

Woodforde regarded me with an intense dislike and a terrifying kind of detachment, as though he didn't recognize me as even being human. I might have been a spider or a cockroach. "Isn't it obvious? She knew too much from the moment she saw this place. I could have told you then what was going to happen to Ursula. There's only one answer. Ursula won't be seen again. Just harden your heart, girl. Family comes first, just as you said. Do you want to see your father swinging from a rope?"

"But Cecil knows she's here!"

"She won't be found here. Anyone who asks can be told—probably by you, my wench—that she left here, that she went somewhere else and you don't know where, and his men can search the place if they like. They won't find her."

"I don't like it!" Jester spluttered. "Killing a woman isn't . . ."

"You nearly killed my mother more than once!" said Ambrosia bitterly.

"That was in hot blood. Sybil could make me so wild," Jester said. "But doin' it in cold blood . . ."

"She's a spy. That means she doesn't count as a woman," Woodforde told him.

"Look, can't we just think about this?" Jester pleaded.

"*Shush!* Listen." Woodforde cocked his head. "Someone's coming."

We all listened. Outside in the attic study, footsteps were crossing the floor. I opened my mouth to shout for help but Jester's hand came around and clamped over my mouth. Someone was moving books on the other side of the hidden door. Whoever it was knew how to work the hidden latch. The door swung open, letting in a welcome breath of fractionally cooler air. And then the way was blocked by, of all people, the large and pink-faced Wat.

18

Convenience Before Morality

"Whass goin' on?" said Wat. I stared at him, trying with my eyes to signal *Run!* but the great booby merely ducked his head under the doorway, which was too low for him, and stepped inside. Light from the door behind him poured in, revealing the tableau within: Ambrosia looking terrified, Jester gripping my arms from behind, and Woodforde standing close by with an unsheathed dagger in his hand. Wat's round blue eyes widened in amazement. "What're you a-doin' to Mistress Ursula? Master Woodforde, you put that dagger down!"

"One step closer and I use it!" snapped Woodforde. "Stand where you are!"

"Ah?" said Wat, bewildered, but did as he was told.

"Shut the door, Ambrosia!" said Jester.

Ambrosia hesitated.

"I'm your *father.* In God's name, girl!"

Ambrosia let out a moan, but obeyed him. She

darted past Wat and shut the door, and then stood with her back to it, barring his way out, not that he showed any signs of wishing to retreat. He rubbed his head. "What's all this, thass what I want to know. Whass all this about?"

"Now are you goin' to say we've to finish them both off?" Jester demanded of his brother. "Be a bit much, in my opinion. I suppose we could say they'd run off together but who's goin' to believe it?"

Woodforde edged behind me and said: "Give her to me. That's it." I felt Jester's hands drop away, but Woodforde took his place, pulling my head back, and once more gripping my chin. He once more put his blade against my throat turning it slightly, however, so that for the moment it would not cut my skin. "It seems I'll have to talk you round," he said to Jester. "I don't know what you're making such a fuss about."

Ambrosia moaned again and Jester made a gobbling noise. Then he burst out with a decidedly down-to-earth and practical objection: "Cut throats mean blood! It 'ud get all over us and it 'ud smell. And besides, in this weather, afore long, *they'd* smell."

"We'll sacrifice a couple of your nice new settles or something. They open, don't they? Stuffed in settles and stowed in here, they wouldn't stink much. Pity you broke the old settles up," Woodforde said matter-of-factly.

"What're they talkin' about?" Wat asked me, understandably unable to grasp that his employer and his employer's brother were discussing our murder, and more in terms of inconvenience than morality. They were reducing us to the level of two sackloads of smelly rubbish. I didn't answer because I had gone rigid with fright and didn't think I could speak, even if moving my throat muscles hadn't felt dangerous.

"We *can't!*" Jester was saying.

"No, we can't!" echoed Ambrosia, looking from her uncle to her father in terror. Even in the dimness I could see that she was white-faced and trembling.

"Oh, for the love of God!" said Woodforde, exasperated. "All right! We'll talk about it." He let out a disgusted snort. "Ugh! This room reeks anyway—I can hardly breathe. Cecil's men have come and gone and we've got these two safely in here. If there's no one else skulking round the premises, we can go into the outer room where there's some air. We can leave this pretty pair here for the moment. I can hardly put up with the sight of them, I don't mind telling you. We need rope. Ambrosia, you slip out and fetch some of that rope you hang out washing on. Oh, do as you're told! And while you're at it, make sure there *isn't* anyone else on the prowl. Make sure that girl Phoebe hasn't come back as well. Roland, where's your own knife? Get round behind that great oaf there and keep him in order with it, same as I'm doing with Ursula here."

Ambrosia gave me a desperate look. "They're my family. I've got . . . I mean I can't . . . Oh . . . hhh!"

She plunged out of the room, with a hand over her mouth, as though she were about to vomit. She just paused long enough to shut the door after her and then we heard her rushing away. I made an attempt to move in Woodforde's grip but the feel of the steel against my skin stopped me. Jester pulled out his own knife and stepped behind Wat, who exclaimed and would have resisted but was halted by a sharp command from Woodforde. "Do you want me to cut this woman's throat in front of you? What brought you back here, anyhow? How did you know about this room? And have you told anyone else? *Answer me!*"

"I paid him off and sent him home," Jester said. "He should have stayed there."

"I didn't want to go home," said Wat sullenly. "That 'ud mean wildfowling with my old dad, that would, an' I don't like it, stumpin' about in the mud on they old stilts. I'm too heavy. They break too easy. Dad don't like me usin' 'em either. But he wouldn't have me slummocking round the house doin' nothin' so I'd have to go with him. An' then I thought: well, all this is funny like; I wonder what's goin' on? An' Mistress Ambrosia was there when you paid me off, Master Jester, an' she looked that upset. I was sorry for her. I thought I'd best come back an' see what the trouble was an' ask if I could help. I went all over the rooms, lookin' for someone an' then I heard a lot of shouting from in here . . ."

My idea about raising my voice in the hope of summoning help had been essentially quite sound, I thought bitterly, if only it had produced a more promising rescuer than Wat.

"And how did you know about *this* place?" Jester shook poor Wat, and let the edge of his knife draw a thread of blood. Wat yelped.

"No, Maister, don't do that! I didn't know I was doin' wrong! I *wasn't* doin' wrong! I only found out a week ago or thereabouts! I come up with a message for

Maister Jester and saw him carryin' something into here. I thought to myself, thass funny, but I thought maybe he wouldn't want me to see, so I crept away again and gave the message later. Only . . ."

"Yes? Only?" growled Jester.

"I come up again next day, just to see—I were curious, like. I didn't mean any harm! Mistress Ursula, tell him I didn't mean any harm! I remembered I'd seen him shove some books aside and push summat at the back of the shelf. So I had a look and there's a knothole. So I put my thumb in it and it slid sideways an' there's a hole I could get my hand in, an' a latch on the other side. The door swung open an' I just walked in. But there was nothing in here to see, so I went away again. I haven't told anyone! When I heard the noise in here just now, I used the knothole again and in I come! Oh, Maister Jester, do let me go and take that there knife away from my throat! You're scarin' me!"

"You'll have to stay scared," Jester informed him. "But maybe you won't come to any harm if you behave. Now see here, Giles, we could at least wait until we know whether . . . well, until you've managed it or not. There's no point in goin' to extremes too soon."

"Too soon? It's too *late*. They know too much already. It's nearly as bad as though they knew it all. I'm not even sure we can trust Ambrosia."

"But we've told her nothing about your scheme!"

"Don't be a fool, man! She's guessed something big's afoot, she said as much and God knows *we've* said as much in front of her not five minutes ago. I just hope she's gone to fetch that rope and not gone running for the Constable of Cambridge. She's taking her time."

"Now who's the fool?" For once, Jester overrode his domineering brother. "She's my daughter. She's got family feeling and anyhow, women do as they're told. And I tell you, I don't believe Ursula there is any sort of official spy; who'd employ a woman for that?"

This time I achieved speech. "Cecil did. I assure you. If I vanish, the hue and cry will hunt you down."

The bewildered Wat said: "Who's this Cecil?" but no one took any notice of him.

"Bah!" Jester said to me. "Women don't spy. They don't act alone. They do what their menfolk tell them, as religion enjoins."

"Sybil didn't," said Woodforde grimly. "Nor does Lady Lennox—or Queen Elizabeth."

"Great ladies—they're different," Jester said dismissively. "They've got power, which they shouldn't have, being nothing but men's ribs, according to Holy Writ. Common women aren't like that. Oh, you get the odd one tryin' to be unnatural. That's what Sybil did. But when I get her back, she'll never do it again, I promise you."

In Woodforde's grip, I shivered, despite the sultry heat of the room. In that short exchange, I had seen, as it were, the underside of Jester's mind. Very likely he did love Sybil in his fashion. Maybe he even loved her passionately. But he also despised women and held them light.

"Well, where has that girl got to?" Woodforde said sourly. "I tell you, if she's betrayed us . . ."

"She's comin' now," said Jester.

Ambrosia reappeared carrying a length of rope. From the greenish tinge of her pallid face, I thought she had been a long time because she had probably stopped to be sick. Following her uncle's orders, she took away the little belt knives that Wat and I both carried, as most people do, for cutting their meat at table, and used one to cut the rope into lengths. Then Jester bound Wat's hands behind him. Wat started to bluster, but Jester struck him on the side of the head, so hard that this time even the hefty Wat reeled. Before he had recovered, his hands were tied. After that, it was my turn.

"Lie down on the floor!" Woodforde ordered me, and helped me by kicking the backs of my knees. "And you!" he barked at Wat. "Unless you want Mistress Ursula to suffer for it!" Wat gave me a despairing look and then obeyed.

"Now their feet," said Woodforde, and with that our captors secured our ankles as well. "All right," Woodforde said, straightening up. "We can leave them there for the time being, while I talk some sense into you, Roland. Come along. You too, Ambrosia. The fact is, Roland, unless you want to spend the rest of your life in exile . . ." They went out of the room, closing the secret door behind them and Woodforde's voice was lost. Wat and I were alone in the stuffy shadows, lying on a dusty floor that caused me to sneeze.

"I don't understand. I don't *understand*. Whass happening? What are they goin' to do to us?" Wat moaned.

"I think," I said grimly, "that Master Woodforde wants to convince Master Jester that it would be a good idea to kill us."

"But *why*?"

"Listen," I said. "I'm not just a cookmaid and my name isn't really Mistress Faldene. I was sent here from the court . . ."

"What, the royal court?"

"Yes. Because the playlet made people there suspicious and they thought . . . thought it might mean some harm to the queen."

"But how could it?" Wat was anything but bright.

"Well, some people thought it might." I didn't feel equal to complicated explanations. "I came here," I said to Wat, "pretending to be just a harmless servant girl, and I've found out that it's true, there is something going on, some sort of plot, to do with the playlet but I don't exactly know what it is. Only, I was caught looking at Master Jester's letters and dragged in here. They were trying to make me tell them what I knew. And then you walked in. I wish you hadn't!"

Wat twisted in his bonds, trying to loosen them, and groaned in misery. "Mistress Ursula, they're not really goin' to kill us, are they?"

"I hope not. But I'm horribly afraid . . ."

I was lanced through with fear. Out there on the other side of the door, our fate was being decided but in a way it was decided already. Whatever Woodforde was plotting was obviously serious. Was he planning to kill the queen? I wondered. Could he and Lady Lennox actually be conspirators? Did she want the queen out of the way to make room for Mary of Scotland, to whom she hoped to marry her son? And was her apparent anger with Woodforde, his dismissal from her service, just a blind?

If so—and it might be—then Woodforde could scarcely let me live. To conspire against the queen, even if the conspiracy were never carried out, was treason, as serious as actually attempting her life. If such a plot existed, even in embryo, and he knew that I suspected it and would report my suspicions, then he had no option now but to murder me, and Wat as well. Once he had talked his brother into cooperating—and I was quite sure he would—we were as good as dead.

Unless . . .

Were there any chinks of hope? Ambrosia was worried about me and probably about Wat. She might evade her father and uncle and release us. She might well want me to escape, in case her father, after thinking it over, began to wonder if perhaps I was lying when I said I didn't know where Mistress Smithson lived, and tried to put me to the test. Or in case I tried to use my knowledge to bargain with him.

If necessary, I thought feverishly, and if I had the chance—if when Woodforde came back to finish us, Jester came with him—I might do precisely that. For some reason, Woodforde's plans—assassination of the queen, I supposed—apparently needed Jester's help, and knowledge of Sybil's whereabouts seemed to be the hold that Woodforde had over his brother. I would be sorry to betray her but if it would save my life and Wat's . . .

If. It might not. If he could, Woodforde would probably kill me before I could speak, because if I did, his power would be broken.

I would try to use Sybil Jester's address to bargain with if I had to but I feared it would be a poor, weak tool. I lay tense, straining to hear any conversation that might be going on in the adjoining attic, but I could hear nothing. The partition and the secret door between the two rooms were stout. Only raised voices would penetrate them. How long would the business of persuasion take? And then what would happen? Roland was right about the messiness of cutting our throats but now that we were helpless we could just as easily be throttled.

Or would they just—leave us here to die? That might please Jester better. Perhaps he would agree more easily if agreeing meant just doing nothing, just forgetting that we were here.

Wat had begun to whimper, like the big child he mostly was. I clenched my teeth so as not to do the same, wondering why I had ever let myself be coaxed away from home and safety. I wanted to be studying Latin with Meg, sitting by the window while the summer breeze blew in, bringing the scent of flowers from the garden at Withysham. I wanted to be on the walls of Blanchepierre, watching the Loire flow past below, standing there with Matthew, feeling his strong arms around me. I didn't want to die. I didn't want to die. I . . .

I opened my eyes. They had adjusted to the poor light by now, and with a new jolt of terror I saw that in one corner was a roundish papery object that I recognized because when I first took charge in Withysham, there had been such an object hanging in a dark corner of a spare bedchamber. It was a wasps' nest. I lay staring at it in fright, until I realized that the room was quite silent. Nothing was humming and no insects were flying in and out. It was a dead nest. My gaze slid thankfully away from the papery globe and then, just below it, I noticed distractedly that there was a low, square door.

Our prison apparently had a cupboard. In the gloom I hadn't seen it before. The attic went the full depth of the house from front to back and the door through which Wat and I had entered was near the front. The cupboard was near the back. It jutted out a little and looked as though its rear wall must be the outer wall of the house. Since the premises were at the end of the line of houses, there was no adjacent property beyond that wall.

I lay staring toward it. It had a lock, quite an ordinary one. It was just a plain, shallow cupboard. Only . . .

This room was made as a place to hide and there're ways out of the house, as well, so that if hiding wasn't enough, if someone needed to get right away . . .

When Jester said that, I had wondered whether he meant that there was a way out of the attic. Could he have meant the cupboard? It would be possible for someone to crawl through its door; it was big enough, just.

If only, if only, we could get free of these ropes. And what was I about, lying here so passively, not even struggling? I rolled over, moving my ankles against each other, trying to ease their bonds. I failed, but in my hidden pocket, the drawings I had stolen rustled and the other contents of the pocket knocked against the floor. I jerked up to a sitting position. "I must be going silly. How could I have forgotten? I've got a dagger! Wat, listen! Stop that moaning and listen. I've got a dagger!"

"Ladies don't carry daggers," Wat said miserably.

"This one does and they haven't taken it. Listen . . ."

"But what's the use of it when we're all tied up?" Wat twisted again, in a further useless struggle. "I can't get free. How'll we use a blade even if we've got one?"

"*Will* you listen?" I kept my voice low, but made it fierce. "I'm wearing an open overskirt and I've got a pouch sewn inside it. It's on the left side. My left, I mean. Can you roll over here and get hold of my overskirt with your fingers? You can use your fingers, can't you, even if they're behind you? You may be able to get the dagger out. Come on, try!"

I had to explain what I wanted twice more before he grasped my meaning, but once he had done so, he tackled the task with energy. It was more difficult than I expected, but eventually he succeeded in turning my overskirt back, exposing the pocket. "Now," I said, "can you feel the dagger?"

Wat's brain was not the brightest I have ever come across but his physical coordination was good. He squinted over his shoulder for a moment so that he could see what he was dealing with, and then, resuming a position with his back to me, groped for the top of the pouch and pushed his fists down into it. The pouch was deep, which I had arranged on purpose, to make it more secure, and my dagger was small, very much a lady's weapon although it had a lethally sharp blade. It took him a little time to find and get hold of it. I was listening all the while for sounds from the other room, afraid that at any moment Woodforde would appear with murderous intent, and only with a great effort could I hold my impatience down so as not to upset Wat.

At last, he gave a grunt of satisfaction and I saw him draw the dagger out of the pocket. "Got it, mistress!"

"All right," I said. "Now can you draw the blade and hold it firm while I try to saw through this rope round my wrists?"

Unsheathing the blade proved to be much harder than dragging the dagger out of my pocket. The hand holding the hilt and the hand holding the sheath needed to move apart in order to draw the blade, and Wat's firmly bound wrists made this so difficult that in the end, we did the job between us, back to back, straining our necks in order to peer behind us while I got hold of the sheath and Wat grasped the hilt. Then we pulled them in opposite directions and the dagger was out.

We then encountered more difficulties. Wat was able to hold the dagger firmly enough, but it was awkward for him and he couldn't see what he was doing. There was more play between my wrists than between his, but the blade kept catching me. The point jabbed into one wrist and then the sharp edge bit into the other, and I felt the warmth of blood trickling down my hands. I tried again, twisting my hands into a different position, but the same thing happened.

"Try it t'other way about," Wat said. "You hold the ould dagger and I'll try and saw my hands free instead."

This was nearly disastrous. Wat cut himself quite

badly. "For God's sake!" I said. "There *must* be a way. There *must*."

"What'll we do even if we do get free, anyhow?" Wat asked, showing signs of sinking back into lethargy and despair. "We goin' to jump on 'em when they come back?"

"If necessary! But what I hope is that we'll escape. There's a door over there." I jerked my head toward the small door. "It may only lead into a cupboard. But it just could be something more than that. Something that Master Jester said, before you arrived, makes me think so."

"That just looks like a cupboard to me," said Wat dolefully. "An' what if it's locked?"

"First of all," I said, "let's get out of these ropes! If only we could . . . I know! Let me pass the dagger back to you for a moment. I want to try something."

I had had an inspiration. If I could push myself somehow through the loop made by my arms and my bound hands, and then as it were, draw my feet back through the loop as well, I could get my hands in front of me instead of behind. Then I would be able to see what I was doing.

Wat took back the dagger in what were now rather gory fingers and I tried my new plan out. My efforts were more ridiculous than anything. In theory, it seemed easy. After all, I was still quite young and an active life with plenty of riding and dancing had kept me supple. In practice, hampered as I was by my skirts, it was nearly impossible. It would have been completely impossible if I had been wearing a farthingale. My cookmaid's skirts at least didn't have that disadvantage but nevertheless, they made me quite bulky enough. After a struggle, I did succeed in pushing my rear end through my arms but the strain on my wrists was agony and my wretched skirts kept tangling round my feet. My endeavors reached an impasse.

Wat watched me anxiously and then actually produced an idea of his own. "Look here, mistress, you can see your feet. You can put them just how you want them. Maybe it 'ud be easier if I hold the dagger and you saw *them* free, and then perhaps you could step back with them one at a time."

He shuffled into position with his back to me, presenting the dagger blade. I managed to kick my feet clear of the skirts, and delicately, gingerly, I began to work my bonds against the blade.

It was awkward but slowly, slowly, it worked. One loop of rope gave way and then another and then all the rope around my feet fell away. "Done it," I said. "Just a minute." Once again I tried to persuade my feet to follow my rear end back through my pinioned arms, but still my skirts seemed determined to defeat me. However, a new idea came to me. I rolled and kicked, flapping my skirts until they rode up, and there were my bloodstained wrists and hands, visible between my parted feet. "Sit still," I said to Wat, "and hold that blade as tight as you can. I'm going to shuffle close up behind you. I think I can do it now."

Another minute, and my hands were free as well. They felt numb and awkward, but I worked my fingers furiously, rubbing and flexing, and then took the dagger from Wat and cut his bonds, too. At least now, if

Woodforde came in, we were not helpless. We could fight and if necessary, we would. We sat side by side, vigorously massaging our feet and our wrists and noting with relief that though we had both cut ourselves on the dagger, and Wat's cut was quite deep, our wounds were ceasing to bleed. There was still no sound from beyond the partition. "Now," I said. "Now for that little door."

19

Jackman's Way Out

I sheathed my dagger, thrust it back into its pouch, and scrambled over to the door. As Wat had surmised, the cupboard was locked. The lock, though, was a commonplace type and I did not think the lockpicks that shared my pocket with the dagger and—just now—the stolen drawings, would have much trouble with it.

Nor did they. Before Wat's astonished gaze, I produced my spindly lockpicking wires and set to work. My hands were shaky with nerves but nevertheless, the lock yielded so easily that I was fairly sure it had been oiled. I peered inside. So, crouching behind me and leaning over my shoulder, did Wat.

To my disappointment, all I could see was the inside of a most ordinary cupboard, maybe three feet by three, and a foot deep. The back of it wasn't the brick wall of the house, but was made of planks, with some shelves attached, on which sat a few cracked and chipped pieces of disused crockery. I could have wept. My only comfort at that moment was the thought of the resistance we could now put up with our freed hands, if Woodforde suddenly came back to kill us.

Wat was evidently thinking along similar lines. "Looks like we'll have to lie in wait and brain 'em when they come back. Any of these things heavy enough, you reckon?" Edging past me, he pulled out a tall earthenware ewer and then, pausing, ran a hand over the plank wall at the rear of the cupboard. "No knothole this time," he said regretfully.

As he backed out, however, I peered in. There were indeed no knotholes in the planking. There was, however, a vertical crack where it looked as though two pieces of planking had been used instead of one longer one. The crack was where the two ends met. On impulse, I reached forward, hooked my fingertips into the crack, and pulled sideways. Nothing happened.

"What you doin', mistress?" Wat whispered, peering over my shoulder.

"Nothing useful," I said, and would have given up, except that Wat muttered urgently: "Turn the other way, mistress. Pull left instead of right."

"It won't go left either . . . oh, wait a minute." I had been using my right hand. I changed to the left one, which gave me a better purchase. A section of plank obligingly slid a few inches, leaving an square opening big enough for a hand to be thrust through.

"Here," Wat said. Dumping the earthenware ewer on the floor of the cupboard, he leaned past me, pushed his massive paw through the hole, and groped downward. "Got it!" There was a click, and the back of the cupboard swung open. It was the same principle, evidently, as the door to the secret room.

"Wat! You're a wonder!" I could have kissed him but this was no time for playing games. Death could walk in on us at any moment. "Come on," I said. "You first, so that I can shut this door behind us. God knows where this leads but it must lead somewhere."

Wat went through on all fours and then stopped. "What's the matter?" I demanded. "Go *on!*"

"Just a minute," said Wat, shuffling awkwardly. Then at last, he went forward and out of my path, and following in too much haste, I first knocked over the ewer with a clatter that terrified me, and then realized too late what had caused Wat to stop. Had he not been there to block the way with his bulk, I would have pitched headfirst down the stone spiral staircase which was immediately beyond the back of the cupboard.

Wat, fortunately, was there to catch hold of me. I twisted about, got my skirt caught on something, wrenched it free, somehow maneuvered my feet in front of me, and slithered down onto the stair.

Peering around, I realized that the back of the cupboard opened straight into what must be one of the ornamental buttress towers at the corners of the Jackman's Lane terrace. This would be the one at the back corner of the pie shop. The towers were evidently not as slender as they looked, though they were scarcely roomy. We were inside a tall brick cylinder, with a stone pillar rising through the middle, around which ran a very narrow, very precipitous, very tightly wound spiral staircase of stone. A pattern of chinks in the wall provided weak light, just enough to make out this much.

I could still hear nothing to suggest that our foes were returning. Delay scared me but if I had time to close the way behind us, I must use it. Urging Wat down a few steps farther, to give myself room, I set about shutting the cupboard.

By edging down a couple of steps myself, I could reach a point from which I could lean into the cupboard and try to lock its outer door again. In this, however, I failed. The lock, which had been easy enough to open, resisted my attempts to secure it. Since I was stretched across the cupboard floor, I was too awkwardly placed to work efficiently and I dared not waste time. Below me, Wat was muttering: "Come on, mistress, do; we did ought to get on!" And he was right. I gave up and slithered backward. As I did so, my fingers unexpectedly touched something soft.

Momentarily I recoiled and then, peering, saw that it was nothing worse than a roll of what looked like quite fresh linen, which had half slid out of the overturned ewer. I finished scrambling out of the cupboard, got myself onto the stairs again, and then, inquisitively, reached in to pick the linen roll up. I found that I was holding a solid object, about two feet long and narrow, apparently wrapped in cloth.

As I drew it toward me, the linen wrappings unrolled themselves. The faint light showed them to be a man's shirt, and inside, to my surprise, was the heavy wooden arm of one of the discarded and broken-up settles from the shop. I recognized the lion's head carved into the end of it. Puzzled I held it up, close to the nearest chinks, and then my whole body went still.

The lion had been eating meat. Its mane and muzzle were darkly stained but under the light there was little doubt about the nature of the stain. It was blood, and not only blood, either. As I moved it I saw something glint and held the carving closer to one of the chinks. There were hairs caught in the dried-up, dark red stain, and a couple of them had free ends, clear of the blood, which were still clean and showed their color. In the bright streak of daylight, they glinted like brass.

"What is it?" Wat asked me. "Mistress, do come on, afore we're caught!"

I cocked my head but there was still no sound from the room behind us. "This . . . it's . . . just rubbish," I said, and made my mind up quickly. My first impulse was to take it with me, but the place where evidence is found is evidence in itself.

I wrapped the wooden arm up and reached back into the cupboard again. I shoved the bundle back inside the ewer, though I left the ewer lying on its side, and then moved down once more, out of the way of the swing of the cupboard's false back. I could close this, at least. Gripping it by its bottom edge, I pushed it nearly shut. Its own latch stopped it from closing altogether but I hopped quickly up a step or two, to work the latch, and noticed as I did so that on this side, the door had bolts, top and bottom. With a gasp of relief, I shot them.

It takes time to tell it all, but in fact we had lingered for no more than a minute, and now, if our captors came after us, their way was barred.

"Now we can go," I whispered.

We moved warily downward. Further gleams of light came in through more little apertures here and there in the stone. The stonework outside was ornamental, I remembered, more so than the tower at St. John's College. Small slits would be lost in the pattern and not easily visible from outside unless one were looking for them.

I was beginning to have considerable respect for Master Jackman, Jester's father-in-law and the ardently Protestant parent of the fugitive Sybil. He had seen the peril coming in time, and he had laid his escape route with remarkable thoroughness. A disguised door, leading to an attic room where he could hide if the heresy hunters came to the house. A second line of defense in the shape of an innocent-looking cupboard with a false back, and beyond that, if he needed to get out of Cambridge and flee England altogether, a hidden stairway to the ground.

We were halfway down when we heard the sounds we had feared: angry voices from above and then a pounding as of fists against the cupboard back. We tried to hurry, though to make any kind of speed on such a steep, tight spiral of a stair was dangerous and difficult; to miss one's footing would be all too easy.

We went as fast as we dared, always ready to put out a hand to help each other. By the time we reached the foot of the stairs, the pounding had stopped and there had been no sound of splintering wood or feet on the stairs above us. The barrier, mercifully, had held.

At ground level, we found a further door, nearly as small and low as that of the cupboard, oddly shaped

with an angle in the middle of it, and provided with a
bolt and an iron latch. The bolt was pushed home. As I
slid it hurriedly back, I noticed that it moved silently,
and under my fingers, I felt the smoothness of oil. Like
the lock of the cupboard, this had been used recently.

I pressed the latch and let the door open an inch or
so while I peered through the gap. Immediately in
front of me was the strip of garden—just grass and
weeds at this point—between the side of Jester's house
and the surrounding wall, but just to the right was a
side gate. "Come on," I whispered, and stepped out,
beckoning Wat to follow. As I closed the door, I saw
how skillfully it was made, of wood faced with thin
brick and how neatly it was fitted, across two facets of
the tower. From outside, the latch was worked from a
tiny lever in a crevice of the ornamentation. The patterned brick and the line of the facet through the middle of the door confused the eye and made the outline
of the door extremely hard to see when it was closed.
Master Jackman had probably intended to use his
secret exit after dark, if he had to use it at all.

"This way," I said to Wat, making for the side gate,
with my hand outstretched to open it, just as dark
shadows loomed up to left and right, and Woodforde's
voice said: "Ah. There you are. You argued too long,
Roland, but it seems we're just in time," and there was
Jester closing in from one side, while on the other,
Woodforde's hands were reaching out to seize me.

The next couple of moments were a blur. I had
never used my dagger in earnest before. I had sometimes wondered if I could, if I would be able to bring
myself to lunge with the blade at a living body. Now

that the moment was here, I didn't even pause to think. On the instant, I had flicked back my overskirt, and grasped the sheath through the fabric with one hand, while I plunged the other into the pouch and whisked the weapon out. I struck straight at Woodforde's right arm. He sprang aside with an oath and the blade went through his doublet sleeve. At the same time, I was aware with half my mind that Wat had raised a mighty fist and landed it on Roland Jester's jaw. The weight of the blow was probably backed by years of banked-up resentment for all the blows Wat had endured in the past. Jester went flat, immediately, and didn't get up again.

Then Wat was at my side, and as I tore my dagger free, he charged forward, got hold of Woodforde around the ribs, and picked him up bodily. Woodforde had his own dagger out by now but it did him no good because before he could make use of it, he had been thrown down on the ground with such force that he could only lie there rolling his eyes and gasping.

Wat, becoming resourceful under the stimulus of excitement, promptly ripped Woodforde's doublet open, tore a piece from his shirt, rolled him over, administering a couple of kicks in the process, and used the shirt to bind his hands and feet. Woodforde started to recover his breath and his powers of resistance, but I went to Wat's aid, pressing my own dagger against Woodforde's neck and recommending him not to struggle.

Jester was just coming to his senses, but he was still dazed and it was easy enough for the two of us to serve him the same way. "Ambrosia can't be far off. She'll rescue them, I expect," I said, as Wat tightened the last knot and I put my dagger away, "so we'd better be out of sight before she finds them."

Leaving our defeated foes, we opened the side gate and slipped out into Silver Street. Our pursuers were for the moment immobilized and could not rush out after us, shouting: *"Stop thieves!"* or demanding that the populace should help them retrieve an eloping couple. We were safe, in the open air, out in a public street, back in the world of the living, back into the midst of sunshine and daily business. People were about, striding, strolling. Two fashionably dressed ladies were walking toward the river with a small dog on a lead, and a crowd had gathered, laughing, around a stall whose raucous proprietor was claiming incredible virtues for his array of pots and pans. I straightened my cap, which had been been pulled awry by my adventures.

"Mistress, where do we go now?" Wat asked.

"St. John's College," I said. "To see the Secretary of State."

20

Murderous Scarecrows

Wat didn't know what a Secretary of State was. As I hurried us back to the main thoroughfare of Cambridge, I tried to explain. It seemed that he had hitherto believed that the queen simply ruled and that was that. The idea that she had councillors who advised her was quite unfamiliar to him. When at last he did, more or less, understand, he stopped dead and said in frightened tones: "But I can't go and see anyone like that, mistress! Wat from the pie shop can't go talkin' with folk like that! An' you said summat about a college. I can't go into one of they places, neither!"

"It's just a building. And Sir William Cecil . . ." I began.

"What? Oh, mistress, you didn't tell me he was a Sir!" In Wat's mind, this evidently made things worse. "Mistress, I *can't!*" He came to a dead stop in the street.

"William Cecil," I said patiently, leaving out the title

and taking Wat's arm so as to get him moving again, "is just a man like any other. He's middle-aged and has gout and he's brought his old nurse to Cambridge with him to look after him. He won't frighten you any more than Master Jester did. A good deal less, I should think, and look how you've just served Jester! You *have* to come. I want you to be a witness to all that's happened today." I considered him anxiously, looking at him sideways as I continued, virtually, to drag him along. Passersby looked at us strangely, but I was too worried to care. The afternoon's events had to be reported to Cecil and placed under his control, and that meant placing Wat under his control as well. What had happened was enough to make even the untalkative Wat become garrulous, and Cecil certainly wouldn't want him rolling around Cambridge like a loose cannon on the deck of a ship, describing the day's events to family and friends. I clearly remembered Cecil saying that he preferred the very notion of plots against the queen to be unthinkable and, therefore, unmentionable.

"If you're there to say that everything I describe is true," I said deviously, "they'll know that I'm not lying or imagining things. I'm just a woman, you see."

With his chivalrous instincts thus aroused, Wat, though still quaking like a blancmange, at last consented to come with me, and stopped resisting my tug on his arm. When we reached St. John's, a groom who was waiting in the street, holding a stolid-looking gray cob with an old footboard sidesaddle behind the crosssaddle, gave us a curious glance and so did the door porter, although to my relief, he recognized me and let me in because he said that he had instructions from Cecil to admit me.

He eyed Wat doubtfully but I said sharply: "This man has something to tell Sir William. I will vouch for him," and he was allowed in as well.

Wat quaked more than ever as we crossed the magnificent courtyard and I really think that if he hadn't felt surrounded by it and intimidated by the dignified porter, he might even then have turned around and fled. As it was, he followed me obediently inside, but kept so close to me that he trod on my heels.

There was a solitary clerk in the anteroom, someone I did not know. He too gave me an odd look. Sir William Cecil was in the lodgings, he said, but was closeted with some people who had been brought to see him unexpectedly. "Master Henderson was here and insisted that they should be seen," he said discontentedly. "And the Fellows are awaiting a summons from him, too."

"Nevertheless, I must ask you, please, to tell Master Henderson that Mistress Ursula Blanchard is here as well," I said crisply. The clerk's gaze sharpened at the sound of my name.

"Ah. Yes, I do have instructions. Wait one moment, please."

He disappeared through the door to Cecil's private rooms. A moment later he came back, dismissed the porter, and led us through into the room where I had talked with Cecil before.

It seemed much smaller this time, because it was so crowded. Cecil was there, of course, still sitting with his bandaged foot up. There was a document-strewn table within his reach. Near Cecil stood Rob Henderson, and there too were Dale and Brockley side by side, Brockley's face even more expressionless than usual, Dale, pale and unhappy, her pockmarks very obvious.

Nanny sat stitching on a stool by the window, and close to her, on a bigger stool with arms, was a woman older than Nanny, bent-backed and evidently lame, for an ebony walking stick was propped beside her. She had a downturned mouth and chilly pale blue eyes set in a white face with an aquiline nose. She had been handsome once in a haughty fashion though now her skin was lined and looked as thin as paper. She wore a costly ruff edged with silver, and a dress of black satin with a wide farthingale pushed into an awkward slope by the arms of the stool. Even the stick was intricately carved and must have been expensive. I could not imagine who she was.

Standing quietly behind her, however, was another woman whose name I knew at once even though I had never met her before. She was perhaps forty years of age and plainly clad. There were worn lines in her face, and the expression in her dark eyes was not passionate but resigned. Nevertheless, there was no mistaking those strong, sweeping eyebrows or those broad nostrils.

"You're Ambrosia's mother!" I gasped, before the clerk could even begin announcing us. "Mistress Sybil Jester!"

Wat was anxiously bowing to everybody in turn. I hastily remembered my manners and dropped a curtsy, but I could hardly take my eyes from Sybil, who smiled at me, somewhat sadly. The elderly lady in black observed in a sour voice: "Will no one have the courtesy to present these persons to me? These *disheveled* persons?"

Cecil opened his mouth to answer but before he could do so, Nanny let out a squeal and pointed a finger at me, while Brockley's blank expression gave place to horror, and Dale gasped: "Oh, ma'am, whatever has happened to you?"

Suddenly, I realized that the porter and the clerk and the people in the street had had good reason to look oddly at Wat and me. Our hands and clothes were smeared with dried blood from our cut wrists and with dust from rolling about on the attic floor, while strands of our hair had been dragged loose by the passage through the cupboard. My reflection in a highly polished walnut press told me that my efforts to straighten my cap had merely given it a crazy tilt. Disheveled was a mild way of putting it. We resembled a pair of murderous scarecrows.

"Nanny," Cecil said, "fetch some soap and warm water. And—er—my clothes brush and my comb." Nanny scuttled out and Dale followed her. "Meanwhile," said Cecil, waving the clerk to return to the anteroom, "I will do the presenting. Mistress Grantley, this is Ursula Blanchard, a Lady of Her Majesty's Presence Chamber and a most trusted member of the court. Who is your companion, Ursula?"

"Wat," I said. "His name's Wat. He works at the pie shop."

"Thank you. Ursula, this is Mistress Catherine Grantley, with whom Mistress Jester has been living.

And now, my dear Ursula, what indeed has happened? What in the world have you and Wat been doing? You seem to have blood on your hands, literally."

"We haven't been committing any violent crimes," I said with a shaky laugh, hoping that punching Roland Jester and knocking the breath out of Giles Woodforde didn't qualify as crimes. "We've barely escaped with our own lives. If I hadn't had Wat to help me, I don't know what would have happened. We've had a most exciting afternoon. We . . ."

I was trying to speak with lightness, to be the capable and courageous agent I was supposed to be but there were dancing black specks before my eyes and in my own ears my voice echoed as though I were in a cave. The next I knew, I seemed to be waking, but for some reason, not in a bed. I opened my eyes to find myself on the floor, with Brockley pushing a cushion under my head, while Rob and Wat stood staring worriedly down at me. "Don't try to sit up yet, madam," Brockley was saying. Somewhere a door latch clicked, and then I heard Dale and Nanny exclaiming in distress. Dale's face appeared above me.

"You were supposed to be back at Master Woodforde's lodgings," I said vaguely to Brockley.

"He didn't obey orders," said Cecil's voice.

"It was my fault," said Rob regretfully. "When we sent Brockley back to Woodforde's lodgings in case his master came home, I went part of the way back with him as I wished to return to my own lodgings. On the way he asked me for news of his wife, Fran Dale, and I told him that you had sent her to Brent Hay to warn Mistress Smithson that Dr. Woodforde knew where she was and that the playlet was a trap."

"He didn't tell me everything, of course," Brockley interposed. "Not that Fran had first been afraid to take the message because, well, because she was muddled about something." Peering upward, I saw Fran biting her lip. There were tears in her eyes.

"I told him that myself, ma'am," she said. "I told him all about it. And oh, he is so angry with me!"

"I've grasped," said Rob, "that there's something private here, which I know nothing about. And I'm not asking."

"Thank you, Rob." I turned my gaze toward Brockley and stared steadily up into his face. "I wish you to forgive her. That is an order," I said, and my eyes passed on the silent message, *You know why.*

He gave me a faint nod, and I knew that the memory of a night in a Welsh dungeon was present in his mind as it was in mine. He put out a hand and touched Fran's arm in a gesture of reassurance. Aloud, he said: "Master Henderson only said that my wife had set off for Brent Hay today. He left me at the gate of King's, and I went in, but halfway across the courtyard, I turned round and came out again and went to the stable to get a horse and go after Fran. I felt worried about her, somehow, as if something wasn't right with her. It can be like that, sometimes, between man and wife."

"Yes, it can," I said, and was glad to see that he was now giving Fran's shoulder a kindly squeeze and that she was responding with a trace of a smile.

"Anyway," Brockley said, "I met her on the road coming back—with Mistress Jester and Mistress Grantley."

"When my gentlewoman companion receives a letter that flings her into a flurry and makes her insist that she should come instantly into Cambridge to find a woman called Ursula Blanchard, of whom I have never heard, and declares also that she is in a state of fear for a young relative I have never heard of before, either, I want to know what is going on," said Catherine Grantley grimly.

"I understand, madam," Brockley put in, "that Mistress Grantley has read the letter you sent by Fran."

"I insisted, but much it told me! I had put forward Mistress Smithson, as I believed my companion to be called, as a candidate for presenting flowers to the queen; now it seems that if she does, she may also find herself returning to a husband I didn't know she had. A brother-in-law called Woodforde apparently knows who she really is—which is more, it seems, than I have been allowed to know! Futhermore, the letter, from a woman claiming to be employed by Sir William Cecil, also inquired if Mistress Smithson, or whatever her name is, knew of any reason why either the husband or the brother-in-law should be laying plots against the queen, and told her that if so, she should speak at once before they ran into further danger, or led someone called Ambrosia—her daughter, apparently!—into danger with them. It made no sense at all, except that it tells me all too plainly that I have been shamefully deceived in *Mistress Smithson.* . . ."

Cecil at this point attempted to say something but Mistress Grantley raised her voice and overrode him.

" . . . All this time, instead of giving honest employment to a poor widow, recommended to me by Dr.

Edward Barley, a man I believed to be a respectable tutor, I have it seems been harboring a runaway wife who has left not only a husband but a daughter to fend for themselves. When I questioned her, she admitted it. Shameful!"

"I fled from my husband because I feared that one day he would kill me," Mistress Jester said in a low voice. "I took the name of Smithson to help me hide from him, rather than to deceive you. Though it is true that I needed a sanctuary, and Dr. Barley said you might not take me in, not even if you knew the full truth."

"No more I would!" snapped Mistress Grantley. "If a woman has taken the vows of marriage, she should abide by them."

"At risk of her life?" I asked her. I reached a hand to Dale, who helped me up and steadied me onto a spare stool.

"If she tries hard enough to please her husband, her life won't be at risk!" Mistress Grantley retorted didactically, and with every word, she banged her ornamented ebony stick on the floor by way of emphasis.

"He turned on me because of something my father did, not because of anything I did!" Sybil cried protestingly. "And attacked me with his fists when I protested!"

Cecil once more attempted to speak but Mistress Grantley, in whose mind age clearly took precedence over such minor matters as the title of Secretary of State, overrode him again.

"Concerning the plots mentioned in the letter, Mistress *Smithson* claimed that she knew nothing. In view of the way she has deceived me, I cannot help but wonder . . ."

"It's true! I wanted to come here to find out what all this talk of plots meant. I am afraid for my daughter!"

"So you say! Well, I wish to know all. I still take the air on horseback now and then, slowly, on an old footboard pillion, behind a groom. If Sybil were so determined to come to Cambridge, I said I would come with her and whatever she found out, I would find out too. On the way, we met this man Brockley, who it appears is the husband of this woman Fran, who brought the letter. He looks," said Mistress Grantley disdainfully, "like a common serving man but had the impertinence to insist that we should all come at once to see Sir William. To see the Secretary of State, no less! Hardly had we arrived, however, before these two other people have joined us. One of them is apparently the woman who sent the letter. *Why* does an employee of Sir William Cecil look as though she has been butchering sheep with the help of a scullion?"

"Will you all kindly be quiet!" Cecil got a hearing this time by shouting. "I want to know what has happened to Ursula and Wat. Are you feeling better, Ursula? Nanny, give her the bowl of water and the comb, and let her clean and tidy herself and then pass them to Wat."

"I'll not give your comb to him! He's likely got lice!"

"No, I ain't!" said Wat indignantly.

I saw Rob and Brockley both suppressing grins. "Damn the comb!" Cecil snapped. "I can afford a few spares! You can throw it away afterward, Nanny. Do as I bid you! Now then, Ursula, will you begin your explanation? And will someone fetch some wine. I think Ursula needs it and probably we all do."

Nanny brought me the water. I washed the blood quickly off my hands, pulled my cap off, and then let Dale tackle my hair while I told them how I had gone up to the pie shop's attic for another look at Master Jester's papers and Ambrosia had caught me. I told how she had shouted for her father, who suddenly appeared from what seemed to be a secret room into which I was dragged. I described the alarming conversation between the two brothers, the arrival of Wat, and how we had been tied up and left, probably to await our doom. "We would neither of us have escaped if we'd been alone. We did it because there were two of us. I had a dagger with me that the brothers hadn't found . . ."

I described how Wat and I had managed to free each other and then our escape through the cupboard and the spiral stairway. With some embarrassment I admitted that we had had to fight our way out of the garden. "Then we came straight here. The talk between Woodforde and Jester is proof enough to my mind that something else is afoot besides the entrapment of Mistress Jester."

"There was no need for a trap," said Mistress Jester. "Not if my brother-in-law knew where I was anyway. And precious little need for secrecy even if there was a trap. Would even the queen have cared? How many people," she asked bitterly, "would criticize a husband for snatching a runaway wife back?"

"No one in his right mind!" snapped Catherine Grantley.

Sybil Jester looked at her. "I think Dr. Barley was in his right mind," she said quietly.

"He was an old man, going senile, I daresay!"

Cecil banged his fist down on the table beside him. "That will do! To listen to you all snapping and snarling, anyone would think this was a bear-baiting pit! It happens to be my private apartment. The Secretary of State's private quarters, to be precise! Mistress Grantley, you will be good enough to hold your tongue. Mistress Jester, *can* you shed any light on the secret business in which your husband and brother-in-law seem to be engaged?"

"No," said Mistress Jester. "No, I cannot. I only know that the mere idea terrifies me, for my daughter's sake, and yes—because although I fled from my husband, he *is* still my husband and I would not like to think of him . . . facing a traitor's end."

"Did you know of the secret room or the stairway in the buttress tower?" Rob asked her.

"No," said Sybil. "Athough my father—who had the house built—did tell me that he had built hidden ways of escape into it. He wanted them in case he had to flee from a charge of heresy. He was terrified of that. He had . . . seen a burning once. He told me that it haunted him; that he couldn't forget it."

"I heard a description of it once," I said. "The uncle and aunt who brought me up forced me to listen. It gave me nightmares." Of all the things I had against Aunt Tabitha and Uncle Herbert, that hideous incident, when they held me so that I could not stop my ears while they poured horrors into them, was and always would be among the most powerful.

"When my mother was alive," Sybil said, "she told me once that my father used to have nightmares, too. He was a good Protestant. And so is my husband—it was one thing on which he and my father agreed. I can't believe that my husband is caught up in a plot against the life of the queen. That is what you fear, is it not? As for Master Woodforde, he has little interest in politics or religion. I think," said Sybil with unexpected, dry humor, "that he worships a goddess called Lady Lennox."

"Lady Lennox wouldn't care if the queen were killed," said Henderson bluntly.

"Lady Lennox isn't fool enough to risk her neck on the block," said Cecil. "If you mean that she is paying Woodforde to act as an assassin on her behalf, I find it difficult to believe. There was nothing at all in the letters you saw that might help, Ursula?"

"Not overtly," I said. "But I think they may be in cipher. I found . . ."

"They weren't in cipher. We tested several of them, from both men, and there was no sign of such a thing," Cecil cut me short. "I told you that."

I opened my mouth to persist but Sybil was quicker. "But my husband and Giles Woodforde *did* correspond in cipher!"

Cecil turned to her. "Did they? But my expert clerks insisted . . . What kind of cipher?"

"Oh, a very clumsy one. They had to write letters a hundred miles long in order to exchange quite short messages. It was a game between them. They started it as boys. They kept a note of the key, in the form of drawings."

"Drawings?" Cecil frowned.

I reached into my hidden pocket and drew out the set of sketches that I had stolen from the chest in Jester's attic.

"Like these?" I asked.

21

Moat, Walls, and Keep

Mistress Grantley took hold of her stick and levered herself to her feet. "I have learned all I need to know. I have not only been lied to by Dr. Barley, whom I trusted, and led into giving my countenance, unawares, to an errant wife and mother, but it seems that the family she comes from is less than respectable. They correspond in cipher and are suspected of treachery. I will take my leave. Will someone be good enough to assist me to the street? My groom is waiting there for me."

"I saw him as we came in," I remarked politely. "By the way, Brockley, where are our horses?"

"I paid a college serving boy to take them back to Radley's," Brockley said. "I will help you, Mistress Grantley, if Mistress Blanchard permits."

"Certainly," I said.

Mistress Grantley gave me a cold glare. "I will accept his aid, but it would have been more courteous to ask me first whether it was agreeable to me. I fancy, however, that he is simply your servant and is obedient as servants should be. I will overlook his impertinence in taking it on himself to decide that we should be brought here. It was the right place, after all." She turned to Sybil and Cecil together. "There is no question, of course, of Mistress *Jester* returning to Brent Hay. She is dismissed. My charitable gifts to the university will, however, continue as before; I do not blame the university for any of this. With Mistress *Jester* I will have no more to do. I am a woman of standing and of moral standards. You must fend for yourself, my lady. Your *friends* perhaps will help you."

"I must ask you, before you leave, to give an undertaking not to discuss this matter with any other person," said Cecil smoothly. "It is state business."

Mistress Grantley, not in the least impressed either by Cecil's position or his air of gravitas, shifted her chilly blue stare to him. "No one has ever challenged my discretion in the past and I trust will have no cause so to do in the future," she informed him, with awe-inspiring dignity. "On that you may depend."

"Thank you. And if there are outstanding wages due to Mistress Jester, I trust they will be paid?" Cecil added.

"I am also an honest woman. The wages, and her personal belongings too, will be dispatched to her if Mistress Jester will send word of where she is staying."

"Show Mistress Grantley out, Brockley," said Cecil. "When you return, you and Wat may go to the buttery and ask for some food. You must need it. My clerk out there will show you the way. You are not to leave the college, however. My clerk will also arrange for you to have somewhere to sleep. Don't look so frightened, Wat. You are not under arrest! I merely don't want wild talk spreading all over Cambridge. You will go home when the queen's visit is safely over. For the moment, go and wait in the anteroom till Brockley comes back. Master Henderson, take Ryder and Dodd and go to the pie shop. If Woodforde and Jester are still there, though I doubt it, fetch them in. If they're not there, give chase. They may have made for Norwich or Lynn in the hope of getting away by sea."

Rob went quickly out. Brockley took Mistress Grantley's arm and helped her from the room and Wat, looking like a worried ox, followed them. The rest of us regarded one another with raised brows. "You have been living with Mistress Grantley for—what? Five years?" I asked Sybil.

"She isn't—wasn't—such a bad mistress," Sybil said calmly. She seemed to have a calm temperament altogether. "While she believed I was a widowed relative of Dr. Barley—that was the tale we told her—she treated me quite well. She is autocratic, but as long as I did her bidding and was respectful, I had nothing of which to complain. She keeps her tenants' roofs in good repair, dresses cuts and burns if her servants hurt themselves, gives them generous presents at Christmas. But—there are things she doesn't understand."

"Obviously!" I said.

Cecil had been looking at the drawings I had stolen. "There is a cipher to break. It looks as though you were right, Ursula. As it happens, because I brought a number of document boxes with me in order to carry on with various items of business, I also have with me copies of the letters we intercepted at Richmond. I didn't expect them to feature in the business but nevertheless, they're stored in one of the boxes, so they're here. Would you put your head out of the door and ask the clerk out there to bring in box number three?"

I did so, and after leafing through the box for a moment he had found what he wanted. He handed me a sheaf of papers. "Here they are. Since I have clerks who are skilled at deciphering codes, I would normally call on them to deal with this, but they are still in Richmond. However, it seems that you and Mistress Jester between you may in any case have the edge on them as regards this one. Are you feeling quite better now?"

"Yes, thank you, Sir William. It was only—I'd had a fright," I said candidly. "I am sorry I was so foolish."

"I wouldn't call it foolish. Where on earth is that wine I sent for? Nanny, go and hurry them up, will you? And ask for some food as well, for the ladies. Now, Mistress Jester and Mistress Blanchard, can you make a start on the deciphering? I, alas, must see the Fellows. I can't keep them waiting any longer, and Dudley is supposed to be coming with them, so I am expecting him as well."

Cecil's quarters included a writing room, to which Sybil and I, attended by Dale, now took the letters and drawings. There was a desk, placed in front of the mullioned window for the sake of a good light, and equipped with inkstand, prepared quills, sander, and paper. There were a couple of side tables too, and several padded stools. The wine and food arrived, and Dale, still subdued, filled glasses for us. "Fill one for yourself," I said gently. "And eat something as well. Brockley has forgiven you now, you know. Was he so very angry with you?"

"We were riding along together, coming back to Cambridge, when I told him, ma'am. He couldn't say much because Mistress Grantley and Mistress Jester were there, but, oh, what he did say . . . !"

"It will be all right now," I said. "I promise. Most men are pleased enough to know that their wives love them, you know. Think no more about it." I paused and reinforced what I had said to her in the lodging that morning. "If I have ever seemed to be too friendly toward Brockley, please excuse me. I am sorry if it gave you pain, but truly, there was no harm in it." That was a lie, but I said it for Dale's sake, and from now on it must become the truth I had sworn that it was.

We set out the food. Dale ate at a side table, while Sybil and I sat down together at the desk with our platters, wineglasses, and documents all arranged before us. I thought with a touch of amusement that to anyone glancing into the room, we would present a most misleading picture. Such an onlooker would see two women quietly taking refreshments while reading letters and looking at drawings. No doubt the onlooker would have smiled fondly, assuming the letters to be from husbands or friends, full of affectionate phrases, dignified pious sentiments, and instructions about family or household business; the drawings to be examples of our feminine pastimes, probably inexpert, but a source of innocent amusement.

The notion that we were a pair of code breakers, hoping to decipher proof of a treacherous plot against the queen, would never have entered such a person's head.

Although he might have been surprised at the lack of feminine chatter and laughter. We had no inclination for either. Sybil, spreading the drawings out on the table, said: "It looks as though they have extended the code since I last saw it. It was clever of you to suspect that these might contain a key, Mistress Blanchard . . ."

"Ursula," I said to her. "Since we are to work together."

"Well, it was very sharp of you, and sharper still to seize your chance and bring them away." Sybil's dark eyes, so like her daughter's except for their gravely tranquil expression, scanned my face. "I must say I admire you. I suppose you have guessed at the principle?"

"I think so. There are twenty-six sheets here. That was what made me so certain. I take it that each is a key to a letter of the alphabet, and each letter must be"—I paused, rubbing my forehead—"am I right? Each letter is represented by a word, or sometimes by alternative words, and these drawings are to help anyone using the code to remember what the words are. The parts of the drawings that . . . that illustrate the words, are very clearly shown, while the rest isn't. Is that it? This first one, which would be the letter *A,* has an apple clearly drawn, and the dapples on the pony, and a church or perhaps a chapel. Is that it?"

"Yes, and either *chapel* or *church* could be used as code words for *A*," Sybil said, "along with *apple* and *dapple*. In the days before Roland and I began to quarrel, I used to help him write and read the cipher letters—I was allowed to take part in the game, as it were. That's how it all started; just as a game between Roland and Giles. I enjoyed it! At first, when they were just boys, they used words that began with the letter of the alphabet they represented, and only one for each letter. Then they decided that this was too obvious—the same words would keep on reappearing and it was difficult to write anything that read like an ordinary letter. So they decided to have a choice of words for each letter, and not all with the same initial letter. They said let's use words which rhyme with the original code word as *dapple* rhymes with *apple*—as you seem to have worked out."

"It's a clever device," I said. "Very hard to come at, without the key."

"It changed over the course of time," Sybil said. "To start with, *weather* was one of the words for *W*, and *rain* was one of the words for *R*, but they found that they wanted to use those words freely sometimes, so they took them out of the code. They settled that *R* should be *river* or *ring*, and *W* should be *weal* or *wander*. Then, in my day, they thought of going a step further and employing words that were linked to the original ones or were more or less synonyms, like *church* sometimes instead of *chapel*. That was Roland's idea. It made the text much less repetitive. One of the words they used to represent *T* was *time*—but they might say *timepiece*, or *clock* or even *sundial* as well! Those two know each other so well that they can manage like that. I'm not sure it would work between people who aren't so close."

"Dear God," I said, looking in despair at the letters on the table in front of us.

"We have the drawings," said Sybil. "And I was quite good at this, once on a time. Let's just try. Roland and Giles had ways of making things easier for themselves by little secret signals. Just before a code word, they would write something carelessly, sloping upward a little instead of on a level. When you were used to it, you could recognize the signal at once. But these letters are copies and I don't suppose the clerks copied little quirks like that . . ." She picked up one letter and then another and sighed. "No, they didn't. Well, we must do without. Let's to work."

"They've added to the words for *T*," Sybil said, examining the sketches, which we had laid out carefully in rows, in the right order, with the letter each sheet was meant to represent noted in the top left-hand corner. "And to some others, I think; *I* and *J* for instance, and also *T* and *M*. The letter *I* was always *eye, ink,* or *ivy*. It looks as if *island* has been added and from the people skating, I would guess that *ice* has, as well. *J* always had *jester* or *jest* and *jay* or *popinjay*—that's the sketch of a jester with a popinjay on his shoulder. But why there's also a picture of a man asleep, I don't know. The drawing for *T* always used to be a sundial—that was the reminder for *time, clock,* and the actual word *sundial* as well. But now there's a woman at a table, combing her hair. The table and the hair are clearly emphasized . . ."

"*Table* would fit," I said. "It begins with *T*."

"Yes . . . yes . . . but I can't understand the hair." Sybil sipped some wine, puzzling. "Could the word actually be *hair*? But that wasn't the way they used to arrive at their code words. It ought either to begin with *T*, or rhyme with one of the other words for *T*, or be an alternative for one . . . can you think of a word that means hair—and rhymes with one of the timepiece words, or else starts with *T*?"

I thought, and couldn't. The drawings for *M*, however, gave me an idea. "If the second drawing under *M* is new," I said, "could it mean *music*? I mean the sketch with the musicians in it. Do any of the letters use the word *music*? I wonder."

Sybil took the drawing from me. "People dancing, and musicians in a gallery—yes, *music* could be the word. But all the people have such wide smiles. That must mean something too . . . *mirth,* perhaps! We'll have to see if it works. I think new words have been added for the letter *U* as well. Because for *U*"—she put down the sheet for *M* and picked up *U* instead—"there are pictures that I certainly remember, of sheep—*ewe* was the original word, and two clasped hands for *unity,* and a lot of funny little stick men dotted about inside a square frame—they stand for *ubiquitous* . . ."

"How could anyone guess that?"

"Well, Roland and Giles didn't guess. These are just reminders to jog their memories if they forgot any of the code words. They were so used to them that most of the time they didn't forget. But there's a new picture of someone chasing a child upstairs, and the child is crying. The stairs and the tears are done very plainly, in dark lines . . ."

"You've just used the word *upstairs*. That starts with *U*," I said. "But I don't know what to make of the tears." I picked up a sheet at random. "Which one's this? It's marked *N*. I can't make this out at all. There's a man hammering something, and above him is a clock with the hands pointing to twelve, and in the lower half of the page there's someone reading a letter to someone else who seems to be trying to snatch it away—I must say your husband can draw!—and also, there's the constellation of the Plow and the Pole Star!"

"The words for *N*," said Sybil, "always used to be *nail, noon, north*—that's where the Pole Star comes in—and *news*. The man with the hammer is knocking a nail in, the clock's pointing to noon, and the letter someone is trying to seize hold of is supposed to contain something exciting. Come. We must be methodical." She drew a sheet of paper toward her, picked up a quill, and dipped it. "Let us list the code words for each letter, as far as we can work them out. We'll sip our wine and nibble our pasties as we go along."

She gave me a smile of sudden and immense sweetness. "At Mistress Grantley's house, all meals are very formal, even breakfast and supper. We eat sitting upright at table and the only conversation is that begun by Mistress Grantley. Most of the time, she prefers to have her chaplain read from the Bible while we eat, so there's rarely any conversation at all. And no one ever, ever, reads to himself or herself, or writes while eating. Believe me, this is a pleasure!"

*   *   *

When we had assembled as much of the code as we could, though there were some worrying gaps, Sybil picked up one of the letters and pushed another toward me. "Let us take a letter each and just plunge in. I'll see what I can make of this."

Glancing over at the letter Sybil had chosen, I saw that it was one of those that Woodforde had written from Richmond. I had read it, briefly, in Jester's attic. The one she had passed to me was shorter, and was new to me. In Jester's house, I had only seen the letters that Woodforde had sent to him, while this was a copy of one written by Jester himself, to his brother. When I read it through, however, I recalled that Cecil had mentioned it. Jester had bothered to hire a courier, he said, in order to complain that the girls who work in his shop giggled too much and that his furniture was getting old!

I studied it carefully. I could see what Cecil meant.

Dear brother,

How are you faring, away at court? I often think of you among the great folk there. Things go on here as usual though Ambrosia and Phoebe are often too frivolous.

I am writing this in the evening, at a table in the shop. The weather is bad and everything was veiled in rain until noon, but it is now late and upstairs I can hear the girls giggling over some jest or other.

A thousand curses—I have just caught my hand on a nail sticking out of this bench—I must buy some better furniture. As I was saying, no doubt it is

natural for young things to enjoy a jest but they have
to be up early and I hope they will soon end their
foolishness and go to bed. Of a verity it is well past
time . . .

Awkward, stilted wording. It looked promising, I
thought. I knew that *weather* and *rain* were not code
words and could be discounted, but the word *table* was
there, and I had noted that *veiled* was a code word for
V. The sheet for the letter V included a drawing of a
veiled woman. *Nail, noon,* and *jest* were all there, too!
As Sybil had done, I took quill and paper and set busily
to work. After a few moments I had arrived, discourag-
ingly, at TVNUJN.

I looked across at Sybil's efforts. "Mine's coming
out as gibberish. How are you getting on?"

"The same." Sybil leaned back, as though the words
in front of her might look different if viewed from a
distance. "I recognize a lot of code words. I am quite
sure that this is a cipher letter but you're quite right; it
makes no sense. Look at this!"

She passed her effort to me. I glanced over the letter
she had been trying to transcribe, recognizing the first
two paragraphs.

My dear brother,
    My thanks for your letter. I am growing used now
to being at court. I have several times seen the queen,
often dressed in white or silver. The food is nothing
remarkable, though. Pease potage appears quite often
at the noon meal. There is much frivolity and jesters
are a ubiquitous feature. I have never liked them

(except for you, my brother!). Sometimes, I think their
humor is too unkind and full of pepper.

We are well housed here. Most people on the floor
where I have my quarters are of good social standing,
and at dinner I am above the salt. Everyone here
dresses very well. Men and women alike are as fine as
popinjays, with their tresses well washed and combed.

"The first code word here seems to be *queen*," Sybil
said. "That stands for Q and most people who are used
to writing and spelling put U after Q, so that the next
code word should stand for U, but it doesn't. The next
one is *silver*, which means S. Then comes *pease*—they
used to use that for P and the drawings show a girl
shelling peas—and then *noon, jesters,* and *ubiquitous.*
They're all code words. *Pepper* comes after that—that's
one of their words for P and that's the next one I'm
sure of, anyway—then *floor*—that's F—and then there's
salt, which is another word for S, and *popinjays* which is
another word for J. And what," said Sybil wearily,
"does all that add up to? QSPNJUPFSJ! You're quite
right, I fear. It's gibberish."

We sat in silence, defeated.

"And yet the code words are *there*," I said. "The
wording's almost sprained so as to get them in! Pease
potage at court, indeed! I *never* saw such a thing at any
table in a royal palace, I promise you! It's a complete
invention and I can only think he did it to bring in a
word for P. Could *tresses* be *T,* by the way? Could that
be the meaning of the woman combing her hair?"

"Possibly. But it doesn't help, even if it is."

Beyond the door of the writing room, I could hear

masculine voices. The Fellows must have arrived. I listened, and recognized Dudley's familiar tones as well; he had a deep voice that was unmistakable. It suddenly occurred to me that the reason why Elizabeth was so enamored of him might be as much to do with his voice as with his handsome face. There were many handsome men at court but how many of them had deep, steady voices like Dudley's? He was an excellent Master of the Queen's Horse because he was very good indeed with horses. No doubt that voice soothed and reassured them.

I wished someone now would soothe and reassure me. I did not want to fail at this and I was beginning to fear that I would, and that Sybil would, as well.

"If your husband and his brother were discussing something very serious," I said slowly, "could they have built a second code inside the first? A sort of second line of defense?" I remembered something. "When Cecil first had these letters tested for ciphers, and came up with meaningless sequences of letters, he asked his clerks to test those sequences again, to see if they were themselves a code."

"Like having a cupboard built as well as a secret room?" Sybil's eyes widened. "It could be, yes. I remember I once heard my father talking to my husband about what he called his hidden way out. I didn't know then what he meant. But yes, he did say he had a second line of defense. He used those very words! Perhaps Roland learned from him to think in the same way, and passed it on to his brother. How would it work with this? Perhaps each letter actually means the letter before it in the alphabet, or after, something like that . . ."

"I hope it's no worse than that, if it exists," I said. "If it's very complicated, we can't do it without professional code breakers. But we could try those two possibilities. Let's see. If we assume that each letter stands for the one that follows it in the alphabet, what does that make TVNUJN?"

Sybil wrote. We gazed at the result without enthusiasm. UWOVKO.

"Try going the other way," said Sybil. "Try going one letter back instead."

This yielded SUMTIM. "It has sensibly placed vowels," I said critically. "But otherwise . . ."

The door latch clicked and Cecil limped into the room. We both stood up but he shook his head. "No, no, be seated." He deposited himself on a spare stool and propped his foot on another. "The Fellows are here and so is Dudley, and I've left him to talk to them for a few moments. How are you progressing?"

"We aren't doing very well," I told him. "The letters seem to have the code in them—the sentences and phrases are skewed, somehow, as if to bring code words in . . ."

"Yes. That impression was there from the start. But it doesn't decode into anything that makes sense?"

"No, it doesn't. We are wondering if there is a code within a code, a second line of defense, so to speak. We're trying that out just now. We haven't been lucky so far. We may have got the idea right, but if the second code isn't very simple, it could be beyond us."

Cecil sighed. "Nothing is ever simple in this world, it seems to me. All I can say is, decode all that you can, whether it makes sense or not, and then we may have to bring in more help. Perhaps I can find someone among those learned Fellows with a liking for encryption. They're all so very learned," he added wryly, "that they frighten me. I may be their chancellor, but Dudley's the Lord High Steward of Cambridge and of the two of us, he's the more at ease with them. When they drift into Latin tags, he can understand them. I can only speak the tongue my mother taught me, alas. We . . ."

"Latin!" I gasped. "Sybil, can your husband and brother-in-law both write Latin? Giles Woodforde can, obviously—he teaches it—and—yes! Ambrosia once said that her father understood it, too!"

"Why, yes. Giles has Greek as well, but they both learned Latin as boys. I didn't, though," Sybil told me.

"Dudley could help," Cecil offered, but I had snatched up the short letter from Roland. "I learned Latin with my cousins!" I said. "And I've been studying it again with my daughter. SUMTIM—that's what we made of TVNUJN, by shifting each letter back. They really did build in safeguards, didn't they? A code within a code and then the whole thing comes out as Latin instead of English. Moat, walls, and then a keep within them! Sybil!" I thrust the letter under her nose. "Which are the next code words in this?"

Sybil took the sheet from me. "*Jest,* I think . . . that's J—let me see . . . '*I hope they will soon end their foolishness and go to bed. Of a verity it is well past time*' . . . *End!*" said Sybil. "That's the drawing of a coffin on the *E* page—so that's *J* and *E* . . . and the next code word is *verity.* That's another of the words for *V*—it's a pretty little picture of a man taking an oath on a Bible. And the last

one's *time*—that's *T*. What have we got? JEVT . . . are
we going back or forward? I can't remember . . ."

"Back," I said. "*I,D,U,S. Sum timidus*. It *is* Latin! *I
am afraid*. That is the message that your husband was
sending to his brother."

Sybil pulled the long letter toward her. "What are the
dates? This looks like Giles's reply. Yes, it must be. What
have I got? QSPNJUPFSJ! Put each letter back one.
PROMITOERI . . . if *tress* or *tresses* does mean *T*, then
back one letter from that is *S*. PROMITOERIS . . ."

"*Promitto eris!*" I yelped. "At least, there ought to be
an extra *T* in there . . . which would have decoded as
U . . ."

"' . . . *jesters are a ubiquitous feature. I have never liked
them (except for you, my brother!). Sometimes I think their
humor is too unkind and full of pepper . . .*'" Sybil read the
passage aloud. "I wonder—could *unkind* be a code
word?"

I caught up the sheet for *U*. "We couldn't make out
what the crying child meant. Could that be a reminder
for the word *unkind*?"

"It might be. So we've got PROMITTO ERIS . . ."

"What comes next?" I said eagerly.

"It goes on about Richmond being a beautiful
palace." Sybil went on reading aloud. "'*I woke at an early
time*'—time!—'*this morning and looked out on to a faery
dawn. Of a verity that is what it was, with just a trace of silvery
fog drifting over the Thames*' . . . time, faery—that's *F*—!"

"A pretty picture of an ethereal female being with
wings," I agreed, picking up the page of drawings in
question.

"And *dawn, verity, silvery*—both *silvery* and *silver* can be used for *S*—and *fog*, that can stand for *F,* too . . . TFDVSF. Go back one . . ."

"*S, E, C, U, R, E!*" I almost shouted. "*Secure*—safe! *I promise you will be safe!* The word for *safe* is almost the same in Latin as it is in English. I think . . ." I wrestled with a part of Latin that was slightly hazy in my mind " . . . I think he's used the adverb—maybe it ought to be *securus*—but the meaning's clear enough."

"The adverb was shorter, I expect," Sybil said. "It's not easy, writing letters in this fashion."

I stared at the list we had made of the code words and laughed. "To get the letter *U,* they'd need the letter *V.* The words for that are quite difficult to drag in! *Verity, veil, vinegar, vanity* . . . I daresay neither of them would worry too much about grammar as long as the meaning was clear!"

"I'm going to fetch Dudley," said Cecil. "Meanwhile, continue!"

He was some time in bringing Dudley. No doubt it was difficult to detach him smoothly from the Fellows. By the time the two of them came back, we had made progress. Dudley and Cecil joined us at the writing desk, a contrasting pair, Cecil drawn with the pain of his gout, Dudley athletic and splendid, dressed as so often in the favorite crimson that set off his dark complexion.

He greeted me with a nod, as someone he knew well, which clearly impressed Sybil, who at the sight of him had instantly got up and dropped a curtsy, and then actually blushed when this magnificent being put out a hand and graciously raised her. Then we looked at the message that Sybil and I had decoded into Latin and that I had then translated into English, and although his brown face did not stir a muscle, I began to feel sorry for the magnificent being.

I promise you will be safe. Consider! If Dudley dies, he cannot marry Mary. My grateful lady will love me again and I will give your wife to you.

"I understand what this is," Dudley said, speaking to me. "I am fully informed, Mistress Blanchard. Cecil dictated a letter to me and sent it to my lodgings this afternoon—and described the latest developments while he was bringing me up to this writing room. A disturbing account, I must say! You have had a terrify-ing brush with death and it seems," he added dryly, "that the same could be said of me. We all believed that the playlet concealed a threat against the person of the queen. But it looks as though the target is myself!"

22

The Dormer Window

"It would appear so," Cecil agreed. "It certainly sounds like it. Woodforde's aim, I fancy, is to please Lady Lennox and your demise would probably please her very much. She is afraid you'll go to Scotland, marry Mary Stuart, and destroy her son Henry Darnley's chances of marrying her instead."

"If she'd simply asked me," said Dudley, "I would happily have sworn on a pile of Bibles that I have no intention of doing any such thing! As the queen herself well knows. Though the suggestion was serious when she made it. You have never believed that, but I can assure you that it was so. I have been much afraid that she would actually order me to Scotland and in that case I would have had to go. I've been in the Tower once in my life and that was enough! As matters turned out, by the time she understood that I didn't wish to go—and that Mary didn't wish to receive me, either—she was relieved. But at the start—oh yes, she meant it. At that time, she was willing to sacrifice me in order to cut young Henry Darnley out. I mean much to her—though not as much as some people think."

I glanced at him curiously. I did not like Dudley for I knew him to be ambitious and ruthless with an icy core to his heart. Yet I also knew that I must not condemn him too much, at least not for the latter, for Elizabeth had that same core of ice within her and I understood it because to some extent I shared it. I could not have worked as an agent without it. Rob knew. He had commented on it during our journey to Cambridge, when he talked of the affinity between me and the wild geese. Now as I covertly studied Dudley, I found that I really was sorry for him. In his way, I think he did love Elizabeth and still harbored hopes of winning her, though I had reasons for believing that he wouldn't succeed.

"She is changing her opinion on the matter of Darnley," Cecil said. "So am I. Before I left Richmond, we discussed him at some length. I have learned recently that although Darnley is officially a Catholic, like his mother, he has Protestant leanings. The queen and I are now wondering if we might do better with him as king consort in Scotland than with some Catholic prince or other—and that would be Mary's likely alternative choice. I didn't, of course, say this to her, but I feel that the Darnley marriage could have one great advantage. It might produce an heir with the right credentials! A legitimate child, descended twice over from Henry VII, would certainly be that and such a child would have to grow up before it could be a rival. By then, I trust, Elizabeth would be too secure to fear it. I'm beginning to despair of Elizabeth herself ever providing us with an heir. I believe I said something of the kind to you, Ursula, before you left for Cambridge. Since discussing it with the queen, I have come to feel it more strongly."

"Yes," I said. "But surely . . ."

"But surely all this is by the way," said Dudley abruptly. "However little Lady Lennox has to fear from me, *she* doesn't know it, nor, apparently, does this lunatic Woodforde. I wonder, Cecil, if your men have been able to lay their hands on the brothers, or not?" He paused, his head on one side. "I can hear booted feet on the stairs. I think we are about to find out."

The tap on the door came almost at once. Cecil called: "Enter!" and Rob Henderson came in, accompanied by John Ryder and Dick Dodd. Cecil looked at them with raised brows.

"Too late," Rob said in exasperated tones. He looked both weary and hot, and no doubt was still suffering from the weakening aftereffects of his fever. "If you left them in the garden at the side of the house, Ursula, they're not there now. We took four extra men and put them round the house and then, with Ryder and Dodd here, I went in through the private door. It was locked and we had to break in. We went right through the house and the garden as well. We found the secret room and the way out through the cupboard and the tower. What we didn't find was any sign of human life. They could have got away either by river or by road."

"My husband kept a boat on the river," Sybil said. "They may have used that."

"Maybe. We sent two men galloping toward Lynn and two toward Norwich, straightaway, and now others have gone after them to help if need be, and to follow the course of the river. We're doing all we can," Rob said, somewhat defensively.

I said: "They meant to kill us, you know. At least, Woodforde did." It was evening now, but still warm. Nevertheless, the gooseflesh came up on my arms. "We've had a narrow escape."

"I trust that they won't have an escape at all," said Cecil ominously. "I hope they are overtaken very soon, Master Henderson."

I took a grip on myself, and said: "Should we decode the rest of these letters? In case there is something more?"

By ten o'clock that night, Sybil and I had finished decoding all the material we had. By the end, we had mastered virtually all of the code words including the additions since the days when Sybil was at home. We worked out that the mysterious sleeping man on the page for *J* meant *jaded*—or *jade*. The Latin was very simple, dog Latin, in fact, with the words more or less in English order. Since Woodforde actually taught the language, he had probably done that to make things easier for the less accomplished Jester. There were a few grammatical errors. There were several of these in the letters written by Jester, but some occurred even in Woodforde's, usually, we thought, for the sake of brevity. It didn't matter. We could always arrive at the gist.

Jester had written twice to his brother while Woodforde was at Richmond, stating that he was afraid, but not specifying why, although he did complain that Thomas Shawe was courting Ambrosia and that this might lead to trouble, its nature again unspecified. In Woodforde's second letter back, he had again told his brother not to fear for his safety, but recommended him to put a stop to Thomas's wooing.

That was all, but with what we had already, it was enough. Once Jester and Woodforde were caught and brought back, a very little questioning should get results. "Woodforde keeps telling his brother that he will be safe—from what?" Cecil said. "Then he exhorts Jester to consider: if Dudley should die, then he can't—obviously!—marry Mary and that must mean Mary of Scotland. In that case, Woodforde's lady will love him again. That can only mean Lady Lennox. Judging from what you witnessed and what Brockley has reported, he's obsessed with her and she certainly doesn't want Dudley to marry Mary Stuart. He ends one letter by saying that he will give Jester's wife to him. Both Lady Lennox's love and the return of Jester's wife to Jester appear to be conditions following the death of Dudley. That's the heart of the plot. We'll get the rest when we bring them in, and bring them in we will, and that before long, I trust."

He contemplated the letters in silence for a further moment and then added: "Sir Robert, it was Woodforde, was it not, who invited you to be the queen's champion in that tiresome playlet—and, therefore, arranged for you to step forward, out to the front of the queen's dais, to act out your duel?"

"I was provided, in writing, with a list of moves," said Dudley. "A very precise list. I imagine its purpose was to position me as a convenient target. Well, well."

"There have been reports from an agent in Scotland that Mary has been in touch with Lady Lennox," Cecil observed. "We haven't managed to trace the couriers or intercept any letters, but I daresay that the subject was the good looks and excellent education of Henry Darnley. Margaret Lennox may well see you as a threat, yes." Cecil looked Dudley up and down in a most remarkable way, one man assessing the stallion potential of another. "The interesting point that we still have to deal with is whether all this springs only from an aberration in the mind of Woodforde, or whether Lady Lennox employed him to murder you."

Sybil Jester had hardly been listening. Her mind was taking another path. "Wherever my husband and brother-in-law are," she said in distress, "Ambrosia must be with them. When you fetch them in, what of my daughter?"

"From what Ursula says, she knows little if anything of the plot," Cecil said. "I think you need not fear too much for your girl, Mistress Jester."

We were all tired. Rob had been dismissed to rest, some time ago. Dale was dozing on her stool. I had tried to bear up, but that afternoon I had not been far from death at Woodforde's hands and it had drained me. Now I felt exhausted, and Sybil's white face and shadowed eyes revealed a weariness nearly as great as my own. "I do believe," she said, "that all this goes back to my father and his terrible fear of being arrested for heresy. You have no idea how *fast* those houses in Jackman's Lane were built!"

"How do you mean?" Dudley asked her. Cecil's explanations had evidently not covered this. Sybil explained how the secret escape route had been provided because of her father's dread that one day he might need it to escape Queen Mary's commissioners.

"In 1556, only months after we moved to Jackman's Lane," she said, "the place actually was searched, by a party of royal commissioners—some of them from London and some from the university. Nothing was found to incriminate any of us though Father had an English Bible and various Protestant works in his possession. He told me afterward that he had hidden them. In the secret room, I imagine, though I didn't know that then. The searchers didn't find it, anyway, though they went through every cranny they could see. I remember how we all stayed in the parlor while they did it. Father was very brave when it came to the point. He told us we had nothing to fear and must not hinder the officials in their work. My mother was some years dead by then. My husband, Roland, was downstairs, serving customers. Father sat reading a book of verse and Ambrosia and I sat with him and I taught her a new embroidery stitch . . . but I remember seeing my father's hands tremble as he held his book. It seemed forever until the men apologized for troubling us and went away."

We were silent. Sybil's eyes were remote as she gazed back into the past. "But when the commissioners had gone," she said, "Father broke down. He cried.

I didn't know what to do. He was my father, you see; someone I'd always trusted to stand between us and danger, someone invincible. But he cried and I put my arms round him as though I were his mother and he were my child. He told me that if he was ever taken up for heresy and threatened with burning, he thought he would lose his mind with terror, and that if it ever happened, he would have to rely on us to get in to see him, and smuggle a knife to him so that he could end his life himself. If not, he said he would beat out his brains against the wall. No wonder there were secret hiding places in the house! Yet—if it hadn't had that secret way out . . . then perhaps none of this would have happened."

"Why do you say that?" Dudley asked her.

"The letters don't say exactly how the deed is to be done, sir, but if you are to be positioned in some special way during the playlet, out in front of the dais, isn't it likely that the idea was to shoot at you, very likely from an attic window above the pie shop and then take shelter in the hidden room? If it hadn't been there . . ."

"One could say *if only* for evermore," Cecil said. "Having a house with a secret way out of it doesn't necessarily turn people into criminals!"

Sybil sighed. "I suppose not. It might not have happened either if Mistress Grantley had never put me forward to present those wretched flowers! Once my brother-in-law knew that I was Mistress Smithson, he decided to use me as a bribe to persuade my husband to help him. A better bribe than money, though money was at the root of it. My father's will turned my husband against me, and so I fled, and thus I gave Giles his weapon. Both he and my husband . . . are unreasonable men. Giles is not balanced concerning Lady Lennox and Roland is not balanced concerning me. And yet . . . oh, my God, I used to love Roland. He fathered Ambrosia! I'd save him, too, if I could!"

"Honorable feelings," said Dudley, "but apart from the plot against *my* life, he and his brother threatened and assaulted Ursula here, and Wat as well."

"And one of them probably murdered Thomas Shawe," I added.

"Though I don't see how," Cecil said. "From what you've found out or seen for yourself, Ursula, Woodforde was in his rooms, suffering from the marsh ague, under the eye of his man at the time when Thomas Shawe was killed, and you told me, Ursula, that Jester was at home under *your* eye."

"I daresay Woodforde's man is in it, too," said Dudley.

"He's left now," I said. "My servant Brockley has taken his place. I suppose we could track the fellow down if we wanted to. I don't think he *was* in it, though."

Cecil glanced at me sharply. "You have a reason for saying that. What is it?"

I hesitated. The moment that I found the bloodstained table arm hidden in the cupboard, an idea had moved in my mind, and gradually, through all the hours since then, it had been clarifying. I thought I now knew who had killed Thomas and how. But I could be wrong. I needed proof. "I do have a reason," I said slowly. "But before I talk about it, there is someone I must speak to."

"Who?" demanded Cecil.

"Well—it's Jem, the groom at Radley's stable."

"The groom at where?"

"Thomas kept his horse there," I said. "And I want to know whether the groom was late in to the work on the day that Thomas Shawe died."

Cecil surveyed me thoughtfully. "You want to know whether a stable groom was on time at his work. Is the groom your suspect?"

"No!" I said, in some alarm. "I'm sure Jem wouldn't harm a fly. I just want to know if he was late that morning. That's all! I do have a reason."

"For a woman," Cecil said, "you have one of the most tortuous minds I've ever come across. The only one I know who is worse is Her Majesty herself. But I've learned to trust your instincts. I'll let you have your way. At the moment I am much occupied and my gout is a nuisance. Report to me when you have questioned this man, and learned whatever it is you wish to learn. For the moment, I must have you and Mistress Jester escorted back to your lodgings. You will not mind sharing your room with Mistress Jester?"

"No, of course not. The landlady may object, though."

"The landlady," said Cecil, "will do as the Secretary of State tells her. My clerk will accompany you."

Cambridge was en fete for the queen. The dais in Jackman's Lane had been hung with brocade of blue and gold, and spanning the streets through which Elizabeth would ride were strings of flags and pennants, some of them elegant and official and gracefully festooned, some of them homemade and haphazard. But it would not matter, for Elizabeth had always appreciated a nosegay of wildflowers as much if not more than any gracious bouquet of cultivated roses; she would probably like the sagging strings of homemade pennants best.

At two o'clock on Saturday the fifth of August, her expected hour of arrival drew near, and the townsfolk gathered in force to greet her. I doubt if there was a stall or shop left open for business. All the tradespeople wanted to see her go by and so did their customers. No one was going to be out buying milk or onions when they could be jostling for a view along her route. The sun shone on an array of best clothes; even humble folk who had no silk or satin could still produce jerkins and kirtles, glass beads and brooches in vivid colors, and they had.

Those who could afford better were as fine as peacocks. I was in green with silver embroidery (though I had my usual pouch inside the overskirt, naturally). Sybil Jester's belongings had not yet arrived from Brent Hay but she and I were much of a size and I had lent her my cream and tawny ensemble, which, she said, was far better than anything of hers, in any case.

The beadles and university dignitaries who had escorted Cecil from his lodgings to Jackman's Lane had taken charge of Sybil and separated her from me. I was waiting just in front of the dais, in the company of Rob Henderson, with Brockley and Dale in attendance.

Cecil himself was already on the dais, ready to step

down and hand the queen to her place when she arrived, and Dudley, after a morning of formal greeting ceremonies and orations, had set forth in his capacity of Master of the Queen's Horse, to meet her at the city boundary and escort her in.

Dudley was in good spirits, Rob told me. The discovery of a plot against him hadn't shaken his nerve overmuch. But neither Cecil nor Rob Henderson himself were in a happy mood. Both were finely clad, Cecil in a formal gown of black velvet and Rob in a dashing black doublet and hose, slashed and striped with gold, and Rob himself was now properly recovered from his illness. Both, however, were annoyed because so far there were no reports that Woodforde and Jester had been sighted. The pursuit along the roads and the riverbank had yielded nothing. Our quarry had either got farther than we thought, or else they had taken shelter somewhere along the way. Cecil had sent messengers off to order searches of all ships leaving port at Norwich and Lynn and no one doubted that the fugitives would be found. Until they were, however, neither Rob nor Cecil were likely to feel happy.

I regretted the escape, too, but to a lesser degree because I had had a small success of my own. The exhausting day when Wat and I barely escaped alive from the pie shop, and the cipher was broken in the evening, had been Thursday and today was Saturday. On the Friday, I had done as I intended and visited Radley's stable to talk to the groom, Jem. He had confirmed what I had guessed. As soon as Cecil was free to listen, I would explain it to him.

Meanwhile, though, the original plans for the queen's welcome were going ahead after all. There was no danger now either to Dudley or to Sybil. She was to present the flowers as planned, and even the playlet was to be performed. Cecil had countermanded his order to cancel it. Young Francis Morland, nervous but determined, was waiting nearby with his band of students. Costumed as outlaws and rustics, they were all assembled in front of the house belonging to the bronzesmith, Master Brady. The locked and shuttered pie shop beside it had now had bars nailed across its street entrances.

Dudley had spared two hours on the Friday in order to practice the pretended duel with Morland, which would be enacted while Sybil was whisked, not into the pie shop, but into the bronzesmith's house instead. Rob and I would join her there, and so would most of the neighbors and we would all partake of refreshments provided by the college kitchens. This was a last-minute plan that Cecil had created. "Mistress Jester was nearly the victim of an ugly deception," he had said. "We will make it up to her—and do it with style."

The refreshments, therefore, included pork and veal pies of Paris with ginger and raisins, all enclosed in delicate pastry, with pastry doves on top; a marchpane model of King's College Chapel, cold capons with a bread and pepper sauce in a separate dish, a honey and saffron quiche, and a magnificent molded blancmange. There was a choice of fine wines, too. All this had arrived in covered trays during the morning, borne by college servants, and it had sent Mistress

Brady into ecstasies involving clasped hands and actual tears of joy.

It was hot. The sun beat down on the dusty lane and my green satin felt heavy. Lookouts had been posted to watch for the queen, and now, in the distance, we heard trumpets welcoming her as she entered the city, and a moment later, church bells rang out all around us, exultantly clanging up and down the scale to add their voices to the trumpets.

The lane was becoming more crowded every moment. A large merchant with an equally large wife and a crowd of children came shouldering past me and Rob, intent on getting a good view. Brockley, behind me, clicked a disapproving tongue and I half turned to exchange rueful, *yes, how impolite,* glances with him. As I did so, the frontage of the pie shop came briefly into my line of vision and my gaze swept casually over it.

It could have been a trick of the light, the reflection of a rippling banner, or even of one of the many faces peering out of the windows across the street. It could have been my imagination.

It was none of those things. I went rigid, body and face alike, and Brockley saw it. "Madam? What is it?"

"Up in the pie shop," I said quietly. "In the attic. Somebody's up there. I've just seen a face glance out of one of those dormer windows!"

23

Desolation

"Master Henderson!" said Brockley sharply. Rob moved quickly toward me and I told him what I had seen.

"There can't be anyone in there! It's been under surveillance ever since it was searched and found deserted," Rob said. "No one can possibly have got in."

"I know what I saw."

"Ursula, are you sure?" He turned and stared up at the windows of the pie shop. Nothing strange was visible now.

"Yes," I said firmly. "Someone's in there. Could it be any of your men?"

"No. I said, the place is deserted and it . . ." He stopped and froze. And then, with somewhat elaborate casualness, turned back to me. "You're right. I saw a movement myself. It's impossible, but . . . wait."

Ryder and Dodd were among the guards keeping the crowd back. Swiftly, Rob made his way to them. A moment later he came back, bringing them with him. "The side gate," he said. "And then the back door. We nailed up the front doors but we just locked the one at the back and we left the side gate on the latch—bait in a trap, so to speak—and posted a watch to guard it. What have they been doing—sleeping on duty? That's our way in, anyway."

I sent Dale into the bronzesmith's house, but with Brockley, I followed Rob and the other men around the corner to the side entrance. Rob checked sharply when he saw that I proposed to form one of the party. "Ursula, you can't come! This isn't fitting for ladies."

"Being tied up in attics isn't fitting for ladies, either," I said. "It's late to worry about that. Look, if Ambrosia is there she may need me. Her mother can't come to her just now but I can represent her. I will keep behind you and do nothing foolish."

"Mistress Blanchard can be relied on, Master Henderson," Brockley said. "As surely you know, sir."

Rob snorted but said nothing more. Very quietly, we unlatched the side gate and went in, moving at once to the yard at the rear. We looked up at the pie shop but there were no dormer windows on this side. Nothing stirred behind the lower windows. Fortunately, there were no longer any poultry to warn our quarry by cackling, since Master Brady had taken charge of them for the time being. As we reached the back door, Ryder said: "But we haven't got the key with us."

I sighed, and fished inside my green satin skirt. "I'll open it for you," I said, and brought out my lockpicks. I'm sorry to say that I couldn't forbear giving Rob a faintly triumphant smile as I let us into the pie shop.

I had some difficulty with the lock and could feel Rob seething with impatience beside me, but after two or three minutes I persuaded it to yield. We filed into the kitchen. It was deserted, the fire out, and the unraked ashes cold. The usual hams were hanging from the beams, though I noticed that one was missing from its hook. I opened the door to the larder and peered inside. I saw a gap on one of the shelves as though something had been removed. Someone had been there, helping themselves.

"They took food when they went," I said in a low voice. "At least, I think so."

"I daresay, but the point is, did they come back?" Rob whispered, and led the way cautiously out into the passage. There was no sign of anyone on the ground floor but once or twice Rob paused to listen, holding up a hand to keep the rest of us still and absolutely silent and the second time he did this we heard something creak on the floor above us. Stealthily, we made toward the stairs.

Then stealth became unnecessary, for a joyous uproar broke out in the street: clattering hooves, blaring trumpets, cheers and whistles, and shouted commands. The queen was coming into Jackman's Lane. As we reached the next floor, I looked into the parlor, found it empty, slipped inside, and went to the window.

Down below, the street was a blaze of color and excitement. Trumpets sounded again and along the lane came a troop of horsemen, armed and accoutred for display. Beyond them, the sunshine flashed and sparkled on something I could not at first see. Then I glimpsed a tall plume of dark feathers with glints of gold, and a moment later, I saw that the feathers were attached to an elegant black hat, which in turn was poised on a head of pale red hair caught in a gold net. A few paces more and I saw that it was Elizabeth, clad in the sweeping black that enhanced her pale skin, seated slender and upright in the sidesaddle of a white mare whose gemmed bridle gave off blinding flashes. Beside her, in vivid contrast, rode Dudley, crimson-clad on a chestnut gelding.

They reached the dais and the horsemen wheeled to face it, forming a semicircle at a little distance. Dudley dismounted and helped the queen to alight. Someone led their horses aside and Cecil came down to offer his hand and escort Elizabeth up to her waiting seat of honor under the canopy. Someone else stepped forward to read an address and Sybil, holding an immense bouquet of summer flowers, was being brought toward the foot of the dais. The crowd was cheering wildly. Rob touched my shoulder.

"There's no one on this floor. Come on. Upstairs. Quickly, now."

We crept up toward the attic. Rob went first, followed by Dodd and Ryder. I came next, and then Brockley, who had indicated to me in sign language that he wished to bring up the rear, presumably to protect me from anyone who might creep out of a hiding place we hadn't found, and attack from behind. We had all kept our shoes on but the hubbub from outside completely drowned any sounds we might make. At the top of the stairs, where they emerged into Jester's study, Rob halted. Ryder and Dodd were hard on his heels. I was still one step down but by standing on tip-toe and craning my neck I could just see into the room.

We were in full view of its occupants, had any of them looked around but none of them had. Ambrosia was sitting by the desk, her face turned away from us and her eyes fixed on her father. The sunlight, slanting through the dormer window, touched her cheekbones and I could see that although her face was apparently in repose, tears were flowing steadily down it. Her father was standing by the window, staring out of it, riveted, it seemed, by the scene below, while Wood-forde, leaning across the lidded settle, was opening one of the casements. On the floor beside him, for some reason, was a lit candle in a holder.

There was a fresh surge of noise below and some laughter, and the voice of Francis Morland floated up. *Your most gracious Majesty, light of our firmament and guiding star that shines through the leaves of the forest . . . the bright eyes of fair ladies . . . heed our pleas and let us take Your Majesty's handmaiden Mistress Smithson away with us as a keepsake . . .*

Laughter, shouts, the clash—in slow and stylized time—of swords. Then Woodforde stooped and from the top of the lidded chest he snatched up something that was lying there, hidden from us by his body. As he leaned across to the window again, I saw that what he was holding was a musket.

I had time to think: of course, a musket. Brockley had found out that in the Lennox household, Wood-forde had joined in military training, and in Cam-bridge, he kept his eye in by practicing with the crossbow. The candle was there to provide the necessary flame. The ball would strike Dudley, but for a moment no one would realize what had happened. The report would probably be lost in the excited hub-bub of the crowd, and though Woodforde could hardly have planned for it, the blood from the wound would be scarcely visible on Dudley's crimson garments. When he fell, everyone would think he had been wounded by accident in the mock duel. There would be confusion and a gap of time before anyone knew what had happened, before men came to search the houses. Ample time for the musketeer to escape into the secret room and the cupboard entrance to the tower.

Except that the room and the tower stairs weren't secret anymore! Woodforde and Jester must be completely insane. . . .

Then everything erupted at once. Rob muttered: "Hold the stairs!" to Dodd and then he and Ryder leaped forward, just as Ambrosia turned, saw us, and screamed, and her father spun around. Woodforde, ignoring them, was thrusting the muzzle of his weapon through the open casement and had caught his candle up. Ambrosia sprang up, apparently to rush to her uncle and drag him back. Rob and Ryder collided with her and the three of them clutched at one another as if in some demented dance. Rob let out a stream of curses. Jester, though he was staring at us all in white-faced horror, did not move.

Woodforde fired.

Or tried to. But there was no puff of smoke, and I saw him try again, and then fling the musket down on the floor in a rage. He shook impotent fists at it and sank onto the settle, his face blank, his fists clenching and unclenching.

Ryder jumped back and Rob, throwing Ambrosia off him, shoved her roughly down onto her seat again. "Women! Always where you're not wanted!" The happy racket outside rose to a chorus of laughter and cheers and then subsided.

"There ain't no need for alarm, anyone," said Jester in a tense, high voice. "I made sure the gun wouldn't work. It was too big a risk. I damped the powder. Did it yesterday and made sure again a half hour since. I'm not putting my neck in the noose for you, Giles. Ambrosia told me that my wife was goin' to present the flowers and she was callin' herself Mistress Smithson. You know that. Well, I worked it out in the end, though I grant you it took me too long. I reckoned that surely I could find out for myself where a Mistress Smithson, so-called, was living, even if she never did present any flowers. I just wish I'd seen it sooner. But I saw it in time to make sure that damned hackbut wouldn't fire, all the same."

"You damped my powder? *You . . . ?*" said Woodforde in a bewildered voice.

"Father!" sobbed Ambrosia. I went to her, avoiding Rob's angry eyes. He turned his rage on the two miscreants by the window.

"As for you, Master Jester and Master Woodforde, both your necks are in the noose . . . believe me . . . oh no, you don't . . . !"

As if impelled by a single brain, Woodforde and

Jester had both flung themselves toward the stairs, where Dodd was blocking the way as ordered. Brockley at once appeared beside him. Jester raised a fist and Woodforde snatched out his dagger but Rob and Ryder were hard behind them and this time reached their target. Rob seized Woodforde's arms from the rear, while Ryder's forearm went around Jester's neck. Brockley sprang to lend a hand and the two captives were dragged, struggling, back into the room.

Dodd, running to the window, whistled sharply out of it before he too joined in the scrimmage. In moments, guards' feet were clattering upward but by the time they arrived, Woodforde and Jester were already facedown with their noses crushed against the floor and heavy knees pressing into their backs and necks. When they were finally allowed to get up, the guards were standing around them, pikes at the ready. All chance of escape was gone. Deftly, their hands were bound and they were thrust side by side onto the settle.

"And there you will wait until Her Majesty has gone on to Queens' and her reception there, and we can remove you without occasioning comment," Rob said coldly.

"It isn't fair! They haven't done anything!" Ambrosia wailed. I patted her shoulder uselessly, but she shook my hand off. "You can't take my father away!"

"There has been a plot," said Rob, "to assassinate Sir Robert Dudley. We understand, Master Woodforde, that your motive is to please Lady Lennox, who fears that Dudley may marry Mary of Scotland when she wants her own son to become that happy bridegroom."

Woodforde gaped at him. "Oh yes," said Rob, enjoying his triumph after that moment of embarrassing muddle. "We know all about it!"

"But my father *stopped* it!" Ambrosia shrieked. "You saw what happened. He stopped it!"

"Only because he no longer needed it to earn his reward," Rob told her savagely. "The reward was to have been Mistress Jester, brought back into this house and into his hands, was it not?"

"I was going to stop it anyway!" Jester shouted.

"Were you?" I asked him. "Your brother was bribing you to help him by promising to restore your wife to you. I fancy you meant to cooperate—because at that time, you didn't know where she was or how she would be restored. Once you knew that your wife and Mistress Smithson were the same person, and you had had time to think about it, you saw that you no longer needed your brother's help to find her."

"I wanted her back! I can't go on without her. Doesn't anyone understand? She's *mine!*" Jester almost howled.

"You can't do this! You can't! My father *stopped* it, he *stopped* it; you can't say he didn't! Don't take my father away!" Ambrosia was nearly hysterical and this time when I made another attempt to put a calming hand on her, she struck out so fiercely that I stumbled aside and was caught by Brockley.

"You must have been crazy to try to go on with it," I said angrily to Woodforde. "After Wat and I had escaped, you must have known that we would report everything to the authorities—including the news of your secret room. If that gun had fired, this house would have been the first to be searched, secret room, tower stairs, and all."

"You don't know everything," Woodforde informed me. "You're not as clever as you think, though you're too clever to be decent for a woman. We'd none of us have been found."

"My father *stopped* it! He damped the gunpowder!" Ambrosia wailed persistently.

I couldn't help but feel sorry for her. I wanted to say to Rob: *But he did damp the powder. Surely it may count as mitigation.* But I couldn't say that. I had stood in the chapel of King's College and looked down on the face of Thomas Shawe, dead before his time and Thomas Shawe's blood cried out for justice.

"Rob," I said. "There is something more."

"And what might that be?" Rob's tone was slightly acid. I could understand. Dudley's life had been saved by Jester, not by Rob, who had collided with Ambrosia before he could get to the would-be assassin and I had seen it happen.

"In the cupboard—the one that leads into the tower—there's a tall earthenware ewer lying on its side. Inside it, there's a bundle wrapped in linen. I found it. I looked at it and then put it back. . . . I would like to fetch it now and show it to you. You may think it important."

Rob stared at me. Then he saw Jester's face. It had been pale before but now it was as blanched as death, and his lips were shaking. Rob considered him curiously and then nodded to me. "By all means, if you wish. The door of the cupboard is unlocked and unbolted, by the way. We came through from the tower when we searched on Thursday, and undid the bolts."

I was not sure if I could open the door from the attic to the secret room but it would have been in such bad taste to make Ambrosia do it that I tried on my own. It turned out to be one of those things that is easy once you understand how it works. The knothole was obvious if you knew it was significant. I put my thumb in and pushed; the opening appeared, and I put in my hand to use the latch. I went in.

As Rob had said, the cupboard was unlocked. I found the bundle where I had left it. I don't like to remember Jester's eyes when I came back and he saw it in my hands. I put the bundle down on the desk and opened it, and the settle arm, with its bloodstained lion head, lay revealed.

"What's this?" Rob asked.

"I think," I said, "that it's the weapon that killed Thomas Shawe. There are hairs stuck to it, caught in the blood, and unless I am very much mistaken, they are his. His hair was that same brassy color."

"But who . . . ?" Rob picked up the evidence and examined it, holding it to the light. "I understood, Ursula, that it was impossible for either Woodforde here, or for Jester, to have killed Master Shawe."

"No," I said. "We all supposed that he was killed after five o'clock in the morning, and at five o'clock, Woodforde was in his rooms—I think that is true and that his former manservant is not concerned in this—and Master Jester was here.

"But all that rests on the testimony of the groom, Jem, at Radley's. He arrives at the stable before Radley himself does in the morning and he said he saw Thomas ride out at his usual time, which was at about five. But I fancy that his master, Radley, was by when he said that. I spoke to him yesterday, however, without Radley overhearing. Jem was forever in trouble for being late and if Radley finds out, he beats him for it. He wouldn't admit in Radley's presence that he'd been late that day. He admitted it to me, though, once I had promised him that I wouldn't tell Radley—and why knowing the truth mattered."

"I expect you bribed him to say whatever you wanted him to say!" shouted Jester.

"No," I said. "Though I would like him to be rewarded now." I had in fact, bullied Jem considerably but I had felt it wiser that no money should change hands. "Thomas took the mare out before Jem got there. So Thomas could have ridden out much earlier. I rather think he did."

Hardening my heart, I turned to the trembling Jester. "I think you met him in the grove, Master Jester. How did you get him there? He would hardly have gone to a tryst with you! Did you use Ambrosia's name instead? Not that it matters. You got him there. You took a weapon wrapped in an old shirt so that if anyone saw you, you were only carrying a harmless roll of linen. But not many people are about so early; I daresay no one saw you who knew you. You went out by way of the secret room and the tower, and when you'd killed him, you came back by the same route, slipped in through the side gate, came up through the tower, and there you were in the house, upstairs, able to come innocently down them just before five of the clock. Am I right?"

"What is all this?" Ambrosia cried out. "Ursula, what are you talking about? Are you saying that Thomas was murdered? Are you saying that my father did it? How dare you? It isn't true; it can't be true! Thomas and I were going to be married. Father, you didn't, you couldn't . . . !"

"Just what did Thomas know that was so dangerous?" I asked Jester. "And how did you know he had arranged to talk to me about it?"

"Father!" Ambrosia shrieked. "Say it isn't true! If it is, I hope . . . yes, I hope you hang! I mean it! Thomas and I . . . Thomas and I . . . !"

"Hold your noise, girl! If you'd been a good, dutiful, obedient daughter, it wouldn't have happened. If Thomas is dead, it's your own fault! Your fine young lover would have been my death and your uncle's!"

Woodforde, who had been listening with the air of one who can hardly believe his ears, at this point shouted: "Roland, be quiet!" but it was as though Jester and Ambrosia, lost in the passion of their private quarrel, had completely forgotten the rest of us.

"I come up here one day and I find you've got that Thomas up here for lovemakin' an' kissin' and I ordered you downstairs and I was tellin' him what I thought of him and what happens? He's grinnin' at me and sayin' he'll have you to wife whatever your father may say . . ."

"Why shouldn't he?" Ambrosia was sobbing out loud. "Why shouldn't we have married? Why not? Why *not*?"

" . . . an' he's fidgetin' about with my things and he opens the lid of that chest there and says, *What's this?*

and picks that old musket out of it that we thought we could store there safe enough . . ."

"Roland!" shouted Woodforde.

"Oh, you hold your noise an' all! They seen you aim that there gun out of the window; not much point pretendin' it doesn't exist! *You takin' up musketry?* that cheeky Thomas says to me, and then I see him frown and look worried, and I know he's already got the idea that there's somethin' behind that there playlet; sharp, that's what Thomas was. Sharp enough to cut hisself. And then I'm in the kitchen not five days later, and I hear whisperin' goin' on in the shop, so I stepped up to listen, just behind that screen thing I'd had put up."

"Did you, indeed?" I said bitterly.

"Aye, I did, I heard Thomas plannin' to meet someone and talk to them about his suspicionings concernin' the playlet! I couldn't hear everythin' he said, but I heard enough."

I remembered how I had twice had to put my finger on my lips to warn Thomas that he was speaking too loudly. Master Jester, it seemed, had keen ears.

"Only," Jester said to me, "I didn't think it was you he was talkin' to. The other person was whisperin' just too low and the screen was in the way, but there was a clerk in the shop as well and just afore he went out, Thomas spoke up in his normal voice and said sorry to him for the noise his friends were makin' in the street, and the clerk fellow said he'd been the same once but folk grow out of it. I thought it was him Thomas had been talkin' to all the time. I didn't know who he was or I'd have gone after him same as I did Thomas. Laid awake that night worryin' about him, I did. I didn't want anyone havin' notions that there was something amiss with the playlet. Thomas hadn't told him owt and I meant to make sure he didn't get the chance, but I didn't like it."

"No one was going to suspect *us*," said Woodforde furiously. "Any talk of something strange about the playlet and I could have admitted the plan to bring Sybil back to you. There was no need for you to panic!"

"Well, I did! If I hadn't wanted Sybil back so desperate, and if you hadn't held out on me about where she was . . . just draggin' me in, danglin' the thought of her in front of me so I couldn't resist . . ." He paused for a moment, his voice choked off by a sound like a sob, and gave Woodforde a savage sidelong scowl. Then he said: "Just as well I let the clerk get away, seein' as it wasn't him at all! But I didn't think Thomas would go tellin' his tales to a woman. I didn't think *women* were hired as spies and pokenoses!"

"Quite a lot of people feel like that," I agreed. "Sometimes it's quite useful. One can avoid suspicion for so much longer."

"You *killed* him!" Ambrosia screamed at her father. "*You* killed Thomas! You talk about loving my mother; you say you can't do without her, but you nearly killed *her;* you drove her away! But I still went on loving you, in a fashion, because you *are* my father, and I went on helping you and looking after you, and then Thomas came and now you tell me . . . you admit . . . !"

Brockley caught hold of her just in time, before she hurled herself on her father with fingers curved like claws to rend his face. I said uselessly: "Ambrosia, I'm sorry, I'm sorry!" I did not try to go to her this time but as Brockley pulled her away from her father, they came close to me and she spat in my face. "It's your fault too! If you hadn't come here, prying and peeping and finding things out . . . !"

"Quiet now. Easy. Easy." Like Dudley, Brockley had a soothing rumble of a voice and was good with horses. His efforts had no effect on Ambrosia, however. "I hate you! I hate my father and I hate my uncle and I hate *you*!" Ambrosia shrieked at me. "I'd like to . . ."

Her voice faded suddenly. Her eyes went from me to the staircase behind me. Jester and Woodforde were staring in that direction, too. I turned, and there stood Sybil Jester. Dale was just behind her.

"When the students brought me into the house next door," Sybil said, "Mistress Brady and Dale showed me up to a bedchamber to wash my face and we could hear the shouting from in there! Then Dale told me that someone was in this attic, and that the queen's men had gone to find out who it was, and that you were with them, Ursula, in case Ambrosia was here and needed a woman's help. I must thank you. I see that Ambrosia is indeed in this room. And Roland too . . ."

Jester, sitting pinioned on the settle, said: "Sybil," and then fell silent. Silence, though, can be strangely informative. His eyes searched her face with a look of desperate questioning, as though seeking her pity, her understanding. As for her, as she gazed back at him, she stiffened and—just a little—leaned away. There was pity indeed in her face but her body spoke of fear. Rob Henderson said: "I have to inform you, Mistress

Jester, that your husband is under arrest. An attempt on the life of Sir Robert Dudley was made just now, from this room."

"I tried to stop it!" Roland pleaded. "I made the gun useless!"

"He killed the man I should have married!" Ambrosia burst out.

"Hush," said Brockley. "Just for a moment. This is between your parents."

Even Woodforde seemed aware of that. He sat in his bonds, taut but quiet. Sybil glanced at her daughter but then her eyes went back to Jester. "I would save you if I could," she said. "But I could never return to you. I will pray for you."

Jester said pitifully: "Will you not at least—touch me once, in farewell?"

"He killed Thomas! You can't . . . !" Ambrosia cried. She tried to break away from Brockley, but he held her firmly.

Sybil glanced at her again. "I lay in his arms the night that you were made, my dear." She looked at Rob. "May I?"

"Yes. I give permission," Rob said.

She crossed the floor to her husband. She was nervous of him, I thought, even now, when his hands were bound behind him and she had friends all around. I noticed that Rob Henderson and Dick Dodd moved close as well, watching her keenly, as though they feared that she might either wreak vengeance on Jester or else save his neck or maybe both at once, by producing a dagger and putting him out of his misery.

But there were no such dramatics. She came up

close to the settle, glanced coldly at Woodforde, who turned his head away, and then looked intently into the face of her husband. Then she laid a hand on his head and kissed his brow. It was the kiss one gives to the dead, the kiss I had given, for Ambrosia's sake, to Thomas Shawe.

"Good-bye," she said. Ambrosia was crying now, but quietly, in a healthier fashion. Her mother went to her, took her from Brockley, and led her away.

As they disappeared, Jester spoke, to himself or to us all, one couldn't tell which. "I saw her," he said. "A moment back, from the window. I saw her give the flowers. Oh, my God, don't anyone understand? If I got married to her 'cos her father was rich, well, we'd not been a wed a week before she had me under such a spell . . . witchcraft, that's what it was. I'm still under it."

Then he fell silent, his eyes fixed on the stairs down which she had gone. I have rarely, in my whole life, seen eyes so full of desolation.

24

The Third Line of Defense

Another scholarly debate in King's College Chapel was ending. The black-gowned disputants on the platform were bowing graciously to each other, having finished an argument on a fine point of theology with honors more or less even.

It was Monday, the seventh of August, and there were still two days of the visit to run. This was the third debate to which the queen had listened; there were yet others to follow, along with a stream of dissertations, receptions, banquets, and plays in Latin.

Elizabeth had been playing close attention to the points for and against the immanence or transcendence of God, even to moving her chair nearer to the edge of her dais and calling to the disputants to speak up, but it was very hot in the chapel and I could see that she was growing tired. Her ladies and courtiers, standing around her, were wilting as well. In such weather, formal clothes felt as though their hems were weighted with lead, and the starched pleats of my ruff were pricking my neck badly. I inched back a step or two, trying to make the best of a faint current of air from a window and found myself next to Rob Henderson, perspiring heavily in violet-colored velvet. He glanced at me sideways and then looked away. I sighed.

Between me and Rob, who had once been my friend, things were not as they should be. I knew why, of course, and so did Brockley, who, when I remarked on it to him, had put it into words for me.

"Madam, you and he came here to find out if there was a plot behind the playlet. You arranged to meet Thomas Shawe . . ."

"And got him killed."

"That wasn't your fault, madam. Don't go blaming yourself. The fact remains, it was you, not Master Henderson, that found a student who had suspicions and arranged for him to tell you about them; it was you that found out that Mistress Ambrosia was writing to her mother; you who found the key to the cipher, you who found the secret room and the tower stairs . . ."

"I didn't find the secret room!" I protested. "I was forcibly dragged into it!"

"But you escaped through the tower, didn't you?"

"With Wat's help!"

"And your lockpicks. You escaped, you found the weapon that killed Master Shawe, and recognized it, and it was you that saw the movement at the pie shop window. Whereas what did poor Master Henderson do? He caught the marsh fever and failed to snatch a hackbut out of Master Woodforde's hand because he and Ryder went and collided with Mistress Ambrosia on the way. You've done sterling service to the queen and to Sir Robert Dudley, but Master Henderson won't forgive you easily, all the same."

Under cover of some polite applause I said awkwardly to Rob: "Is there any news of Mattie?"

"No," he said shortly. "At least, yes; she is well. But the child is yet to be born."

When the debate was finished and we left the chapel, he withdrew from my side and was lost in the crowd. I was free now to return to my lodgings, for the queen was to dine privately with the vice chancellor and I would not be needed until a reception much later in the day. Rob must be going to the lodgings as well, but evidently not with me. I found Dale awaiting me and we made our way back together. Since Sybil Jester was now living at the pie shop, I was surprised to find her in the entrance hall, talking to Rob, who had evidently arrived just ahead of me. When he saw me come in, Rob moved aside.

"Mistress Jester has come to visit you, Ursula. I'll leave you with her." He gave me a stiff bow and went upstairs. I gazed after him with regret and then turned inquiringly to Sybil.

"Can you find time to ride just outside the town with me, Mistress Blanchard?" Sybil asked. "I have to go to the house of Dr. Edward Barley, to do something for Ambrosia. Dr. Barley has left her all his books and I must look at them and have them packed up for her. She can't go herself; she is ill in bed. I wonder, too, if your manservant could help with the packing up and arranging for a cart to collect the books. Dr. Barley had quite a big library. His housekeeper is still there and will give us a meal, I expect . . ."

I had been looking forward to a rest and the thought of a ride through the heat of the day was exhausting, but Sybil looked at me so appealingly that I said: "Yes, very well. What is wrong with Ambrosia?"

"Prostration, poor lass," said her mother, and with a small, significant movement of her head indicated our landlady, who was standing in the doorway to her private rooms, arms folded and ears visibly flapping. "To be young isn't always to be strong. Their energy flags sometimes where ours wouldn't. I have already arranged to hire a horse from Radley's. You keep your own horses there, I believe."

"Brockley is there at this moment, looking after them," I said. "He has little faith in Radley. He will advise us about the cart."

We were on the way to the stable when Sybil said: "Now that we are out of other people's hearing, I think I can tell you. You know that Thomas Shawe and Ambrosia considered themselves betrothed?"

"Yes." Enlightenment came suddenly. "Is she . . . ? I mean, did they . . . ?"

"She is," said Sybil, "and they did. She is carrying Thomas's child."

"I saw her faint once," I said. "And she was sick when her father and uncle made her help them bind me and Wat. I should have guessed before. Is she in danger of losing it?"

"I think not, but I have put her to bed for safety's sake. Oh, she will be all right, Mistress Blanchard. So will the child. She made no mistake in choosing her man, or the family into which she hoped to marry. Thomas's parents came to Cambridge after his funeral, to attend to various matters he left unfinished—bills to be paid and so on—and while they were about it, they waited to see the queen. They are still here and they know that Thomas wanted to marry my daughter. He had hinted to them that he wished to marry, and he and Ambrosia exchanged letters which were found among his things. Master and Mistress Shawe wanted to see the girl and her parents and they called on me . . ."

"How very difficult! What did you say?"

"I told them the truth," said Sybil frankly. "There have been lies and deceit enough. They were extremely shocked, especially to learn that their son probably did not die by accident. I felt that I owed them some honesty but I expected them, when they had heard my story, to turn their backs on us and walk out. But they didn't. They questioned me at some length and then Ambrosia, separately, and decided that we were not responsible for the actions of her father and uncle. Ambrosia's baby is all that is left of Thomas. They are willing to adopt it. Ambrosia can go to them and stay until the child is born. I shall put it about that I have sent her to relatives until her father's trial is over. When she comes back, she can resume life in Cambridge. There is money in trust for any children that she has. This child will have a family, and a future."

"You intend to stay in Cambridge yourself?" I said.

"What had I to do with this scandalous plot?" inquired Sybil tranquilly. "I had run away years before, after all! As for my daughter, she is still a young girl. Thomas's parents don't blame her for what her father and uncle did, and why should anyone else? There will be gossip and a few pointing fingers for a while, but that will pass. I intend to reopen the pie shop tomorrow. Wat and Phoebe are there now, setting all to rights. I have an idea," Sybil added with a smile, "that those two will make a match of it one day."

I said: "You are making a brave new start. But it can't be easy."

"No." Sybil sighed. "It is not. I have to endure the thought, all day and every day, that my husband has been taken away on a charge of treason, and his brother with him. I fled from Roland because I feared him and believed I hated him . . . but when I think of him in a cell, awaiting trial on such a charge, and with such a death beyond it . . .

"Believe me, I have cried for him, the silly, obsessed fool, and in time to come I foresee I shall cry still more. I have even cried for Giles Woodforde, and I really do hate *him,* for this is all his fault. On the day they die, the pie shop will be closed and I will pass their last hours in a church, praying for the solace of God for them and for me and for Ambrosia. I would rather stay in the place I know and keep myself occupied. The whispers *will* die out in time. And to have something to do," said Sybil with forced cheerfulness, "can keep one from thinking too much."

I had no idea what Dr. Barley's house would be like. It turned out to be a cottage with a huge thatched roof that seemed to weigh the walls down. The dormer windows of the upper story peered through the thatch rather than out of it. There was a small garden, front and back, not well kept, with straggling weeds among the gillyflowers and sunflowers and pansies. The herb patch alone was well tended. The place was already a scene of activity, with two carts outside being loaded with furniture, which was being brought down from the upper rooms.

"Barley's kinsfolk," Sybil said. "He left them the rest of his goods. The cottage itself belongs to Mistress Grantley and she wants all trace of him out of it as soon as may be. She is still angry with him even though he's dead—for foisting a wicked runaway wife like me on to her! His man of business, who came to the pie shop to explain the terms of the will, told me about that. He was a tall, thin, solemn fellow and in sympathy with her, I think. He had the impertinence," said Sybil with feeling, "to *preach* to me on wifely duty, and him a celibate! I told him to mind his own business."

I laughed, liking her for her even temperament and her courage. For all her troubles, there was humor now and then in her deep-set dark eyes, a spark of mirth I had never seen in Ambrosia's. Sybil responded to me with a smile. "One must not be crushed down. Or obsessed, either. That was the trouble with both Giles and Roland and also, I believe, with their mother before them. They would fasten on things, on people, and refuse to let go. Ambrosia has something of the same nature. I fear that life will never be easy for her."

Her face became grave again. "She has decided to be angry with you, Mistress Blanchard, to blame you for Thomas's death, and I am afraid that she will never change her mind. It would be best if you didn't meet her again. She can't help herself, I think. But I am not like that."

"I have a conscience over Thomas's death," I said. "You can tell her that, if you like."

"I will, but it will make no difference. She *knows* it wasn't really your fault, you see. But she will not be reasonable. Just like her father."

Barley's housekeeper reminded me of Cecil's nanny, although she was a couple of decades younger and much thinner—in fact, decidedly spry on her feet. I had sent Brockley cantering ahead to announce us and she came out to meet us as we pulled up at the gate.

"There's a bit of common land with tethering posts at the back where the horses can go. We've got long tethers handy for visitors' horses. So many of the doctor's old pupils used to come riding to see him. Now, Mistress Smithson . . . no, it's Mistress Jester, isn't it, so Mistress Grantley says. I don't understand why there's been a muddle over your name, my dear, or what Mistress Grantley's got against you, but there it is—not that we need worry. Dr. Barley liked you so I've no quarrel with you and Mistress Grantley's not here. I just wanted to say that there's food nearby. Got to give a bite to these as well," she added, waving a hand at the hired men who were at that moment stacking bedsteads and presses behind a team of dozing oxen. "Come you in and take something, and then you can see about the books."

"We've ordered a cart for tomorrow morning," I said as I dismounted. "Today Mistress Jester wishes to see the books and pack them up in some sort of order."

"Whatever you like, whatever you like. Packing them'll take some time. Such a man for books, he was. I used to think if he got any more of them, he'd have a job to get to his bed between the piles on the floor!"

We didn't see the books at first because our good hostess, whose name was Mistress Cottrell, was anxious to serve us with mutton pie and homemade elderflower wine. We had it in a cramped little parlor, while she trotted in and out with extras and talked incessantly about "poor Dr. Barley," of whom she had obviously been very fond.

"Poor dear man, I can see him sitting at his desk now, pouring himself a glass of wine, or maybe I'd pour it for him. He used to be well looking as a young fellow, he told me, but to me he'll always be little Dr. Barley with his bald head and his ring of white hair round it, and his nice pink face, though his physician said once his color was too high. So good-hearted, too, never short-tempered, and never said I was nagging, either, when I urged him to take his medicine regularly. I did the same thing for my poor late husband and he *did* complain that I nagged, though I meant it for the best. But the both of them would get that short of breath if they didn't take their doses."

"The steward who used to run my manor Withysham has a similar illness," I remarked.

"Has he, dear? I kept Dr. Barley's medicine up in his bedroom on the windowsill and I'd see he had it, every night, regular," Mistress Cottrell said. "Nasty stuff it was, but it did some good, I think, right up to the last and then it failed him. I've thrown it out now."

With the meal behind us, we were able to examine the books in Dr. Barley's bedchamber and his study. Mistress Cottrell had exaggerated the number of them, but he really did have some piled on the floor of his bedchamber, probably because there were no shelves in the room. When she took us to his study though, we found some shelves there and they were all full. He had no doubt been collecting books throughout his life. Most were printed but we found two or three illuminated medieval manuscripts, which he had probably gone without meals and new clothes to afford.

The study was comfortable, evidently a place that he had loved, but it was even more cramped than the parlor, since the desk and the two well-cushioned chairs, not yet removed, were much too big for it and nearly filled it up. The shelves were fixed to a wall behind the desk and the only shelf space not occupied by reading matter was across the corner of the room, and held a wine flask, with glasses placed beside it.

"That's red Rhône wine in that flask in front," the housekeeper said, when she saw me looking at the shelf. "Oh, he liked his drop of wine. 'Mistress Cottrell,' he'd say to me, 'I sometimes think my wine does me more good than my medicine.' But neither physic nor wine did him any good the day he was took ill, with throwing up like I'd never seen before."

Mistress Cottrell, remembering, began to cry, and Sybil and I hastened to comfort her.

"He *did* like his drop of wine," she said, sniffing. "He didn't care for my elderflower, but Master Woodforde—well, he was Dr. Woodforde rightly, only somehow hardly anyone ever called him that—that was a friend of his from university, used to bring him fine wines from France and Italy and all over, to try every now and then. That Rhône wine that's up there now, he brought that out here just the day before poor Dr. Barley died, and they drank of it together, here in this very room, using the desk as a table, just as they always did."

"Woodforde was here the day before?" I asked in surprise.

"Why, yes, my dear. I was glad that Dr. Barley had had a chat with a friend for the last, and at least he didn't have a long miserable illness and a deal of pain. Though the stairs were hard for him in his last months. He'd come down in the morning and haul himself up again at night and that was all. I've tried to think that it was all for the best."

"Did they both drink the wine?" I asked.

"Oh yes!" Mistress Cottrell was pleased to talk about her ex-employer and saw nothing strange in my questions. "Master Woodforde brought a flask of it in his saddlebags, riding very slow, he said, not to jolt it, and the two of them sat here and drank it all. I poured for them my own self. Master Woodforde

stayed all afternoon and then left to go home. Poor
Dr. Barley was took ill that night, and sadly sick, but
seemed to be better by the morning. And then, later
that day . . ."

Shaking her head in sorrow, the poor woman was
completely overcome. Well, the wine could hardly
have been poisoned, I thought, not if Woodforde had
been sharing it himself. The moment Mistress Cottrell
had spoken of Woodforde being there only the day
before Dr. Barley died, I had come alert. If I had been a
hound, my ears would have pricked. But the thought
that had come into my head was horrible. Dr. Barley
sounded such a pleasant and kindly soul and I couldn't
bear to think of him being another of the ruthless
Woodforde's victims.

For Woodforde might have had a motive. Woodforde could well have known that his niece was still
writing to her former tutor and once he found out that
Mistress Jester was visiting Barley, the possibility that
she was in touch with her daughter would have been
all too obvious. That wouldn't have suited Master
Woodforde at all. What if Ambrosia discovered that her
mother was the woman who was to present the flowers to the queen—and was to be brought straight into
the pie shop! Sybil had been Woodforde's lever, his
means of controlling his brother.

And he had not mentioned that he had seen Barley
on the very day before the tutor's death.

It seemed unlikely, though. He might have brought
a vial of poison with him, but poisons are not as easy to
come by as all that, unless one knows how to brew
them from plants. I wondered if an academic like

Woodforde would know such things. Failing that, he would have to buy it from somewhere and apothecaries have a way of remembering sales of poisonous substances. No. Barley's death had surely been fortuitous. God had called him. Woodforde must have been relieved. Perhaps he had thought it merely wise not to mention the time of his last visit, or perhaps, busy with his own machinations, he had simply forgotten exactly when his last visit was.

We set about packing the books. We had brought some sacks with us and we stowed the volumes into these, securing them firmly with twine, ready to be collected the next day. At last, we took our leave and rode back to Cambridge. I dismounted at the lodgings and parted with Sybil, who rode on with Brockley to Radley's. In the entrance hall of the lodgings, I once more found Rob Henderson. He eyed me with a slight smile, which, however, was more malicious than friendly.

"I've been to the pie shop," he informed me. "Following up something Mistress Jester told me this morning before you got here. She'd been questioning her daughter, it seems, about that odd remark that Woodforde made when we caught him—that if his plan had gone through, we would never have found him."

"Oh?" I began to draw off my stiff, embroidered riding gloves, wondering why being a lady of position meant wearing such inconvenient objects in hot weather.

"Did you know there was another secret room in that place?"

"No. Is there? Where?"

"There's a funny kink in the passageway downstairs, where the storeroom juts out, as it were. It's misleading. It tricks the eye so that you don't realize that the length of the passage between the store and the door of the kitchen is a good bit *too* long, even if you take the larder into account. At the back of one of the larder shelves there's a knothole like the one that opens the hidden attic room. This one lets you into a space between the larder and the store. It's a nasty little place; only about eight feet by four, with hardly any light and not much air, except from a few cracks up at the top of the pantry wall and chinks that were left on purpose in the brickwork. But it's hidden enough."

I remembered, when we crept into the pie shop after seeing that movement upstairs, that I had looked into the larder and seen that things had been moved about on one of the shelves. I remembered too, returning from that invented errand to buy peppers and mushrooms, and finding Roland Jester in the pantry, looking flustered. He had at once started shouting at me and saying that we had plenty of peppers and mushrooms, and flourishing them at me. But had he, perhaps, just been into the room behind the wall and was he afraid I had seen something odd?

"Sybil said that her father was truly terrified of being taken up for heresy," I said slowly. "He had one line of defense after another. As we said about the ciphers—moat, walls, and keep."

"Very likely. Well, that nasty little hole is where Woodforde, Jester, and Ambrosia hid when the house was searched, after you and Wat escaped. And that was where Woodforde meant them all to hide after he'd shot Dudley. It's got a table and bedding and buckets and candles in there, all ready, and they could have got food from the larder, of course. They'd have skulked there until things became quiet and they could slip out and get away by night. So at least," said Rob, smiling at me with his teeth but not with his eyes, "I have managed to find out one thing that you didn't discover, my dear Ursula."

"Rob, don't."

Rob didn't deign to answer, but as he turned to go upstairs, I said: "I know you're worried about Mattie. Everyone who cares about her will be praying for her and the child, you know. I'm quite sure that . . ."

At the foot of the stairs, he paused and glanced back. "Have done with patronizing me, Ursula. I have no time for it. Oh, I nearly forgot. I am charged with a message for you from Cecil. Woodforde is pleading— demanding, almost!—to be allowed to see Lady Lennox. He wants a final meeting with the object of his passion, just as his brother had with Mistress Jester. When the court returns to London, his wish is to be granted. We shall both be allowed to eavesdrop on that most interesting meeting. I am very grateful to Cecil and to Dudley for their graciousness in permitting me to join you!"

I watched him go upstairs, his back rigid, and felt myself grow cold and tired. I had looked on him, for so long, as a friend but the friendship was over and with it, I supposed, my friendship with Mattie.

Well, when all this was finished, I would collect

Meg from them and soon, soon, Meg and I would be on our way to France, to Blanchepierre and to Matthew. I would leave Brockley and Dale behind at Withysham. No one, ever again, would suspect me of being too friendly with my manservant; nor would anyone resent me for being too successful an agent of inquiry. I would become Madame de la Roche, wholly and completely. For the rest of my life.

25

Queen of Ambition

"We've questioned Woodforde and Jester," Cecil said in a quiet voice, as together with Dudley, Rob Henderson, and myself, in private audience with Elizabeth, he told her all that had passed in Cambridge. "They have talked. They might well have got away with it. According to their original plan, Jester would have been out in the street in front of his shop, in full, innocent view of everybody, and Woodforde would have fired his musket from the attic, and then, while everyone was still wondering exactly what had happened, he'd have been away through the secret room and into the tower and wouldn't have emerged until he felt safe. The houses nearby would all have been searched but I don't suppose we'd have found him. As things were, they meant to rush down the stairs and get into the room behind the larder. Oh yes, it could have worked!"

"When I became involved in that playlet," said Dudley grimly, "I allowed myself to be fooled." The expression on his haughty face was that of an offended falcon. "And I am not in the habit of being fooled. I would prefer that this should not be bruited about too widely."

"There we agree," said Elizabeth seriously. "But there is one thing we badly need to learn. Just how far was Lady Lennox involved in this?"

"That," said Cecil, "we intend to find out before long."

It was not in Elizabeth's nature to say in so many words: *I was wrong;* still less to apologize for even the most disastrous misjudgments, at least not in public—though it may be that she and Dudley, in private, said something of the kind to each other. After all, they had both encouraged the playlet and refused to see its dangers, and because of that, the queen's sweet Robin had come close to being shot dead in a Cambridge street.

A few days after that private interview, however, she did make an opportunity to thank me for my work in Cambridge, without referring to the details. She chose a casual moment, while leaning back in her chair to watch some of her ladies practice the figures of a complex new dance. The heat wave was over, and under the windows of the gallery in Whitehall Palace, where the court was now ensconced, the Thames was rippled by a brisk wind. Elizabeth had a fine wool shawl over her loose gown of ash-gray satin.

"I am grateful, Ursula, for all you did in Cambridge," she said softly. "I am touched that you were willing to put up with such ill-usage for my sake. I have to thank you, but I have waited to do so when Master Henderson is not present. He feels, I think, that your exploits somewhat outdid his."

"That was only chance. He fell ill. As for me, I am always glad to serve you, ma'am," I said conventionally, although it was in fact the truth. There was that about Elizabeth that made people unable to be neutral about her. They loathed or loved her, feared her or defended her, and either way acknowledged her magnetism.

She was not beautiful in the ordinary sense of the word. Women who were called beautiful mostly shared certain features: a glossiness of lip, and a softness of mouth and chin; a come-hither shimmer in the eyes. A latent willingness to surrender.

Elizabeth's lips were dry and her eyes always wary. Her pale, pearly face was sharp-pointed like a shield, and in many ways a shield was exactly what it was. Behind its protective facade, she thought her own thoughts and hid her emotions. I sometimes thought that the secret of her magnetism lay in precisely that; one could sense that the thoughts were deep and the emotions strong, yet she rarely let anyone know what they were. She drew people to her, or frightened them into angry retreat, because she was a mystery.

"I believe," she said now, "that Lady Lennox is shortly to be brought face-to-face with the man Woodforde. I wish I could be there to overhear, although I have no doubt, Ursula, that Cecil and you will ably represent me."

"We will do our best, ma'am," I said.

* * *

The dancing ended. I had asked permission to with-
draw afterward, as far as the other ladies were concerned because I was preparing to leave the court and
return to Withysham, by way of Thamesbank so that I
could collect Meg. I would have to ride with Rob. I
hoped that on the way, I might yet put right the cold-
ness that had fallen between us. It had saddened me,
but so far Rob had not softened.

Elizabeth, however, knew well enough that I was
not really going to spend the afternoon in helping Dale
to shake out dresses and fold them into hampers for
the journey. Instead, I was going to the Tower with Sir
William Cecil, though Rob had asked to be excused
because: "Ursula did most of the investigating; it
should be solely her privilege." The words were gracious; his eyes were not. I was sorry.

It was an odd sort of privilege. I wasn't looking forward to it. I had visited a Tower dungeon once before
and I would never forget it. I was relieved when, on
the way there, Cecil told me that we were not going
into the dungeons. "Eavesdropping isn't so very easy
down there but it's been deliberately provided for in
other places. It's often useful to overhear what prison-
ers imagine to be private conversations with their visitors. Lady Lennox and Giles Woodforde will meet in a
Tower room. It's not very large, partly because the timber partition at one end is a thin false wall. There's a
narrow space behind it with just room for two or three
people, and anyone placed there can hear everything
that is said. There's a door into the hidden space from
an adjoining chamber and it has a small window."

"Secret rooms everywhere I turn," I remarked, somewhat sourly.

The eavesdroppers were even provided, I found, with a couple of stools, and there were holes in the partition through which it was possible to peer into the chamber beyond. Cecil's gout was better but he still preferred to sit, although I remained standing. Lady Lennox appeared first, escorted by the Lord Lieutenant and superbly dressed as usual, in an elaborate blue and silver ensemble. The Tower chamber was indeed small and when Lady Lennox was standing regally in the middle of it, her vast farthingale almost seemed to fill it. It was not in Lady Lennox, I thought, to tone down her apparel out of respect for the plight of a prisoner.

She waited, hands linked before her, while the Lord Lieutenant went out again and called down the stairs. Then came the sound of guards ordering someone to get a move on, there, hurry up, we ain't got all day, and Giles Woodforde was hustled in. The door slammed behind him and was locked, leaving the two of them, as far as they knew, alone together.

They had tidied Woodforde up, or so I supposed. His straggly dust-colored hair had been trimmed and he was wearing a clean brown jerkin and hose. His face had been washed and so had his bare feet. But he was gaunt from two weeks of prison fare and constant dread, and his bony wrists were crimson-circled from the gyves. He stood trembling, just inside the door until Lady Lennox, after staring at him coldly for all of half a minute, said acidly: "I am here at the queen's bidding because a prrrisoner had asked to speak with me. Now I find that the prrrisoner is you. *You!*" The disgust in the last word would have curdled milk and Lady Lennox's Scottish *R*'s fairly rolled with fury.

Giles Woodforde threw himself at her feet. She stepped hastily back but he scrambled after her, clutching at her ankles, pulling at her silver-embroidered hem, kissing her shoes. "Oh, my lady, my lady, you're my last hope! I did it all for you . . . at least I tried to do it . . . I'm sorry I failed; I'm so sorry. Please forgive me. Speak for me! You're a great lady. If you speak . . . if you plead . . . if you say you'll take me into your house and be surety for me, surely, surely . . ."

"What in the name of God," said Lady Lennox, "are you talking about, you atrrrocious little worrm? Get up! Get up, I say! Ugh! Leave me alone!" She jerked her skirts out of his fingers, and stooping, administered a violent smack on the side of his head. "What is all this? What have you done, or tried to do? Get *up*!"

"I was going to kill Dudley!" Woodforde babbled. He came to his feet, not so much from choice as because Lady Lennox had seized his hair and literally hauled him up by it. "So that he would be out of your way, so that he would be out of your son's way! I know you were angry because you heard that the queen had offered Dudley to Mary of Scotland. You said so in front of me, more than once! You said the queen was scheming to make sure that your son could never marry her. I thought . . ."

"You vile little toad of a man! Dudley will never leave Elizabeth. I've always known that! And what is Dudley, by birth, comparrred to my son with his rrroyal blood? Elizabeth's schemes made me angry but I always knew they'd fail! I don't need a dirrty little assassin to clear the way for my son! He can do his wooing for himself. If he chooses, he will make me queen mother of Scotland without *your* assistance!"

"But I did it for *you*! Oh, my lady, think what they will do to me if you won't help me! My lady, my lady!"

"I know exactly what they'll do to you," said Lady Lennox disdainfully. "Of courrrse I do. I'll be there to watch. *Guard!*"

When Woodforde was taken away, screaming and howling as though the knife were in his guts already, I sank onto the other stool and would have liked to block my ears but didn't because this was the world in which I worked—partly by choice, at least—and I would not shield myself from its horrors. But when Lady Lennox had been collected by the Lord Lieutenant and had also gone away, I said to Cecil: "I don't think I shall ever forget that—the *sounds* he made. Like . . . like an animal bellowing in terror."

"No, you won't forget," Cecil said. "Nor should you."

"I know. But—I will not witness his death, or Jester's."

"I too," said Cecil, "avoid such things. The burden is heavy enough as it is."

We sat on for a moment, in silent concurrence, until we were sure that Lady Lennox was well out of the way. Then we emerged, to join our waiting escort, mount our horses, and set out for Whitehall.

On the way, Cecil said: "She is not implicated. But she is a queen of ambition if ever I met one. I shall

warn Her Majesty that Lady Lennox had better be
watched and should be clapped into the Tower if she as
much as breathes a wrong word in time to come. We
may grant Darnley permission to go to Scotland—his
father has already asked to go and I think Her Majesty
will agree. But we shan't let Lady Lennox go. As I
think I once said to you before, she will be our surety.
While we have her, Darnley may become king consort
of Scotland, but he won't conspire with Philip of Spain
for an army to make him king consort of England!"

I didn't envy Cecil. His was a hard task in a hard
world. I was glad I would be away from all this soon. I
would be in France, at Blanchepierre, with Matthew,
settled at last in a permanent way of life and in time,
my days at the court of England, in the service of Elizabeth and Cecil, would be no more than a dream.

When I arrived back at Whitehall, I met Rob on my
way through the garden. Calmly and politely, but still
without a sign of his old friendliness, he told me that
he had had news from Thamesbank. Mattie had had a
baby daughter two weeks early, but safely. She and the
child were well. "Mattie would have liked to call the
baby Ursula," Rob said. "A pretty compliment to you.
But if you will forgive me, Mistress Blanchard, I
would prefer to call her Elizabeth. I am writing to tell
Mattie so."

"A wise choice," I said mildly. I went on to my
apartment, and found that I too had letters awaiting
me, two of them, though the messengers who brought
them had already gone. Both were from Blanchepierre.

One was in Matthew's hand; the other in a writing
unfamiliar to me. I opened Matthew's first. It was

dated early in August and spoke of a waning both of the summer heat and of the plague epidemic. Soon, darling Saltspoon, he said, he hoped to be sending me word that I could come home in safety, bringing Meg with me. All was in readiness for us and every day would seem like a year, until we were together again. . . .

Then I opened the second letter. It was from Armand, Matthew's uncle, who was also a priest and lived at Blanchepierre with us. It seemed that the very day after Matthew's letter had been sent, the heat had been renewed and so had the plague. It thrived in hot weather. People from outside had to come to the château sometimes, to bring in food. A drover bringing cattle in had collapsed in the courtyard. He had been carried to a hayloft and had died there, and two men at Blanchepierre had taken the disease as well. One of them was a groom who had helped to carry him to the loft. This groom, before he sickened, had spoken to Matthew about a lame horse. The second Blanche-pierre victim was Matthew himself.

Within four days after his letter had been dispatched to me, Matthew de la Roche, my dearly loved second husband, was dead.

I did not sleep that night. A little to my surprise, I didn't develop a sick headache, which was my usual response to violent emotion, but I sat up all night, by the window, listening to the hoot of passing owls and the murmur of the soft summer breeze, and thinking, thinking, of all that Matthew and I had been to each other; of our passion and our quarreling, of our days together in Blanchepierre; of the stillborn child that had nearly killed me; of my love for him, and the love of England and Elizabeth from which he had never weaned me; of what my future now would be.

It was hard to believe that I would never again see his dark, narrow eyes sparkle with laughter; never again hear him call me by his special pet name of Salt-spoon.

I would not consider the other thoughts, deep in my mind: the fact that I need not, now, face another pregnancy and risk my life in childbed. At this, I would not look. I would not admit that for me Matthew's death was anything but unrelieved calamity.

I would never now go back to France. Matthew had not left Blanchepierre to me but to a cousin of his, evidently assuming that if I lost him, I would not want to live in France but would wish to stay at Withysham, and that Withysham was adequate provision for me, which indeed it was.

I will not speak of the next week or two; indeed, my memory of that time is vague. People were very kind, including the queen. I was allowed to keep to my chamber as much as I wished; prayers were said for me in chapel, asking God to comfort me and heal my grief.

The grief was the worse because Matthew was already buried before I even knew he was dead. I had had no means of saying farewell. I had had no opportunity to place the kiss for the dead on his forehead; no chance to shed tears by his grave. The queen, when I asked, refused to give me a passport for France.

"It is better not," she said. "The place you need now

is your own home, Withysham. You should go there as soon as you feel well enough to travel." She regarded me with those remarkable golden brown eyes of hers, which could be both kind and implacable at the same time. "When you were here so briefly before you set off for Cambridge, I think you told some of my ladies that at home in Withysham, you had been studying Latin with your daughter. I urge you to resume that. There is healing in such occupations. I speak from experience."

I had been right when I wondered whether Elizabeth, to whom the worlds of marriage and motherhood were closed, had sought and found a refuge in the life of the mind. I think she did. I could only hope that I would, too.

And so to Withysham I came, in the late September of 1564. Behind me in London, I left two men who were doomed soon to die, and I had brought them to the scaffold. Though my conscience about Woodforde and Jester was not too troubled. One memory that kept on recurring was that of Dr. Barley's book-crammed study with the flask of dark red Rhône wine on the corner shelf, and his housekeeper, the spry, loquacious Mistress Cottrell saying that Woodforde had been there on the day before Dr. Barley died.

He had brought wine with him and shared it with Barley. He could have had little chance of bringing poison to put in it, or so I thought at first. Unless . . .

I found at Withysham that my aged protégée, the Welshwoman Gladys, had behaved circumspectly while I was away and had caused no trouble. She greeted me cheerfully, with her fanged smile, and showed me some new medicinal plants that she had grown in the garden, which would be good for coughs and colds in winter. On impulse, I picked her brains.

"Gladys," I said, "are you still making infusions of foxglove for the steward, Master Malton?"

"Yes, I am. And it works, indeed it does, as well as anything could!" Gladys bridled slightly, fearing censure.

"I heard of a physician in Cambridge who uses it, too. But I wanted to know—what happens if you take too much of it? Would it make you ill?"

"'Course it would," said Gladys. "Lots of things do, if you take too much. You take foxglove for a toiling heart and it'll ease it, in the right amount. Take too much and you start throwing up and likely you'll die."

I never reported my suspicions. There was no need. Woodforde was as good as dead already. Besides, I couldn't be sure. But the pictures kept coming into my mind: of Woodforde arriving with his wine, talking to Dr. Barley, poor ailing Barley who found the stairs such a trial, and saying, perhaps, *I'd like a look at such and such a book . . . you keep it upstairs, don't you? No, no, I'll find it. I know the stairs are hard for you. . . .*

If he knew the house, he might know of the medicine on the windowsill in Dr. Barley's bedroom. As an educated man, he might know little about the practical work of brewing potions, but still have some knowledge of medicines in general. I could see him, in my mind, climbing the stairs, perhaps taking a little empty vial from his belt pouch, filling it from the medicine flask. And coming down, and sharing the Rhône wine with his friend, and finding an opportunity to slip the contents of the vial into Barley's glass of deep red wine, whose color would mask it. I didn't know what the medicine tasted like but a few pinches of spice might have solved the problem of taste. And then Woodforde went away and Dr. Barley . . .

Became sick and the next day, died.

The idea wouldn't leave me. I believed that Woodforde was capable of it and he certainly had his reasons. As for Jester, he had killed Thomas Shawe and had confessed to it. They were as murderous as each other, those two. Jester was more apt to murder from fear while Woodforde was content to kill for expediency, that was the only difference.

If I could not quite forget Woodforde's cries as he was dragged away from Lady Lennox, well, I still need not lie awake and think about them. On the day of his execution, which was also Jester's, I did have a sick headache, but it passed.

Hitherto, I had only known Withysham in summer. Autumn that year was beautiful for a while, with the trees turning to gold and red, and lively winds to tear at the leaves and fill the air with a dancing largesse of bright leaves. But when the trees were bare, the days turned gray and hushed. Underfoot, the earth was muddy and the evenings darkened early, filling the old house with shadows. In this house, I had been married to Matthew; in this house I had lain my first night with him. Here, too, I had schemed to flee from him, and done so, because Elizabeth needed me. But I had torn my heart from my body when I did it and I had been glad, at last, when we came together again. I would have been happy, in time, at Blanchepierre, I told myself, and surely, I would have had children for Matthew, and survived it.

Well, the dream was gone. I tried my hardest to fill my days well. My aunt Tabitha and uncle Herbert paid me a formal visit of condolence and we sat in the hall exchanging correct sentiments. Aunt Tabitha never omitted the social proprieties. I was glad, however, when they went away.

I had not after all ridden with Rob to collect Meg from Thamesbank. The news of Matthew's death had thrown all arrangements into confusion. In the end, I had gone to Withysham first and then sent for Meg. Rob dispatched her to me with an escort but neither he nor Mattie came themselves. But Meg was well, and glad to see me. Together, she and I resumed our studies.

As I had once planned to do in France, I began to look for a tutor so that we could take up Greek. I took an interest in the house and the kitchen and began teaching my daughter to cook. I also introduced her to advanced embroidery stitches. I did write once or twice to Mattie, giving her news of Meg, and Mattie wrote back, but I knew our friendship was withering, because Rob would not forgive me for being a more successful agent than he was.

Which was absurd, for my days as an agent were over, just as my days as a wife were over. I had Meg and I had the company of Brockley and Dale, who would have to remain with me now, although I was careful, very careful, to keep my distance from Brockley. I must make a new life and it must be the life of a widowed matron, a dignified chatelaine, the lady of the manor of Withysham, of whom no scandalous word was ever spoken, for I must not hurt Dale, and one day Meg would grow up and perhaps go to court, and I wanted her to have every chance of a good marriage.

In December, although I was wearing black, Yuletide still had to be celebrated in some fashion and with a huge effort, I arranged for the usual green branches to be brought indoors and for the usual feast to be served. I think Meg enjoyed it. I can't say that I did. I was aware, all the time, of Dale and Brockley watching me anxiously, as though I might suddenly collapse. I felt sometimes as though I might, but came through it all without drama.

January was gray and bitter. I tried to take an interest in plans for changes to the garden when the springtime came. About the middle of the month, I was walking one morning in the grounds with Dale and Meg, pointing out the places where I thought this or that might be planted, when Brockley came out of the house to tell me that, just as she had done before I went to Cambridge, Aunt Tabitha had called on me. She was waiting in my parlor, where there was a fire. Would I come?

When I entered the parlor, I stopped short, startled. This was not the Aunt Tabitha to whom I was accustomed. This was a version of my aunt that I had never seen before, with an old cloak thrown on anyhow, and graying hair looped untidily under a cap that did not look entirely clean. And a look in her eyes that was quite new to me—of desperation and appeal.

"Ursula!"

"Aunt Tabitha? My dear aunt, how cold you look. Please come and sit by the fire."

"Ursula, I can't waste time on politenesses. We need your help. Our son . . . your cousin Edward . . . he has gone to Scotland and . . . I think he's gone to do something . . . something that people might say is wrong . . ."

"To do with Mary Stuart?" I asked sharply.

"Yes. Yes! He's been before. Your uncle and I have been worried for a long time. I wanted to ask your advice in the summer, before you went off to court but I didn't know what to say. I didn't think I could trust you. Not after what you did to my husband. Only, now . . . we're frightened. His wife is frightened too and . . . Ursula, you're the only person now that we *dare* trust. You're family. We want you to go after him and bring him back and . . . stop him before it's too late! It would be in the interest of the queen . . . yes, I know we're Catholics, but we can't let Edward risk himself like this . . . young people can be so passionate . . . Ursula, please help us!"

Lady Lennox, I thought wryly, was not the only one who could be called a queen of ambition. I too had my ambitious longings.

I was glad of this. This was the summons back to my own world, of secret missions and adventure and the subterranean labyrinth of scheme and counter-scheme that lies below all the dignified and glittering affairs of state, the audiences and receptions and banquets—the council meetings and the festive processions.

It was the summons back to a world where to win

prestige might mean alienating old friends like Rob Henderson, but where the prestige rested on defeating such fierce challenges that nothing, not even Rob's enmity, could destroy one's satisfaction. I was of the temperament that could not win such satisfaction from a well-planned Christmas dinner or shelves full of preserves, and if that was wrong, well, it was the way I had been made and those who disliked it had better address their complaints to the Almighty who made me.

It was like a sudden jolt, a surge of excitement, and a rush of new, hot blood through all my veins. It was like the call of the wild geese in the cold, wide sky.

I motioned Aunt Tabitha to a seat and without taking her eyes from my face, she accepted and sat down. I sat down opposite to her. "Now," I said. "Tell me everything. If it is in Elizabeth's interest, I will help you if I can."

SCRIBNER HARDCOVER
PROUDLY PRESENTS

PAWN FOR A QUEEN

FIONA BUCKLEY

Now available in hardcover
from Scribner

Turn the page for a preview of
Pawn for a Queen. . . .

It had happened so quickly. Only twenty-four hours before that dismal dawn start, I had woken to what I thought would be an ordinary day at home. Before midday, I had been confronted in my own parlor by an Aunt Tabitha I hardly recognized, dressed in an old cloak that she must have snatched up without looking at, and with her gray hair escaping from her cap, and a desperate expression. "We need your help. Our son . . . your cousin Edward . . . he has gone to Scotland and . . . I think he's gone to do something . . . something that people might say is wrong. . . ."

"To do with Mary Stuart?" I asked sharply. Mary Stuart was Queen Elizabeth's rival for the throne of England and she was in Scotland. And the Faldenes had conspired on her behalf on a previous occasion.

"Yes. Yes! He's been before. Your uncle and I have been worried for a long time. I wanted to ask your advice in the summer, before you went off to court, but I didn't know what to say. I didn't think I could trust you. Not after what you did to my husband. Only now . . . we're all frightened. His wife is frightened too and . . . Ursula, you're the only person now that we *dare* trust. You're family. We want you to go after him and bring him back and . . . stop him before it's too late! It would be in the interests of the queen. . . . Yes, I know we're Catholics, but we can't let Edward risk himself like this. . . . Young people can be so passionate. . . . Ursula, please help us!"

I asked her to tell me what she meant. "If it's in Elizabeth's interest, I will help you if I can."

"It *would* be to the queen's advantage," said Aunt Tabitha earnestly. "We want Edward to stop what he's doing—stop completely. Ursula, come back to Faldene with me. Your uncle's there, and Helene, Edward's wife. They want to talk with you too. Come *now*," Aunt Tabitha implored me. "Then I won't have to explain it all twice."

An hour later, I was in Faldene House, sitting by the hearth in the great hall. The fire was well made up against the cold, and on a nearby table stood glasses and a wine jug, meat pies, and sweet cakes. A hovering servant girl was ready to refill glasses and offer the dishes.

Aunt Tabitha set great store by the social niceties. Her servants were so well trained that they were sometimes attentive to irritation point, and my aunt would always proffer refreshment to a visitor, no matter how odd or harassing the circumstances. When the Faldenes went in for conspiracy before, Uncle Herbert had been arrested, and according to my kitchenmaids, who had kinfolk in service at Faldene, she had even offered food and drink to the men who came to do the arresting.

My uncle owed that unhappy experience to me. When I was at court, I had done rather more than walk, dance, and ride with Queen Elizabeth, and occasionally, as a privilege, carry her prayerbook and hand it to her in chapel. I had also undertaken a number of confidential and sometimes dangerous tasks for her Secretary of

State, Sir William Cecil. Withysham had been granted to me in payment for one of those tasks. It was my success in another that had led to Uncle Herbert's removal, for several months, to the Tower of London.

In other words, I had first stolen his daughter's betrothed and then sent my uncle himself to jail. It was hardly surprising that he detested me. Nevertheless, it was through the episode of the Tower that he and my aunt had learned of my secret other life. Now I sat sipping their wine and thinking that all this had an ironic side to it. In this hall, I had been shouted at and bullied and even beaten; in this hall, I had wept with pain, trembled with fear, and seethed with rage that I dared not express. Now I was the one with the power. Today, they were in such desperation that they wanted to call on my services themselves.

It was plain enough, of course, that my cousin Edward was in some way breaking the law. That gave me a qualm, but if whatever was required of me really was in Queen Elizabeth's interests, then surely I could do it, and keep my family's counsel as well. For one thing, although in the past I had suffered unkindness at their hands, I had not actually *wanted* to send my uncle to the Tower and certainly didn't wish to do so again. Whatever pain he and my aunt had caused me in my childhood, I had already done them more than enough harm to outweigh it.

Also, like it or not, Aunt Tabitha was right: the Faldenes were family; and as I had never known my father, they were the only family I had. Big, fleshy Herbert Faldene, with his inborn stinginess and his gout, was nevertheless my uncle, my mother's brother, and his son Edward, Helene's husband, was still my cousin. Anyway, there were children involved.

When the rest of the family had joined me by the fire, Helene was the first to speak.

"You have come to see us at my mother-in-law's plea. Does that mean you will help us? I beg you that you will, madame." Helene had been brought up in France and had retained French mannerisms. Marriage, indeed, hadn't changed her at all as far as I could see. She was still the same lanky young woman I had first met three years ago, with the same pale complexion, mousy hair and round shoulders. "I have two little girls," she said. "If anything befalls Edward, they will be fatherless." She also retained the high-pitched and self-righteous voice that had always set my teeth on edge.

"It is a dreadful thing for children to be deprived of a father," said Aunt Tabitha.

"He would be a martyr," said Helene, "and that is noble—but . . ."

I couldn't quite resist letting them know that old hurts still rankled. "You feel that the substance might be better than even the most admirable shadow?" I said caustically. I turned to Aunt Tabitha. "I had no father," I said. "And my daughter, Meg, lost hers and much you cared."

"Please, Ursula." It was extraordinary to hear that tone of appeal in my aunt's voice.

My uncle was less restrained. "Your mother was always gentle in her manners, I'll grant her that. You must take after your father—whoever he was," he said. He leaned toward me as he spoke, his stiff, heavily padded red doublet creasing across his ample stomach. His right foot, sliding forward, bumped into the table leg. He yelped. "Damnable gout! It's the curse of my life. Despite the fact that we didn't know who on earth your father was, my wench, we gave you a home and an education. You owe us something. Without a good upbringing, you would not have been acceptable at court. Do you forget that?"

"Herbert, I beg you!" Aunt Tabitha protested, and Helene, taking out a handkerchief, wiped tears from her eyes. Her distress was obviously real, and in spite of myself, I felt sorry for her.

"You are our only hope," she said tearfully. "Please don't fail us!"

"I spoke my mind," I said. "I admit I have a sharp tongue." My second husband's nickname for me had been Saltspoon. My saltiness was part of my attraction for him, although from the moment we were wed, he did his best to make me sweeter. Poor Matthew.

I would never hear him call me Saltspoon again.

No use to think of Matthew now. "Tell me the full story," I said. "My cousin Edward, I take it, has been dabbling in . . ." I was going to say *treason* but checked myself ". . . in politics."

"As did your French husband, Matthew de la Roche," said Uncle Herbert. "In fact, they were in touch, working together."

The story came out, told by first one and then another. Being Catholic, my family did not regard Queen Elizabeth as the rightful monarch since their Church didn't acknowledge that her parents, King Henry the Eighth and his second wife, Anne Boleyn, were ever lawfully married. For Catholics, the true queen was Mary Stuart of Scotland, an undoubtedly legitimate descendant of King Henry the Seventh.

"As you well know," said Uncle Herbert grimly, "I was imprisoned for the crime of helping to gather money for her and collecting information about English households willing to support her claim. Ah, that Tower! The cold! I confess it—when I was freed, I feared to go on with the work, but my son Edward volunteered in my stead and his contact was Matthew de la Roche."

"I was so proud of him," said Helene mournfully. "But . . ."

"I knew that Matthew was engaged in dealings of this kind," I said. "But we never discussed them and I had no idea that he was still in touch with Faldene."

"As part of his work," said Uncle Herbert, "your husband compiled a list of households friendly to Mary and sent it to Scotland. Edward was one of his informants, one of many, of course. When the civil war broke out in France, the work virtually came to a halt, but last year, after the war had ended, Edward went to France."

"He didn't go on . . . on political business, not at first," said Helene. "His purpose, madame, was to sell my property there. We hoped to use the money to buy a house here."

"Edward, as you know," said Uncle Herbert, "is not our eldest son. Faldene will eventually go to his elder brother, Francis. Edward and his family are welcome here while we live, but they cannot stay here forever."

"Edward managed the sale and brought the money home," said Helene. "But while he was in France, he also called upon your husband, the Seigneur de la Roche."

"Did he? I had no idea." I spoke bleakly, thinking with sorrow how much Matthew and I had had to conceal from each other. "I suppose I had come back to England by then," I added.

Matthew and I had lived together in France for a while, and my visit to England the previous spring should have been only a brief absence from him, to deal with a family matter. But first one thing and then another had intervened to keep me on this side of the Channel, and then the plague had come and taken Matthew's life.

"I expect so," said Helene. "It was in May." I nodded. "Anyway, your husband was pleased to see Edward. Seigneur de la Roche wished to set the work going again and to prepare a new, up-to-date list."

"The list would certainly have altered during the interruption of the civil war. Some people would have died and others would have changed sides," said Uncle Herbert. "Very often," he added sourly, "those are the ones who are living in what used to be abbeys. They are afraid that if Mary Stuart were to come to power, she would want to restore the stolen buildings to the Church. I daresay you understand, Ursula. After all, Withysham was once an abbey."

Aunt Tabitha rolled her eyes, and I found myself giving her a reassuring smile. "It's all right," I said. "I am not going to take offense. Please go on."

Edward had apparently agreed to communicate with some of Matthew's sources of information in England. He would write to some and visit others personally. He had been educated in Northumberland and was acquainted with a number of the said sources in that district. He had agreed to visit these himself in order to coax worthwhile offers of support out of them. Having obtained as much information and as many promises as he could, he would send a report to Matthew, who would meanwhile have collected extra details from various other people with whom he was directly in touch. He would complete the updated list and dispatch it to Mary. "For the time being, we put off looking for a house of our own," said Helene. "Edward had much to do. He had many letters to write and he had to take great care in choosing trustworthy messengers."

"He dismissed his valet," said Aunt Tabitha. "He found the man reading his correspondence and suspected that he was a government spy. A shocking thing. Such a betrayal of trust."

"There is more than one kind of treachery," I said, and saw them flinch. "What happened next?" I asked.

"I became frightened, because of the valet," said Helene. "It looked as though Edward might be under suspicion . . ."

"To begin with," said Aunt Tabitha, "Edward didn't tell us of his meeting with your husband in France. We didn't at first know that he had begun the work again or realize why he had sent the valet away." She beckoned to the hovering servant girl. "The wine jug needs refilling. And go and make sure that my guest's manservant has had proper refreshment."

"Please, madam, do you wish for any further cakes or pasties?"

"Yes, yes, by all means." Aunt Tabitha waved the girl impatiently away. "What was I saying? Just after the valet was dismissed, Edward traveled north to see his contacts there in person as he had promised to do. He told *us*— his parents—that he was simply going to see old acquaintances in Northumberland. But while he was away, we saw that Helene was very anxious over something. She was pregnant at the time and she was so worried that it made her ill."

"I kept fainting," said Helene miserably. "And weeping."

"At length," said Aunt Tabitha, "we persuaded her to tell us what was wrong and then we learned why he had really gone to Northumberland and also that he intended to visit Scotland as well—and that before he left, he had had reason to think that his valet was spying on him. We agreed with Helene that this must mean that someone somewhere suspected Edward. We were greatly alarmed. That was when we first considered coming to you—except that we were afraid to trust you."

"I had never been easy in my mind about Edward's work for Mary Stuart," said Uncle Herbert. "But he was so eager . . ."

"And I encouraged him," said Helene, sniffing. "As I said, I was so proud of him. But not after the business with the valet! I tried to dissuade him from going north and I was so thankful when he came safely back. I implored him to take no more risks. He said he wouldn't. He said that he had learned some very useful facts. He had only to put them together with the reports he had asked for, from other people in different parts of the country, and then he could prepare his final document for Matthew and his task would be done. The other reports had mostly come while he was away, so he was able to get on with that without delay. And then—"

I interrupted. "How did Edward communicate with my husband? Or indeed, with his contacts elsewhere in the country?"

"We have reliable servants here," said Uncle Herbert. "They carry messages within the country. For keeping in touch with Matthew de la Roche, in France, we used Matthew's own couriers. There were two regular ones. They even kept to their normal schedule throughout the time of the civil war. They traveled back and forth between France and Scotland. One was an itinerant tooth-drawer and the other was a peddler. The tooth-drawer went on foot; the peddler had a mule. They were excellent couriers because they were so ordinary. They were the sort of folk no one ever notices."

I said nothing, but inwardly I sighed. Matthew and I had disagreed about so much, but I had truly loved him, and curiously, one of the most endearing things about him had been a kind of innocence. Matthew genuinely believed that Mary Stuart ought to be queen of England and that if she became so, she could simply tell the English to return to what he called the true faith, and that would be that. The truth was that Mary would never gain the throne without a vicious and gory civil war, and if she won it, then England would be wide open to emissaries of the Inquisition with all its attendant horrors. I could never make Matthew see it. When I tried to point these things out, it was as though my words just slid off from him, turning away like beggars from a closed front door.

Now, I thought, my uncle and his family were displaying the same streak of innocence. From working with Sir William Cecil, I knew very well that ordinary men making commonplace but frequent journeys were the likeliest bearers of treasonable messages and that they were far from unnoticed. Cecil had a payroll on which literally hundreds of harbormasters, innkeepers, and ships' captains were listed, and they kept him informed of who traveled on what routes and how often. I had no doubt that the journeys of the toothdrawer and the peddler had been noted long since. What Helene said as she resumed the story confirmed it.

"I was afraid that Edward would be angry when he knew that I had told his parents what he was about, but when he came home, he just shrugged and said that he had expected them to guess, anyway, since he had used

Faldene servants to carry messages back and forth," she said. "He made his report—it was in the form of a list of families and what each family had offered—and waited for one or the other of your husband's couriers to arrive. The peddler usually came back from Scotland in early August and the tooth-drawer perhaps a week or two later. But they didn't come, and then a messenger brought word of your husband's death to Withysham, and as a matter of family courtesy, the news was passed to us by your steward, Malton. Edward was upset. He didn't know what to do. He had no idea who had replaced Matthew de la Roche, if indeed anyone had! But soon after that, another messenger, a stranger from London, came to tell us that the tooth-drawer and the peddler had both been seized on their way south and were in prison in London. And then . . . then . . ."

"Edward became so anxious about his new list," said Aunt Tabitha. "De la Roche had intended the information eventually for Mary Stuart in Scotland—in Edinburgh—but De la Roche was dead . . ."

"And Edward decided not to worry about the extra items of information that Matthew had collected and to take his own list to Scotland himself," I said helpfully. "Am I right?"

"The man from London refused to carry it," said my uncle. "He said it was too dangerous, that the arrest of the other two couriers showed that too much was known. But Edward left yesterday, despite all the pleading of his womenfolk."

"Father-in-law, you yourself begged him not to go!" said Helene.

I glanced toward the tall windows that looked out to the front of the house. The sky beyond was iron gray, and the ride from Withysham had been bitter. "Why so much haste? If it's as cold as this in Sussex, the snow in the north is probably six feet deep."

"It wasn't haste, precisely. He didn't mean to travel *ventre à terre*," said Helene. "He said that if the weather slowed him down, it couldn't be helped, but go he would, just the same, simply to be done with it. He promised to take care, and to call on his friends in the north, as before, as though he were just making social visits . . ."

"Such a likely thing to do, in January!" snorted Aunt Tabitha.

". . . and just make a brief visit across the border, deliver the list, and come back," Helene finished. "But . . ."

"The valet," said Aunt Tabitha, "and the two couriers who were arrested; all this has made us sure that Edwards is most likely being watched, has perhaps been followed. We did indeed argue against it, but he wouldn't listen and set off yesterday, as your uncle says. We were up most of last night, fretting and worrying and in the end, we decided. Someone must go after him, catch him before he crosses the Scottish border if possible—and make him see that it's too perilous; he must come back and—"

"Tear the list up," I said. "That is my price. On that, I insist. If necessary, I'll steal the list and tear it up myself. I'll probably have to. If he won't listen to you, why should he listen to me?"

"He knows what you did to me in the past, for Queen Elizabeth's sake. You can threaten him," said my uncle candidly. "None of us can because he knows we would never carry the threat out. You, on the other hand, might. You might also be better than any of us at such things as stealing lists. You're our only chance, anyway. I can't go. My gout won't let me. My elder son,

Francis, as Edward once did, is gaining experience of the world in an ambasssador's entourage and is in Austria. I can't even inform him, let alone call on him for help. Your aunt isn't strong enough, and Helene has her children to care for."

"One barely a year and a half old and little Catherine not yet three months!" said Helene. "If anything happens to Edward now, they won't even be able to remember their father! Madame, he is not, as I told you, traveling in great haste, and he means to linger a day or two with more than one household in Northumberland. If you tried, we think you might be able to catch him up. Will you try? Will you?"

"It's your kind of task, isn't it, Ursula?" my uncle said. "I never thought I'd see the day when I had to ask you to use your curious and frankly, in my opinion, your dubious skills for us. . . ."

"Herbert!" wailed Aunt Tabitha.

I looked out of the window. The winter dusk was already gathering. I said: "Today is nearly over. But I can leave at first light tomorrow morning."

I had better reasons for agreeing than they knew. I knew a good deal about the current political situation. A young man called Henry Lord Darnley, a Tudor descendant and a cousin of both Queen Elizabeth and Queen Mary, was due at any moment to start out for Scotland, ostensibly to see his father, who was visiting the family estates there, but in reality to present himself to Queen Mary as a potential husband.

He was being allowed to go only because he was a slightly less lethal prospect than a marriage between Mary and some Catholic prince with armies at his command. Even so, a Mary Stuart reinforced by a Tudor-bred consort could be very interested indeed in having up-to-date details of people who might help her to raise an army on English soil. It was my duty to get my hands on that list if I could and destroy it.

And I had another reason for agreeing. I didn't say yes simply because it was my duty or even because Edward was family (though I did have a glow of satisfaction over my own good-heartedness).

It was the excitement that drew me. I did not have the kind of nature that could be satisfied forever with well-planned dinners and linen rooms full of faultlessly folded sheets interleaved with dried lavender. Plenty of people considered that wrong in a woman—there were times, indeed, when I thought so as well—but it was the way I was made. Queen Elizabeth and Cecil had recognized it and made use of it.

This particular opportunity had come to me in a time of grief and loneliness like a summons back to life. It was like the call of the wild geese in the cold, wide sky, a sound that I loved.

Or so it seemed when I was sitting by the hearth at Faldene. The mood didn't last through the cold early start next morning. Then, as I rode reluctantly through the gatehouse arch of Withysham, I wondered at myself. On more than one occasion in the past, I had determined to give up my perilous way of life. Every time I made such a resolution, I seemed to break it five minutes later. A new task, a new set of challenges, would call to me, like the siren voices of the wild geese. It seemed that I would just never learn.